I0661492

THE BLACK MASK LIBRARY

THE EARLY YEARS (1920–26)

The Man in the Shadows: The Complete Black Mask
Cases of Terry Mack *by Carroll John Daly*

THE SHAW YEARS (1926–36)

Blood on the Curb *by Joseph T. Shaw*

Black Harvest: The Complete Black Mask
Cases of Jules Tremaine *by Norvell W. Page*

Boomerang Dice: The Complete Black Mask Cases of
Johnny Hi Gear *by Stewart Sterling*

Dead Evidence: The Complete Black Mask Cases of
Harrigan *by Ed Lybeck*

Laughing Death *by Raoul Whitfield*

Luck: The Complete Black Mask Cases of
Oscar Sail *by Lester Dent*

The Price of a Dime: The Complete Black Mask Cases of
Ben Shaley *by Norbert Davis*

South Wind: The Complete Black Mask Cases of
Jerry Tracy *by Theodore Tinsley*

THE LATER YEARS (1936–51)

Dead and Done For: The Complete Black Mask Cases of
Cellini Smith *by Robert Reeves*

Let the Dead Alone: The Complete Black Mask Cases of
Luther McGavock *by Merle Constiner*

Murder Costs Money: The Complete Black Mask Cases
of Rex Sackler *by D.L. Champion*

THE MAN IN THE SHADOWS

The Complete Cases of Terry Mack

CARROLL JOHN DALY

introduction by Evan Lewis

cover by Fred Craft

BLACK MASK
2021

BLACK MASK® is a registered trademark of Steeger Properties, LLC. "Three Gun Terry" is a trademark of the Literary Estate of Carroll John Daly. Authorized and produced under license.

Texts and illustrations © 2021 Steeger Properties, LLC. All rights reserved.
"Introduction" appears here for the first time. Copyright © 2021 by Evan Lewis. All rights reserved.
"Three Gun Terry" originally appeared in the May 15, 1923 issue of *Black Mask* magazine (Vol. 6, No. 4). Copyright © 1923 by Pro-Distributors Publishing Company, Inc.
"Action! Action!" originally appeared in the January 1, 1924 issue of *Black Mask* magazine (Vol. 6, No. 19). Copyright © 1924 by Pro-Distributors Publishing Company, Inc.
The Man in the Shadows originally published in 1928 by Edward J. Clode, Inc. (New York). Copyright © 1928 by Carroll John Daly.
"About the Author" originally appeared in the April 1927 issue of *Black Mask* magazine (Vol. 10, No. 2). Copyright © 1927 Pro-Distributors Publishing Company, Inc. Copyright renewed © 1954 and assigned to Steeger Properties, LLC. All rights reserved.

No part of this book may be reproduced or utilized in any form or by any means, electronic or mechanical, without permission in writing from the publisher.
Visit STEEGERBOOKS.COM for more books like this.

Table of Contents

Introduction

CARROLL JOHN DALY was responsible for a string of firsts in the field of hardboiled fiction, and all of them appeared in the pages of *Black Mask*. "The False Burton Combs" (Dec. 1922) is recognized as the first story featuring a hardboiled narrator. "Three Gun Terry" (May 15, 1923) featured the first official hardboiled detective. "Knights of the Open Palm" (June 1, 1923) introduced Race Williams in the first hard-boiled detective series. And "The Snarl of the Beast" (serialized June-September 1927 and appearing in hardcover later that year) was the first hardboiled detective novel.

All but one of those works can be found in the first two volumes of *The Collected Hard-Boiled Stories of Race Williams* published by Altus Press. What's *not* there is that historic first appearance of Terry Mack, the detective who beat Race to the punch by a mere two weeks.

As you'll see in this collection, the Terry Mack of "Three Gun Terry" was indistinguishable from Race Williams. But after that he went his own way. The heroes of "Action! Action!" and the novel *The Man in the Shadows* were so different from "Three Gun Terry"—and from each other—as to be almost independent characters.

WHILE GRUDGINGLY ACCORDED his "firsts," Carroll John Daly has generally been bad-mouthed by mystery historians. The criticism is not altogether unjust, but it's often based on a scale placing Dashiell Hammett at the top and

Daly at the bottom. And that's where it gets tricky. As Stephen Mertz pointed out in his article "In Defense of Carroll John Daly" way back in 1978 (google it and see), Daly was more popular than Hammett with *Black Mask* readers of the day, and arguably a greater influence on the writers who followed.

And much as Hammett would have hated the notion, he was influenced by Daly, too. The early Op is a nearly invisible observer. Over the next several years, through the clamoring of Daly fans and the urging of "Cap" Shaw, Hammett injected ever more action and fun into the stories. The Op reached his full potential in 1927 or '28 with adventures like "Corkscrew" and "$106,000 Blood Money," displaying his personality in almost every line. Without Daly leading the way, Hammett's Op masterpiece *Red Harvest* might never have been written.

So what made Daly so popular? He was simply one hell of a storyteller. He could grab and hold the reader's attention with the best in the business. He was like the guy on the next bar stool, spinning adventures so outlandish and colorful you're rooted to the spot until he turns you loose.

There's an unholy joy in Daly's prose, a wild abandon and a freedom from convention. So what if the plots are creaky, the characters one-dimensional and the dialogue melodramatic? Daly wasn't trying to write great literature. He was having fun and getting paid for it, creating urban fantasies that swept his readers along on a thrill ride. Steve Mertz called it "blood and thunder" writing, a description that's hard to beat.

That blood and thunder is on full display in the two *Black Mask* adventures presented here. The third work in this collection, *The Man in the Shadows*, is another matter. It is probably the prime example of Daly attempting to write like a normal person, and seeing the lightning in his bottle grow dim.

MANY BIOGRAPHICAL SKETCHES of Daly have been written over the years. I wrote one myself forty years ago, and all the known facts were there. New information finally came to light in 2016, with the publication of *Them That Lives By Their Guns*, the first Altus Press volume of Race stories. Professor Brooks Hefner did an excellent job of corralling old information and adding enlightening details from his own research. So I'll discuss Daly's life only briefly, and refer you to the professor for the rest. Our focus here will be on the years leading up to "Three Gun Terry" and the five-year period between that and *The Man in the Shadows*.

The most important facts are these: Joseph F. Daly and John Brennan were partners in a New York law firm, and both had political connections to Tammany Hall. Joseph married John's sister Mary, and their son Carroll John was born in Yonkers on September 14, 1889. The boy was just eleven when his parents died, and he moved in with his well-to-do Uncle John. He was well cared for, and eventually attended De La Salle Institute and the American Academy of Dramatic Arts.

Carroll John had dreams of being an actor, and even once organized a short-lived stock company. Instead, he went to work as a law clerk in his uncle's office. At age 24, he married Margaret Blakely, and a year later she presented him with a son. He also worked for a time as a stenographer, stock salesman, real estate broker and manager of a fire-alarm company. Somewhere along the line he got into the motion picture business, working his way from usher and projectionist to assistant manager, and eventually owner of several movie theaters, one of which was the first on the Atlantic City boardwalk.

At about age thirty, Daly decided to become a writer. Luckily, his uncle agreed to stake him, and he started pounding the typewriter in earnest. The first thing he ever wrote, he claimed, was "a 90,000 word novel full of dazzling words out of a thesaurus." That novel was never published, but it taught him to use plainer language. His first sale has yet to be identified. The earliest I've seen is "One More Thrill" in the *Chicago Ledger* for August 27, 1921, but there are other intriguing possibilities. "A Pursuit to the Death" by "Sergeant Daly" appeared in the Mar. 15, 1919 issue of *Mystery Magazine,* and "The Kid" by "John Daly" was published in the Dec. 1, 1920 issue of the same mag. Could those have been early pseudonyms for Carroll John?

More sales followed, in *Brief Stories, People's Favorite Magazine, 10 Story Book, Wayside Tales* and *Saucy Stories.* Daly's first appearance in *Black Mask* came in October 1922 with "Dolly," a tale of obsession and insanity, and his first important *Mask* story, "The False Burton Combs" followed in Dec. 1922.

THIS UNNAMED NARRATOR known as the False Burton is clearly a progenitor of Terry Mack and Race Williams, but he stops short of calling himself a private investigator. In all other respects, he operates exactly like Terry and Race. Having tired of the traditional adventurer role of helping governments out of trouble, he's found it more lucrative to prey on criminals and turn the tables on blackmailers. "I ain't a crook, just a gentleman adventurer and make my living working against law breakers," he tells us. "You see, I'm a kind of a fellow in the center—not a crook and not a policeman. Both of them look on me with suspicion, though the crooks don't often know I'm out after their hides. And the police—well they run me pretty close at times but I got to take the chances."

As has been often said, Daly's new hero was basically a Western gunslinger transplanted to the streets of New York. But he was more than that, thanks to his innovative narration. The False Burton speaks in what Daly saw as the language of the streets, tossing in a lot of "ain't"s and a little underworld slang for seasoning. This was enough to make it the first hardboiled mystery story, but it was still not as streetwise as those to come.

Two of Daly's next tales, "A Gift from the Gods" in *People's Story Magazine* (Jan. 1, 1923) and "Not Reel Life" in *Argosy All-Story Weekly* (Mar. 3, 1923) feature what is likely Daly's first series character, a tough-talking kid named Chester Robinson. These stories are narrated in relatively staid third-person, but Chester and his young co-stars make their own contribution to the developing style, conversing in the sort of gutter English that will come to fruition with Terry and Race.

This gutter vernacular is also present in Daly's next *Black Mask* story, "It's All in the Game" (Apr. 15, 1923). Unlike the False Burton, the narrator of this one is purposely illiterate, substituting *is* for *are, them* for *those, come* for *came* and *a* for *have.* And this story makes an even more important leap, providing a direct link between "The False Burton Combs" and "Three Gun Terry." Once again, the hero preys on crooks, but this guy *might* be an actual private detective. He has at least two—and maybe three—separate identities: Members of the underworld know him as racetrack tout Sam Smithers; his "real self" (name uncertain) lives in the Westchester Hills with a crippled sister who thinks he's a detective; and he has a private detective agency in the city, under the name Frank Atkins. "Leastwise," he tells us, "I had a little office and it helped the game I was in." So is he really a detective, or not? He's just so cagey that we don't really know, robbing him of the honor of being the first hardboiled private eye.

A bit of Daly's real life crept into this tale. The same year he bought a home in White Plains, some 25 miles from the city, in those same Westchester Hills. He and his wife would live for the next sixteen years.

That same month in *The American Magazine* (April 1923) Daly again used his illiterate, present tense narration in "Paying an Old Debt," featuring a kindhearted burglar. Then it was time for "Three Gun Terry" to take the stage.

ONE OF THE many mysteries in Daly's work is the precise relationship of Terry Mack and Race Williams. There's no question the two were cut from the same cloth, but are they really two separate heroes, or the same guy with different names? All we know for sure is that two weeks after Terry Mack was introduced in "Three Gun Terry," the same essential character, bearing the name Race Williams, appeared in "Knights of the Open Palm." And six weeks after that, Race returned in "Three Thousand to the Good."

Which story was written first, and which submitted first to *Black Mask?* We just don't know. "Knights of the Open Palm" was written at the editor's request and slated for the special Ku Klux Klan issue. "Three Gun Terry" could have been purchased before, after, or even at the same time, and still be published first. But as you'll see in our discussion of "Action! Action!", it seems likely the name Terry Mack was conceived first, so we'll proceed on that assumption.

Both Terry and Race have signs reading "Private Investigator" on their office doors. Both live in ground floor apartments, offering easy emergency exits. Both charge an extra $250 for each on-the-job killing. And most telling of all, both have chauffeurs named Bud (as did "Frank Atkins"). All of that points to a simple name change. Why? Maybe Daly just thought "Race Williams" sounded a little cooler. You'll note that "Three Gun Terry" features a minor character named Williams, who may have provided the spark.

In a short piece in the June 1, 1923 *Black Mask*, the same issue that featured "Knights of the Open Palm," Daly spoke of Race much like Robert E. Howard did of Conan. "Just take Race Williams—put him in need of money—hand him a situation and let him work out his own salvation. It's up to him. We live on the fat of the land or starve together." Race had already become a force unto himself. In a later article, Daly said, "I tried to corner him, tried to make him squeal, surrounded him with desperate gunmen and—he liked it. And I couldn't fool him. I couldn't lead him up to a door and have a man hiding behind that door to trap him. Not this Race Williams. He wouldn't go in. He laughed at me and kicked down the door and walked over the man I had planted to trap him."

In that 1923 piece, Daly discussed his writing method:

I just sit down at the typewriter and pound away. Of course, I have a character and situation but seldom more. I may work for hours and never get anything and then again it may come in the first few pages. It's that creepy feeling which makes me jump from the machine to see that the doors and windows are locked—when that comes I know I have it. Then I write. Two or three nights and it's done; perhaps twice or even three or four times as long as I wish it. Then comes the real work. REVISION! And that is work. How long that will take? How much burning of the midnight Edison no man can tell. But in that writing and re-writing again really lies the bread and butter of the fiction builder.

The notion that Daly spent a great deal of time on revision may come as something of a surprise. Much of his work gives the impression of being slapdash or simply off-the-cuff. But he again stressed the importance of revision in his 1947 *Writer's Digest* article "The Ambulating Lady," so I guess we have to take him at his word.

FOLLOWING THE APPEARANCE of "Three Gun Terry" and the first two Race stories, Daly apparently took a break from his hardboiled hero. Eleven months passed before Race returned, while Daly went in other directions. Along with three non-series tales for *Mask,* stories appeared in *Top-Notch, Action Stories, The Open Road* and *Sport Story Magazine.* He made four more appearances in *Argosy All-Story,* one of which again featured Chester Robinson. For *People's Story Magazine,* he partnered with CC. Waddell on "Two Gun Gerta," a wild and woolly novel-length Western set in contemporary Mexico. Stylistically, most of these were a far cry from Terry and Race.

A possible explanation for this break can be found in "The Ambulating Lady." When the first Race stories (and presumably those featuring Terry and his nameless progenitors) were purchased, *Black Mask* editor George Sutton was on vacation, leaving the magazine in the hands of associate editor Harry North. On his return, Sutton wrote Daly, saying that had he been in charge, those stories would never have appeared. But he'd since had a change of heart. "I don't like these stories," Daly recalled Sutton saying, "but the readers do. I have never received so many letters about a single character before. Write them. I won't like them. But I'll buy them and I'll print them. If you do bad work you will be the one to suffer. You can make money with this boy Williams, every one seems to like him but me."

From this, we might infer that in late 1923 and early 1924, further adventures of the Race/Terry character were not welcome. Once Sutton changed his mind, the floodgates opened, and Race returned to *Mask*, appearing with increasing regularity.

An exception to this eleven-month hardboiled drought was "Action! Action!", the second story in this collection, which we'll discuss in a moment. Another *possible* exception is "Modest Terry" in the February 1924 issue of *Detective Tales*. At the time this present volume goes to press, all efforts to locate this story have failed. "Modest" is a term sometimes the Terry/Race hero uses ironically to describe himself—because he's anything but. Did the title "Modest Terry" refer to Terry Mack? Could Daly have sent his hardboiled hero to *Detective Tales* because *Black Mask* no longer wanted him? I don't know, but I'm mighty curious.

"ACTION! ACTION!" APPEARED in the January 1, 1924 issue of *Black Mask*. As the second Terry Mack story to see print, it occupies the second spot in this collection. But it was tempting to place it first, because I'm about ninety percent convinced it was written well before "Three Gun Terry" and "The Knights of the Open Palm." I wouldn't be surprised if it was submitted to *Mask* even before "The False Burton Combs" and "It's All in the Game"—and rejected.

The prose of "Action! Action!" is generally more crude than that of the other stories, and the punctuation is some of Daly's worst (and that's saying something!). Some sentences are decipherable only if you supply your own commas.

And while the narrator calls himself Terry Mack, he's not the same guy we meet in "Three Gun Terry." This Terry Mack is *not* a Private Investigator, and shows no sign of having been one. Like the False Burton and "Frank Atkins," he's a former globetrotting adventurer. He's tried to make a living preying on New York criminals, but found pickings slim, and is about to return to his old profession in South America when a new opportunity arises. In the end, we see fate leading him in an entirely different direction, and it seems unlikely he'll ever become a New York private eye.

If it's true that "Action! Action!" was written first and failed to sell, Daly would have felt free to recycle the character name for "Three Gun Terry." As for it being rejected, that seems entirely possible, too. Daly claimed to have had fifty or a hundred stories rejected before selling one, but he kept sending them back out. One in particular, he said, was rejected by the same magazine four times before being accepted. So after George Sutton lifted the ban on the Terry/Race character, what would be more natural than to send a rejected story back to *Mask?*

THE NEXT GROUP of Race Williams adventures, beginning with "The Red Peril" in June, 1924, showed Daly still honing his skills. In the eight Race stories appearing over the next year and a half, Daly gradually moved away from his present tense narration and intentionally bad grammar. By the end of 1925, shortly before Joe Shaw came on the scene, Race's speech had reached the form that would carry him along until the mid-forties, when—in the keen-eyed view of Steve Mertz—Daly smoothed it out even more.

The period between June 1924 and the publication of *The Man in the Shadows* in 1928 was a busy one. While Race Williams accounted for about forty percent of the output, Daly spread his seed far and wide. July 1925 saw the four-part serial "The Man With the Twisted Face," in *Western Story*. Like *Two Gun Gerta* (published in hardcover in 1926), this was set in the Wild West of present-day Mexico. Daly enjoyed this setting, sending Race Williams there in both "Them That Lives by Their Guns" and "Alias Buttercup."

Two stories in *Argosy All-Story* could easily have appeared in *Black Mask*. "The Gentleman from Hell" (January 31, 1925) stars a Race Williams clone named Tracey Young. And "A Sentiment Job" (April 11, 1925) features an "unofficial" investigator with the same narrating style.

In August 1925, the four-part serial "The White Champion" began in *Flynn's*. Narrator Stacey Lee is a slightly more sophisticated version of Terry/Race. Like the False Burton, "Frank Atkins," and the Terry of "Action! Action!", Stacey came to New York after many years of adventuring. But instead of preying on criminals, he invested in the stock market and began the climb to respectability. When his investments go sour, he's ready to chuck it and resume his adventuring ways. But in the nick of time (as in "Action!) he's given another chance to make money with his guts and guns. Like Terry/Race, he deals with both polite society and the underworld. And like the Scarlet Pimpernel (and later Zorro, the Phantom and the Spider) he understands the power of advertising, pasting white stickers on his kills. The serial was published in hardcover as Daly's first solo novel, *The White Circle*, in 1926.

Another series character also made the scene. Known to friend and foe as "the Bible stiff," Doc Fay runs a halfway house in the Bowery, offering succor to denizens of the streets. Fay himself is a reformed gunman/adventurer type, who finds it necessary to employ his old skills to keep his new charges on the straight and narrow.

In November 1926, in a case of mistaken identity, Daly was arrested and hauled from his home to the Manhattan city prison known as "the Tombs." The guy the cops were really after was John T. Daly, wanted in California for mail fraud, who had visited White Plains earlier that year and stayed at a house on Daly's street. After spending a night in jail— and $50 to raise his $1000 bail—Daly finally got his day in court, only to be told it was all a mistake. He was irate, telling a reporter, "I can assure you that those who put me in this predicament will have cause for regret." If they ever did, we have no record of it.

Meanwhile, Daly kept busy. Race Williams starred in his first *Black Mask* serial, "The Snarl of the Beast," in 1927, and it was quickly published in hardcover. Daly also appeared in *Triple-X, Detective Story, Crime Mysteries, North-West Stories, Illustrated Novelettes* and *Complete Story Magazine*, and made return appearances in *Action Stories* and *Sport Story*. He employed a variety of styles in those magazines, but nothing I've seen bears much resemblance to the novel that appeared in 1928, *The Man in The Shadows.*

THE MAN IN THE SHADOWS is a mystery. Or, more properly, a mystery novel wrapped in a riddle inside an enigma.

First, the *riddle:* Who wrote the dang thing? Daly, surely, wrote most of it. But even if old Carroll John rose from his grave and swore on a stack of Bibles he penned the whole shebang, I'd have my doubts.

Then, the *enigma:* Why, among Daly's eighteen books, was this the only one (with the possible exception of Murder at Our House in 1950) that appears to be a hardcover original? Daly was first and foremost a magazine writer, and knew it. What possessed him to play novelist?

My first reaction to the opening chapters was that I seeing the hand of an editor. If this truly was a hardcover original, the publisher might have wanted to make Daly's rough prose more palatable to the book-buying public. But as I read on, the feeling grew that those chapters were written by someone else and merely *revised* by Daly. Certain passages are just too smooth, too glib, too subtle or too clever. Daly had fun at the typewriter, making him fun to read, but his skills had limits.

The plot structure is unDalylike, too. We meet almost all the supporting characters, with the plot and backstory firmly in place before the detective arrives on the scene. It feels as if someone else laid that groundwork—right up to and including the appearance of the hero—before Daly really got down to business. The choice of Terry Mack to fill the detective role was obviously Daly's, but the character is far different from the one we met in "Three Gun Terry."

This Terry Mack does share a few of the other's characteristics. The New York police don't like him, calling him a common gunman. He's proud of his skill with a gun (though he carries only two), and knows when to shoot: "Why first, of course," he says. "You must always shoot before the other fellow." But otherwise, he's just not the same guy.

The new Terry Mack speaks drawing room English, and acts like a perfect gentleman. "Terry was not a detective for the excitement it afforded him," Daly tells us. "To him it was a cold and practical business." He has studied medicine, and once refused an offer "to head the investigation department for a nationally known railroad." At one point, we're told he spurns such fripperies as fingerprints, but at another we see him trying to solve the case with his brain. There's a scene where Terry feels fear, and another where he's even afraid to use his guns. Does that sound like a Daly hero to you?

What we have here, I believe, is a detective envisioned by someone else, and Daly trying to cram his Terry/Race hero into the other character's shoes. The classical mystery plot calls for a classical detective, not a Western gunslinger transplanted into modern society. The story forced Daly to trim Terry's ear back, with mixed results. It reminds me of Hammett's attempt to rein in the Continental Op in *The Dain Curse.*

Not all of Daly's work was slam-bang action, I'll admit. When he wanted to, he could slow things down and write in a more sedate style. Some stories even fall into the Old Dark House category, as we find here. And there are elements that *do* feel like genuine Daly. The backstory of old hatreds in a far-flung locale, for instance, was a device he used more than once (inspired, no doubt, by such works as *The Sign of the Four* and *The Valley of Fear*).

But I still believe those first seven chapters were provided by someone else.

So, back to question of authorship. When I raised the issue with pulp reprint mogul Matt Moring, he suggested a line of inquiry: Who, among Daly's fellow *Black Mask* writers, was he friendly with? One answer, Matt said, was Erle Stanley Gardner. Could it be as simple as that?

It's an intriguing idea. Gardner was a lifelong friend and admirer of Daly, and those early chapters offer several Gardner-like lines. One of the earliest reads, "It was a fine morning; it was a fine car, a fine stretch of beach, and perhaps the finest summer home in South Newton." Daly just didn't write like that.

There's this opening to Chapter VII:

> Ardath Johnson could be described in one word. You might write pages and say less. You could not say more. She was real. Pretty? Yes, at first glance; but after you knew her a while she was beautiful. Beauty may be skin-deep with some. Not so with Ardath. There was something beneath that soft delicate skin; something that looked out from the depths of those sparkling brown eyes. Even the little turned-up nose had characteristics entirely different from other little turned-up noses. It was an inquiring little nose. Twenty, black bobbed hair, straight and slender—and we are back where we started. Ardath was REAL.

And this too-subtle description of Ardath knowing "the secret of high finance":

When the worst came to the worst, she just crept into her father's arms and waited for the investment to pay dividends.

When we first we meet Terry Mack, we get something this typical Gardner exchange:

> "Want to take it easy and see the country?" the chauffeur inquired.
> "I want to see as little of it as this car is capable of showing me," Terry said.

There's also the subject of food. Gardner's characters take a great interest in it, where Daly's never seem to eat. When Terry Mack arrives in town, he considers breakfast, but dismisses it as "a thought of the stomach rather than the brain." And besides, "he didn't like the look of the dingy all-night restaurant across the street. It would be a shame to mistreat an appetite such as his."

In 1928, Gardner had three series going in *Black Mask* (Ed Jenkins, Bob Larkin and Black Barr) and was also appearing in *Flynn's*, *Clues*, *Top Notch*, *Argosy All-Story*, *West* and *Ace High*. A fast and extremely prolific writer, he could have dashed off seven chapters without leaving his chair. Then, having lost interest in the project, he could have bequeathed it to Daly to finish as he liked. Daly already had three works in hardcover, and was likely itching for more, while Gardner did not make the leap to novels until 1933. Pure speculation? You bet. But it would account for the drastic change in style and the likelihood that the story did not have its birth in a magazine serial.

Of course, the man behind the mask, if there was one, needn't have been Gardner. C.C. Waddell, Daly's collaborator on *Two-Gun Gerta*, could have been the culprit. It's also possible

Daly's publisher, Clode, could have acquired a partial manuscript and passed it on to him to finish.

From Chapter VIII onward, Daly seems to be at the helm, though somewhat restrained by the established tone and form. As usual, his personal history shows through, as he frequently compares "real life" with actions on the stage and screen. He even used the old gun-in-the-chair trick that often saved the bacon of Race Williams and Satan Hall.

Reviewers at the time praised the book as "a rattling yarn" and "a good straight detective story," with "heaping measures of mystery and suspense," in which "a pugnacious young detective" solves "a baffling mystery." But most seem to have gleaned this information from simply looking at the dust jacket.

A reviewer for the Atlanta Constitution made this all too obvious. The jacket copy reads, "Terry Mack, private investigator, who has solved so many intricate problems, here again leads the reader through an amazing series of tense and dramatic scenes to a most unexpected conclusion." Swept up in this spirit, the reviewer waxed on in the same vein: "The plot is too clever for the comments of a critic, the characters are too real to be described, and the story is too thrilling and exciting for anyone to discuss, but the reader. The beginning is a tragedy, but the ending will not cause you to lose any sleep."

The dust jacket also said, "Mr, Daly really thinks 'The Man in the Shadows' is his best detective story." Pure applesauce!

SO THAT'S IT. I'm done. No more yapping. No more wild and crazy speculation. I'm turning you over to Mr. Daly. It's time to meet Three Gun Terry, Primal Terry and Sophisticated Terry, and do some speculating of your own.

Three Gun Terry

MY LIFE IS my own, and the opinions of others don't interest me; so don't form any, or if you do, keep them to yourself. If you want to sneer at my tactics, why go ahead; but do it behind the pages—you'll find that healthier.

So for my line. I have a little office which says "Terry Mack, Private Investigator," on the door; which means whatever you wish to think it. I ain't a crook, and I ain't a dick; I play the game on the level, in my own way. I'm in the center of a triangle; between the crook and the police and the victim. The police have had an eye on me for some time, but only an eye, never a hand; they don't get my lay at all. The crooks; well, some is on, and some ain't; most of them don't know what to think, until I've put the hooks in them. Sometimes they gun for me, but that ain't a one-sided affair. When it comes to shooting, I don't have to waste time cleaning my gun. A little windy that; but you get my game.

Now, the city's big, and that ain't meant for no outburst of personal wisdom. It's fact. Sometimes things is slow and I go out looking for business. About the cabarets; in the big hotels and even along the streets I find it. It's always there. I just spot some well-known faces playing their suckers, and that's my chance. A bit of trailing; I corral the bird, offer my help, and then things get lively. Blackmail it is mostly, but it doesn't matter to me. And then the fee; a hard-earned but gladly paid fee—that's me! I'm there forty ways from the ace.

So it comes that things is slow, and I'm anxious to chase

down and corner a little of the ready. I guess I blow in nearly twenty bucks, jumping from joint to joint; but it's expense money, so I just shrug my shoulders when nothing turns up. Oh, I see crooks galore, but they ain't having no more luck than I am; which ain't the usual run of things.

Along about one-thirty I start for home—I got a car, but I ain't using it—the subway is my ticket that night. I just come out of a high-class robbers' den over on Sixth Avenue, and start toward Broadway; it's Fifty-sixth Street that I trot down, and it strikes me a wonderful place to pull off a murder—dark and quiet.

Then, when I'm halfway down the block, a woman shoots out of a brownstone front and skips down the steps toward a waiting taxi. She's just about to pull open the door and jump in when I see her draw back suddenly, stand undecidedlike a second, and then, turning, make a sudden dash for the steps. But she's too late. Two chaps hop out of that taxi and go after her. Now, I don't say that she mightn't 'a made it, for she had a start on them, but another lad steps out of the basement way and heads her off.

And let me give those boys credit for working fast; they sure turned the trick like professionals; there ain't no more than a scream and a couple of kicks when them birds have whisked her up and run her into the taxi. A crank of the motor, and the car is speeding away. Is that young lady lost forever? Not so you could notice it, she ain't! If they worked fast, so did I. I couldn't stop them—not me—but I had run across the street and as the car shot past me, I made a grab and swung up on the spare tire.

As we turn into Sixth Avenue, I see a window go up in the brownstone house, and I think I catch a shout. Then we ride.

Things weren't so dead after all, and it looked as if I might get some return on that twenty.

There's three men and a driver, and you think the best thing I can do is to holler at the first cop we pass. But not me! He might stop us, and then again he might not. Also, I might get shot off the back of that speeding car, which was not exactly my most cherished thought. Besides, at the best, the police could only make a capture and give me a vote of thanks, with a misspelling of my name at the bottom of the page of the evening papers. No, I'm not looking for honor—there would probably be jack in this for yours truly.

It ain't cold, and the ride ain't so bad; not so good either, but then I couldn't be particular. As far as being worried about the end of the trip—not much! There were four of them—all armed I guess—but then I had a couple of guns of my own, and I'd be the one with the drop.

At last the ride was over, and we pulled up on a lonely street in the Bronx. It was an empty street, but on the next block was a row of two-story frame houses. I guess they didn't want to attract attention by arriving in style and would hoof it the rest of the way. There is some delay about them getting out of the cab, and I drop off the tire, and stretch my legs, and shake out enough kinks to account for a fifty-mile trip in a lizzy; also I might make mention of the fact that I played with my automatics—being overfond of such toys on certain occasions—and this was one of them. Of course, those birds couldn't know I had come along with them; they was too busy with the struggling girl when I swung aboard. So everything was rosy.

At length, they opened the door, and after stalling around a bit, one of them got out and leaving the door open beat it up the street. I guess he was going to get things set before he took the girl in. Well, I give him a chance. I like to do things right, and I waited to see which house he went into. Then I stepped around from the back of that car and slipped in. Yep, just slid right in and took the empty portable seat which he had left.

I get a laugh yet when I think of the expression on them lads' faces—the two of them, with the girl bound and gagged between them. There in the pale light of a dull moon, she sat, every muscle tense—her eyes wide and frightened.

But the two lads—regular tough birds they were too— no, their muscles weren't tense, they just sat there loose and staring, their eyes near popping out of their heads. Prepared! Why one of them held a gat right on his knees, but he never made no move to use it. Not that he got the chance, for I had rapped his knuckles with the barrel of my gun—not the butt but the barrel—and his gun just slid down his feet, to the floor. Of course, it's a bit risky using the barrel for such things; once in every so often the gun goes off, 'specially a light shooter like mine; but then you can't really bother about such little accidents; you can see where it would be his hard luck, not mine.

Say, there wasn't a yip out of either of them—their hands went up with such a goodwill that I thought they'd stick them through the top of the car. Very obliging they were, and I hadn't said a word yet. I just grinned. As for the lad in the front— well—I had the other cannon poked so hard into his spine that he was sitting straighter than he ever sat before in his life.

"Young lady," I says to the girl. "You got to help, as I can't keep more than half an eye on the driver—so just please close your left eye if he don't keep his hands well up and empty. That's the girl," I added as she nodded. "If you wink the left, I'll plug him. And don't be overparticular—I'm not of a sentimental nature."

Now most of this was only for effect. I didn't really think that the girl was able to help much, but it would give the chap in the front something to think about and make him behave. I didn't need much time because I work fast. Even this kind of a situation wasn't new to me.

In thirty seconds, I had them gunmen standing on the sidewalk, their backs to the car and their hands stretched toward the heavens, like they were listening to Walter Camp.

"Now," I says to the driver. "Let the hands drop and we'll go—back to where you came from. And pray that nothing happens to your car. For the first time that she slows down, I'll drill a hole in the back of your neck and do a little driving myself."

I didn't have to shout at him—you see, the window was down, and his attention was perfect.

And now for the first time, one of the lads on the pavement got his wind back and opened up.

"Better stay out of this," he warned me. "It will mean death for you—sure."

He spoke in broken English and his voice trembled with rage.

"All right Mr. Wolf," I chirped cheerfullike. "But Little Red Riding Hood and me will trot along. If she wants to come back to you later—why, well and good." Then turning to the driver I said sharp, "Let her go!"

And the driver being a man of sound judgment, we went.

I let him drive along for about a mile, and then I stop him and frisk him for a gun; he only has one, which shows a poor eye to the necessity of his profession. After that, we shoot along real merrily, and I give my attention to the girl. I guess it took about ten minutes to get her all straightened out, for I had to keep an eye on the driver, and take a look behind every once in a while. By the time I was finished, we were well down in Harlem.

Say, but that girl was scared; why, she didn't do nothing but hang close to me and keep her head up against my chest as she clung to my coat. And she was mighty little and mighty young too, I think, though I couldn't tell much about her, there in the dark of the cab. Somehow I felt almost like a father as I patted her little dark head and ran my fingers through her soft black locks. I could 'a laughed, but somehow I didn't. It certainly did seem strange to find myself putting my arm about a kid again. I don't know when I did it last—if I ever did it. And there I was, telling her that she was all right, and that I'd take care of her and—and—oh—just acting like a regular nut. What I should 'a been doing was questioning her and finding out just what her old man was worth and how much there would be in it for me. But somehow I didn't do anything but just try to comfort her like she was a baby.

After a bit, she calms down and gets out her handkerchief and snuffles a bit, but she never says a word, just clings to me like some frightened animal.

And then, when I'm about to ask her a few questions, the car suddenly comes to stop and I see that we have turned into Fifty-seventh Street and have stopped around the corner from Sixth Avenue.

"What's this, my lad?" I hail the driver. "Your memory is sorta weak, but mine ain't—come shake a leg and drive us around the block."

"This is as far as I go," he says sulkylike.

But at the same time there seems to be a note of determination in his voice.

"Oh, is it?" And I lean over and tickle him with the gat. "Come, I'll count just ten, and if we ain't off, then I'll give you the surprise of your life—and your death too." And I ain't bluffing either. I never bluff. And not being a chap what wastes time I start in counting:

"One, two, three, four, five." I run them up fast. I ain't no moving-picture director looking for suspense.

Would I have plugged him—well, he didn't wait to find out; he wasn't curious.

"Wait a minute, boss," he says. "I want to say something."

"Make it snappy—and if you ain't inclined to do what you're told, make it prayers."

"There's a cop down the street," he chirps. "If you don't get out here I'll holler to him."

It sounded like he meant business, too, though I couldn't get his game. Also, his English is pretty good.

"Call a cop! You!" I laugh. "Ten to twenty years for kidnapping—that's what you'll get."

Then he turns around sudden and looks at me.

"You ain't no Italian," he says, after a long look.

I only laugh. I'm too old in the game to take offense at such slander. Besides, there is something deadly earnest in the way he speaks.

"I guess you ain't in on the game. If you was, you wouldn't ask me to drive to that house, and you wouldn't go within miles of it yourself," he says half aloud.

"I wanta go home—I wanta go home!" The girl suddenly

flings both arms about my neck. "Just around the corner!" She points down the street. Her voice is low—hysterical—foreign.

I shake the girl off and give him the once-over, and then I poke him with the gun.

"Now drive," I says. "Or I'll find a way to make you and the car move so fast that it will surprise both of you. Six, seven, eight—" I start in where I left off. I'm mighty sore and mean business—besides, I can see the cop coming down the street.

And then the girl suddenly takes things out of my hands. She opens the door and slips out, and is around on Sixth Avenue before I know she's gone. That settles the argument with the driver—I'm out and after her. One last look at the car, and the number is firmly in my mind as it goes rapidly down the street.

I'm only about ten seconds behind as she turns into Sixth Avenue, and then I swing around the corner myself and stop dead. There ain't a person in sight; the street is quiet and deserted.

It didn't seem possible that she could have made the length of that block in that short time, but I took a run down to the corner of Fifty-sixth Street to make sure. I could see well down the street—clean to Seventh Avenue—and there wasn't a soul in sight. I sure was stumped. She must be hiding in one of the hallways along the avenue. But why? Anyway, I'd take a look. And just then along came a cop. Now I ain't afraid of any cop—not me. But they sure ask embarrassing questions, and I don't stand in good with most of the dicks. I've made good when they have failed so many times. So I just loitered around and played safe. And this bull is a good-natured fellow, who smiles at me and says, it's a fine night, as he goes by. He's trying all the doors and is mightily slow about it, and all the time I'm expecting him to come across the girl. But I just stand there and stretch and look around; then I light a butt and walk slowly about.

But that cop was a gentle trusting soul, and pretty soon he shoots across the street and passes down the next block; and he's faster there because there ain't no one to see if he tries all the store doors. Things look good, and I decide to have a peek.

There were several dark entrances to the flats above the stores—dirty, ill-smelling hallways that I'd have to look into. I just come out of one of them when I hear a voice, and there she was, popping up from behind a newsstand that had been pushed flat up against the building for the night.

"What are you doing there?" I says, some relieved and some mad.

"Oh—has he gone? I was frightened," she whispered as she come timidly out and clutched me by the arm. My, but she was a slim, delicate little thing.

"Who went?" I asked. "The lad with the car—yes, he went, all right." I still felt a bit sore about that.

"Oh no—not him—the policeman."

"The policeman," I exclaimed. "Why, what would you be afraid of him for? He'd be a good friend of yours—anyway."

"Oh—no, no. Uncle says no. I have had a lot of trouble since I have been in America. At the convent, things were so different, and I was so happy."

"How long have you been over?" I asked, to try and get her mind working easy; she was beginning to tremble again.

"Over?"

"Yes—in America?"

"Oh!" she said. "Three weeks—nearly."

"Is that all? You speak mighty fine English—almost as good as mine."

Why, there wasn't hardly any accent at all, just enough to make it sound attractive.

"I always knew the English, I think—my mother was an American—she died when I was a little girl."

She kind of sniffled a little.

"Never mind," I said. "You'll be with your father in another few minutes. It's your father that lives here?"

I paused; we were in front of that same brownstone front again—the one she had run out of earlier in the evening.

"I have no father—he died—a little while ago—and I came here—to my uncle."

I looked down at her again as we mounted the steps; she seemed so young.

"How old are you?" I asked. Fourteen, I guessed.

"Nineteen—almost twenty," she told me.

I whistled softly. Well, we never can tell, and the next minute I was ringing the doorbell. A moment later, an electric light flashed on above us. I felt that someone was observing us from within, and then the door was flung open.

Two men, fully dressed, whom I took for servants, stood one on either side of the door, and a tough-looking pair of citizens they were. They looked like they'd cut your throat in a minute. But that didn't bother me; a minute would have been too long—I'd 'a got them both—besides, just at present it seemed to me that these birds would be on my side of the fence.

And then, as we stepped inside and the door closed behind us, a stout man of about fifty, all dolled up in a trick bathrobe that would knock your eye out for color display, came down the stairs.

"Nita!" he yells. Then both clinch, and everything is jake.

After that I'm forgotten, except for those two rough-looking lads who watch me mighty careful—and what's more, I'm watching them too. There's a lot of Italian flung back between uncle and niece, and then I guess he starts in to question her; then they clinch again, and she beats it up the stairs.

Then the fat lad takes a tumble to himself and comes across the hall and takes me by the hand.

"The señorita calls you friend—she has told me of your chivalry, and I cannot thank you enough."

With that, he drags me by his cold, clammy hand into his library, and we both sit.

For a couple of minutes he just sits and looks at me and his smile grows bigger and bigger, and then fades and comes again. But he ain't fooling me none. Of course, I'm the light-haired boy with him now. I can see that, but behind that smile I can also see that he's a tough egg. His smile is broad enough, but then, I've seen too much of life. This bird I spot for a bad actor. And he's a buck with uncertain age, one of them half-bald fronts; he might be ten years older than what I think him, and then again he might be ten years younger.

So he has me tell him the whole story of the night's events, and he smiles some more, and I gather that he's thinking up an explanation of some kind. Then I pull a wisecrack, and I see that he's puzzled.

"You don't have to explain to me," I tell him. "I ain't interested unless—unless I got to be."

Well, that took the smile clean off his slate, for I suppose he was hatching up a barrel of lies. Then he starts to walk up and down the room. After a bit, he stops and looks down at me.

"You don't want to know about this—why—and why?" was the best he could get out.

"Not a word. It came out all right and I'm satisfied, if you are."

That fetches him up fine, and the smile comes back, and I see that he's getting ready to dismiss me without a yip. But he don't yet; he rings a bell and orders some refreshments—which is some pretty fair wine and a half-dozen slim sandwiches.

"You are a remarkable man—a real gentleman," he starts in to make a speech. "It is not often today that we find young men, who for the love of adventure and for their pride in the strong for the weak, succor women in distress. I wish I could reward you, but a gentleman cannot—"

And that's where I bust in on him. I don't want him to commit himself, and I see no reason why he should waste all them flowery thoughts. So I up and give him another shock.

"My reward for tonight's services—now that you suggest it—is exactly two hundred and fifty dollars. Fifty for the night's work and two hundred for the successful finish. I generally charge a little more at the end, but seeing how I came in uninvited—"

But I didn't get any further.

"Am I to understand that you wish money—money for what you did?" And his eyes grew big, and his wine slopped over his glass a little. I had touched him this time, for the foreign accent crept into his voice for the first time, and I knew that he was the brother of Nita's father. Before that, I wasn't sure which side of the fence he was on.

"Sure," I said. "You don't take me for no Sir Lunchlot, do

you? This is business with me." And to keep him from having a stroke of apoplexy, I tell him my trade.

At first, I think that he's trying to hold out on me, but then I see that he's just thinking. His eyes go up and down, and his mouth too, for that matter; then his eyes get small, and he looks closely at me. Whatever he sees don't start a row, for he turns and, ringing a bell, tells the chap that comes to the door to send the señorita down. I get that much even if it is Italian.

And in about five minutes she comes in, and she's a wow. I didn't get a good look at her before, and I tell you it's a lucky thing that I ain't romantic. She sure was one swell-looking dame. Even me, a hardened citizen like me—yep, I was nearly ready to take ten dollars off the bill if the fat lad had suggested it. She sure looked grand, all fixed up.

But he didn't make a crack about money; he just talked to her for a bit and they seemed to be having a bit of a row about me. At length he gives a wave of his hand that she shall go, but she don't—she just stays there. He says something, and she stamps her foot, so I see that she ain't so timid when she's in her own house. For a minute, I get the idea that they are arguing about the price, and she don't look so beautiful, for I can't tell which side she's taking.

At length the old bird gives in on some point and turns to me.

"We'll pay you what you ask and—perhaps much more."

Things are looking up. I just nod.

"Yes," he goes on. "There will be money for you if you are as brave as the señorita says you are—but you must be very brave."

Now he's hitting my gait and talking turkey. So I just smile and tell him:

"Show me the coin, and I'll make the boys at Valley Forge look like pikers."

Then his shrewd eyes went over me again, and his lips opened wide and his teeth showed, but no smile came this time—just a bit of a dental display—he couldn't make a go of the smile because he had forgotten to open his eyes wide enough. Then he took another drink and without further preliminaries opened up; yep, opened up considerable. But he talked so fast that I couldn't get for sure which was the bull and which was the real thing.

"It is this way," he makes a break. "The señorita, Nita Gretna, is my niece. She is my brother's child; Michel Gretna who, if he had lived, would have been recognized as the world's greatest scientist. Well, he made a formula—a formula of great value. The result of it will someday—I hope—startle the world. It is for his daughter—the glory, the honor and the money. To a friend who was his assistant, he entrusted this sheet of paper; this young man, Manual Sparo, brought it here to America. Certain things about it were not quite clear; Manual would work on it—perfect it before he married the señorita and turned it over to us. And when all was ready and the great moment at hand, enemies who desire this paper more than life—great powerful enemies—fell upon him and bore him away."

"Then they got the formula?" I said. Of course, I felt that they didn't, but he paused so long that it seemed up to me to show a little interest. And this talk of marriage was sudden.

"No—they got it not," he said backward. "Wild horses would not tear the secret from him, and the formula was hidden away. Tonight, the señorita went out in answer to a message which she thought came from him. She was indiscreet and should have consulted me, though she says she could not find me. What they would have done with her, I do not know; frighten her, perhaps."

"But they talked of torturing me to make him tell—"the girl started, but the uncle stopped her.

"Tut—tut," he said. "You were frightened and nervous." He turned to me again. "We will pay you much for that formula."

"Do you want me to know what the formula is about?" I got to admit I was curious; it's as well to know how valuable your services are. Besides, I didn't quite like the whole story—it sounded fishy, at least parts of it.

"I do not think that that is necessary. For the paper we will pay much money," he repeated.

"How much is that?"

I don't take much stock in promises.

He thinks a while.

"A thousand dollars," he says at length.

Well, he might have said ten thousand; it wouldn't 'a made no difference to me. I don't work on that kind of speck'. I draw a regular salary. So I up and give him an earful:

"That may be all right," I say, "but I have a regular charge. Fifty dollars a day, and five hundred bonus when I deliver the goods; also, I am willing to take all sorts of chances, but if I get pinched, it's up to you to hire the best lawyer that money can buy—also, I get thirty bucks a day for every day I spend in jail. And for every man I croak—mind you, I ain't a killer, but sometimes a chap's got to turn a gun—I get two hundred dollars flat. It ain't that I don't count this as part of my services, but there's a certain nervous shock to it—and besides, they're your enemies and should be cheap at that price. Also, your game must be strictly honest—I ain't no crook."

I tell you his eyes sure did open wide enough now—wide enough to pop out of his head, almost. He sure was hearing a trunkful, and I could tell that I wasn't falling none in his estimation. I generally let the killing business go by the boards until the time comes, but this time I didn't. You see, if I had to hunt around Italian joints, there was almost sure to be some gunplay and—and I got to protect my interests.

After a bit he says:

"You make this quite a business, but a man would be a fool to sign up to any such agreement."

"Oh, you don't have to sign nothing," I tell him. "When you agree, we just shake hands like a couple of gentlemen. And that's that."

His smile this time was a real one.

"But that protects you not at all," he twists up his English again.

"It gives me all the protection I want. It makes me feel that I've done the right thing."

"But if one don't play fair, what then?"

"Then..." I rubbed my chin. "That's the only point I forgot to tell you. You see, that only happened once and—but why go into unpleasant details; let's just say that they buried him anyway."

This time he actually rubbed his hands together, and chuckled. These foreign gents sure do have a real appreciation of art.

And then, when he's all set to agree to everything, the girl suddenly breaks in with an Italian marathon. I don't think he agrees with what she says, but she turns to me anyway and says:

"Uncle is doing all in his power to recover that paper of my father's, and now it is my turn. I will shake you by the hand, and I will pay you for this service; it is my turn to do something, Señor—" She pauses, and knowing the proper thing to do I get up and bow.

"Mack," I says. "Terry Mack."

And with that she puts out her little hand and mitts me.

It was near four when I got home, and nearer five before I got to bed. Yep, I sat up there in my big easy chair and killed nearly a double deck of butts; I had something to think about, you'll admit.

In the first place, even with the long talk I later had with the fat bird, whose whole moniker was Gustave Gretna, I didn't get any information worth a hill of beans. He made it clear enough that he didn't want the police to know anything about the game. He said if they did, why, the Italian government would mix up in it and make him turn over the formula for about one-tenth of what it was really worth, and he didn't want his niece to lose all that money. I also gathered that she was worth considerable change in her own name. But with real dope, that lad wasn't there at all. Oh, he talked a lot, but he didn't say anything, and of course it was my game to look wise and act like I could settle everything in no time, which was probably what I would do once I got started.

As for the girl, well, she puzzled me; yes, and bothered me some too. When the uncle went upstairs to get the two hundred and fifty bucks for me, which he kept in the house, she spilled out some conversation that even rattled me.

"I am not going to marry this Manual Sparo," she tells me lowlike. "I think I am going to marry someone else—oh—I hope I am. He is an American and—and I love him." With that, she kind of ducks her head and turns red.

"Good for you," was the best that I could pull off—I didn't quite like the way she looked up at me through them thick lashes of hers.

"Yes," she goes on. "But I don't know if he loves me—what do you think?" And she turns them big, black glims of hers full on me. "He's so brave and so handsome and—but I have known him such a short time." Then she breaks off sudden, for her uncle is coming down the stairs.

"Terry," she whispers, leaning over and laying a little hand upon my arm. "You are hired by me, you know, and I want you to promise that you'll see me once every day—without fail."

With that, her uncle trots into the room, and I must say he was a welcome sight.

Now, that's part of what I was thinking over, alone in my room along about four-thirty in the morning. She loved someone else—and that someone was an American—and was brave—and she lived in a convent all her life and had never been out of the house alone since she came to this country—and—and she had called me Terry. Well, I didn't need no more than three guesses. That dame had fallen for me, and fallen hard.

Of course, there wasn't nothing so terrible strange about that, except that I'm off dames—they don't go well with my business—good or bad—women don't have no place in my life. And yet as I stretched myself and looked my reflection over in the glass, something seemed to say: "Why not?" A home in sunny Italy, an open garden beneath—but rats—I snuffed out my last butt and climbed into bed. No more thinking then. I don't do nothing but sleep once I hit the covers; I used to plan then, but queer ideas come to you in bed—great and glorious ideas—but when you turn them over in the morning they ain't worth a thing—you just find them a waste of time.

But the next morning, when I have breakfast, I do a bit of real brain work. You see, Bud brings me my coffee and chops—Bud is my man, my valet, my chauffeur, my assistant—in fact, Bud is the whole works; not much of a thinker, but he can carry out instructions to the big T.

The first thing I figure on doing is having a talk with that taxi lad who drove me and the girl the night before; he was a real funny citizen, and the way he had acted bothered me some. Of course, you might think that would be a tough job, but not for me; it would be easy. I know the ropes in the underworld and the way to get my hooks on these lads. You see, I had the number of the car, a fake number to be sure, but then me and the bird what drove it would know and that was enough.

Along about two o'clock, which is about an hour after I finish breakfast, I trot down to Larkin's Saloon in the Thirties. Now, this Larkin sells booze, but he's also a dope peddler. I've done him more than one good turn because I can use him a lot, and he's always ready to turn a trick for me, if none of the boys— his boys, that's what he calls the crooks—suffer by it. Larkin has a suspicion that I'm a big gun in the dope traffic, and since it leaves a good impression on him, I let him have his think— yes, and help it along. And this same Larkin has got a system of communication that ain't been beat from here to Frisco. So I brace Larkin.

"Larkin," I says, leaning over the little desk in that tiny private room of his, just off the corner of the old bar, "Larkin,

I'm looking for a gink what drove a car last night—number 19964—fake, I guess."

Larkin don't say nothing, but just screws up his face and wiggles his fingers, which I know is the sign to slip over the regular fee, so I dig and produce the ready.

"I can only do my part, Mr. Smith." Larkin makes it a point of calling everybody Smith—it don't make no difference how well he knows you. "The word will go about, and of course I can guarantee that no hurt will come to the—the boy?"

"Absolutely. I'm looking for information with money, not force—at least when I use your system, Larkin. I always play fair with you."

He just nods.

"You may expect him at eleven, if he's alive. In my little room, eh—that'll be ten dollars more." His palm is itchy, and though he keeps his hand by his side, his fingers go nervously back and forth.

"I'll pay now," I tell him. "You can give it back to me if he don't show up." I knew that old boy's weakness.

"Good," said he, and taking the money, we both walked out of the little room. He ain't much of a talker, is Larkin, but he's clever, or maybe just shrewd in his own way.

When I leave that joint about ten minutes later, I see the number 19964 in small figures over his cash register. But it was big enough to read, and I knew that that same number would be in more than a hundred places within the next two or three hours. It was so that Larkin worked his system; the chap what drove the car would see it and know what it meant. Larkin had called, and he would answer. Yes, there had been something in that chauffeur's eyes which told me he would come—I couldn't be mistaken about them same eyes.

After that, I take a bit of a walk, and then I beat it up to the brownstone house on Fifty-sixth, partly to keep my promise to the girl, and partly to see if I couldn't unbutton something of real value out of her Uncle Gus. And that bimbo meets me with a sure-enough startler. Señorita Nita had gone away!

Suspicious! I should say I was; if my face ever betrayed anything, it betrayed it then. But I like to think it didn't; I have a regular poker face and am mighty proud of it.

"Where has she gone?"

This seemed a natural enough question, and I put it to him suddenlike.

But he didn't show any more expression than an oyster.

"Off to Lake—but there, she's away for a rest—Manual and she are to be married soon. I might as well tell you that the gang of cutthroats who were after that formula took fright last night and Michel has returned. You believe me, of course."

And he pulled that last sentence louder than any of the rest; and to me it sounded like he was giving it as a signal or warning to someone listening. But he smiled all over as he watched me closely. I could see that he didn't expect me to believe him, and wouldn't believe me if I said I did.

"No—I don't get you," I says. "What's the lay?"

"It is enough that you should know that everything is now all right. The formula is back—your appearance of last night was of great value. Nita is pleased and has left this for you."

He brought forth a wad and counted a number of bills out on the table.

But I wasn't watching him. I was looking over his shoulder, and I was sure that the curtains moved behind him and that someone peered in. There was something intensive and strained in the whole atmosphere of that room, and I knew, just as well as if I had seen it, that a gun was behind that curtain.

"Ah—you don't believe." He stretched out the money toward me. "Will this five hundred make you believe and—and forget? Nita and I will not need you now—you understand—we are paying you this for silence."

The constant use of that plural "we" grated on my nerves. I guess it was done to hand me the impression that his niece and he were acting in consort, and that she was all right, but it hit me exactly opposite. But then the waving curtain with death probably lurking behind it! It was best to play the game into his hands.

"For five hundred dollars I'll believe anything," I chirped with a grin. "Trot over the coin. When I wish to be, I am as silent as the grave."

He fell for it, and why wouldn't he, after the way I had represented myself last night. I was nothing more than a gunman in his estimation. It was quite evident that he didn't see the ethics of my profession and the good that I did—but I made up my mind that he'd see it later. You see, he had forgotten one thing: I had been hired by the girl—not him. He'd change that grin of his when he seen how a real gentleman played the game.

Then he up and patted me on the back.

"I knew you for a sensible rascal," he said. "Someday we may use you again—Nita and I."

So he bid me good night, and it was all I could do to keep from backing out of the room. I tell you it took real nerve to turn and walk to the front door and then go carelessly down the steps. I sure had a longing to put a bullet through that curtain. But I had five hundred dollars, and a mighty mean suspicion—also, I knew for a certainty that I was going to do that girl some good yet. As for her Uncle Gus—well, of course I didn't believe a word that hummingbird told me.

There was plenty to think about as I went down the street; there were the girl's last words to me, of the previous night, about seeing her every day. Did that just mean that she had fallen for me, or did it mean more? Did it mean that she was growing suspicious about her uncle? Well, I like to think that it meant both.

And there was more than just a feeling of money, and a feeling of pride to make good to the girl who had hired me. For one thing, I never fail—for another thing—well, somehow I just seemed to want to know that that little girl was all right. If I had 'a been sure of my ground and really thought it would 'a done her any good, I'd 'a thought nothing of forcing the truth out of her uncle or—yes—of bumping him over the hurdles. And the gun behind the curtain wouldn't 'a made no difference neither. I knew the gun was there, just as well as I knew that that fat crooked Italian had lied to me.

For the first time in my life I'm worried, and what's more I'm followed. I look at my watch; it ain't but five o'clock and there won't be nothing doing until eleven. Of course, I could shake off the lad what's following me—there ain't nothing to that—but I think it will leave things clearer for me if I can send him back to Uncle Gus with a good report. There ain't really nothing for me to do. I could go and search the house in the Bronx, of course, but if I had thought there would be any chance in that direction, I'd 'a been up there before I went home in the morning. I know that's useless; that gang was out of the dump twenty minutes after I lit out in the taxi—any cluck would know that.

So I play a high-class joint for a feed and spot a dapper little foreigner, sitting over in one corner, as my meat. But I don't give him a tumble; just act like a lad who was out for a good time—blowing in Uncle Gus's jack. I gotta laugh when I think how snug they're feeling and I figure along about midnight I'll have my fingers in their pie up to my wrists. Yes—all I want is plenty of leeway, and then, when I get my earful, there sure is going to be some fireworks.

And I'm right; that lad ain't got the sticking power. He follows me home, and twenty minutes later, when I look out the window, that street is as deserted as a poetry graveyard.

It's near eleven when I slip out of my apartment window—which is on the ground floor for just such occasions—and Bud meets me with the car around the corner. Away we go to Larkin's, and pulling up about a block away, I hop out and beat it for the saloon.

My bird's there; Larkin gives me the high sign as soon as I bust in the door. Into his little private room I slide and shut the door. My man looks up—a little frightened, but smiling just the same.

"Good!" I says. "The system worked."

"Larkin wanted me to see you and—and here I am." I could see he wasn't going to be none too cordial.

"Know me?" I sit down.

He just shows his teeth and nods his head.

"How deep were you in last night?" I ask.

"Deep enough," he answers.

"Want to double-cross?" I ain't going to waste time if he seems agreeable.

"Not me," he grins.

Then I look at him close.

"Snowbird, ain't you?" I shoot at him sudden. Those eyes couldn't fool me. It was those same eyes which had told me he would answer Larkin's call—Larkin was pretty well looked up to by the hopheads.

"What's that to you?" His eyes blaze a bit and the smile does a fadeout.

"Hard guy, eh?"

"Dick, eh?" he retorts.

"Ask Larkin—you know better."

"Did!"

I see he's a man of few words and we ain't getting no place, so I open up on him, tell him what's under my hat; that if he don't give me the information I want, I'll see that Larkin cuts off his supply. The thing registers a bit, and I see him get white under the gills, so I guess Larkin has tipped him off that I'm a big gun in the traffic. But I don't get much out of him; I see that he's in deadly fear of this Uncle Gus.

"He'd kill me in a minute," he says, his eyes wide with terror. "All I'll say is that he used to run a fruit stand down in Mott Street—just before the girl come, he fixed up the house on Fifty-sixth Street and then—no! My God! No! He'd find out who told and—no—not another word."

He wasn't smiling no more now; his face had turned a chalky white, and his teeth were chattering. In another minute, he had gone all to pieces like his kind do—he was between the two fears: of Larkin cutting his supply and Uncle Gus cutting his throat. Changed? Why, you wouldn't know him for the same man—cringing and whining and kneeling at my feet. But nothing came out of him, and then he suddenly turns, and I see him roll up his sleeve and give his arm a long scratch with a safety pin; then into the blood went a few drops from a tiny bottle. Blooey! Just like that he was himself again—and any chance I had, which wasn't much, was gone. But I was working on another idea.

"A hundred dollars for the information—where is the girl?" I rip out quick.

"The girl—again—"

Then he stopped short, but he eyed the money which I held in my hand longingly. But he wouldn't open up, so I pulled my best and last card; time was passing and something was telling me that the girl needed me.

"I tell you how you can avoid all trouble—with the gang and with Larkin," I told him. "Give me the name of one of the gang. One that knows all, and one that I can reach tonight—now. I'll get the information out of him just the same as I would have gotten it out of you, if I hadn't passed my word to Larkin." Oh, I felt like shoving my gun down his throat and getting the truth out of him. But my word had gone to Larkin and—well—I couldn't break it. I know that don't sound like common sense, but we'll call it my weakness. Terry Mack's word is good, and weak or not, it always will be good.

I see I had him interested, and I took out three hundred and offered it to him. Then I told him if this Gustave was sure to find out everything, why, he'd find out that it wasn't him that told, but the other fellow.

"Ain't there some fellow—just give me his name and address—just one who knows what's going on tonight—perhaps you have an enemy—someone what done you dirt." And that caught him.

He grabs the bankroll and spills a mouthful.

"Daggo Joe," he says, and gives me an address which is less than five blocks away. "He's there now alone—and will be there until six-thirty, when he goes on duty."

"Good," I eye him, "and if you have lied to me, why I'll hunt you up and make you eat every one of them bills and then—then I'll cut them out of you again." Which may sound like a lot of wind, but it was the kind that he would understand best, and I don't know but what I meant it.

With that, I beat it over to the Thirties and step up and down in front of Daggo Joe's for a few minutes. You can't fool these birds and give them a surprise visit; they have a way of knowing you're coming. And this Daggo Joe knew, for I seen a figure at the window which I spotted for his, and then the light went out in that window. But I want him to know that I'm coming and coming alone—he won't beat it—not him; he'll stay and play it foxy on me—kind of get revenge for the previous night. So eleven-thirty finds me entering the dusty old building and climbing the stairs to the third floor, where this Daggo Joe parks his noble person.

Of course, my electric flash covers every jump of them hallways; there ain't a chance for a lad to jump me in the dark—also, my gun is mighty convenient. When I reach his door, I tap lightly, and there ain't no answer, but I know that he's listening in there, and I know that he takes me for a soft one announcing myself like that.

I don't waste much time, but try the door—just a turn of the knob, and it gives—the door ain't even locked. Do you get the game—well, I do. He wants me to walk right in so he can croak me off. It nearly makes me laugh—the simplicity of the whole thing; why he's almost like a kid.

And I know just where he's standing, as if he told me so himself; he's behind that door, and he's got a blackjack or a knife in his mitt. And then I start to do what any dick would do, and just what Daggo Joe figures I'll do—push the door open slowly. That's what ninety-nine in a hundred would do—play the game very cautious.

So I push the door very softly, and this Joe waits behind it, all smiles, I guess. Then I suddenly up with my foot and give that door a kick—a real healthy kick. If I do say so myself, that's the only way to enter a room what you got your doubts on.

Bang! Crash! You could hear his head connect with that door in one heavy thud. After that, there was nothing to it. I had my flash out and my gun on him, and the door closed and locked before he knew what had happened. It was five minutes before he recovered enough to speak. He didn't fall to the floor—I guess his head was too thick for that—but he slumped up against the wall and stayed slumped while I lit the gas.

"Howdy, Joe," I says, as I took the blackjack from his useless fingers and chucked it under the bed. And then, while he was recovering his manners, I dumped some water from the pitcher over his head and watched him swim ashore.

"I kill you yet," he says in a feeble voice, as he clutched at his aching head.

I could have laughed, but I didn't; there wasn't time. I saw now that that duck was able to talk and understand me, which was more to the point. I wasn't there for any fooling—not me—he had information that I wanted, and I hadn't passed my word that there'd be no force used.

"Joe," I says, whipping my gun into his stomach. "I want you to blow the whole game—first, where's the girl—quick!"

There was nothing gentle about me then—I'm a different man when it comes to business—that's why I'm a success. I always play that the end justifies the means.

"I tell you nothing!" He pulls himself up straight and folds his arms across his chest. "Your girl, eh—pretty soon they be through with her—and she my girl—the—"

But he never finished that string of dirty epithets. I up with the butt of my gun and gave him a swipe across the face that made his lordly air look mighty cheap. And right here come the tactics that you may not agree with. You may question the ethics, but the results are good. Poor morals perhaps, but good, sound, common sense.

It ain't pretty to tell, so I'll skip over it. But I beat and choked the truth out of him, anyway.

His tongue was hanging out, and he was black in face and pretty near gone when he nodded he'd tell. And tell he did.

"You'd torture that girl," I said. "And I'll torture the whole truth out of you," and I thought of that poor little kid and meant what I said. I don't bluff, and that gink knew it when he opened up.

It was in spasmodic jerks, and between the real fear of me and the imaginary fear of Gustave, he give me the lay of the game. Here's what I get:

In the first place Gustave ain't her uncle at all—his real handle is Boro, and him and her uncle ran a fruit market together down on Mott Street. The uncle had already kicked off when the word came that Nita was coming to America. This Boro got hold of the letter, fixed up the house, and posed as the uncle, whom Nita had never seen. It wasn't hard; he used to write all the letters for her uncle—that bird couldn't read nor write, and didn't feel overproud about letting his family know that America hadn't done much for him.

Nita comes and falls heavy; then comes this Manual Sparo, and things ain't so good; he spots the game at once. But he's a bit of a crook himself and loves Nita, so he offers not to spill the beans if he can marry Nita and connect with half of the formula money with Boro, the fake uncle. The uncle agrees, but Nita ducks on the marriage, and Boro, getting frightened that Manual may cash in on the formula, kidnaps him and tortures him to tell where he's hidden the paper.

Enough of that—he won't tell, and Boro hits on the plan of torturing Nita—for deep down in his black heart, this Manual really loves the girl.

That would hold me for a while—Joe didn't know what the formula was about, but he knew there was much money in it. A final shake and he tells me where the girl is hid. And that stumped me—she was right in that house on Fifty-sixth Street, and they were dead set on getting the formula that night.

The dirty swine; I just looked down at him—if he'd 'a smiled then I'd—but I had seen to it that there wasn't enough left of his map to smile. So I just cracked him over the head once—one good one that would put him to sleep for the rest of the night. I didn't want him to come butting in on the grand finale. Leaving him lying on the floor, I beat it; locked the door on the outside and, slipping the key in my pocket, turned the corner and whistled for Bud.

We sure made time uptown. It would be too late to call for help, and besides, I didn't figure I'd want none. When I left the car on Sixth Avenue, about a block away, I said to Bud:

"Give me an hour, and then if you don't get word from me,

why—send the police—tell them it's murder."

"Police! Police!" Bud's mouth opened wide.

"Yes—police," I says. "It's the first time you ever had that kind of an order, but obey it to the letter—let the police know and then beat it."

Not that I thought that there was a chance of failure—I never fail—but that girl was trusting me and I was— But I turned my back on Bud and beat it down Fifty-seventh Street. It was like I was a bit ashamed of showing weakness.

So I pick my distance and make my approach from the other street. I duck through an alleyway, hop a high fence and land in the backyard of the house next door to the gang's. I got to figure out the best way to make it. Oh, I'm going in all right if I have to bust straight through the big French windows in the front with a gun in either mitt. But that's my last stand. I ain't one that goes in for dramatics; not me. I got the two big guns and one little one—the little one I always have—it's a sleeve gun and is used in an emergency; also, I have my flash and am ready for business.

I guess I take about five minutes studying all of them rear windows: I want to make sure that there ain't anyone spying out the back; it don't seem likely, but then I don't take no chances. There are only two lights—one high up which you can hardly see—the other one comes from a window about seven foot from the ground. I think it's the kitchen. Now, there is a water pipe running up to the top light, but I ain't no acrobat. Another look around, and I jump the adjoining fence and land in the yard of the brownstone house.

Edging up close to the back of the house, where a lad at the upper windows couldn't see me without raising one and looking out, I try to peer in the kitchen window, and it's a success; the shade is up just enough to look in under. There's one man in there, a dirty-looking bird, and he's in his shirt-sleeves and fiddling around the coal stove.

Now, there ain't no trick ways of entering houses without people knowing it when they are awake—least I don't know of none. Open windows are nice, but you don't find them in a joint like this one. I'm good with a gun, and in my line that's near enough, but I might say that I have brains too and know how crooks think. For another thing, I ain't a lad what waits around all night for what is called an opening. I don't spend the rest of the night planning when some client's life is at stake, not me; I earn my money and act.

So—I just up with my fist and knock lightly on that kitchen window. If that boy goes for help, I'll be in that window before he ever comes back, for there ain't no bars on it. But if he ain't scared and uses his think box, he'll get to figuring that only a friend would knock. And that's what he done—he comes to the window and looks out.

It's dark, and he can't see nothing but my outline, which I stand there and let him see. Then I lift my hand cautiously like and signal him to lift the window. He stands undecided a minute, and then plays into my hand—he opens the window, but I ain't altogether in luck, for he don't stick his head out. He whispers something in Italian. I don't get what it is, but I make a sucking noise which he can take to keep quiet, and I hand him up a slip of paper which I pull out of my pocket. Out comes his hand to grasp it, and then—with all my strength I take hold of his wrist and pull. Say, there ain't a shout out of him as he comes out that window. But there is one unfortunate circumstance which I had hoped to avoid. I don't figure enough on the play of his heels—they crack that windowsill some wallop, but no glass breaks. He don't holler none as he lands; guess he's too surprised, but he sure did kick up the woodwork. One belt on the head, and the cry dies on his lips, and I'm up and over that sill and into the kitchen. Down comes the shade again; from an upper window someone might see the light and the shadow of the limp body on the ground below.

Just a jump and a brace and a swing, and I'm standing in that kitchen; believe me, I didn't waste no time. I wasn't going to get caught half in and half out of that window. Now, if any of them lads wanted to take a potshot at me, well and good—I was ready. Let them come. I was now in a position to return the compliment; in fact, I was perfectly willing to *start* the show. A fellow don't have to take a shot at me to arouse my interest; you don't have to give me a good moral reason to shoot. Show me the man, and if he's drawing on me and is a man what really needs a good killing, why, I'm the boy to do it.

Well, luck is with me or with them; you can take your choice, for I ain't dodging no gunplay, but there ain't a sound in the house. I'm inside, without anyone being the wiser.

I stand around for several minutes, though, to make sure, and then I hear a tap tap of feet in the room above me—just pounding on the ceiling—slow, like slippered feet that were treading heavily up and down in the same place. It would stop and then go on again, but listen as I would by the kitchen door, there was no other sound of life in the whole house. Still, that didn't mean so much. It was an old house and the walls were thick, and sound don't carry much—but it sure was a deathly stillness and that tap, tap, tap just above me.

I took a look around the kitchen to see if I could find out why that lad was down there, and I did—my heart missed a beat, which is something for my heart to do, I can tell you. What had I seen—well, I had seen two pokers flaming red hot, there in the open stove. Now, if it had 'a been one, it might have been there by accident, just dropped in when I knocked on the window. But two, I knew they were being heated for some purpose, and it was the realization of that purpose which made my heart give a sudden beat and a quick jump. The pokers were to be used to torture the girl and....A sudden scream—a woman's scream of terrible agony or fear came sharply through that heavy silence. I was out in the hall in a moment—it was Nita who had given that piercing shriek.

But I didn't lose my head none. Like a cat I went sneaking up the heavy wooden stairs, my sneakered feet making no sound there in the darkness. Oh, I had my flash, but I didn't use it. I ain't much stuck on suicide.

But the cry don't come again, and I reach the second-floor landing. I grope about in the darkness, following the banister along the hall, for that cry had come from someplace near the top of the house. Then, when I'm about to start that second flight, the tap, tap, tap comes again, and I stop dead listening. The sound is right behind me—just about in the middle of that hallway. Then I turn and catch a tiny speck of light creeping under a doorway. I sneak toward it carefully and listen again—the tapping stopped, but I hear a moaning now, and then a feeble foreign voice.

I push my hand along, feeling for the knob, and my fingers strike a panel—a sliding panel—just a tiny one, like they have in the speakeasies. I work it slowly just a crack and peer in.

The room is only lit by a candle, which stands on an old table right in the center of the room; the rest of the place is bare, and then—came the groan again, and I see a figure laying on the hard boards, in one corner of the room.

There ain't a spot in the room for a cat to hide in, so I turn the knob; the door opens and I walk in, shutting it gently behind me. One look and a flash of light tells me that there ain't no cause to fear that gent lying in the corner—his hours are on the run; just another groan, and I don't need to be a doctor to know that that guy is going out.

Right off the bat I spot him as Manual Sparo, and I'm right. He half turns his head, and his eyes are glassy and he don't seem to be sure if there is someone in the room with him or not; then he mutters something, but I don't get him.

"Speak English," I says. I'm none too gentle because it won't do him any good now, and if he has anything to say I want to get it before he slips over.

"I'll tell—I'll tell," he says, in good English. "The girl don't know—I wouldn't tell her. The formula's in one of Boro's books—downstairs—third shelf—*Modern Italian Poets.* I tell you the girl don't know—spare her."

And his voice is getting louder with the final effort. Partly because I'm afraid he'll spill my chances all over the house, and partly because I feel sorry for the poor cuss, I up and tell him that I'm the rescue party.

At first he don't understand, but then things kind of get into his head and he grabs me by the hand. He knows I'm friendly, and he takes me for his brother back in Naples. So half in English and half in Italian, he gives me a lot of chatter. But I gather enough to learn this: They had carted him down from the Bronx early that morning, and they told him that they would torture the girl if he didn't tell. He wouldn't tell, and they sent the girl in to him; and he started to tell her where the formula was, and then he changed his mind. Some of the birds were trying to listen outside and got enough to make them think that he had told her—that was about two hours ago. He guessed that they were torturing her, and he had been knocking on the floor with his bare feet—he was ready to blow the game and save the girl, which I don't think would have helped her none.

And you should'a seen him; his whole body had been hacked at, and his feet and hands burnt to the bone; he had grit, that boy—they didn't get nothing out of him, with all their deviltry. Yep, he had grit and bullheaded stupidity.

Now, you see, I just about did the right thing when I choked the truth out of that murdering villain a short while before—this was no crowd to fool with.

"How many are there in the house?" I said, lifting up his head so that he could breathe better. "How many?" I repeated again a bit louder, and then I look down at him.

There I'd been, listening to his story and trying to ease him up a bit and—well—he had gone out on me—living through all that he did, and then kicking off sudden like that. But I just shrug my shoulders—I can't expect all the luck—the poor devil was better off; he'd never have walked again anyway; that was certain. I let him down easy; he was a bad egg, but way down in his black heart he had loved the girl, and even if it was a selfish love, why—oh, well, I let him slip down to the boards easy.

I straightened up for one last look around that room, and then that shriek—that terrible cry—came again, a bit longer, more penetrating and piercing. This time I didn't wait to take things easy; I just dashed out of that room and up the stairs, my flash going full blast. And it was a good thing I had it, too, for it shines right on a lad sitting on the top of the stairs. Oh, he fired—yes—and I don't know what kind of a shot he was under ordinary circumstances. My light, a mighty powerful one, too, had struck him right between the eyes, and he didn't see none too well, or he shot in a hurry. Anyway, he only shot once—none never do shoot more than once at me. I guess our guns spoke together. I felt nothing and I didn't need to give a second look to him. When I fire, there ain't no guessing contest as to where that bullet is going. Often I poke for the heart, 'specially if there is any distance to cover; its surer. But this was shooting uphill like, and the light was directly on his face, so I let him have it there—someplace about the center of that ugly map of his.

There ain't much to that sort of shooting; you just kind of see a hole for a second; a tiny speck of red, and then the face fades out of the picture. So I just step over him as he rolls down the stairs.

Of course the shot is heard, and another bimbo ducks out of a side room, just as I make the landing. He don't do no shooting—he don't even get a look—just a spurt of flame and I get him. He falls pretty, blocking the doorway which someone is trying to close, but having no luck. And then for the fireworks!

I got the jump on them now; I've made a mighty good impression, and it'll have a good moral effect; there is nothing like following it up. Two of them dead—oh, they're dead all right—none ever come back and fire just one more shot after I plug them. Once I hit a lad, he stays put. So I jump to the door, kick it flying, and, dropping my flash, I stand there a gun in either fin.

And then things ain't so good; to this day I can't explain how they happened to be so well prepared. I just stand there like the avenging angel, with a smile of greeting, when something like a ton of brick comes down and cracks me on the head. I remember firing at a sneering brown face and muttering number three as the clouds come down—after that, curtains—everything goes black.

How long, I don't know, but I come to after a bit and sit up. I ain't tied or nothing—just dazed—I see near a million stars and then I see worse. Over in one corner of the room I see Nita, and she's bound hand and foot on a bare hard bed. There's Boro and another lad close beside him, and one stretched dead out in the center of the floor—so I figure that even with the weight on my head, my aim was good because he ain't dressed like the bird I copped in the doorway.

And Boro is playing the game hard now, and there ain't no smile on that mean, wicked kisser of his. He has a gat stuck close up against my chest, which don't give me much of a chance even if I did feel like pulling something—which I don't. It's a good thought, but my brains are dusty—hitting on one cylinder like. But there's one thing they overlooked, one thing what brings a gleam of hope. They got both my big guns, yes—but their search hadn't been a good one, or was it the way I was lying? Yep, tucked up my sleeve is still the little automatic twenty-five; it's little, yes, but as I get the feel of it there, it seems as big as a cannon. Just let me get my head clear and give me a chance to drop my hands, and those birds will receive a treat—a little treat what they won't enjoy long.

I can shoot in a split second on an open draw—none faster. I'll pull a gun with anyone, even if he comes from the cow country; and I'll beat him to the draw too—there ain't no two ways about that. But on the sleeve business—oh, I'm fast—like lightning—but it takes a second, a whole second, and that's some time in a matter of life and death. But to pull my arm down and shoot takes one full second; I know, I've timed it.

But Boro has that gun bored into my chest and my hands shoved up in the air; through instinct, I guess, for there ain't no will to hold them there, for I don't hardly know what I'm doing. But I was trying to think—place exactly where I was—what was happening—and behind it all was the reassuring pressure of hard steel just below the elbow.

"Get up!" says Boro, and though his hand is steady, his voice trembles with rage.

And I get up. I can see he's mighty willing to shoot and wonder why he don't. Then he backs me up against the wall.

"You say everything is all clear downstairs, Pedro, and that no one heard the shots," he says to the only other lad left, but he keeps his gun and his eyes on me while he talks. I guess his English is for my benefit, though why he wants to shower me with happiness, I don't know.

"No one heard," Pedro answers, and his English is punk.

"Go fetch some rope," Boro chirps, "and we'll tie up this swine—but first—well, you shall see something amusing when you return, Pedro—and Pedro, another hot poker—very hot—it is for his eyes."

So Pedro beats it. Well, you don't need three guesses to tell you that I'm going to take chances at the first opportunity, or without any opportunity, for that matter.

Boro holds me, with his gun, against the wall a moment, and then he backs away about three paces.

"You are one who shoots well, but so do I," he sneers. "Watch—first I will cripple you. The arms and then the legs—a bullet for each; and then when Pedro returns, it will be the eyes, but that will not be so pleasant—you would play a game with Boro, eh?"

Get what he was up to; why, he'd just stand me against the wall and wing me, and then burn out my eyes. I tried to think. I said to myself, now or never, and did nothing. I was like a man in a dream, and a mighty bad dream—just acting mechanically.

Bang! He had fired. There was a sear of red hot flame just below the elbow, and my left arm dropped to my side. I heard Boro laugh and Nita give a little smothered cry—just the quick intake of breath.

As the blood streamed down onto my wrist, my head seemed to clear, and then my brain hit suddenly back to normal. I was Terry Mack again, and believe me that is something.

Bang! The report came again and I thought it was too late, but no—his bullet had jammed against the hard steel of my little twenty-five, without ever touching my arm.

I don't know if he saw me smile as my right hand started to slink to my side. I think he did, for he was suddenly raising his gun again when I fired. But he never used it; Boro had fired his last shot.

The tiny splash of red appeared for a moment between his eyes; he stood so, his great eyes bulging in surprise more than pain—the surprise of death—then without a groan or a cry he pitched his length upon the floor. He didn't roll over and give a last convulsive groan or a kick—some may do it—none that I ever hit at that range. Boro died standing; died before he fell, and when he fell, there was not so much as a wiggle of his fingers.

As he hit them boards, the door opened and Pedro appeared for a moment in the aperture—but only for a moment. Why I didn't wing him I don't know—but he was gone—whining like a dog as he ran down the stairs, and that was the last I ever heard of Pedro. Of course I bolted the door before I went over to the girl. And I spotted the weight, too, which had put me out of business—it was fixed so that the rope didn't loosen it from the ceiling until someone pressed a catch near the door. Oh, it was good stuff all right, and I admired the pretty way it was pulled off.

I guess I must have staggered across to the girl—my arm didn't bother me none, but my head had gotten about as big as a church again. But somehow I released her. It seemed like I was two persons, and I'd ask my other self what I'd do, and my other self would answer me. Like this it went:

"And now, Terry, my boy, what's on the program—they've all gone, you know."

And then I'd answer:

"Get a knife, Mack—there's one in the corner there—and cut the rope."

And I did, and afterward Nita told me that I talked to myself like a man in a fever. It was then that I told her about Boro not being her uncle at all, and about Manual being dead, and all that I had learned from Daggo Joe. But I never mentioned the formula; somehow I kept that to myself. And she wasn't hurt at all. Her feet were all right, for they had only just started the torture and hardly touched her tender skin. She had cried out more in deadly fear than in pain—but her mental suffering must have been terrible just the same.

It was she who took the chances, while I just sat there on the floor and mumbled to myself; she went downstairs and got water and bathed my head and tied up my arm, which proved to be only a flesh wound, and not much to bother about at that.

And then, when I come about all right, she turned around and fainted on me. I tell you it was a tough proposition, there with her in that house of death. But I was as clear as a bell now; it's wonderful what water will do for a man, and I tell you it's been a good friend to me in many an emergency.

Water helped her, too, and just as I got her able to sit up and was thinking of helping her downstairs, there came a ringing at the doorbell, followed by a heavy pounding on the door. I left her a moment and, opening the door, listened. The rapping came again, louder than before; and then came the crash of an ax, and I remembered—the hour was more than up and Bud had sent for the police. Good old Bud—I felt like wringing his neck; I wanted to do some talking with a first-class lawyer before I paid my social obligations to the police.

I turned to the window and looked out—there was the lead pipe, the one I couldn't climb up, but I felt that even with my bad arm I could slide down it—especially now that I had the proper incentive behind me. You see, this was no kind of a situation for Terry Mack to be found in. The girl would be all right—they couldn't possibly suspect her of all that slaughter.

"It's the police," I told her in a hurry. "You'll be all right, but for me—a quick getaway. You can tell them about me, but I'll hang low till my lawyer has proven a case against this gang. If they got me, they'd frame me sure—they love me like poison—

you'll be O.K. Nita—I'm going to duck."

And then she up and staggered across the room and threw her arms about my neck and hung there; in fact, I had to hold her—she was so weak that her hands couldn't even retain their grasp about my neck.

"Don't leave me, Terry—you're all I got—and the police—oh, Terry, I'll die if you leave me."

And that shows you what fear of the police the fake uncle had instilled in her.

And right there is another thing that I can't explain. Maybe it's weakness, but I like to think it ain't, though I can't account for it. You might think that I had done enough for this girl and earned my pay—well, perhaps I had. But there was soft little hands about my neck and silken hair against my cheek—great innocent, childish eyes looking through pools of water into mine—and—well, I stayed—yep, I just played the fool and stayed.

So it was I held her in my arms when half a dozen cops busted into the room. My cap is still sticking on my head, and I retain sense enough to pull it down close to my eyes.

Then there is questions and warnings and one thing and another. But I don't need no warning—my trap is shut tight—I'll have my mouthpiece when I do any talking, and he's a good lawyer, too. As for the girl, well, she opens up a bit but don't say nothing about the formula, which I think is wise but don't get her real reason for it; though I put it down to the money what's behind it, and her distrust of the police. And I tell you another thing—they are some surprised cops after they look that house over. I hear some of them in the backyard, where they have found the first lad what I socked.

Then in walks Detective Sergeant Quinn, and I know that things are going to get lively. This same Quinn has been trying to hook something on me since George Washington was a boy.

"And the story goes that this one man killed these four—pretty thin," he says, and then he walks over to me. "We'll just have a look at that mug of yours, my man."

With that he jerks off my cap, and me and Quinn look straight at each other.

"Good evening, Sergeant." I can't help but grin. Quinn's fizz is a scream.

"Terry Mack! Terry Mack!" he says twice as he steps back, but he can't hide the feeling of joy that comes over him. "Well, after all it does look like it might be a one-man job—with Mack that man," he says to one of his men. "Hooked at last!" His ugly face screws up in satisfaction. "We'll trot this pair out—separate them—you can keep the girl here until after the coroner comes. But keep your eye on her, and trot this fellow along."

Just as the cop comes up to me with the cuffs in his mitts, I turn to the girl!

"If you have any friends, know of anyone in the city that can help us—now's the time—we're in bad."

And I meant every word of it. I knew the police system, and knew that they'd put me through the jumps before I ever got my lawyer.

Nita seemed to recover somewhat.

"I know one who would help me—who would do anything that I ask. Can—how can I get him?" She was looking at the ceiling while she talked.

That's what I wanted; I wanted her request registered while all them cops were in the room. One of them would be looking for Quinn's job, and if Quinn did anything to hamper the cause of justice, one of them might be glad to blow it—secretly.

"Quick," I says. "Who do you know—who that can help us on the outside?"

"I know Mr. James Roland Williams," she said quietly, though her voice shook a bit. "I think he would do anything for me."

Quinn drew back; I gasped! And why not? James Roland Williams was the commissioner of police.

"Well—well—we'll see about that in the morning." But I noticed that Quinn's voice lacked its usual air of authority.

"How about it now—Quinn?" I chimed in. "This young lady is not used to being treated like a common crook, and from what I know of her friendship with Mr. Williams, it might cost you your shield."

Of course, I didn't know nothing about it, but it didn't strike me as a good time to show my ignorance.

Quinn just scowled at me and told me to hold my tongue, then he turned to the girl. Her honest, quiet air of refinement evidently impressed him.

"Do you know him very well—Miss?" He added the "Miss" after a moment's hesitation.

"Oh yes—I should say—oh, very well indeed." She nodded her head.

"Well enough to disturb him at this hour of the morning?" Quinn bent those hard, stern eyes of his full upon her. "You know, he only got back from a trip south last night."

"No—I did not know that. But it does not matter. He would be glad to come to me at any hour—he has told me so—told me—oh, please call him." Her voice broke.

Another glance, and Quinn turned toward the door. He paused undecided a moment, and then:

"Who shall I say—what name?" he said, and his manner was almost courteous.

"Sen—Miss Nita Gretna—Nita will be enough—he will come at once." There was a certain calm dignity in her manner.

One more close scrutinizing look, and Quinn turned again and left the room.

"And make it snappy, Quinn, even if you are getting a bit on for so many stairs."

I could not resist the temptation to call after him as he descended the stairs. I could see now that pretty soon everything would be jake, and I'd be the light-haired boy; a commissioner has a way of hushing up unpleasant events. Of course, I never doubted the girl—just one look at those clear, honest glims of hers was enough to convince anyone.

It was five minutes later when Quinn returned, and although he had run up the stairs his face was white—white with anger.

"Take them away!" he roared. "Keep them apart—watch that girl." He pointed a finger which shook with rage at Nita. "What do you mean by lying to me—Mr. Williams never heard of you. And he had other things to say to me, things that you'll pay for, my fine girl. Take them away!" he spoke to his men. "And keep an eye on that gunman—Terry Mack." With that, he showed us the width of his shoulders as he stamped viciously from the room.

As for me, I didn't look at the girl—she must'a felt pretty cheap, I thought. But what a superb bluff she had made! That innocent-appearing kid had looked the tough Quinn straight between the eyes and handed him out that earful of bull—and me—oh, I fell for it too.

But I shrugged my shoulders as they slipped on the bracelets and led me away.

"Holler for the best lawyer you can get," I called back over my shoulder to Nita. "We'll see it through together if they don't railroad me. And if you need any money, why—why, I got a bit saved up."

And that last line will pretty near show you that my head wasn't altogether clear yet.

And there you are; I spent the night behind bars. I didn't like the ride they give me neither. I should have been taken to an uptown station, but they booked me further downtown, which sure did look bad. You see, I had a sneaking fear that they might jump me through the hoop; there were several little things that the bulls would have liked to have gotten out of me. I ain't afraid of nothing, mind you, but I was a bit worried; this third degree which you hear so much about ain't all wind—not by a jugful it ain't. I know them birds.

Of course, I was searched all right, but there wasn't a thing on me. I had dropped that sleeve gun when the cops broke in the door, and frisking me was about as exciting as searching a Sunday school superintendent. But this Quinn was a lad who would railroad a bishop, if he felt like it, and—and I ain't no bishop.

A cop what knows something about medicine looks over my arms and sniffs at the wound and says it ain't nothing—so I don't even see a doctor. But I guess he's right, and although it smarts a bit, there ain't much to it as for my head—well, it's a pretty tough head, and I ain't looking for any sympathy, and what's more I don't get any.

I slept pretty well, though, for I felt they'd be too busy to put over any rough stuff that morning; just like a baby I sleep until breakfast. The turnkey was agreeable, and I got a pretty good breakfast. But I didn't like the idea of eating there—I should 'a been brought before a magistrate—the whole thing didn't look good.

At eleven o'clock a dick comes to my door and has it opened and smiles in at me:

"Come on Terry," he says. He's grinning from ear to ear and looks real friendly, which, of course, makes me suspicious. But he walks me right out of the side door of the jail and lands me on the street. Then he hands me out my things that they took from me when I was booked.

"You're sure in luck this time, Terry," he says. "You fitted in right last night, and Quinn is having forty fits—that car there is waiting for you." And he indicates a big touring car with the jerk of his thumb. "Good luck, Terry, you're a game boy, if a tough citizen, and I don't hold anything against you."

I take his outstretched fist and turn toward the car like I had expected it to be there; they ain't going to faze me.

"Good-bye and thanks—" I wave to the dick from the back-seat.

"Casey's my name," he says, "Richard Casey!"

"Casey it is."

I shake again as the car speeds away. Then I look around a bit to get my breath; it's an expensive car all right, and there ain't no one but me and the driver. But the chauffeur don't seem to need any instructions, so I don't say anything. Just sit tight; that's my game.

Right up to the restaurant entrance of the Bolton Hotel we pull, and I hop out as live as life. I even start to enter the front door when a great big strapping boy of about twenty-five comes running out and grabs me by the hand.

"Mr. Mack—Mr. Terry Mack!" He smiles all over as he pump-handles me. "I'm James Williams—James Roland Williams, Jr. How's the arm?" he asks suddenly.

I almost forget myself for the moment:

"You're the police commissioner's son!" I guess I kind of gasp.

"That's it," he laughed. "Nita has told me all about you. She forgot the Junior last night when she rang up. You see, father was south when I returned from Italy, and I didn't get a chance to tell him the good news. Besides, there really wasn't any until this morning. Nita slipped away from me on the dock; she was to let me hear from her when she would say yes. She said it this morning."

He laughed again.

But I was to lunch with him and Nita, and there she was, waiting for us in a little private dining room upstairs. She didn't seem much the worse for last night. Young Williams said he wouldn't let her remember; he'd keep her going under high pressure until she forgot. Of course, his old man would see that everything was fixed up properly, and not a reporter had found out who had done the bumping off, nor that Nita was mixed up in it. The papers had just set it down for a general feeling of discontent among the Black-Handers.

And then I learned that he had met Nita on the boat, and that a wedding was all cooked up for the next day.

"It'll just be a quiet affair." Williams smiles all over his good-natured map. "Nita don't know anyone but you, so you'll have to show up." Then he tells me the church, and both of them get my promise to be on deck at eleven the next morning.

"Yes," she looks up at me from across the table, and I notice that there are dark rings under her eyes and that her fingers are twitching nervously. "We must have you Terry—it could not be a wedding without you and—oh—that old formula." She half closes her eyes. "I guess that it is gone forever."

And that's where I shine once again:

"Oh, is it?" I said. "Not so you could notice it—it ain't. Miss Nita, I was hired by you to get that formula, and I most generally get what I go after."

Then I turn to young Williams. I don't give him no information, but just make him promise to go and bring that copy of poems about them Italians to me, without opening the book, and I give him full instruction as to the lay of the book.

It ain't nothing to him, being the commissioner's son, to step right in and turn the trick, and in a half-hour or less he's back with the book. I open it, and there's the envelope. I guess I play the actor a bit when I hand it over to Nita, unopened. There sure was a certain air of satisfaction in that delivery.

Do their eyes open? Well, I should smile; Nita breaks the seal and opens it. She reads it a minute and then chirps:

"That is it." And leaning over the table she takes a match and lights the thin tissuey paper that she holds in her hand. We just sit and stare as she drops it in the plate—a burnt, blackened, unrecognizable mass.

At first I just scratch my head; it's like seeing all your good work literally going up in smoke. Then curiosity gets the better of me for once, and I break my rule about not asking questions.

"Would you mind telling me what it was?" I can't help but ask; you must remember that at least five met their deaths on account of that same piece of paper.

She gives a wan little smile:

"All I know is that it is a formula—a chemical for making poison gas—a gas far stronger and more deadly than any used in the last war, or ever invented. I understand that a small quantity dropped in a container, from a plane, would be enough to wipe out hundreds upon hundreds of people. It may be worth much money, and I do not doubt that it is—but—but it is worth more to humanity there in that dish." And she stirs up the ashes with her spoon.

Personally, I don't take much stock in such sentiment, and I look at Williams to see how he's taking it. But he's only looking at her, cowlike and grinning. Well, he's either dough-heavy or he's in love—or I guess both, for he looks like money and I think the car is his.

And then when I'm leaving them, Nita up and throws her arms about me and kisses me—yes, kisses me full on the lips.

"Oh, Terry, Terry," she says and her voice breaks a little, "you've been more than a father to me—much more."

More than a father! Grandfather, she must mean. But I don't say that. I look at Williams to see how he's taking it, but it seems that his only aim in life is to carry a perpetual grin, which he does to the queen's taste.

"There—there! Be a good girl," is all I say as I pat her on the back. And wasn't that a fool remark for a full-grown man with all his senses!

So I left them.

I guess it's near three o'clock when I see Bud and wrap myself into my easy chair. You see, my arm's all right, but I feel like taking it easy. And then along about eight that night Bud brings me in a envelope.

It's a check, and a good big one; I can see at a glance that everything has been taken into account, and she ain't forgotten the little matter of the four lads what got bumped off. And then the bonus—guess the extra was for Boro. But the check was big—very big—yet I can't honestly say that it was more than I was worth.

So I smoke and think; after all, it was an American that she loved and she hadn't fooled me none. Well, that little garden and the sunny sky of Italy had all gone blooey. I stood up and looked at myself in the glass—not a gray hair appeared—so she might have spared me that father scene. Did I feel bad—not me. I was mighty relieved; for a time, it looked like that dame was going to hook herself onto me for life. With a shrug of my shoulders, I picked up my hat and coat.

And how did I take it? Why, like the gentleman that I am. I just went out and bought her the very best wedding present that the swellest pawnshop in the city could produce. And believe me, that little gift, marked with the best wishes of Terry Mack, would hold its own alongside of anything that she got.

Action! Action!

Is it action you want? Well, you've got your wish. This story is action—barrels of it— from its title to its very last word. Start it and you won't have to worry about what to do with the next hour of your time.

TEN DOLLARS DOESN'T go far in the big city but with the lid down tight it will buy one swell feed and that's just what I was doing with my last ten spot.

In a way it was like taking the final plunge, for my life had been quiet and uneventful of late. The ordinary business life was not for me. That very night I had decided not to settle down; back to the real living for me—what might be called the adventure stuff though I had gone into it on a business basis.

Tonight I'd go and see Devlin, park my noble person in the best hotels and live on the fat of the land. I think it was a South American scheme which he had on tap; he wanted me—needed me. I pull a mighty mean gat and down there a quick shooter and a quick thinker is worth a greaser army.

And then I looked up and saw the face at the window again.

He was a little runt and well plumed; there was money in his make-up but not in his face. He was new rich; you had only to lamp him once to know that. I was near the window and this was about the fifth time that his flat, red nose was screwed close to the glass. Those glims of his were on me; there was no getting away from that.

I half raised my coffee cup in salute, just to let him know that I was wise. Then I looked indifferently about the room. There was no danger from this bird. I have enemies, yes; plenty of them but people bent on vengeance don't spend the best part of the night watching you load up. No—there was no danger from the nose at the window. Hence the salute with the invitation in it.

I wasn't surprised a few minutes later when I saw him slide into the seat opposite me.

"I'll take the check—Mr.—Mr. Mack; isn't it?"

His short, stubby fingers crawled across the table and fastened on the little pink slip which had enough figures on it to warrant the use of an adding machine.

"No, you won't."

I just shot my hand out and plucked the pasteboard from his grasp.

"You have the name right—Mack—Terry Mack—and he pays his own checks; at least at the start he does."

Not that I was touchy on these little matters of etiquette. Oh, I intended that he take the check alright. But I'd let him see the manner of man he was dealing with first. This lad had the look of business about him and he might as well know that he wasn't dealing with any second-story worker. That check would serve a complete college course to him later.

"I hope you don't mind my sitting in with you like this."

"Not at all," I nodded. "It must have been cold outside." I turned the check over and looked at the addition.

"Have a cup of coffee," I suggested.

I'd gamble two bits on this fellow anyway.

"You have been recommended to me—highly recommended, Mr. Mack," he opened up when he took his face from the cup. "I think that I can put a little money your way."

"Little won't do!" I shook my head. "I'm off for South America very shortly."

"But I understood from…."

"So did I," I helped him along. "It was only tonight that I decided. The city has not been kind to me. No sir, it treats me like a step-child. It's a false alarm; the money isn't here."

And I was givin' him facts then. The lure of the old life was calling me; the life where a man's pockets were filled by the quickness of his trigger finger. Yep, it was pleasant to think of. I was going back.

"It is final?"

His voice was anxious as he leaned over the table and I caught the full reflection of his face in the light of the little table lamp. He was a squared-jawed important little fellow of about fifty and his diamond pin and larger finger rocks told of money—not class you know—just money.

"No, it's not final."

I watched his nose ring the cup. "But it's near it, mighty near it, and you'd have to talk real money. What's the lay?"

I suddenly decided not to waste more time. Anyway, I wasn't much interested.

He sat up straight when I put the question and then came suddenly forward again, his elbows on the table.

"I have heard, Mr. Mack, that you are quick with the gun and—and in a good cause ready to use it. For such a man I will pay much money."

And that was the first time I noticed his foreign accent. I give him a quick glance. He looked enough like an American but I placed him as part Spanish; his eyes were dark and shifty, and his English was a bit off color at times.

"What's the lay?" I ask him again, lighting a butt.

"You don't ask who I am, ehe?"

And seeing that he expects an answer I give him one:

"No, I don't," is the whole of my oratory.

"I am John Rogo."

He raises his head and throws out his chest like he had handed me a knock-out. But I couldn't roll over and kick; the name meant nothing to me. He might be a boot-legger or a head waiter or any other well known character but I couldn't do a fade out. Still he was my guest; at least to the extent of a cup of coffee and I had to play the polite so I let him fall as easy as possible.

"Mr. Rogo," I says, "I'm sorry. But your handle don't mean nothing to me. Still that don't distract from your greatness. I'm not up on the Who's Who and it would take a Morgan or a Rockefeller to get a rise out of me."

"I thought you would know."

His chest caved in and his face slipped a little.

"But it is enough that I am rich and can pay you well and that my daughter needs your protection."

Now, that was real talk you got to admit. He almost told the whole story in that one simple sentence. Later he gets down to business and turns out an earful which is like sweet music. His pay is big, the time unlimited—perhaps a week, perhaps a year but when he is satisfied that his daughter is free from all danger I come into a bank roll.

And let me tell you this much. It was a piece of change that would make my South American handout look like German marks in comparison.

His story was a good one and I liked the way he told it; he had guts for such a little runt.

There were five of them who had gone into the thing in Africa some twenty-five years ago. They had found some British Government land that appeared thick with diamond dirt. A hundred thousand dollars' worth they nailed amongst them.

Well, the others had stuck him; killed his brother, knifed him and cleared out with the rocks. So they left him out there in the wilderness to die.

There was more to the yarn of course but all told it was one sweet story of treachery, low cunning and murder. But the poetic part of it was that the mine they left him wasn't just a worthless dump. The old servant who nursed him back to life gave him the secret of a real bed at the foot of the hill far into the ground. It is enough that years later he was rich—dough-heavy beyond the expectations of any of them. And now those dear old boys were blackmailing him and threatening him for an honest divvy of the coin.

He had no fear for himself and that's what made me coddle to him; he had spunk—that lad.

It was his daughter who worried him and his description of that frail would make your mouth water for beauty and your flesh creep for unfaithfulness. She was twenty and for all John Rogo could do he couldn't get her married. Not to the lad he had picked, anyway, though I took it that he wasn't over particular.

Somehow he was set on getting her married. The why of that I couldn't get. She had been engaged to half a dozen of the cake-eater variety but she always dropped them heavy before the wedding march come off.

But that wasn't so important. The former partners of his were on the war path; that is two of them were—the other one was dead. But these two were enough; from all accounts they had more roughnecks working for them than a shad has eggs.

They wanted two-thirds of his money and they threatened to hang crepe over his daughter's head. Twice they had attempted to carry her off and both times they meant business—two guards that he had hired had been killed.

Now he had come to me. My reputation had made him shake a leg. Some South American exporters had given him one grand earful of my accomplishments. And if the truth must be told they hadn't misled him none.

This Rogo knows values and he ain't no nickle nurser so before we finish our second cup of coffee I've turned over the check to him. Yep, the sad news is his; all expenses go with the job. He tells me there ain't no present danger for his daughter though he don't tell me why and I don't ask him. I ain't nosey when I'm well paid. But he wants me on the job. "The blow may fall any moment, but I'll have warning," and he shakes his head and looks troubled.

So it is that three days later finds us driving into his country home which goes by the fancy name of Three Pines. The name is high toned but has a deal more sense to it than a lot of them swell monikers. There are three great pine trees right by the gateway; one on each side of the entrance and one on a little grass plot right in the middle of the driveway. Artistic perhaps if you got an eye for beauty but dangerous on a dark night if you're bent on speed.

And the girl! She's there on the big veranda to give us a welcome. You see, she ain't in the know. She's to get the idea that I'm a visitor—a landscape artist to fix the place up. That's a rich one for me but it's Rogo's idea and I guess it's as good as another. All I got to do is park my tongue and look wise.

Now, I ain't much on women; in my business they ain't conducive to long life and liberty. Fellows I used to know in South America, right down high-class chaps, got to whispering things in the ears of dark eyed señoritas and shortly afterwards they turned up corpses. That is some of them did; others turned up missing or married.

It's just as bad either way you take it. Their gun eye was gone; they'd get a thinking how the wife would look in black or something. Leastwise I know of three what went out because of poor shooting. There ain't no other way to account for it.

But I got an eye for beauty and never let my business take on a sordid hue. And this dame is what is commonly called a fine piece of goods; there ain't no two ways about that. She's half Spanish and half American and whole flapper; just a slip of a kid with great black eyes and brownish red, bobbed hair. Not a bit of harm in her.

She's just bursting with verve and go and it really is a shame that someone don't bump off that gang what's thinking of taking the joy out of her life.

Of course she's a heart breaker. Why not? The kid's young and what's Romance but youth. Peggy is her handle and she turns out a real good little sport but a tough one to order about. She's set on having her own way about things and most times she gets it.

The first thing I do is go over the whole house from cellar to attic. If a gun breaks in there I'm going to know where to look for him. Also I make it a point of seeing all the servants. In an emergency a fellow wants to know who he's shooting.

Oh, I ain't looking for no general gun play but that don't matter. I'm thorough and that's partly why I'm a high priced man and mostly why I am still a man and not worm seed. Rogo likes the way I do business. He ought to. I like it myself.

"I'm not going to be driven from my home," Rogo tells me that night when Peggy has hit the hay. "I'm afraid the blow will fall now any minute. If Peggy would only marry Leo—then—ah—but I fear—"

Then he switches suddenly.

"I hope to get a bit of sleep while you're here. I've given you the room next to Peggy's and across the hall from mine."

"Rest easy."

I just hold up my hand. I want him to realize now that I'm there his fears is groundless.

And now for the catch in the whole business what don't please me none too well.

The next day I meet a cousin of Rogo's what's a steady free boarder at the house. This is the lad what he wants to marry Peggy and his plans are as easy to see through as a plate glass window without no glass. But unless some influence is brought to bear that ain't written in the stars this bozo ain't got a chance. He's dead from the neck up; dressed all up like a floorwalker and talks like time didn't mean nothing in his life.

His eyebrows keep going up and down which seems to be his idea of being high toned. He's got lace curtains all over his chin which are trimmed up like the stage doctor. Altogether he's a scream. But his eyes are small and mean and his nose is spread out all over his pan. His signal is Leo Loft and it fits him as well as another. And this is the lad what takes Peggy out and watches over her.

If there's any real danger old Rogo's been playing in more luck that he knows anything about. This lad is big—immense, but I put him down as a false alarm.

But lately the only thing he had to fear are threatening letters. And I sure got to admit that them letters are annoying. They pop up like a regular Broadway mystery play. The second day I'm there there's one under his plate at breakfast. Rogo just turns white about the gills and stuffs it in his pocket.

An hour later me and Leo and him have a little council of war in the library. Leo's eyebrows are going a mile a minute when he learns that I am in on the show. Rogo does the explanation and although I can't be sure, it's like he was giving a sinister message to Leo.

"Mr. Mack has had some experience in this—this sort of thing and has been kind enough to offer me his assistance."

He casts a quick look at Leo and then colors a bit like a child who has spilled the beans.

"Mr. Mack will only advise you to see the police," Leo sneers.

But all and all it's a remark with some sense to it. One of them things you can't never explain.

And Leo sure draws a bull's eye with that little bit of wisdom. Rogo goes white and then red and then jumps Leo.

"Haven't I told you that the police must have nothing to do with this. Sometimes Leo I think that you know more—"

Bing! he takes another tune almost at once and his voice is sure apologetic.

"A man in my position can't afford such notoriety and have this whole diamond business hashed over again."

Pretty thin, I think. Rogo's past is evidently not written in the golden book. Most men that have made money can't pull up the shades too high.

Then we all have a slant at the letter. It's cheap stuff but this shot it gives time. If he don't put up two-thirds of his bank roll they will take his daughter. Yep, it gives him ten days and you don't have to work your imagination overtime to get thinking that this letter might be considered as a threat. And Rogo's kisser spells disaster; it's written all over his map that these lads don't bluff.

Somehow I don't like the sneer of Leo's so I wait till he trots out before I open up with any more conversation. Then I ask Rogo:

"How are you supposed to put up the coin? A man don't drop half a million under a stone by the roadside you know."

He scratches his chin and then decides to open up a little.

"The thing has been run on a business basis," he tells me. "It started less than a year ago. Aron De Lasko, a well known foreign banker in the city, called on me. He spoke of the claim my former partners had against me as though it was all an honest business deal."

He stood up and paced the room a moment his face haggard and drawn.

"This De Lasko is back of the whole thing I know; it is he who is to take the money. He says that he knows nothing but I am sure that the others are helpless without him. His hand is a far reaching one."

And now you see the whole game or as much of it as I saw which leaves considerable in the dark you'll admit.

Why didn't Rogo out with the truth to me? What was he hiding and where did Leo Loft fit?

Rogo and Loft had been alone that morning for upwards of an hour. What would he tell this bird that he wouldn't tell me?

But I only shrugged my shoulders. I was hired to protect the girl and not stick my face too deep into his business.

But that there was dirt behind his silence I never doubted. Let this gang come for the girl and we'd ring up the curtain on the first act with the local undertaker playing a leading part.

But before I leave him Rogo lays his hand on my shoulder and says real solemn:

"Be ready, Terry—the danger draws nearer but thank God I am to have warning before the final blow is struck."

So I wander out into the garden behind the house and get a thinking. I wonder how the letter is planted under the plate; it must be an inside job sure. I don't take much stock in this mystery business nor do I weep tears of joy over the good and faithful servant stuff; I've bought too many of them myself. It sure does strike me that some good and faithful has turned this trick. And just as I pulled out a butt and lit up Peggy herself shoots out on me from the thick trees.

I pinched the butt and put it back in the box for I guess I know how to act in class. There weren't no use in getting this dame down on me. It was my job to trail her about and see that she didn't get suddenly jerked off the earth by these letter writers.

"Go on with the smoke," she laughs. "I like it but—it's a bit early for me."

So I lit up again and gave her a smile; she had sense and I thunk then her old man ought to put her wise to the whole layout.

"Leo and I are going motoring," she says. "Want to come along—he has something very important to tell me. Better listen in."

"If you don't mind," I do the polite.

"Well, you have been trailing along pretty steady."

She looks up at me out of them big brown eyes. Darned if I don't believe she's got the idea that she's vamped me.

"Yep—" I look off over the house. "I was just wondering if it was alright you—you being engaged."

Now, I don't know just how this would stand in the book of etiquette but it was a thing that needed answering. I wanted to be in on the know if there was to be peace and quiet around this little domestic establishment.

"Which one of the many are you referring to?"

"This Leo Loft was my guess," I come straight out with it.

"You talk like a fairy tale," she chirped. "Mr. Mack, I'll have you understand that I don't intend to do any circus act."

And with that she outs with the glad tidings that she wouldn't be found dead in a ten acre lot with that bird.

"I think that's the question he's going to ask me today though I have turned him down half a dozen times. I wish you'd stick along; sometimes I'm just a wee bit afraid of him. He has such influence with father you know. And once when I spoke to him about our being cousins he said—"

She breaks off suddenly for Leo is coming down the path. Oh, he was one tough egg in his own estimation. Peggy was strong for the hero stuff and he played it up every chance he got. It wasn't my lay to cross him so I let him bluster and took my laugh inside. He was big and husky weighing all of a hundred and ninety I guess.

Leo pulls a dirty look when he sees that I'm coming along and then when that don't do any good he speaks out:

"I just thought I'd be alone with you today, Peggy," he says as he looks daggers at me. "The thing I must tell you is important to everybody."

And the way he spills it you'd think he was the Prince of Wales. But I look at Peggy and she wants me to stick. She chirps something about it being necessary for me to look over the surrounding country and then asks me if I can drive.

So we start out with me at the wheel and Leo and Peggy in the rear and this lasts for about fifteen minutes when she decides to drive herself. The end of it is that she mixes things up so that Leo's alone in the back seat. Mad? You can hear his breathing above the purr of the motor! She gives me the wink and then speeds along without a peep out of the heavy villain.

But ten minutes later Leo horns in on her; whispers a lot of things close to her ear which I don't get. Peggy turns red and pulls up the car.

"Mr. Loft has something to say to me," she says real dignified as she hops out of the car. "He and I shall take a little walk. I would hear it all."

My but her voice is cold and although there ain't tremble in it I get the idea that the girl's a bit worried.

And I'm right for as they pass through a cluster of trees she casts a look at me over her shoulder. It's one of them looks what says, "Stick close!" And I just stick. Not keep them in view mind you but kinda wander along after them. It's a cinch she won't travel far with that he-goat.

A couple of minutes later I spot the two of them in a little clearing. He's talking earnestly to her and she's looking right up at him. Her eyes are blazing and her chest is going rapidly up and down and then she does it. She ups with her tiny hand

and slaps him across the face. Yep, from where I stood I saw the imprint of her little fingers just above his whiskers.

At first he steps back kind of surprised like but when she hands him a left he gets ugly. Both his big hands shoot out and he pins her little ones; then he takes them in one of his and holds her so. She pulls and struggles but don't scream.

There's hardly a sound as I slip over the soft grass toward them; just in time too for he's leaning forward his free arm about her neck. There ain't a bit of doubt but that lad's going to kiss her.

It's then that she cries out

"Terry! Terry!"

And it's music to my ears to hear how easily that name slips out of her. Why, it's like being a kid again. But of course a man in a business like mine can't take these little side affairs seriously.

And does he kiss her? Not a chance! He just pecks at the back of my hand as I wipe it across his mouth. It ain't none too clean either sein' I had rubbed it in the dirt as I snaked over.

That's only part of the fun. Was there a fight? not so you could notice it. Friend Leo couldn't even talk. There wasn't a word out of any of us as I led the girl back to the car—Leo trailing. No, excitement you understand, everything peaceful and quiet.

I drive back to Three Pines and although there ain't a yip out of any of us I know how the girl feels. More than once she gives my arm the slightest little press. She don't need to say nothing. I know the thanks is there.

Now, when we turn in at the gates I don't drive to the garage but straight up to the front door.

"I'll put the car away," I say to the girl. "You get out here."

She don't saying nothing at once; just looks back at Leo. And he ain't getting out but sticking close. There ain't no use to argue with Peggy—she decides to stay too.

We might leave the car right there and let the chauffeur cart it in. That's the regular and usual thing but then I don't think that that is good stuff today. Leo's got over his surprise and I figure he's set on being mussy. So I shrug my shoulders and haul the car down to the garage door.

Peggy hops out and me after her. Rogo's chauffeur and Leo's chauffeur is both standing in the doorway. I think for a moment that Leo will have to play the gentleman which he ain't.

Without a word to friend Leo I take Peggy by the arm and start toward the house. Bing! Like that, the big stiff jumps out of the car and grabs me by the shoulder.

"You can't get away like that."

He twirls me around, snarling like some animal. Then turning to his own driver he chirps some mighty good news.

"I'm leaving here—leaving at once. Get my things ready."

With those joyful tidings he swings back to me again.

"Before I go I'll teach you a lesson—thrash you within an inch of your life."

Yep, he yells it loud enough for them in the next county to hear. He's a good half head over me but I ain't making no attempt to get away. I'm just figuring how far this bird will get before I flop him on his neck.

Under ordinary circumstances I'd a just tapped him on the bean with my blackjack and let it go at that. But just then I didn't think that would be good policy. Peggy liked the hero stuff and if I beaned him so, she might take me for a roughneck.

"Ain't he funny?"

I turn to Peggy as he stands there blustering and shaking his fist in my face. But in that turn I slip a pair of knuckle dusters on my right mitt—yep, you guessed it. I'm planning to use them brass knuckles on Mr. Leo Loft.

Oh, I ain't much of a boxer but Leo is mad and his first swing is wild. I take it comfortable like on the side of the neck.

And that's all of that. I just up and sock him one right on the button. A short armed jab to the chin always does the trick. Leo just kind a sags in my arms and I let him slip gently to the ground.

"Better take care of the old master," I says to his chauffeur as I start off towards the house with Peggy.

Did I make a hit with the frail? You said a trunkful; she just spills smiles all over me.

"Oh, Terry, Terry—you're just wonderful."

She says softly as she hangs there on my arm. Terry again— get it? After that it's Terry and Peggy steady. Yep, all brought about by a little pair of brass knockers.

But I smile back at her. Wonderful is right. I'd just like this dame to see me really in action once. She'd get an eyeful I'm telling you.

"And that," I says to her. "That is the end of Leo the Lion Faced boy. Don't you worry about him, Peggy. If he ever bothers you again I'll tap him in a different way."

And I don't know but what I meant it. I was getting mighty sick of that lad and no mistake.

Peggy runs right into her father and I see that she's going to hand him a line of chatter that will wipe Leo's matrimonial aspirations clean off the map.

As for me I trot up to my room and read a bit of Keats Poems. A college professor once told me that there was a whole education in that one book. He ought to know of course but to me it was pretty thick stuff. Still, I was half way through it and when I start a thing I finish it. I wasn't going to let nothing stand in the way of my education even if I didn't know what the damned thing was all about.

Half hour later I see Leo drive off in his car bag and baggage; he's just slumped there in the back seat. I guess he's still wondering what hit him. He sure will hear little birds singing for the rest of that day.

I don't see Peggy again all that afternoon and it's five o'clock before Rogo asks to see me in the library. Gad, but he's a changed man; one slant at him tells me that he's spent a pretty rough afternoon.

"Terry," he begins when he stops his pacing and flops into a chair. "I said that I would have warning before real danger. I have had it. Leo has left the house. I hoped that his love for my daughter would protect her."

"Him!" I can't help but laugh. "Why he couldn't protect anyone. I just put him out like a light."

"Yes, yes, I know."

He sort a buries his head in his hands.

"Peggy has told me and you were right of course. I see now that she could never marry him. Terry," he braces up a bit. "I have lied to both you and Peggy. Leo Loft was not my cousin. He was the nephew of Aron De Lasko."

And then he came out with some real dope. He had met Leo Loft in the South last winter. Leo knowing nothing had fallen in love with Peggy. It was then that Rogo took him into his confidence hoping through this marriage to save his daughter.

"They'll kill her—or carry her away now sure—unless I pay—even then I don't know. But I do know now that Leo Loft is not the man for Peggy. God, but I am glad that her mother died."

Get it! Here I had sat with my back to that lad all the way into Three Pines that afternoon. He didn't know me and I didn't know him which probably saved us both a bullet.

I thought him just a weak sister and he thought me just a fool landscape artist what was sticking his nose into Rogo's affairs. Rogo had only brought me into it before him so that he might understand that if Peggy was suddenly spirited away and he (Rogo) killed that there was an outsider who would report it to the police.

Of course I saw the whole game now. Leo had planted that letter so that Rogo would use his influence with his daughter and use it quickly. Rogo knew it too but couldn't say anything but he tried to return the warning by showing the letter to me in the presence of Leo.

"Take a grip on yourself Mr. Rogo," I says patting him on the back. "They can't just bust in here and kidnap or kill your daughter. This ain't no Treasure Island outfit you know. Turn them down flat and if they come why just sit back and watch me work. Why man, yu're paying me good money and Terry Mack is the boy to earn it. If they ain't just bluff we'll make them wish they were. If the worst comes to the worst you can always go to the police. Swiping a few British diamonds won't cause you much trouble if you get a good lawyer—I know one swell mouth-piece."

Of course I knew with me about there would be no occasion for the police but I just wanted to buck him up a bit. He sure had fell in at the chest now when the crisis came. As for me—well, I like action and up until now it had all looked like a garden party.

But the police didn't buck him up none. In fact he fell flatter and I see there was more in the wind than what he had told me. Yep, the mention of the police knocked him so flat that he come out with the truth. This gang had made a try for his daughter some months ago; before Rogo had brought Leo Loft into his house. The long and short of it was that Rogo had killed one of his former partners.

"Do they know?" I asked.

"One of them does," he nodded. "Mathews—a partner—I've been mailing him money to keep it from De Lasko—it's this De Lasko I fear."

"Still, in self defense."

I rubbed my chin.

"That is some time ago and I have said nothing—and the diamonds on top of that."

And paying him the money, I thought to my self. I didn't mention that to him but he sure had messed things up.

"It's too bad you didn't stretch this Mathews also." Is the best I can tell him.

But he shudders and I can see that this killing business is working on his mind; him not being used to it I guess.

Well, I haven't much use for the police myself so I tell him to buck up and remember I'm there. "Oh Dry Those Tears," went strong with me for about ten minutes. And then he takes a hitch on himself and comes around pretty good. Too good in fact. He gets them glims of his upon me; shrewd little eyes they are and I know he's going to try and put something over on me before he unloads it.

Am I right? Listen! and just try and swallow his proposition.

"Terry," he says, "I'm getting on in years and at the best—well my heart isn't good. How would you like to have one hundred thousand cash and above half a million when I die."

Now, you'd think I'd jump quick at that wouldn't you? Well, you're wrong. Not me. Chaps ain't handing out money like that unless there's a catch in it.

But I give him look for look. He ain't balmy; his head's level so I ask:

"What's the lay?"

That's always a safe question.

"Terry," he says real serious like. "Peggy spoke very highly of you. She admired you this afternoon. She likes heroes. You would make her a good husband."

Of course I expected a wild one but nothing like that. He's calm now too—the light in his eyes is just one of hope. But I don't fall in his arms and embrace him. Not me! Nor, I don't spout foolish questionings about not understanding him neither. His language is clear but he's thinking backwards some place. This marriage of his daughter ain't no new idea with him. I simply pull a poker face and play for him to lead.

"Mr. Rogo," I says. "You hired me to protect your daughter at a certain price. I'm here now to earn that money. I'm not a crook and I'm not what's commonly known as a killer. But if anyone attempts to take your daughter from this house without her consent I'll shoot him dead on the door step."

Am I talking to impress him now or to raise my price? Not

me. I'm talking gospel. I'm a one price man. I let that much sink into him and then I speak again.

"You have told me as much or as little of your business as you've seen fit. I ain't asked no question and I don't intend to. But you have some idea that your daughter's marriage will protect her. You don't seem to care to whom—take me for instance—I'm not the man for Peggy; not by a long shot and I know it. That's from her end of it. From my end of it—well, I'm not a marrying man. If there is anything you ought to tell me better out with it now before the fireworks begin."

He hemmed and cleared his throat and opened his mouth a couple of times. Then he walked the floor a bit and paused for a couple of minutes while he looked out the window. When he turns he's made up his mind what he's going to say:

"You misunderstand me Terry."

He walks over and takes me by the mit.

"Peggy likes you—I can read your character in your fine open face. I thought only of the safety of my little daughter. You would be great protector to her."

Then he paused an' studies me a bit. If he reads anything in that fine open face of mine he's got a double vision. I got a clean platter on me when I want to. After a bit of hard looking he finishes:

"There was nothing else in my mind—absolutely nothing."

His eyes met mine and steadily but I knew that he lied. What was on his chest I couldn't think and I didn't try too. Nor did I bother to tell him that there had been a time when I might have married a Grand Duke's daughter if I had had a mind to look for a soft berth. Soft then but now—I lay awake yet nights thinking of what might have been.

I don't say nothing. I let him do all the talking and it's only in preparation for what's to come. He'd have a regiment of guards in the house if he could trust them. And then he hands me a laugh by asking if I am armed.

Well healed! Humph! Two guns and a blackjack is my regular outfit when I'm busy to say nothing of the knuckle dusters which is carried for little light pleasantries. Then Rogo plans to leave for the city the next day; he figures it will be safer than away out there in the country. But I don't know; I feel pretty much at ease any place.

Peggy is down with us to dinner and she's as gay as if nothing had happened that afternoon. Too gay in fact and I don't like the way she looks at me nor her idea of playing and singing to me after dinner. I never did go in for music, leastwise that kind, and the looks that she deals with it ain't seen outside of the movies. It makes me feel like pulling her ears. She's too nice a little kid to be trying that vamp stuff. As for trying it on me! Well, she might as well make faces at Grant's tomb.

Rogo don't tell her nothing but hustles her off to bed early which is about ten o'clock. Then he gets me alone and is as excited as an Irish election.

"They rang up," he tells me his voice all a tremble. "I'm to lose Peggy tonight. We'll both keep watch—sit by her door all night."

And then he'd up and pace about and mutter to himself. All that I can say don't to do no good for he's made his arrangements without consulting me.

Manual, the chauffeur, is to stay in the house that night. He knows enough to understand that he is needed and that Peggy is in danger.

"But we don't need three men sitting up," I try to quiet him. "Besides they ain't going to do nothing to-night. They wouldn't give you warning. It's the old game Mr. Rogo; they simply wish to create an impression of fear. Perhaps get us all tired out and make the attempt tomorrow night—or on the way into town in the morning. Use your head. One man's as good as three to give the warning. If you like I'll sit up all night."

He took me up at once; agreed with everything I said but wouldn't hear of my sitting up:

"No," he shook his head. "We'll need you tomorrow and you must have your sleep. Manual can stay up. He's a quick, sharp young fellow and I've just raised his salary."

With that he called Manual out of the kitchen. Manual looked good. He was young, tall and broad. How he fitted with a gun I didn't know but he sure looked good for a rough and tumble. And he seemed willing and anxious to do anything he could. Kind of gripped his hands tightly when he heard that "Miss Peggy" was in danger.

I didn't question him; there wasn't no use. Rogo had him in the family for the past five years besides I let Rogo run the show. He just had to. And right here I got to admit that I didn't see any danger. One cry and I'd be on the job. Oh, I ain't blowing about myself. I don't need to. My record is good. I carry fourteen shots in them two automatics of mine and fourteen shots is fourteen hits. There ain't no two ways about that. I don't go for to miss; not me.

So that's the lay of it when we trot up to bed about ten minutes to twelve. I spot the time for I seen Manual safe in a big chair by Peggy's door and Rogo in his room. Then, as I turn into my room, the great clock in the hall tolls off the hour.

Do I lay awake and worry? Not so you could notice it I don't. I hit the hay; in five minutes I'm asleep. Plenty of good healthy honest sleep is first class nerve tonic. When I tell you that I ain't got no nerves you can imagine how I pound the mattress.

And then I wake up sudden. Oh, there ain't nothing startling on hand. But someone has walked across the floor downstairs. It's a soft stealthy tread but I hear it plainly enough. Why you could drop a feather on the floor above me and I'd come to quick enough; yep, if I planned to when I went to bed.

A minute later I'm out in the hall on the first landing. Not a sound!

"Manual," I breathe.

No answer. I flash the light for a fraction of a second. He ain't by Peggy's door. Then I douse the glim; footsteps is coming up the stairs. They ain't so catlike and quiet as they had been neither. I wonder. Bing! Like that I flash the light. I'm right. It's Manual.

"What were you doing downstairs?"

I give it to him sharp like. I haven't much use for a man what don't obey his orders to the letter. And Rogo had told him to sit tight.

"I just went through the house. Nervous like!" Manual admits.

"Did you hear something—some noise that made you look about?"

"No," he shakes his head. "I just had to look. I got restless sitting here with everything so still. I tried all the windows and looked over the grounds."

"Anything unusual?"

"Not a thing."

I turn back to my room and then hesitate. Then I feel like he does. Nervous like.

"I'll just take a look in Miss Peggy's room," I tell him as I softly push the chair away from the door.

"The door's locked."

He's just full of advice.

So I climb on a chair and give a look over the transom; there's one on every bedroom door on that floor. She's sleeping there like a two year old, one arm thrown up over her head—not a care in the world. After all I think it's a good thing she ain't been told nothing. But if she guesses there's something wrong I don't know. She must for she ain't no dumb frail.

I ain't generally fidgety but somehow I'm on edge that night. At all events I give Manual an earful about staying by the door and if he does get another burning desire to look around the house why to call me. If anyone should be downstairs they'd crack him for a row of bamboo canes in a minute.

It's the same way when I get back in my room. I just stand there undecided a moment and then I open up my own transom. With that open and my ears I figure I'll hear Manual breathing. One look at my watch marks the time at one-thirty—with that I hit the sheets again; two minutes later I'm off once more.

How long I sleep there ain't no telling. But I sit up sudden— real sudden this time. Something has struck the floor right at the foot of the bed. There's a scream too—a sharp, piercing scream that seems to echo far away into laughter.

Then everything is nice and quiet again; a voice seems to say lay back Terry and take it easy. Then I go falling back and off— just into easy slumber. I half say to myself; nothing's going to bother me tonight. So I'm just about to pass out of the picture for a while when I get it.

This ain't no dream; I've been drugged—or something. Someone has chucked something over that transom.

God! but it took a power of will to jump from that bed and make the window. But I done it—just fell there and laid my head half out in the cooling breeze. Not doing nothing you understand; not thinking nothing; just lying there sprawled half across the sill. But the night air is beating into my lungs.

At first it is just as if I'm holding my own, not going forward or backward—a half state of coma. Then the air wins out and things outside begin to take shape. It seems kind of brilliant at first—like the moon is bright, awful bright just in one spot where I'm looking. Come real shapes then—the three big trees—yep—I can just see enough of the front of the grounds to spot them great pines. They seem all in together and then they separate and stand out individually.

Oh, I'm hazy yet but not full of no more pretty dreams. I know something's wrong—deadly, terribly wrong. Both my guns is there in the bed too but I ain't sure just where the bed is—nor my searchlight—nor the electric switch.

But the air is working fast and when I come around a bit more I realize that I'm pounding my temples and talking to myself. But I'm coming around mighty fast.

I clearly see that it ain't no moon that I'm looking at. Not by a damned sight it ain't. And just as I figure that out and begin to understand the two big headlights of a high-powered car move from the front of the house and slip silently down the driveway toward the pines.

Like a flash it all comes to me. Peggy is being carried away.

With that thought I'm my own man again. Yep, Terry Mack is on the job. I find the bed and my guns quick enough now and in a second I'm back at the window again. The big car is just turning out the gate.

Could I have hit it? There ain't a doubt. My head would have to be pretty bad to make me miss anything I can see. But my head's clear enough to do a little quick thinking.

That car ain't no more than a blotch against the night. A shot couldn't cripple it and like as not I'd hit Peggy. Besides it would let them know that we were warned. No sir, I had no desire to hurry them. I just let them ride.

Two minutes later I'm out in the hall trying to bring Manual around. The smell of gas is strong but I've got most of the windows and doors open and all the servants downstairs running around doing nothing. Manual comes around all right but Rogo is too far under to get a yip out of.

"Can you drive a car—are you able to drive a car?"

I try to shake some sense out of Manual's head. If he can drive all right—I need him. If he can't—why I'll go alone. I can drive anything.

When Manual understands I mean business he gets into action and the two of us beat it out to the garage.

"Take care of Mr. Rogo and keep your mouths shut," I yell to the servants.

Of course I seen that Rogo's alright—he's just doped up good and proper.

Manual is there. He gets the car a rolling in jig time and we go shooting down the road. Me doing the directing—him the driving. I know this gang alright. They'll beat it for the city without a doubt and it's a pretty straight road all told. I figure they won't rush things trying not to draw attention to themselves as they pass through the little villages.

Do we travel? Why, we must hit over fifty through the night. Manual is for taking it easy but I won't let up on him. In way of encouragement I give him a few gentle jabs in the ribs with my gun. It does him good and the speed keeps up. I don't ask him no questions as to what happened. I don't care; that will come later.

And then we spot them. There ain't a doubt of it. Away down in the valley I see them cutting through the little town of Merser. Six people in the car it looks like as they pass under the big light in the center of the square.

"Take it easy now, Manual," I say. "We'll sneak up on them and do a little shooting. If you handle the car right why I'll come near getting four of them before they can stop and fight it out. There's a lonely stretch of road about seven miles beyond; that should be the ticket."

"But we are two and they are so many."

Manual don't seem anxious for the fray.

"Don't you worry about that," I tell him. "Keep going and watch me work. We'll have Miss Peggy back for breakfast."

Was I trying to cheer him up? Not much I wasn't. I was talking like a book. No second-story black-mailers could go and steal a girl from under my nose—not much they couldn't. I was coming with death—there ain't no two ways about that.

Seven miles is right! Just in that lonely patch of country road we nail them—slip right up to about fifty feet of them before they know who's coming.

"Keep this distance," I give Manual the dope as I swing out on the side of the car crouched low.

And then the lads in the car ahead begin to get worried. They suspicion that all ain't right behind. One of them stands up and takes a look. That's my cue. The road is level and I fire. Did I get him? You said it. He just drops back into the car. If he groans we don't get the music. But I know it's a hit. They're all men in the back; the headlight lets me know that. So I blaze away.

Oh, they're on that things ain't so good now and return the fire. But our lights blind them while for me they're a good target.

One of them shoots well and puts out one of our lights but after that they speed up; their artillery ain't done no damage.

"Easy does it, Manual," I chirp and we out and after them.

Of course they keep a shooting but outside of some busted glass everything is right with us. Then they duck around a curve and we lose them for a moment.

As we shoot the curve I let drive again. Suddenly our car lurches—Manual shouts—it swings back in the road again but I ain't in it. I just remember thinking as I shoot through the air and into the ditch that it is lucky we are making about twenty and not fifty.

After that it's curtains for me. Everything goes black.

Now, the spot I landed in was a mighty soft berth if you were just going to lay down in it—mostly mud and water, more mud than water though. Still at the rate I was traveling when I hit it I'm thankful that I didn't break my neck.

When I do come too I'm lying there on the roadside and a couple of men are looking down at me. Not doing nothing you understand just looking down. That's the way with most fellows that help you in an accident.

They're mighty relieved when I come around and sit up and

look things over. I don't pull the "Where am I stuff?" Whenever I come out of a trance I know enough to keep quiet. They help me up and walk me around a bit which shows that no bones ain't broken though I'm mighty stiff all over.

The end of it is, that when they find out I'm a guest of Rogo's they offer to drive me to his house.

I'm pretty cagey with my talk. In my business it's what you don't say and not what you say that counts. But I get that these two chaps were out to a dance and hustling home when they heard the shots which they took for blowouts.

One look at our car which had crashed against a tree would make them believe anything and that was the stall what Manual had given them. He whispered that to me the first chance he got.

As for Manual nothing had happened to him as far as I could see but I didn't question him any. My thinkbox was far from clear anyway so I kept my trap tight.

When we got back to Three Pines and thanked those lads and let them go without even a bit of breakfast I had a talk with Rogo who had come around all right and was now pulling his hair and acting foolish.

"Mr. Rogo," I says to him as I lay there on the bed. "I know just how badly you must feel. You counted on me and you think I've failed. That's the bunk. I'll get Peggy back for you sure. But—my head's dizzy and won't work right. Give me three hours. Two to sleep and one to think. Come back then and we'll dope things out and be ready for some action."

In three hours I'm as fit as a fiddle—perhaps a second-hand fiddle but pretty good just the same. And Rogo comes back. He has some brandy for me which I pass up but encourage him to take. Coffee hits me—good and black and about three cups of it. Liquor don't make a steady hand. The coffee does me good and the brandy fits Rogo to a T.

He's had a talk with Manual. Manual thinks he must have slept by Peggy's door and someone sneaked up and shoved the ether or chloroform over his face. Then according to him, they chucked a can or bomb of some kind of gas over my transom. All the crooks and cops seem to be using gas these days. As for my landing in the ditch that was easily explained. A bullet from the fleeing car had gone through his right arm.

"Now," finishes Rogo. "There is nothing to do but pay the money—even then I fear for Peggy—this Leo."

"Keep your shirt on," I tell him. "You're traveling a bit too fast. I must admit that I haven't done a lot of good but this Manual sure did turn out one lemon—to say the least. You can't do nothing till you hear from them anyway. In the meantime—well—I'll get up."

And I did. I went through my suitcase and loaded up another nice automatic for the one I had lost there in the mud. Then I trotted out to the garage to have a talk with Manual. And there he sat with his pipe in his mouth like the big calf that he was. His right arm is all bandaged up and he carries it in a sling. He's mighty surprised to see me around so quickly and hopes I felt better and that I have no internal troubles from my shock.

I thank him and show interest about his arm. Not a word about the punk way he carried out his orders. I just show sympathy with him.

"What does the doctor say about your arm, Manual?" I ask him.

"Oh—I didn't see a doctor. It's only a flesh wound."

I shake my head.

"That's bad business; it might cause blood poisoning. However, I know a little about wounds. Let me have a look at it."

"There is no use—no use," he stands up and backs away a bit. "I'll see a doctor tonight I guess. But I won't take the bandage off now."

"Oh yes, you will, Manual. We can't have a good and faithful servant suffering silently like you are. Come take it off and give me a look at it."

My voice ain't pleasant either I'm telling you. I'm going to have a look at that wound of his and have it quick.

Oh, he reads the danger in my eyes. He goes first red and then white and then turns quickly toward the little shelf where he keeps his tools. His left hand just shoots out and grabs a wrench when I lean on him. Just a tap behind the ear with the butt of my gun does it and Manual falls pretty right by the doorway.

A minute later I've unwound the cloth from his arm. One look is enough—I'm sorry I didn't hit him harder. The low skunk. I'm right about him. There ain't a mark on his arm at all.

I pull up a chair and lighting a butt sit down to wait. Must of banged him harder than I thought for it's near twenty minutes before he comes around. Then he sits up and blinks; there I am facing him, playfully fingering my gun.

"Manual," I say slowly. "How much did you get for the dirt? What did they pay you to sell out Miss Peggy?"

He just sits there staring at me.

"Come—what did you get?"

I'm ugly now and mean business.

"I'd think no more of shoving this gun down your throat and emptying it than I would of eating breakfast."

Did I mean it? Was I bluffing? What do you think? Well, Manual thought right; he come out with the truth:

"A thousand dollars—Mr. Leo Loft told me and I—"

He was whimpering and crying like a dog now. And he sure had cause too. When I thought of this cur turning that sweet little kid over to that gang why my finger itched on the trigger. And my guns are built light—it don't take much itching to make them spout.

"You went downstairs and telephoned them—that time I heard you early this morning."

I give him a lead to shut off his waterworks. I wanted information and he wanted to plead for his life. Yep, he sure thought I was going to croak him there. That's funny, ehe. Well, I thought so myself for a time.

But there was no real dope in him. These lads knew better than to trust a mut like that. It's too bad Rogo didn't. Five years in the family and he sold his soul for a thousand berries. One of the good and faithful gone wrong.

There was no use to threaten him; this bird was willing to tell all he knew. But he had never met any of them but Leo and the only address he knew was De Lasko's and you could find that in the telephone book. But I did learn that it was to De Lasko he telephoned and that when he went downstairs he left a window open for the gang to enter.

And I had Manual on my hands; just a whimpering for another chance and swearing to do all that he could to save Miss Peggy. Maybe he meant it. I don't know. But I'm not of a trusting nature. Rogo might be willing to listen to his prayers and take him to his bosom but more than likely he'd cut his throat.

So, I did the best I could have done unless I croaked him right there. I give him ten seconds to make tracks. And that was the last I saw of him. He never stopped to put on his coat, just ducked around the back of the garage, jumped the stone wall and beat it.

Then I took the sad news to Rogo; he had to know—he was so trustful.

Rogo sat in the library, his head in his hands. More trouble! De Lasko had just telephoned him; he had twenty-four hours to pay.

"And where do you meet De Lasko?" I ask him.

"Right at his office. He simply told me that his clients had every reason to believe that I would pay what I owed within twenty-four hours. 'Your daughter has told them so,' he sneered over the wire. I know that he heads the whole plot."

And I knew it too now but I didn't say anything. I was busy thinking. A lot can be done in twenty-four hours.

"Oh, Terry, if Peggy had only married—most anyone," he cuts in upon my thoughts.

And this time I was tempted to ask:

"What good would that do?"

He sat up straight when I put the question, his dull eyes suddenly flashing.

"What good would it have done? What good? Why, I would have known that my little girl was safe. With someone to take care of her I would have gone and killed this De Lasko. I would have shot these men down until I in turn was killed. A good husband could have protected Peggy against the others—a man who had no fear in calling in the police. Yes—I should have killed till I was killed."

His head went into his hands again and he groaned aloud. Yes, as I said before this lad had guts.

Still, I couldn't see any special danger to Peggy. These birds wanted money—nothing else. If they killed Peggy their chances of raising the wind was gone.

They might marry her to Leo of course but then they couldn't hide her all her life. I didn't see much of a complication there. I'd bump Leo off and make her a widow without losing no sleep over it. If he forced the girl into this marriage he needed a killing.

But what bothered me most was the kid herself. I ain't generally worried about such things. But she was such a lively, innocent bit of a girl. That's what bothered me the most. For once in my life I was really personally interested. I felt that a little shooting would combine business with pleasure.

Of course I had an idea running through my head. If the worst came to the worst I know just how to act. I ain't no fancy detective and don't know much about clues and one thing and another. I got a different way of working when things come down to hard tacks. At present I thought it better to wait. A letter might be delivered and I'd keep a careful eye out for the bearer. It wouldn't do no harm to try and choke some information out of him.

But though I hung around the hedge by the roadside, no one approached the grounds and then about dinner time with nothing doing along comes a telephone call. I'm with Rogo in the library when the ring comes.

He beckons over and I listen in.

"This is Mathews speaking," comes a sneering voice over the wire. "We have a little entertainment for you John Rogo. Listen carefully and see if we are just trying to frighten you about your daughter."

Then there's quiet on the wire for a few minutes. I'm beginning to think he's rung off when I hear a voice. It's a very low voice—pitifully low. Even me, who ain't got no nerves, feels my heart give an extra jump—a good one too. The voice is Peggy's there ain't no mistake about that.

"Oh, daddy—daddy! Save me—they are torturing me—burning me— Daddy—daddy! Terry—help—help—hel-p!"

The voice kind of chokes off into a sob—a groan and then one terrible appeal of agony.

I still hold the receiver as Rogo flops to the floor. Then comes the man's voice again.

"Listen to the cry of your daughter—John Rogo. Better pay. Raymonds is dead—your hired gun man did that. We know all about him now. Peggy is paying the price. Later you will hear her squeal again—her flesh is soft and tender and burns easy."

Then a laugh—low, blood curdling laugh.

"No use to trace this call. Even if you did try and let the police know you could never trace this call."

There's a click as he finishes and I know he's hung up.

Rogo's in a dead faint. I pick him up and carry him upstairs to his room. Then I have the servants hustle some brandy to him and I beat it downstairs again.

Central tells me that she can't give me the number that just called. It's against the orders.

"Well," I try to make my voice cheerful. "You better look that call up for your own benefit. I'll be arranging to have it turned over to me. And you might let me have your name—ehe?"

She does that and I hang up. If the time comes I'll buy that information from her; there won't be no trouble about that. I've done it a hundred times in the past. What bothers me the most is Mathews assurance that we can't trace the number.

Rogo's a busted down old man when he comes out of his faint. I never see such a change in my life.

"Go see—De Lasko. Tell him I'll raise the money tomorrow—at least all I can of it. I don't trust him—any of them. Take what precautions you think necessary. I am helpless now—Terry. Go! Save my daughter."

And he fell back on the bed and turned his face to the wall.

I could hear him sobbing loudly as I went down the stairs. But I cautioned the old butler not to leave him for a minute—to watch by his door until I returned.

Yes, Rogo was right. I was going to see De Lasko. Two hours later I park Rogo's runabout on a side street and hoofing it around the corner ring the bell at De Lasko's.

Oh, I would a like to have hopped in a window and surprised him but it wasn't safe. The house must be pretty well guarded especially if he had learned who I was. But I figure there is no danger at the front door. He'll be expecting Rogo or his representative.

If I have any idea of shooting up that dump it fades as soon as I enter the house. It seems to be just full of cutthroats. Two big loafers are sitting in the front hall and they sure have the look of regular guns. There's another one by De Lasko's private study and I don't know but a half a dozen more upstairs.

I guess he knows my business is action and prepares for it. But he sees me alone in his study and lets the servant close the door. I got to admit that he takes a chance and that Rogo could a got him easy if he didn't care what happened afterwards.

Aron De Lasko is a big guy with a little mustache; as smooth as oil and to all outward appearances a polished gentleman. He greets me cordially enough and even asks me to have a cigar. I watch him take one and light up so I do the same. This bird ain't got nothing on me.

He's a close mouth and after about five minutes of silence I see that it's up to me to begin.

"They're torturing the girl already, ehe?" I come to the point.

He elevates his eyebrows as he looks me over:

"I don't understand you. I know nothing about any girl nor do I want to learn about one. Mr. Rogo sent you here with some money—am I right?"

His shrewd, crafty eyes knit closed as he taps the table with his exposed left hand. The right hand is in his lap and I figure there's a gun there though I don't know.

Well, I see that there is nothing to gain by threatening or blustering with him. I guess I'll let him think the money is coming and put him in a good humor. All I really wanted was one look at his ugly mug for I intended to make this lad squeal as soon as I could get him away from his friends.

Give me five minutes alone with him and none of his gang around and I'd force a bit of information out of him. If I didn't he was a tougher bird than I had yet met. I got very persuasive ways I have.

But I just look at him and smile, take a different tack with him.

"Mr. Rogo will pay his—debt."

I permit myself to grin broadly.

"You and me are simply business men and can not let sentiment interfere, ehe?"

He kind a nods and his lips part so I go ahead.

"Now, Mr. De Lasko, you know my business. I ain't hiding nothing. I was hired to protect the girl and get big money for it. The girl's gone and I fail—no money—get the point."

"Go on," he says. "You interest me."

Yep, I'm hitting his talk now.

"Of course you and I have little interest in this girl business. We are both set on making money. But you can't get yours without me—see."

And I jab my finger toward him.

"So."

The frown comes back again.

"So, is correct," I tell him. "And Mr. Rogo can't be frightened any more because he's in bed. If there is any listening to do on the phone I'll do it.

And let me tell you—there will have to be a lot of screaming to appeal to me. Do you get that, my friend? Rogo is going on my advice. You can kill the girl without getting a tear out of me. It ain't my funeral. But I ain't going to lose money on your account."

It hurt me to talk like that about poor Peggy. I was just itching to pull a bit of lead on him. But he read nothing in my face.

He leaned far over the table now and studied me carefully. It was several seconds before he spoke and then his voice was cold and threatening:

"Mr. Mack," he bent quite close. "Let us for a moment throw aside the veil. I know you and your breed—money. You are no more than a hired assassin. You have already killed one man.

What is to prevent you being carried from this house—dead.

He waited a moment; if he was watching for my face to turn white and my hands to tremble he'd have some wait.

"What's a dead man between friends?"

I shrugged my shoulders. I wasn't going to weep over the lad I had kicked off. It was all in the game.

"You can't get along without me," I tried to smirk like he did.

He tapped the desk a bit and then come out with what was on his mind.

"You wish to be paid by—my clients as an agent—that is it, ehe? Very well, you deliver that money here and I shall give you—say five hundred dollars."

"A thousand or nothing," I told him.

"You would betray your friends for a thousand dollars?"

"No betrayal about it."

I shot my eyes over to the big safe behind him.

"For a thousand dollars I will use my influence with Mr. Rogo. As far as anything happening to me here. Piffle! I have not the same fear as Rogo. If I don't return to a friend in a certain length of time the police will be notified of the whole business. I can't always be thinking of other people's affairs you know."

He smiled now, understandingly. It was nothing surprising to him to see me willing to do Rogo; he was used to buying men's honor.

"Very well," he nodded at length. "When the business is closed I shall give you the thousand dollars. The word of De Lasko has never been broken."

But I give him the laugh:

"I'll go your word fifty-fifty. Five hundred of it now."

He watches me a moment and then comes suddenly to his feet.

"It's better so."

I hear him mutter. I suppose he was figuring that he'd have a hold on me. Then he turns to his safe. He figures, with the house full of guards and me a double crossing crook, that he ain't in no danger.

Oh, I'll admit I was a fool to try it. Everything was against me. I've always maintained that women have no place in a life like mine.

But I was thinking of Peggy as I crept softly over the thick carpet and struck him on the head. It was my blackjack this time. It's well cushioned and does the work with less noise. Besides I coughed as I struck him down. It was well done even if I do say so myself. My arm was under him as he keeled over—not a sound—not a groan as I laid him on the floor.

If it hadn't a been Peggy I was thinking of I'd a waited until he opened the safe. Truth is truth!

My game was to slip him out the window, take him off in the car and find where Peggy was being kept. Oh, I'm bad when I'm mad. There weren't no doubt but I'd get the truth out of him.

I listen by the door—not a sound. Then I go to the window and look out. It leads into a little court and—well I never would have suspected it with the inside of the house so well guarded. You guessed it. Two lads were standing just below the window. I let the curtains drop slowly back; they hadn't seen me. Of course I might have shot both of them but that would have only started a riot.

So I turned back to the study and looked around. Just to

one side of the safe was a little curtained doorway. I looked into the little room which it hid. There were two doors in that room. One I opened and it led up a narrow stairway; the other disclosed a good sized closet.

Returning to the study I picked up De Lasko and bundled him into the closet. Then I returned to the window again. The two guards were still there. The window was slightly open at the top. Picking up a paper weight I hurled it out the window. It struck against a lamp post just over the court wall. The two men below jumped at once to investigate.

As soon as they were away from the window I up with a chair and with all my might hurled it through the window shattering the pane. Bing! Like that I ducked back into that little room behind the curtains and hid in the closet.

Did I start something? Well, I should snicker. There was some excitement.

"He's drugged the boss and taken him out the window," I heard one of them say.

At that there was a general dash for the outside of the house. That was my cue. I figured no one would think to look upstairs—nor would they look in the closet yet. I thought too that everyone above would come downstairs.

And I guess I was right for as I staggered up those narrow back stairs with the helpless body of De Lasko over my shoulder I didn't hear a sound above. Panic is what I wanted to create and I sure did.

Three flights I bore him and I want to tell you that last ladder-like ascent to the attic was some job. Few men could do it in the time I did under the best of conditions. But not a soul did I meet.

And I wasn't there none too soon either. That's the bad feature of a cushioned billy; the impression ain't so lasting as the butt of a gun. De Lasko was groaning when I dropped him behind some trunks and carried others over and placed them against the door in that little, low ceilinged, side attic room. I carried them trunks mind you—not pull them across you know. I wasn't inviting no visitors from below.

De Lasko was beginning to groan real loud now so I shoved a handkerchief in his mouth. Then I looked around the attic while I waited for his eyes to open. There was one window which stood about three feet from the roof of the opposite house. The roof across was flat and an easy jump for an active man. I marked this well. That would be my getaway.

I also found some rope and a couple of trunk straps. De Lasko was recovering and beginning to move about when I took the rope and straps and trussed him up.

He sure was a pleasant sight when I got finished with him and sat him up against a trunk. My only trouble now was that I had to work fast. When that gang below got over their first excitement they would begin to realize that I couldn't have spirited De Lasko away. Yep, I was playing against time—the time to put the fear of Terry Mack into De Lasko's soul.

Five minutes later he's opened his eyes and the look in them tells me his head is clear once more. Surprise first—then fear—then the color returned to his face as he looked about and realized that he was still in his own house. That give him confidence and no mistake: I seen the light of hope come back to his eyes. I couldn't see his mouth but I knew there was a sneer there just the same.

Bing! Like that I made up my mind to wipe that look clean

off a his pan. Things were getting quiet downstairs so I figured they were holding a council of war.

"Aron De Lasko," I sit down on my haunches before him. "You say you know something about me. Let us hope you do. It'll save you considerable health and me considerable trouble. In the first place I've got more than a business feeling for this girl—Miss Rogo. Come where is she?"

With that I scrape the mouth of my gat across his forehead. It leaves a nasty scar there I'm telling you. But what of that? I haven't carted this bundle of mis-deeds up in the attic to play the gentleman.

"If you're willing to tell—nod your head."

I watch the red welt raise up on his head.

He shakes his head determinedly but I notice that the look of confidence has gone and the red from his cheeks is upon his forehead where my gun went over.

Oh, it ain't considered just what's right—not real hero stuff to torture a helpless man. I suppose according to the ethics of the thing I should kiss him good night or tell him a funny story. That's alright and very pretty in books and I like to read about it just as much as anybody else. I sure do consider it an honorable and noble pastime. But then I ain't honorable and noble and don't lay no claim to it.

Will I torture him to get information? You said a trunkful. I just remembered Peggy's cry when she called that they were burning her. Ethics! Pity! I just set my flashlight down between us and gave him another ugly gash right up his left cheek. And it wasn't hard to do neither, and didn't turn my stomach none. If anything I took pleasure in it.

I ain't asking for your opinion of me, mind you. I'm just stating facts and if it ain't a pretty tale skip a bit.

I got him now. I can see that the sweat is standing out in great beads on his forehead. Then I turn my head away and pulling out my knife open it.

"Aron De Lasko—will you tell."

I just shoot the words at him and stick my face close to his. He can have three guesses whether I'm fooling now or not. And everyone of those guesses will be right. If his face is hard so is mine. If his heart is black so is mine at that time. If he don't care for his own soul why I'll take a chance with mine. I mean business and Aron De Lasko knows it.

Yep, he nods that he'll tell and I stoop down to loosen the gag in his mouth.

It's then that I hear footsteps on the stairs followed quickly by the turning of the attic door knob. But I got it well barricaded and it'll take them a few minutes to get in. There isn't any general pounding at the door—just the slight turning of the knob and no more.

I hope De Lasko don't hear and I count on getting his gag off and getting the information of Peggy's whereabouts before the gang rush me. They ain't sure where I am and it would courting death to rush the door.

I kneel quickly beside the bound man and pull off his gag.

"Where is the girl?" I whisper.

And then I jump back and up suddenly. The cur has lied to me. And what's more he must have heard the knob rattle. Yep, he lets out a most ungodly scream for help. Fear, pain, hope, all are in that cry. The gang behind the door hear it—small wonder the cry must have echoed through the entire house. Crash! His boys are throwing themselves again the door.

I turn and put one shot right through the door about five feet above the floor. I figure right. Things quiet down at once. Then I turn my gun on De Lasko. Another cry stops right on his lips. He's looking at death and his face is deadly—not white you know—more yellow but for the bright red scars.

"De Lasko you're going out. Once more I ask you where is the girl. Speak quickly."

But I've overshot the mark this time. De Lasko ain't the man I took him for. He tries to speak but can't and I—oh—I can't wait.

Of course it would be natural to put a bullet through his head. I nearly did it but somehow I couldn't. It's one thing to cut a man up to get needed information but another thing to bump off a helpless man. I guess it's a weakness but—well I couldn't do it that's all.

But before I beat it out that little window I give him an earful that he'll do well not to forget.

"De Lasko," I says. "You're a beast and I'm a beast. We should understand each other. If anything happens to that girl I'll find you again and the next time well—I'll cut out that black heart of yours and throw it in your face."

It sounds like cheap melodrama, ehe? Well, maybe. I don't know. Still you can't tell what a man will do under certain circumstances and I sure had a fondness for that poor innocent little kid.

With that I'm out the window; one leap carries me to the house opposite. I know these type of houses and don't waste no time. I duck to the front and drop over onto a little balcony. The window before me is half open. I raise it and hop into the room. There's a scream. My flash goes on and lights on a woman in bed.

"Where's the door?" I says—"The door to the stairs. Come, point it out and no noise."

Scared stiff—perhaps but she points to the proper door and I skip out of it. I hear people moving but pay no attention to it. A quick getaway is my game now. I'm down those three flights in no time. Nothing on the door but a chain and within thirty seconds of the time I left De Lasko I'm out into the night.

My gun's in my hand as I duck around the corner but I don't meet nobody. Just as I find my car I hear the tooting of a police whistle but I don't wait to do no explaining I beat it.

And that's all for that night. I ring up Rogo and tell him to be of good cheer. With that I roll off for Three Pines. I got to have some conversation with that telephone operator in the morning.

Rogo is still confined to his bed and it's a good thing too for the telephone rings twice that night and I do the listening. It's that gang of cut throats every time and you'd need a strong constitution to stand what I heard. They are sure doing everything but killing poor Peggy. It would kill her father to hear the moans that come over that wire.

But she's a brave girl and once she shouts out that she's being kept in an old house far from any other place. That's all she knows I guess. God, the last time I set that receiver down I cursed myself for not putting De Lasko out. It looked like he was getting hunk on what I done to him.

Then I get what sleep I can—I'll sure need it.

The next morning a little after eight I'm down at the telephone exchange in the little village of Thurston. I stand by the door with a taxi driver I picked up. He knows Miss Wilsons, which is the name the dame I'm looking for gave me.

Pretty soon she comes and she's alone. I just take her to one side and work quick. A flash of a fake detective badge and the slipping of a real twenty into her hand does the trick. She gives me the number and what's more she gives me the address—this dame is good. I slip her an extra ten.

And when I find the place in the city I'm stumped. Knocked flat! It's an all night restaurant!

I just flop down there at one of the tables and have a cup of coffee—black. My first thought is that the girl in Thurston sold me. Then I start to think. The voice on the wire had been so certain that we couldn't trace the call. Why? It was tough on me. I ain't use to problems. I generally go straight after things and get them—mostly with a gun. But here was a situation where my trigger finger wasn't worth a continental.

And then I had a stroke of luck. A chap slips into the restaurant and hops right into the end telephone booth. Nothing strange about that, ehe. Well, it was one of them ducks what had sat in De Lasko's hall the night before. He don't see me but I get up and walking to the booth look in. I'm close too and I distinctly hear him call 638 Thurston—that's the Rogo number.

Enough—no one is watching me as with one quick movement I slide over the door and squeeze in.

"Hand that receiver to me, Bo."

I stick my gun against his ribs hard enough to lift a grunt out of him. My lips is smiling for the benefit of any who may look in but my voice is like a sleigh where there ain't no snow.

"Not a yip out of you brother."

I take the receiver from his ear and listen in.

"You know me of course."

I keep talking to him softly.

"If you have an itching to feel for your gun why think of De Lasko—and leave it itch."

But talking to him is just a waste of breath. His map tells me that there ain't no desire for gun play in him. His mouth just stays open and his eyes bulge.

So I keep my glims on him and my listener at the receiver. Then comes the voice of him they call Mathews. He's talking to Rogo's butler; and the old butler is speaking as I told him to. He won't call Rogo to the phone—says he's ill in bed.

"Is that cheap gun man Mack there then."

With that Mathews spits out a string of oaths about me. I take note of them with the mental resolve to some day shoot every one of them down his throat with his teeth.

The butler again obeys orders and tells him that I'm out in the grounds but won't come in. With that there is more cursing and the faint voice of Peggy like she was calling from another part of the same room.

Surprised! You said it. I'm no better off that I was before and what's more I'm half sweating to death in that little box with one of the dirty gang.

I can't force no information out of him there and I can't very well put a bullet in him just for luck. Besides there ain't no information in him I think. This De Lasko is one slick bird and just keeps a lot of Dumb Isaac's working for him.

This lad is afraid of me and no mistake. He volunteers the info that he don't know nothing and that he's just sent there at certain hours to call 638 Thurston. But that booth is getting like a Turkish Bath steam room so I frisk this lad for his gat, pocket it and give him the air.

And he takes to it like it was something what he never expected to breathe again.

And then I'm stumped. A good dick might think it out but not me. I have one good quality. I know my limitations. Give me a gun and a man to shoot at and I'm there forty ways but—

Enough! When a good general physician is up a tree he goes and sees a specialist. That's me!

Now, I know a dame what's the cleverest rock smuggler in this country and she's got a head on her that ain't equaled from here to Frisco—yes and back again. She's often tried to get me to go in with her but give it up when she sees I ain't a crook.

Still we're good friends and I've often helped her out when she needed a man who wasn't afraid of nothing. I know she'll be glad to turn a trick for me so I go and see her.

Myra's her name and she's got a swell house in the Eighties.

I kill a butt with her and tell her as much of the game as she ought to know. The telephone part I play up strong. Where can that call come from is what I want.

Does she hem and haw and promise to look into it? Not her. She listens and gives me the laugh.

"Poor, stupid—good old Terry," she says. "The whole thing is simple. I've worked it many times. This crowd have tapped the house wire; just run a wire off to someplace not far distant. You can be sure it's near for the job is not an easy one. When they want to talk to you they set a time and a confederate does the calling from some distant point. You can easily locate the wire and follow it—though it will take time if it's grounded."

Good old Myra! I promise to do something for her some day and beat it. Relieved? I'm just like a kid again. I can feel action in the air. "Revenge is sweet" is right. I'll put this gang out like a light now. I know now that everything is Jake.

All the way back to Three Pines I keep spitting on my hands and rubbing them together. I ain't superstitious or anything like that but when I do that it's a sure sign that the curtain is going up on the last act. I never knew it to fail.

Rogo's dressed and wandering about the house though he ain't fit to be. But I give him the glad tidings and take some of that hazy, vacant dimness out of his eyes.

"The place must be close," I tell him after I locate the wire which runs down the outside of the house and is mostly sunk into the ground. "Try and think of some deserted old place near here. It'll take hours to trail along that wire."

"The old Redmond Mansion," he says after studying a bit. "It's about three miles from here—right back through the forest behind the house."

Then he gives me directions how to drive to it and what the old dump is like.

"You better get some—some friends to go with you," he advises. "We have to save Peggy at all costs now—even police."

"Friends won't do," I tell him. "Their kind would only blackmail you for the rest of your life. Besides I don't need them. But you are right about Peggy, she must be saved at all costs. If you don't hear from me by eleven o'clock tonight tell the police. At least you know just where she is now."

"But I'm going with you," he starts in to insist.

We had a go at that for about five minutes. Of course he wasn't strong enough and besides he would only be in the way. But I settled the whole argument by just refusing to go until I went alone.

After that I had him. There was nothing to do but wait for

dark. Every once in a while he would get worried and insist that I get some friends to go along. He wouldn't mind the blackmail. Finally I squashed that by telling him the truth. I had no friends in my business. I was a success because I played it alone. So that ended that.

The sun was just sinking when I started off. One look back at the Three Pines as I turned out at the gate disclosed Rogo, old and bent, standing on the porch. Those last few days had sure knocked him for a Rip Van Winkle. Outside of the movies I had never seen such a change.

I sped up on the motor for the next few miles and then I took it easy. It was perhaps an eight-mile drive around the tiny forest. About half a mile from where I figured the house would be I parked the machine off the road and into some under-brush. Then I hoofed it to the top of a great wooded hill and climbing a tree looked down.

Right below me is my meat. It's a swell place for the devil's work, to be hidden down there some two or three hundred yards from the meanest kind of country road. And there ain't another house in the valley—not for a couple of miles at least. But it suits me if it suits them. You could fire away there for half the night without causing no outside interest.

I'd a liked to have brought the car nearer because if I'm on the wrong track there will be a lot of time wasted. Also I half wished I'd taken a chance on following the wire and played safe but the parting advice of Myra had prevented my doing that.

"If there's a wire they'll have it watched somewhere; because they will figure that is your only chance of finding them."

And Myra was there with the dope. Also a car makes a certain amount of noise and is easily spotted.

So I shrug my shoulders and wait until there is just enough light to find my way. Then I cut down through the woods to the valley below. Darkness gets me half way down but I slip along; I got a good sense of direction.

It's pitch black when I reach the bottom and now I got to go careful 'cause there's a clearing of about fifty feet around the house. I just snake through the forest from then on. My little bag of tools—what certain gentlemen use in their line of business—is strapped to my back now and I've stuffed it with grass to keep it from rattling.

Then I hit the clearing; more to the side of the house then behind. I breathe easy. For a time I thought I'd overshot the mark. The house stands big and black and silent. Not a light in it. I wonder if I've drawn a blank.

Then I get a thrill—a thrill of joy. A figure, dimly outlined in the darkness of the night passes slowly around the mansion. It pauses a minute. Another comes from the opposite direction. They meet; whisper a bit and pass on.

Things are not so good. I realize at once I've got the right place, but I also realize that, even out there in the wilderness they guard against danger. This De Lasko is sure one tough egg.

For a while I just lie there and watch them. Want to see how often they meet and if they got to report inside every so often. In half hour they meet about three times and don't take no interest in the inside of the house at all. And what's more there ain't a light in that house—not that I can see anyway.

It's rough laying there. A dozen times I could of copped off both of them. I did wish that some kindly disposed gentleman would invent real noiseless shooting irons; the only kind

I ever tried went off like a cheap tin whistle. It might work in a boiler factory but....

But I see I got to start something. I ain't attending no peep show. With that I slip around back of the house for at that point the two outside guards will be furthest away from each other.

There's a little porch there and the next time a lad passes I skip to that porch and am all set. Oh, I know it's a quick job but it's a job I know.

There ain't much credit in that kind of work, maybe, but the art comes in when you strike. I use my blackjack, of course, and the next guard that comes around gets it right smack on the button. Not a groan; I've hit him clean as a whistle. He falls pretty—the soft grass deadening the impact of his body.

The next lad isn't so good. I got to get him as he turns the corner and can't strike clean. It takes two cracks to do it, but his cry is only a feeble one, and I figure they won't hear it. Events show that I'm right.

I might tell you I just let them lie there and broke into the house, but if you stopped to think you'd know that quick wallops like that are not lasting. But I'm telling the truth and not trying to set myself up as a model of all the virtues. Remember this ain't no story with a moral; it's fact, gospel.

I didn't have nothing to tie those inactive gentlemen up with so I did the best I could. To smooth off the rough edges of this yarn I'll just say I tapped them lads again—behind the ears with the butt of my gun this time. Couldn't have them bobbing up demanding an explanation at a critical time you know— they were good for the night now and no mistake.

With that little pleasantry attended to I went around to the side of the house and took a slant in one of the windows. There was a light there, only distinguishable when your nose was flat against the glass. It come from the second story some place; just a faint ray piercing the blackness.

There's a big tree, elm, I think, on this side of the house and one of its branches hangs over against the roof of the house. That's my lay and I shin up it; after the first rough climb it's easy. As I go up I see why there ain't no light from the second story windows. They are boarded up tight.

Of course I could have made my entrance from the ground but that ain't my way. If they miss the guard they'll be expecting visitors. Good enough! They'll be looking for them from below not from above.

It ain't no trouble to slide along that big branch and drop softly onto the roof. It's cagey work though. The shingles is rotten and I'm in danger of dropping in on them too sudden like. But I find what I'm aiming at; a little railed off platform and a trap door.

I out with my burglar outfit and go to work in the dark. I can't chance the flash. But the wood is old and I pry the rusty rivets lose like an old timer. Ten minutes later, after dropping a moistened bunch of grass to gage the distance, I take off my shoes and swing down to the musty attic below.

The floor is full of crevices and the light comes up from below. I got to be mighty careful that I don't kick fragments of rotten wood between them cracks. A bit further along there's a big gap and the light coming up makes things fairly clear. I creep toward it and discover that two of the planks were missing which makes an opening in the floor about two foot wide. I don't take a chance in looking down there but stretching out full length poke through one of the smaller cracks.

One slant and I pull a sigh of relief. I guess I didn't know how much my heart was in my work before. The first thing that my eyes spot is Peggy. And my blood runs hot; she's a different Peggy now. No longer is the sweet smile about her lips; they're drawn tight and white—kind a plaster white. And her great laughing eyes are dull and listless; looking straight ahead with a vacant stare. Her hair is all loose and hangs down about her knees as she crouches there on some filthy sacking. I see too that her face is bare and that ropes are tied tightly about her swollen ankles and fastened to heavy stone weights.

About half the room or less is all I can see but as my eyes shift and trace beyond Peggy I see two men. One comes over and stands before the girl and after leering down at her a moment, speaks:

"Real burns tonight my pretty one," he sneers and I know the voice was that of Mathews which I'd heard over the wire. "Your father is either a heartless man or he does not believe. But tonight we shall send him a little token—that pretty finger there—which Leo was glad to kiss—once."

With a laugh he turned away to the man whose back was to me. The man swung about. It was Leo Loft.

"Love and hate are much the same, ehe, Leo?" Mathews says with a coarse laugh.

"I could cut her throat and end it."

It took a rise out of me just to hear the way Leo said it. He sure was a changed man. His face was not blank and stupid now; it was mean and crafty and his eyes were alive and crazed. It seemed to me that there was a flood of madness in them— hate at any rate.

And then he stepped over and stood before the girl.

"I would have married you once," he fairly hissed the words. "Now, for all your money I wouldn't have you. And the cutting of that pretty finger belongs to me."

The great beast just stood there rubbing his hands together. It struck me then that I had sized up this bird all wrong.

Worn, frightened, and suffering the tortures of the damned Peggy raised her head. For the fraction of a second there shone the old time flash in her eyes. Defiant words were on her lips but she lacked the physical strength to utter them. The old stuff of a spirit greater than the flesh!

Leo raised his foot as though to kick the helpless girl but Mathews interfered:

"Your uncle will be here any minute," he warned. "You may do what you wish then I guess. He hates them all too. Gad! I saw the scars on his face last night; he'll wear them to his grave."

"Which won't be long," I thought to myself.

Yep, I was counting on a clean sweep that night. As for Leo—well—he had stood in the shadow of death when he raised his foot. It would be bad policy to shoot him down then but if he had touched the girl I'm afraid sentiment would have turned the trick. And that shows you how women can ruin everything.

Five minutes later De Lasko and another walk suddenly into the room. That made four. But the rough part of it was that I couldn't train my guns on more than one of them at a time. The big opening was plenty large enough but the room below wasn't built right. And this De Lasko was sure a sight for sore eyes. His scars were livid now and I got that pleasant feeling of a job well done. Then the man spoke:

"The guards! They are not about!"

He was nervous; not suspicious yet I don't think.

"You should be more careful. Where are they?"

The faces of the other two went white; they knew where those watchers should be. But they never got a chance to answer him.

As for me! I got a real shock now. John Rogo is standing there in the open doorway; hatless, white hair matted upon his forehead he stands there a revolver of ancient vintage held in his shaking fingers.

Of course there is a general drawing of weapons but Rogo shoots first. I just hear him call: "De Lasko!" and fire.

I see his gun spit but if he gets his man I can't tell. De Lasko has passed out of my line of vision.

"And now Terry earn your money," I say to myself as I leap through the opening.

"Action! Action!" I shout as I drop to the floor below.

Not that I want to play the dramatic you understand. I just want to rattle these birds and perhaps save Rogo's life.

I hear more than one shot as I land. Then both my guns spout death. Mathews and the lad what come in with De Lasko drop with a couple of bullets right smack between the eyes. Oh, they're dead alright. You don't have to hold no coroner's inquest when I mean business.

Rogo's on the floor; dead or wounded I can't tell. Leo I don't see but De Lasko is to my left. He fires. There's a hot sear across my cheek. I swing sudden—take a bullet in the left shoulder and cop him straight between his evil eyes. I guess he dies standing.

His mouth is half open, to curse, or plead or cry. Now, I ain't one to waste lead but I take another shot at him. Right down his throat I fire taking a couple of his front teeth with the bullet. Call it fate, superstition or my poetic nature. I don't care. I just had to do it that's all. There ain't no explaining some things.

Since I dropped into the room not more than ten seconds have passed. But I realize that Leo is gone and that I want him bad. I rush into the upper hall in time to hear the front door slam below. Leo is giving me the slip. I duck into a front room in the hope of getting a shot at him from an upper window; too late I remember that the upper windows are boarded up.

Then I'm down the stairs and out the front door but there ain't a soul in sight. A chug chug of a fastly moving motor tells me that Leo has shown a clean pair of heals. I turn back toward the old house.

"Mr. Mack!" a voice calls as I start up the porch steps.

I twirl about. Out of the darkness comes old William, the Rogo's butler.

"I couldn't wait down the road any longer, Mr. Mack," says Butts. "I heard the shooting. Mr. Rogo—is he all right?"

Old Butts has been in the family for upwards of twenty years and is pretty well in the know so I tell him:

"I don't know but Miss Peggy and her father sure need attention. Did you drive Mr. Rogo over?"

And when he says he did I tell him to drag the car up to the house and wait there. With that I beat it inside and up the stairs. I guess the whole gang is accounted for.

Rogo is sitting up now and Peggy has crawled to his side and got her arm about him. He ain't even shot. Tells me that someone socked him on the head. I take it that was Leo as he made his escape. But Rogo sure has got one welt on his dome as big as a hen's egg. I got to help him down to the car. Peggy insists that I take him safely out first.

Then I come back for the girl and cut them ropes off a her in jigtime. When I help her to her feet she can't stand. She tries to walk but almost faints. One look at the soles of her poor little scorched feet tells the story.

"Leo did it," she tells me. "They would hang me up by my wrists and put the phone close to my lips. Then when I didn't cry out Leo lit matches and held them against the bottom of my feet. I couldn't help but cry out then."

Think of it! The lad what I wanted most had got clean away. Or had he? As I carried Peggy down the stairs and out to the car I swore to shoot that mutt down the very first time I seen him. Yep—even if it was in the center of the Grand Central Station at dinner time.

And Peggy wants to know if I've been hurt. I tell her no of course but just imagine that slip of a kid thinking of me at a time like that. Why she ought to be having hysterics and going on terrible. Instead she's as calm as what I am and believe me, I never show emotion.

Butts drives the car and I make him go around and up on the hill where I parked the runabout. There sure is going to be one nasty investigation when the dead is found in that house.

"Cheer up, Mr. Rogo," I tell the old man who is as doleful as a wake. No one will suspect us and this Mathews—the only bird who has a real line on your past—is well—persona non grata."

Oh yes, I spill a little French now and then.

But Rogo shakes his head. He sure is one sad old bird. In my way of looking at it things have gone off pretty good.

"Leo is free," he chirps like an undertaker. "He hates us all. I saw it in his eyes tonight."

Think of that! I wonder what kind of a slaughter he wants for his money. But I don't say nothing. We've reached the runabout now and I jump in it and follow them home.

Peggy's put to bed and old Rogo even had to be given a lift on the stairs. He won't hit the hay himself but sits in a big chair by the girl's bedside while her maid rubs ointment on her poor blistered feet.

As for me I got more work to do. But I ain't bothering then about that. I'm just figuring that that telephone wire might give the police considerable food for thought.

"Don't go to bed yet, Butts," I whisper to the old servant as I leave the father and daughter alone.

Half hour later I slip from the darkened house and Butts drives me back to the old mansion of death. The moon's out now—it being about eleven thirty. I chase Butts back with the car telling him that I will be along later. Being a good servant he beats it along without giving me an argument.

Then I locate that wire and start into work. I sure do intend making a good job of it. It's only hidden in the grass at most places but crossing the road it's sunk deep and takes a heap of pulling.

At first it hurts my wounded arm a bit and starts the blood flowing again but after a while the pain goes away. I work faster and easier. It's funny but I catch myself singing kind of while I work. There don't seem to be really any danger and I got a comfortable and happy feeling; just keep gathering up wire, rolling it, and when it gets too heavy to carry I chuck it into the thick brush.

My feet get lighter; much easier to carry, like I was walking in the air. Once I think I see a figure and take a pot shot at it. Then I laugh. It must be just fancy for whom would dare to bother Terry Mack at his work in the night?

"Who'd dare bother Terry Mack."

That sounds pretty good and I make a song out of it shouting it louder and louder. And every once in a while I pound my left shoulder just to convince myself that there ain't no pain.

Why it seems like I ain't in the woods over five minutes when I spot Three Pines. There is Butts—yep a great light is coming in the sky—no, I see three Butts, each one bigger than the other until the center one stands out as large, as the great house itself.

Butts is talking to me too—all three of them. But what the devil they are saying I don't know. And I wish he'd take that great hand of his off me. It weighs a ton. I never felt such a heavy hand. I shout at him—at all three of them—bawl them out but my voice seems weak and like it come from a long ways off.

Then I'm in the large hall of the house and that hand still keeps pushing me down—down—down. After that blackness. Damn Butts! I've fainted like a woman. Women again!

I'm in bed when I come to again. Peggy is there and she's walking about too. Gad, but I think that her feet got well quick. And Silent Smith is there too. Smith is my doctor in the city; a chap what will take a pound or two of lead out of a chap and not go around blowing about it. Then I sleep again.

The next time I open my glims I'm my own man. Blood poisoning and everything else has been my ticket. A month has been plucked out of my life and nearly the whole life if what Smith has to say is true. Rogo had sent for him when I muttered his name in my first sinking fit.

Peggy's feet is better and Rogo is okey; he give me the dope as to what's gone on. The papers were full of "The House of Mystery" for a while but they put it all down to bootlegging.

Investigation showed that De Lasko had been mixed up in several rum deals. At least we're not suspected. It was five days before the police found the bodies which accounts for no talking. The two lads that I had clouted must have come around the next morning and beat it. There has been narry a peep out of Leo.

And as soon as I sit up darned if Rogo don't come around and spout that marriage talk again:

"I spoke to you once about marriage," he says. "That was when Peggy needed you but now that you need Peggy why—why I'm of the same mind. You're rough Terry but I wouldn't want a better nor a cleaner man for my little girl."

"Need her! Need her!" I exclaim.

Where did he get that stuff? Of course she had nursed me and all that but—

"When you were delirious you said things—many things, Terry."

"Mr. Rogo." I was real serious now. "I'm a man of few words and I won't go into reasons. You understand of course that they could not be unfavorable to Peggy. But I shall never marry Peggy. Let that be an end of such talk."

And that shut him up tighter than a loan shark. What I said in delirium and what I said now were two different things.

Later I find out that all arrangements have been made for a cruise through the Mediterranean. Passage was booked aboard the *Catonia* and a room had been reserved for me. So I put the dampers on that quick.

Peggy was always with me and the way she looked at me give me the creeps. Nothing designing you understand, nor pity neither. Just sweet! But it bothered me though it was deadly dreary there when she wasn't around.

After I sat up in the garden she took to reading to me and the things she read were good. But one day when I was sitting there she started reading something different. Familiar and rotten it was. Then I recognized the guff. My book of poems!

"I found this in your room," she says. "Why you read such rot I can't think. A great, he-man like you."

"Throw it away," I said and then without thinking I added. "You ain't so much different than me then—I couldn't fathom it neither."

With that she tossed the book into the bushes and come over and sat down beside me.

"Terry," she began, taking my hand and holding it like she done when I was very sick. "There is something that must be said between us and you must listen and answer yes or no. Certain words were spoken when you were very sick. Your language and your education are nothing to me. They are small matters indeed but your heart and soul are big and any girl might be proud of you. Terry if you really wish to marry me I'll be a very happy girl. Think how hard it is for me to speak this way and remember what it may mean to both of us. Please just answer yes or no."

"No," I answer without even thinking.

I've done too much thinking of late. Women and me ain't—

But she picks up a book and starts to read like nothing had happened. And from then on she was no different than she had always been. I guess she didn't feel her loss very keenly but then women are all the same.

One month later I was on my feet and prepared to leave. Going to South America I told them but that was wind. I wanted to get away. Sickness had turned my head. I was getting full of fool ideas. My poetic nature was getting the best of me I guess.

Rogo told me at parting:

"If you change your mind your room on the boat will be waiting for you, Peggy wouldn't let me cancel your passage."

Peggy drove me to the station and insisted on holding my bag until I boarded the train. And then she done it. The thing what caused all the trouble. When I went to lean down for that bag she suddenly threw her arms about my neck and kissed me—yep—kissed me full upon the lips.

"There!" I heard her say as the train pulled out. "If you lied when you had your senses and told the truth when you were delirious that will bring you back to me. Remember! The boat sails the tenth of next month."

That's that. The train shot around the bend. Oh, I know the thing was silly and childish still that kiss sure was a pretty fancy and I didn't hold it against her none. Not me!

Of course I don't budge out of the city for the next month. Rogo's paid like a gentleman and I live like one. But the old town ain't like it use to be and I don't gather no pleasure in running around. The country has got me I guess; with its quiet and vigorous air and—oh—and other things. No, it won't do. It's just like it was a couple of months ago. I need action.

And then one morning I read that the *Catonia* is sailing that night at ten o'clock; the late sailing's a good idea—passengers wake up next morning far out to sea.

That night I take in a show. It's supposed to be a knockout but it don't fit with me. I leave after the first act. Then comes the feeling that I got unfinished business to attend to. I'd like to know that Rogo gets away alright. So I jump a taxi and make the dock.

I spend a five spot and nail a position behind a load of boxes where I can watch the people slip on and not be seen myself.

Pretty soon Rogo and Peggy come along; they ain't no servants with them. The whole trip was originally planned for us three just to have a good time together—yes, and perhaps a wedding before the end of it. I watch them go on. It takes a strong will not to follow but boy I sure got one strong will.

I've seen enough but I wait to let the ship start. And then comes the bell and the visitors are hurrying ashore. It won't be another minute now; they are getting ready to lift the gangplank. It won't be but another minute now. I look out over the river and then back to the *Catonia*.

Startled!

I jump back, near overturning a box. A late comer, muffled to the ears though the night is warm, is hustling up the plank. Half way up he turns and takes his bag from the taxi driver who has followed him. The arc shines full upon his face. You hit it. It's Leo, The Lion Faced Boy. And there is that look in his eyes which I seen in the old house two months before. Hatred, murder—madness. Yep, if ever I saw a balmy look it's in Leo's glims that night.

The gangplank is in and tugs take the ship out in the river. The lights on the dock get smaller as we turn and head toward the bay. How do I know? Why, do I need to tell you that I'm with the ship? You said it. I made that plank by the fraction of a second.

Of course I ain't got no ticket but what of that. I grab a room steward and cross his palm with paper.

"My friends are aboard." Then I tell him my name. "They didn't half expect me." I go on. "Quite a surprise this. They have the ticket."

Then I tell him that he's to keep a tight trap until I pull my presence on them next morning.

Is he friendly? I should snicker. Any one what can pay for a room and keep it reserved, even though he mightn't use it, is squirrel food to him. To him I'm dough heavy and he beams on me like I was the returned prodigal. He leads me to my nesting place which is one swell lay out.

Alone, I stretch out and think. Action is what I wanted and it looks like action is what I'm going to get. Then I spot a great bunch of flowers. There's a card tied to them. I get up and lamp it.

"To Terry in case he remembers and comes. And I don't like Keats either."

There ain't no name signed to it. There don't need to be. I know without the help of mind reading that it is Peggy's fist.

Eight bells is striking twelve o'clock when I lock the stateroom door and slip onto the deck. I just drift aft and get the air; kill a butt and think. The first stop is the Azores Islands. You can't get away from that.

One bell strikes and then two. The people thin out. There ain't but three left. Three bells toll one thirty and I got the deck to myself. I'll stick it out a while. It's nice out there; a little breezy for a straw lid so I duck back in the shadow of a bunch of steamer chairs what ain't been laid out yet.

And then she comes. Yep, trotting along down the deck like she was half expecting to see someone. Peggy passes on the off side of me and going to the stern leans over—studying the wake of the ship I guess.

I smoke on unseen. My brains are dusty; there ain't no plan struck me yet.

She turns half sideways after a while and stays there motionless as a statue. I wonder what she's thinking and if I'd better speak now or wait until the morning before I tell Rogo that Leo is aboard.

I'm within twenty feet of her, the chairs piled high running within five or six feet of the stern rail. My eyes shift and lazily slide along the rail.

There—not three yards from Peggy, a white hand stretches itself up from below and rests upon the rail. Some one is skimming up from the deck below.

Do I think it's a deck hand out for a little nocturnal exercise. Not me! I know before ever the face appears that it will be Leo. And it is. He climbs up on that deck with no more noise than an eel. The girl's eyes are on the sea; Leo's eyes are on her and my eyes are on him and the knife which he carries in his right hand.

I could of shot him down; no trouble about that—just a report, a splash and the cry of "Man Overboard!" But that one report would spoil her whole trip. It would be hard to explain to the captain that I was trying to shoot a few flying fish at that time of the night.

As Leo moves along the outside of the rail I move along the inside; he makes one foot and I make three. Is it just coincidence that I'm there when he comes? Not much it ain't. I've been expecting him but he ain't expecting me. If there's any coincidence it's all on his side of the fence.

Oh, it ain't even a close call for Peggy. I got him covered all the way and if he turns or hurries things I'll shoot. But he don't turn my way; his eyes flashing like a cat's in the darkness he edges closer to the girl.

When the knife goes up high to strike I get him. Oh, I'm not laying to make it dramatic; it just happened that way. I don't go in for no play acting. Not me! I just finish my man. One swipe with the butt of my gun behind his ear does the trick. Leo is knocked for a flock of sea gulls.

No scream mind you—just a dull thud—a weak groan and a hole in the ocean. The Lion Faced Boy has pulled his last dirt. In this world at least.

Peggy swings around as I slip my gun to cover. She has heard the crack. "What's that!" And then, "Terry!"

There's a glad ring in her voice.

I'm looking straight into her eyes now and I see that she's been crying.

"Oh Terry! I didn't think you would come."

She breaks off for a second. "Then—then—the kiss—it did bring you after all."

She half laughs—half cries.

See the hole I got myself into. This poor little kid had had enough trouble without my starting in now to kill her whole trip. That's what I'd a done if I up and told her that I'd just crashed Leo to the sharks.

Then she come nearer and laid both her little hands upon my shoulders. Her black eyes is boring right into mine:

"And since I brought you back to me I'll have to make sure of holding you."

Bing! Like that she threw her arms about me and kissed me again.

The moon came out brighter and we still stood upon the deck; six bells struck the hour of three and we still stood upon the deck. Then just to show her that there was no hard feeling I leaned down and kissed her myself. I hadn't counted on this but fate and my poetic nature turned the trick. And I guess I know how to play the gentleman.

The Man in the Shadows

Terry Mack, private investigator, who has solved so many intricate problems, here again leads the reader through an amazing series of tense and dramatic scenes to a most unexpected conclusion.

1

The Dead Man On the Beach

THE DEAD MAN lay on the beach. His glassy, sightless eyes stared unseeingly over the distant stretch of blue sea into the first brilliancy of the morning sun. His left hand gripped tightly at the stiff linen collar of his white shirt as if he had clutched frantically at his throat before he fell; attempted before death stayed his purpose to tear the collar from about his neck. His right arm was stretched by his side, the hand turning slowly, methodically and grotesquely as the foaming water of the pounding ocean swept close to the body and sportively played with those dead, bent fingers.

Far back from the sandy beach and across a stretch of well-kept lawn stood a large house, called Shadow Lawn. But neither the man who played the hose upon the grass nor the one in rubber boots who polished an expensive motor could see the silent, dead thing upon the beach. For a boat house, well back to where the sand met the grass with an intervening wall of loose stones, hid the body from view.

At precisely ten minutes of seven o'clock the owner of that house stepped from between the French windows which opened upon a tiny stone porch, and nodding to the gardener stopped for a word with the chauffeur who still labored over the big sedan.

"Always up early, Crimons," he smiled, "and always busy."

"It's a fine morning for it." The man called Crimons gave a

final rub to a brilliant headlight, touched his bare head and wiped his hands upon the chamois. "She was a sorry sight, sir," he shook his head. "The roads were thick with mud when I drove Miss Florence in from town."

"Late, Crimons—wasn't it?" The man raised his head, sniffing in the clearness of the morning air and the salt-laden breeze from the ocean. And when Crimons turned a slight red and stammered something about not knowing the hour, he smiled good-humoredly.

"It doesn't really matter. I wasn't thinking of Miss Florence. She's quite able to take care of herself. But she must remember that you are alone here now and that I leave for town at eight-thirty." But he breathed deeply, and the shrug of his shoulders was not of indifference; rather, the act of a man who attempts to shift a burden.

Crimons touched his bare forehead again as the master of Shadow Lawn turned down the narrow gravel path toward the boat house and the beach.

It was a fine morning; it was a fine car, a fine stretch of beach, and perhaps the finest summer home in South Newton. Clarence Belford Johnstone could not resist the impulse to turn by the stretch of stone which served as a breakwater against the winter storms and look with pride upon the well-kept lawn, the thick shrub and the freshly painted house. He had not always been rich, but his mythical fortune of years before had laid a foundation upon which a real one was built. When he came back from that gold boom of years ago, fanciful stories had preceded him to Newton. His fellow citizens were out to welcome one who fantastic accounts recorded as a man who had struck it rich and sold out for a cold million to a San Francisco syndicate.

This report he neither affirmed nor denied, but if he leaned toward either it was more in the nature of a denial. A denial, if honest in its purpose, yet was so confused by the respect of his fellow citizens that it was taken for a modest admission of success and a tactful desire to minimize his great good fortune.

There was no romance to that Klondike strike of thirty years ago. The thing had practically proved a bust, yet through the failures and murders and suicides Clarence Johnstone had seemingly been successful. His forehead wrinkled as his thoughts went back to those days now; hazy was the recollection of the biting cold, the long nights of fever, the two dead men in the fuelless shack, and the terrible hours of struggling in the storm. Two dead when relief came; the months in the hospital, and the sudden death of another of those youthful partners in the rush for wealth. With the death of Frank Marion came some money and the responsibility of a baby girl. With the rumor of his vast fortune Clarence Johnstone had returned to Newton and discovered the truth of the proverb that wealth begets wealth—even if that first wealth is born only in the imaginations of friends and acquaintances.

That he did not spend money lavishly brought only nods of approval that wealth had not turned his head. That he lived modestly in the home of his mother until her death only made of him a dutiful son. That he did not invest, or was not reputed to have made large deposits at any of the three banks in a neighboring city only enlarged upon the gossip that he was a far-seeing man. He was wise and conservative; a financial genius whose three years of previous training as a clerk in a bank of a city across the river had built up within his shrewd brain an understanding of money matters. Thus stood Clarence Johnstone in the estimation of his fellow townsmen.

So, when the city of Newton opened its first bank Clarence Belford Johnstone at the age of thirty-three became its president. That was twenty-seven years ago. Newton's population had jumped from 6,800 to a little beyond 200,000. And the citizens of that growing city, at least those who remembered, looked upon the first president of the first local bank, which now was a pretentious trust company, as more than partly responsible for the increasing prosperity of the city.

Clarence Belford Johnstone looked back again at the handsome summer home that his mythical fortune of years ago had helped to, if not actually built. Nothing succeeds like success—and on the first of that month he had reached in reality that million dollars which the love of romance had credited to him thirty years before. He sighed just a little as he passed along the wooden runway by the boat house and onto the beach. After all, the time between the dreams of youth and the reality of age is long indeed. He was sixty years of age and never felt better in his life. That is, physically. Mentally he was disturbed. The actions of his adopted daughter, Florence, had bothered him at first—but now her attitude was to cause sleepless nights and nervous days. He wondered could she actually be mixed up in the past; associated with such a scoundrel as he had forgotten for nearly thirty years and now remembered again. There was the card he had received in the mail only the day before. A card that would have puzzled most men, but simply drew into heavier wrinkles the high intelligent forehead of Clarence Johnstone. For on that card was a single line. It read: THE THREE OF SPADES IS OUT OF THE PACK AGAIN.

He wasn't sure who had sent it, but he was sure what it meant. And now, with Florence almost putting her suspicions into words, suspicions that he had robbed her dead father, the message took on a sinister aspect indeed. Well, he had done the best he could. He had sent for help; his letter had been dropped in the box last night. It would be on the morning train to New York City. Clarence Johnstone sighed. It couldn't be delivered for another twenty-four hours.

Thrusting back his shoulders he turned toward the sea, looked out over the vastness of the ocean, and spreading his arms far apart breathed deeply of the salt air. After all, it was good to be alive—then his eyes dropped slowly to the stretch of sand and fell upon the dead thing on the beach. His arms remained so—stretched out toward the sea a moment—then fell to his sides. He half turned toward the boat house and the board runway; swung back and looked straight down at that dead body.

An unusually large wave, hurtling unexpectedly upon the very crest of a smaller one, swept up beyond the man's head and shoulders. The head half turned, the feet moved as if resisting the pulling of the sea; then the face of the dead man swung toward the boat house, and the wide, surprised eyes of Clarence Johnstone looked upon the glassy ones of death.

Fascinated, he stepped forward. He could not be sure, of course; did not even recognize the man as he drew closer. But the horror in his face, which now took the place of the surprise, was not caused by the glassy eyes nor the resisting legs, nor the twitching of the fingers as the water rushed back into the sea. As Johnstone came within a few paces of that grotesque figure, his eyes were riveted upon the whiteness of the water-soaked shirt; the pale red that even the great Atlantic had not eradicated—and the hilt of a long knife, the blade of which was buried in the man's chest.

He stood looking down at the face of the dead. It was familiar; yes, he was sure of that—but where had he seen it before? It must be he—of course, who else? But time had not dealt kindly with the man; Clarence Johnstone knew that the dead man was at least three years his junior, yet he seemed an old man—a very old man.

He looked more closely at the man now—the stain of red. And he saw it! A cold hand shot over a suddenly moist forehead—a closed fist shot to his eyes and tried to wipe away the mist that suddenly obscured his vision. He felt giddy as the blood rushed to his head, and his shoulders swayed slightly as he bent over the body. With an effort he drew himself erect—turned and stumbled toward the boat house. For he had seen something besides the hilt of a knife protruding from the dead man's chest. The knife had been driven through a playing card. Plainly, cut squarely in the center by the knife, was the three of spades.

Twice Clarence Johnstone tried to cry out but the words stuck and made only a gurgling sort of noise deep down in his throat. When he reached the side of the boat house he recovered his voice—but he did not use it. For a moment he stood there wiping his forehead with the back of his hand, before he thought of his handkerchief. Then he sat down upon the wooden steps. The blood had ceased to pound in his head. He held his right hand out before him. The wrist and hand seemed steady enough but the fingers trembled violently; he could not control that.

The police would have to be notified, of course, but why couldn't it have been some one else who found the body? Would his condition be a natural one under the circumstances? Was he showing altogether too much emotion? No, he thought not. He was no longer a young man. The sight of a dead man on the beach in front of his own home was enough to upset any man. He would be questioned; asked if he knew the man. Truthfully he could say that he did not recognize that drawn, lined face with the shaggy gray hair and the sunken, lifeless eyes.

And the playing card! The police would ask about that, of course. Would he tell them the truth? If he did, what? Nothing could happen to him. It would be unpleasant, certainly. Suddenly he thought of his adopted daughter, Florence, and his promise to her dead father that he would care for her as if she were his own child. She had been keeping very late hours the past month. There was a steady staring, almost suspicious look in her eyes, and her latest request to have the two letters that her father had written years before was puzzling. He had tried to question her and recalled clearly her sudden outburst of anger, if not actual hatred, as she turned contemptuously from him.

Clarence Johnstone clenched his hands tightly together, stepped back on the beach, and looking up and down the stretch of lonely sand cautiously approached that dead body again. He had not decided exactly what he was going to do. That is, consciously he had not. But subconsciously the thing was in his mind. Though he did not know it, he went toward the body with the one set purpose. He must remove that card.

He understood that he must not put a hand upon the dead

man; knew instinctively too that he must not touch the handle of that knife. He must touch nothing that would be found by the police. The sweat broke out on his forehead again as he reached the body and bent over it. He looked back over his shoulder at the house; just the roof of it was visible above the boat house and no one could see him from the grounds. He was thankful too that the season was early and the big gray mansion of his neighbor was not yet occupied.

It was useless to attempt to take what he wanted without looking at the body. That would be the height of folly. His hands shook now, and his fingers trembled violently. Could he get the card away without touching the knife? Was he making a mistake by taking that card? No—no harm could come of that, for only the man who put it there would know. And the knife would cut the thin pasteboard easily enough if he worked the card gently up and down against the sharp edge of the blade.

Slowly he stretched out a hand and touched the card. He sighed his relief. It was wet and soggy and parted like tissue paper as he gently pulled. It was done. He had not touched the body; at least, he did not think that he had. But there was blood upon his fingers. He looked down at the card and there was no blood on the corner that he held. Taking out his handkerchief he wiped his fingers carefully, folded the soft linen twice about the moist card and placed it in his pocket. Then he turned and hurried toward the boat house, and this time he found his voice and used it as he ran.

"Crimons! Harris!" he called hoarsely, as he turned along the side of the boat house. And his shout died, for the door of the boat house, which was closed when he had passed before, was now open and there was a window in the boat house that looked directly out on the beach—and the thing upon the beach.

Clarence Johnstone leaned against that swaying door for support. So the chauffeur, Crimons, and the gardener, Harris, found him as they ran toward the boat house at his first frantic cry.

The two servants were not surprised that their master should take the finding of the body as he did.

"It froze my blood in me." Crimons had described his reaction to the other servants, and Harris had not been ashamed of the fear that gripped him.

"Pushed my heart into my mouth, it did," was the way Harris put it.

Nor did either of them think it at all extraordinary that Clarence Johnstone had insisted that they search the boat house, nor did they notice his relief when he saw that the big canoe was slap up against the window, shutting off the view. Nor did any of the three excited men observe that on the bow of the canoe was the outline of a hand and fingers clearly marked in the dust which had gathered over the winter.

2

—

Shadows

CLARENCE JOHNSTONE WANTED to be alone, to think; yet, the thoughts that persisted in thrusting themselves forward were too fantastic to be considered. Though he tried to push them aside as ridiculous, he knew that the playing card could not be accounted for as just a coincidence in the death of the man upon the beach. He tried to figure out how a man should act in such circumstances—finding a murdered stranger in front of his own home. He had given the orders, but it was his butler, Jenkins, who rang up the police, and Crimons, the chauffeur, whom he had seen going toward the beach with a white sheet in his hands.

He finally decided it would not do to be alone. He must face his family, make a pretense of eating breakfast, and after interviewing the police go to the bank as usual. He must act surprised, of course, and slightly shocked—but nothing more.

Florence, his adopted daughter, who now bore his name, was the only one at the breakfast table when he somewhat unsteadily pulled out his chair and sat down. She was a strikingly beautiful woman, thirty-three or four, dark, with an olive complexion that must have been inherited from her mother who had died at her birth. Certainly her father had been light. Clarence Johnstone remembered him well, now. He wondered too why she stared at him so; still, she had seemed to stare at him a great deal lately—but this morning the natural dark shadows beneath her eyes seemed deeper and rather to distract from her beauty than add to it. And there was a pallor to her face that was accentuated somewhat by the heavy blackness beneath her eyes. She did not speak—just looked at him. He grew restless under the steady scrutiny and was glad when Old Martin came into the room.

Old Martin shuffled across to his seat at the table, his shoulders bent, his head forward—so that his chin almost touched his chest, those expressionless colorless eyes resting first on Florence and then on Clarence Johnstone.

"Good morning." He jerked his head quickly to the left and right, and sitting down began hurriedly to attack his grapefruit. He did not lift his head and did not raise his eyes.

The presence of Old Martin, figuratively spoken of as Mr. Johnstone's secretary, but literally known as a victim of the gold rush of thirty years ago, and a companion at that time if not a servant of Clarence Johnstone, left one vacant chair at the table. This belonged to Clarence Johnstone's daughter, Ardath. Mrs. Johnstone had died ten years before, and since then Florence, the adopted daughter, had taken over the duties of the household. She had never married.

Clarence Johnstone tried unsuccessfully to finish his fruit, and pushed his eggs aside with a feeling almost of repulsion. The silence became oppressive; he was conscious only of his own loud breathing, the soft tread of the butler's feet, and the almost deafening, sucking noise as Old Martin ate his grapefruit. Finally he could stand it no longer.

"Miss Ardath, Jenkins." He raised his eyes to the butler, then lowered them again. What right had the man to be so white? "It is not like Miss Ardath to be so late. Still in bed?"

"No, sir—she's not. That is, sir, she's not in bed. She's on the beach."

"On the beach, with—" Clarence Johnstone's head jerked involuntarily erect. He didn't consciously leave his speech unfinished. The final words simply would not come.

"It's—it's covered, sir," the butler explained hastily. "Crimons threw a sheet over it, and—the police are already there."

"You've been to the beach?" Clarence Johnstone could not altogether hide his surprise.

"Why—yes, sir, we just ran down. Crimons lifted the sheet and let us all—"

"That's enough, Jenkins. We will not discuss this—this tragedy. You will send for Miss Ardath—at once."

"She returned to the house, sir. After her bath and—"

"I'm ready for breakfast." The voice came from the doorway as Ardath Johnstone burst into the room. "Isn't it thrilling, Father—a murder right on the beach. Crimons thinks maybe it's bootleggers. But they didn't leave any card or—"

"Card—card! What are you talking of, child?" Her father's face went from a pale white to a pasty yellow. He felt a foot strike him under the table and turned sharply. It was Old Martin. Those expressionless eyes were on him. Was there a warning in them? But he could not tell that—there never was anything to read in those vacant, colorless depths. They weren't glassy exactly, yet there was a dull glitter to them which reminded Johnstone, with a shudder, of the dead man on the beach. But Ardath was talking.

"Certainly—a card." She laughed. "What's the good of killing a man if it doesn't act as a warning to the others? All the books—and even the papers now print such things. 'Traitor' or

'Vengeance' or—oh, some foreign word. But there was nothing, and—"

"Ardath," Clarence Johnstone tried to put some of his accustomed vigor into his words, "we won't talk about—about the happening of this morning."

"Not talk about it!" Ardath's great brown eyes went wide. "Why, everybody's talking about it. All the servants have been to the beach, and most of them had a peek. Jenkins saw to that. Didn't you, Jenkins. You're quite the—"

"We will not talk about this tragedy—at breakfast." Clarence Johnstone modified somewhat his former command, and seeing the question hovering on his daughter's lips, continued, "There's your sister to consider."

"Oh, she doesn't mind," Ardath shot in. "She was down too—I saw her standing by the boat house." Seeing the sudden color in her father's cheeks and mistaking it for anger, she snapped, "Oh, all right—the water was beastly cold this morning."

"You weren't in—not this morning!" This time her father's surprise was natural enough.

"Why not?" She looked at him somewhat defiantly. And when he did not answer, "People are killed every day. I read once where there are ten thousand murders a year—one every hour—in the United States. Suppose we gave up our pleasure and our habits for all of them! Of course, if they all happened out on our beach it would be annoying. There, Dad—" she suddenly jumped from her seat, and running to him flung her arms about his neck, "it's so hard not to talk about it. Nothing ever happens here—and now—" she pouted up at him.

For a minute, perhaps, her father patted her head in silence, then he spoke.

"I know, I know." He tried not to make his voice impassioned. "But we'll have to talk about it all soon enough." And as those brown eyes sought his steadily, "There's Florence to be considered—we don't all take these things the same. You see, death is very far from you—but very near to me." And he could not control the slight shudder that suddenly ran over him as he realized perhaps the significance of the words he himself had spoken.

"You need have no apprehension as to my emotions." For the first time the dark-eyed woman spoke. "But your father is right, Ardath. It was he who first found the body. It has been a shock to him; a shock that you cannot fully understand."

Clarence Johnstone raised his eyes to those of his adopted daughter. Was there hidden meaning in her words? Had there been hidden meaning in her actions for the past few months, anyway? Never perhaps had he gotten very close to this girl. But there had always been a trust and confidence in him. It was only lately that those cold black eyes had watched him—distrustfully, almost with a touch of hatred.

But there was nothing in her face now; cold and passionless, she met his gaze until it was his that dropped. Finally he rose, looked once at the silent figure of Old Martin, and carefully picking his steps walked to the library. Although their eyes apparently had not met, Old Martin understood. His withered, bony fingers lifted his coffee cup and he gulped down the contents. Then he slowly came to his feet, let his colorless eyes drift from the girl to the woman, jerked his head up and down, and turned toward the hall door.

"Father's terribly down in the mouth, Martin." Ardath smiled up at the old man. "Cheer him up."

"Cheer him up!" The old man laughed—a gurgling, grating sort of laugh. "Cheer him up, is it? Not in this—" he stopped, ran a bony hand across his forehead, muttered something under his breath and shuffled from the room.

3

The Past Again

CLARENCE JOHNSTONE PACED back and forth in the library when Old Martin entered. He turned sharply, motioned the old man to a seat and continued to walk.

"You were down to the beach, Martin?" he asked suddenly.

"I was that." The old man sat motionless, his eyes staring before him.

"You saw the—body?"

"I did that."

"The face?"

"The face—yes."

For some time Clarence Johnstone paced the room in silence and when he spoke again his voice shook.

"Well—why don't you say something? Is it possible you don't know?" He looked doubtfully at the old man.

"No, it ain't possible. It ain't possible that neither of us don't know. I knew the fingers before ever Crimons lifted the sheet. He held them like that the night—Fitz and Morrow died; twitching they were then, but he didn't die. He lived for this. Do you think we too live for—for this?"

"Nonsense!" Clarence Johnstone snapped out the word, but no relief showed in the other's face. "I thought it might be he; are you sure?"

"Sure!" For the first time that expressionless old face jerked erect, the bony hands clutched at thin knees, and dead eyes flashed. "I'd know him in hell." He spat the words out. "And him who sent him, and, yes—and killed him." His final words were very soft.

"Were the police there—yet?"

"That they were—all over the place. Inspector Thurston."

"They—questioned you?" Clarence Johnstone stopped in his walking and stood before the old man.

"They asked me if—if I recognized him."

"What did you say—what did you say?" Clarence Johnstone bent forward and clutched Old Martin roughly by the shoulder.

"I didn't say nothing—not me," he chuckled. "I looked vacant-like and shook my head. I wanted to know what you'd say—if you wanted to forget the dead."

"Why should I want to forget the dead?" Clarence Johnstone said, almost hurriedly.

"I don't know—if you don't." And then very slowly, "Miss Florence was on the beach last night."

"Ah!" The other gasped, but more in horror than surprise. "You don't think she knows. She couldn't. But there's the card." He walked to the little safe in the wall, spun the dial, and jerking open the door pulled out the blood-stained handkerchief and showed the card to Old Martin.

Old Martin gazed at it but no emotion showed in his wrinkled, pasty skin. Withered lips smacked—but nothing more.

"Well?" Clarence Johnstone regarded him a moment before returning the card to the safe.

"It's bad." The old man wagged his head from side to side. "But I expected it. He's been out this five year—pardoned. He wasn't the man to forget. Not Nixon Carleton. It'll be the love of money and the love of vengeance—but the love of money will come first. Somehow he's stretched out his hand and fastened it on Miss Florence. I can't think differently. I told you again and again. There's only physical violence to fear from him—but with the girl— There's your promise to her dead father. 'Like your own daughter' I think the words were."

Clarence Johnstone thought a moment. Should he go straight to the police with the whole story? Yes, undoubtedly he should. But would he, if it was Ardath who had acted lately as Florence had acted and who had been seen on the beach by Old Martin?

"Well," said Martin suddenly, "do we forget the—the killed man on the beach. If he was in with Nixon Carleton and came wanting money, I daresay he deserved what he got."

"Good God!" Clarence Johnstone's face went ashen. "You don't think I murdered him?"

"I didn't call it murder and I don't think nothing. I've always let you do the thinking. You thought years ago and you can think now. I'll say what you say."

Clarence Johnstone regarded Old Martin fixedly. He wondered what was on the old man's mind after all these years. Silently, faithfully, he had done his bidding in all things. And now—suppose he was to deny all knowledge of this crime, the dead man himself, of the card upon his chest—what would Martin's attitude be then? Would he believe that he had other motives than the one to protect the daughter of his dead friend? And believing that, what would he do?

"Martin," Clarence Johnstone laid a hand upon his shoulder, "you've been with me here, thirty years. There was no question of burying a past, no idea of your keeping silent. We had gone through much together; things that those of to-day could not understand. Have you been satisfied? Have you ever thought that I was rich and you were poor? Have you ever thought that you were entitled to your share in my prosperity? Have there been nights when you have dreamed that things might have been—well—just the opposite?"

"Why, no." While there was no change in that thick corrugated skin, there was a bewildered surprise in the voice. "It's the harder task that's yours. You knew what to do then, you know what to do now. I'm grateful—and happy, if at times I can help. But—why I'm here; well, I like to think it's friendship. As you say, they were hard days."

Those lifeless, colorless eyes seemed to rest full upon the gray ones of Clarence Johnstone, yet he felt that they were not looking at him—just staring vacantly into space. Sometimes he thought that the old man was growing weak in the intellect—at other times, that he was very shrewd indeed.

"Yes, yes." Clarence Johnstone dropped into a chair. He wondered if he had not better face the thing at the beginning; tell the police the truth and what he feared. Like a moving picture, the events of thirty-odd years ago passed vividly through his mind again.

There were eight of them together in that Klondike rush. Nixon Carleton and even Fitz and Morrow had been taken in at the last moment, when it was found necessary to strengthen their little party if they were to guard the claim that seemed so rich. For the law of the Klondike was the law of strength. But the gold failed in its promise of great wealth. Thirty thousand dollars, the labor of eight men for six months, and they had dug well into the hill.

Winter was coming and the loneliness of the snow-covered north swept down on them. Yet they would not allow themselves to believe that the claim was hopeless, dared not leave it unprotected until they were sure. But one thing they must face, and that was the necessity of sending some one into town for food—a hazardous trip but certainly not an impossible one.

One week later, at six o'clock at night, eight men stood around the rough board table, prepared to draw cards to see which one of the party would take to the trail and bring relief. They dared not wait longer. The mercury had already dropped; the gray of the sky and rising wind forbade delay. Night was chosen for the departure so that the lonely traveler could avoid any of the roving bands of desperate, disillusioned men that might still be lurking like hungry animals hidden in the vast waste of barren land. Also, a start at night would enable the traveler to reach the most dangerous part of the passage in daylight.

The pack of cards lay upon the table. They were spread out, face down, for each man to draw. Darrow, the man who had lain dead on the beach, drew first. It was the nine of hearts. He breathed deeply. Surely, with so many to draw, the journey was not for him. For the holder of the low card was to make the trip. Fitz and Morrow leaned toward the table together. There was not a second between the drawing of those two cards. The eight of clubs and the six of diamonds went to them respectively. Frank Marion and Clarence Johnstone drew in quick succession. Frank Marion, Florence's father, pulled the five of clubs while Clarence Johnstone turned up the king of spades. That left Harry Urskine, Old Martin, and the scowling-featured Nixon Carleton.

Harry Urskine drew himself out of that trip with the queen

of diamonds while Old Martin seemed to make certain of the journey with the four of hearts. Nixon Carleton alone was left to draw.

Clarence Johnstone remembered clearly the face of each man at the table as Nixon Carleton leaned upon it. His words, too, were burned into his memory.

"It's cold outside, Martin," he said, with a shrug of his shoulders. "Let us hope—" his long, slender fingers shot toward the pack, hesitated a moment, then jerked a card quickly upward and slapped it over upon the table. He cursed softly a moment, then laughed. The card that he had drawn was the three of spades.

None liked Nixon Carleton; few trusted him—but all admitted to themselves at least that he was after all the logical man for the journey. He was older than the others, knew the north and had prospected up and down the Klondike and made the trip to the little village of Tuscal many times.

It was Clarence Johnstone who weighed him out a portion of the precious gold. There would be bread and meat, and a dog sled needed to convey it back to the hut. No one envied him his trip. All turned to the window; the wind was increasing and the snow was beginning to fall. Mechanically Old Martin gathered the cards together and put them back in the old box They were ragged and worn and had been good companions.

It wasn't until the following night that Old Martin discovered the truth. There were now two "three of spades" in his precious pack of cards. On top of that, the gold was gone—the bag still remained in its hiding place, but it was now filled with sand and broken rock. All knew, at least those who were able to know, understood that Nixon Carleton had concealed a three of spades in his hand. The law of the north was the law of vengeance—but that little party of prospectors had other things to give their attention to that night. The remaining food had been poisoned. It simply reeked with arsenic.

Fitz and Morrow died that night. Darrow, the dead thing on the beach, had recovered in the little hut. Harry Urskine lived through the agony of that trip across the frozen waste and was a prosperous business man to-day. Martin and Clarence Johnstone had eaten none of the food. Martin stayed at the hut to nurse the sufferers, and though a blizzard was now raging outside Clarence Johnstone went to seek aid. His quest was hopeless from the beginning, but the hand of God or fate or simply luck led the half-frozen, half-demented man to a party of trappers. He gasped out the condition and location of his companions and knew no more until he regained consciousness in the hospital.

Fitz and Morrow stayed in the north; a bit of wood and some loose stone for a time marked two graves. Harry Urskine and Clarence Johnstone recovered in the hospital. It was there that Frank Marion turned over his savings and the baby girl to Clarence Johnstone. Then he died.

Nixon Carleton's criminal activities were well known in California. It was there he was taken, tried and convicted. He received life imprisonment. Carleton vowed vengeance—but the heavy iron gates and the great stone walls made his words empty threats indeed.

That was the story of the north which raced over in Clarence Johnstone's mind and was reflected perhaps in the dull, sluggish brain of Old Martin. A dream still to Old Martin—a sudden reality to Clarence Johnstone. With the death of

Darrow on the beach, was the past going to flash back into his life? Would all the horrors of those nights, with the murders of the wilderness, sweep down on him again?

He tried to reason things out.

Nixon Carleton! That was over thirty years ago, and Nixon was older than he. There had been the talk that Nixon Carleton had a child of ten or twelve, whom he had not seen for years then. Nixon, if he still lived, was close to seventy. Was it possible for a man of that age to—? But who else? Clarence Johnstone shuddered. The thing seemed so impossible. And Florence, his adopted daughter! That she could be mixed up in the thing was incredible—and yet. So his thoughts still ran riot through his head when Jenkins, the butler, tapped upon the door.

"Inspector Thurston to see you, sir," Jenkins said.

"Yes, yes—to be sure, Jenkins." Clarence Johnstone hesitated a moment. He would have liked more time—then, "You can show him in here, Jenkins." He looked toward the little safe and thought of the blood-stained handkerchief and the card within it, and changed his mind. "I'll see him in the reception room, Jenkins—at once." He spoke almost sharply as Jenkins turned in the doorway, waited a moment, then closed the door behind him.

"You had better see this first." Old Martin laid a hand upon Clarence Johnstone's shoulder as he crossed the room. "It arrived with the morning mail though it bore no stamp."

Mechanically Clarence Johnstone gripped the envelope which Old Martin thrust into his hand. Nervously he broke the seal and drew out the contents. There was a white sheet of paper folded about a small stiff object. Clarence Johnstone turned pale and gripped at the table for support. For the white sheet of paper concealed the three of spades. And it was the three of spades that Nixon Carleton had turned up on the crude wooden table in the north thirty years before. There was no writing on the paper, but across the face of the card was typed: "Think of your promise to the dead and the daughter of the dead, before you speak out. She will suffer."

And that was all. The card slipped from his fingers. He stood so a moment, clutching at the table. Nixon Carleton was alive, and somehow the girl he had promised to watch over and protect as if she were his own daughter had fallen into Carleton's hands. How? In what way?

It was Old Martin who picked up the card and placed it carefully in his pocket.

"Come." Old Martin took him by the arm. "You weren't afraid of him then—why now?"

"I was a young man then." Clarence Johnstone spoke mechanically. "I'm an old man now."

"True—we don't get any younger as the years go on." Old Martin nodded. "You're an old man—but he's an older one—Nature plays no favorites. What are you going to say?"

"I don't know. I don't know."

For perhaps five minutes the two old men remained silent.

"Come," Martin said again, and this time Clarence Johnstone heeded his words. He brushed a hand across a damp forehead, thrust back stooping shoulders, and walked steadily toward the door. He wished now that he had sent his suddenly determined note to New York sooner—a day sooner at least. But the thoughts that crowded into his mind now! No, he couldn't have thought of them sooner. It took a dead body; a blood-stained knife through a playing card. Even now he only half believed. Thirty-odd years was a long time.

4

Police Inspector William Thurston

INSPECTOR WILLIAM THURSTON stood with his hands behind his back, an unlighted cigar in his mouth and a hard, almost cruel expression in his steady green eyes. He was the type of man whose age is uncertain—anywhere from forty to fifty would have fitted him without question. He was not a bad-looking man and only missed being handsome by the fact that his eyes were set just a trifle too closely together.

It was with his accustomed, quiet, unassuming dignity that Clarence Johnstone stepped into the room. The faithful Martin was close on his heels.

"It's a dreadful affair, Inspector." Clarence Johnstone shook hands with the police officer. "Is the man—known in town?" It took an effort for him to speak that final sentence. It seemed so like taking the fatal plunge that he had not really quite decided upon.

"I think not," Inspector Thurston said briskly. "I'm sorry to bother you, and sorry the thing had to happen right at your door. But duty's duty. You found the body, Mr. Johnstone?"

"Yes, I found it." Clarence Johnstone dropped into a chair, his face slightly pale but his eyes steady.

"You didn't know the man, of course?"

Clarence Johnstone hesitated, but it was the "of course" that decided him.

"No, I didn't know him." And it was surprising the way the lie reacted. He had expected that his voice would tremble, but it didn't. A feeling of relief came with the lie. The color came back into his cheeks, his fingers ceased to shake, and his hands grew steadier. Once the decision was made, he felt the better for it. It was easy and it was safe. If they did find out the identity of the man and his close association with him in the Klondike, he could be as surprised as they. Certainly there was nothing odd in his not recognizing him. He doubted that he would have known him anyway if it wasn't for the three of spades. Besides, he could also deny that he looked closely at the man.

Just one thing bothered him. The question had come suddenly, before he anticipated it. Thurston couldn't suspect. No—he dismissed that thought. Old Martin had already been asked the same question, and the others, too, he thought. It was most natural. The first thought, the identity of the victim; the second, the identity of the murderer. But they would not ask him that, of course.

There were other questions. Many of them seemingly trivial enough, yet Clarence Johnstone gave each one careful consideration.

"We think bootleggers are responsible for this—this tragedy," William Thurston went on. "The family, of course, we'll dismiss, and Mr.—" he hesitated a moment, and then, "Martin. How about the servants?"

Clarence Johnstone nodded. He liked the idea of bootleggers.

"All my servants have been with me for some time." He thought a moment. "Of course, we do not keep a gardener in town—but Harris has been well recommended."

"I have talked with Harris." Thurston nodded. "Have any of the servants acted oddly? Late hours or—?"

"Nothing odd that I have noticed." Clarence Johnstone was becoming more and more at his ease. "Of course they have their nights out, but as to the way they spend them or what hour they return, I do not know. You might question Jenkins concerning the servants?" There was just the slightest semblance of surprise in Clarence Johnstone's voice, as if he perhaps reprimanded the Inspector for thinking that he kept tabs on the servants. Old Martin smiled and nodded his approval.

"I have seen Jenkins and I will see him again," William Thurston went on, in no way abashed. He consulted a little book, flipping over the pages. "Your daughter, Miss Ardath, heard nothing in the night. Miss Ardath is down on the beach with the doctor now." Then suddenly, "Your other daughter, Mr. Johnstone. She was out rather late last night."

"Yes—I believe she was."

"You don't know where she was?"

"No—certainly not. But she will tell you, if you wish." And he wondered if she would tell him. And he wondered, too, if for some inexplicable reason Inspector Thurston suspected Florence of knowing something of the crime. Even Clarence Johnstone's knowledge and fears had not carried his excited thoughts to that extent. But the next words of the Inspector dispelled his fears.

"I've questioned Crimons, the chauffeur," he said. "He heard nothing. But he left Miss Florence at the house last night and put the car in the garage. It is just possible that at that time the crime was committed. There might have been a shout—or a cry of some kind."

"I'm sure she heard or saw nothing," Clarence Johnstone said, somewhat stiffly. "If she had she would have told me."

"I'm not sure of that." William Thurston shook his head. Clarence Johnstone came upright in his chair. He could not keep the words back.

"What do you mean." His voice was thick and his lips trembled. All his previous fears of this encounter with the police were renewed again. He was conscious of the hand that Old Martin placed upon his arm, and the bony fingers that tightened upon his sleeve.

"Gave you a turn, did I?" Thurston laughed, and again only his lips smiled while the eyes remained steady. "I'm not suspecting the young lady, Mr. Johnstone—but though I'm not married myself, I have many friends with grown daughters. And they're not in the habit of telling their parents the hours they come in. Now it's quite possible that she—"

"She returned very late." Clarence Johnstone wished to leave him with the impression that Florence herself had given him this information.

"What time?" Thurston looked up, but he didn't wait for an answer and Clarence Johnstone did not offer one. He knew that the Inspector had already questioned Crimons, the chauffeur, and must have learned the exact time of her return. While he—well, Crimons had not told him what the hour was; and certainly Florence had not confided in him.

Thurston changed the subject suddenly.

"Was there any reason for your going to the beach at such an early hour this morning?" The question seemed innocent enough, yet Clarence Johnstone's head went up.

"I am on the beach every morning by seven o'clock," Clarence Johnstone answered.

"Just for the exercise—and air?" There seemed an indifference to the other questions now; more as if he made a statement than asked a question. Certainly the man wasn't there to exchange pleasantries with him. But he answered him.

"Exercise and air—and to win a bet." Clarence Johnstone smiled—and it was a soft, wholesome smile. "My daughter, Ardath, is to take a dip in the ocean every morning at seven o'clock. She must not miss a day for thirty days. So far it looks as if I shall be money out of pocket. She has not missed a—" And Clarence Johnstone stopped. This time it was he who was putting a social stamp upon an official visit.

"So—" The big cigar raced across the Inspector's mouth. "That will be all, sir. It's a difficult job, for after all, I daresay it's an out-of-town job." He turned toward the door, swung back again and spoke. "Oh—before I go I'll be having just one word with your elder daughter—Miss Florence."

Again the hand fell upon the shoulder of Clarence Johnstone. By this time Old Martin's caution was unnecessary. Clarence Johnstone showed no emotion. He stepped to the door and pressed the button. An interval of silence, a low knock and Jenkins entered.

"You may tell Miss Florence that we wish to speak to her, here—now," he said simply—then he spoke to the Inspector.

"By the way," and he turned his head directly away from Old Martin, "this is an unfortunate affair, Inspector Thurston, and I know how deeply your time is taken up in Newton. I've sent to New York for a private detective."

Inspector William Thurston swung sharply about; his face was grim and hard.

"You don't think we're capable, Mr. Johnstone?" He snapped out his watch. "It's hardly nine o'clock—really, you didn't give us much time."

"You misunderstand me, Inspector." And Clarence Johnstone was his old self as he laid a kindly hand on the Inspector's arm. "The girls are a bit nervous—we'll all feel better if the house is—sort of, guarded. After all, you could not spend your time here, you know."

"No?" Inspector William Thurston scowled for a moment, then his frown lifted. "We'd of been glad to station a man here, Mr. Johnstone—and will yet, if you desire it. There's really no reason for this expense. If you have any apprehensions—any reason to expect a recurrence of the tragedy, why—"

"Not at all, not at all." Clarence Johnstone cut in hastily. "I have the greatest respect and confidence in your police department. I daresay there is no reason for alarm, and I mustn't let the nervous whims of the girls take men from their duty. After all, it was on my grounds and I feel a responsibility in the matter; an anxiety, too. We often use private men at the bank, you know—and without any reflection on a very efficient force."

"It's rough on the department, that's all." Inspector Thurston's cold, green eyes regarded the banker. "And the name of the Agency that is sending this man."

"Agency? I'm not sure it is an Agency. But the man's name is Terrance Mack."

Inspector Thurston started.

"You know of him?" Clarence Johnstone questioned.

"Yes—nothing good of him either." The answer was emphatic. "He holds a license as a detective, to be sure. But he's a common gunman. And, if I may say so, hardly the type of man you'd want about the place."

"Too bad—I didn't know." But Clarence Johnstone did not seem to be unduly disturbed. "You know him, then. Inspector."

"Only by reputation," the Inspector hastened to explain. "The New York police don't like him—and don't tolerate him."

"Ah! Well, I'm glad to hear that your knowledge of him is not personal. We mustn't listen to what others have to say. The police, I believe, are never partial to—"

"You put through a call for him this morning?" Inspector Thurston interrupted.

"Not exactly. You see, I didn't know of the man myself. My lawyer—or rather, a lawyer attended to that for me."

"I see," said Inspector Thurston; but it was quite evident that he did not see at all.

Further conversation was interrupted by the entrance of Jenkins.

"Miss Florence is not about," Jenkins said.

"Very well." Clarence Johnstone divided his speech between the Police Inspector and Jenkins. "You will give her my message when you find her, Jenkins—send one of the maids along the beach."

"She's not on the beach, sir. She has gone into town."

"With Crimons?"

"Taxi, sir. And Cora tells me she has taken a bag."

"To be sure." There was no emotion in Clarence Johnstone's voice. Since taking the first step things seemed easy. He turned to the Inspector. "Miss Florence has gone to town. I had forgotten, but I believe she spoke of an appointment with her dressmaker. If you wish I will try and have her located."

"It is entirely unnecessary, Mr. Johnstone." Inspector William Thurston half raised a hand. "I daresay we'd be wasting our time. And now, if you'll excuse me, I'll join Doctor Howard on the beach." He turned before he passed out the door and spoke over his shoulder. "Private detectives are not always to be trusted—and they pry into people's business a great deal. It comes in handy for them later. Good day, Mr. Johnstone." And he was gone.

"That's over." Clarence Johnstone turned to Old Martin.

"Over—yes. And what's this talk of a detective?"

"That," said Clarence Johnstone, rubbing his hands together, "is plain genius. Coming events cast their shadows before, Martin. I had decided how to act yesterday, before the—it was found on the beach." He shuddered slightly. "Harry Urskine was in the bank and he put the thought into my head. I wrote to this man at once. He was to come here as a visitor. But that would look strange now—very strange indeed to the sharp eyes of Inspector Thurston. He might recognize him, and one does not call in detectives before a crime is committed—unless one expects that crime."

"Then you expected—this?"

"No, not this—not this. But we know the nature of the man we have to deal with. Darrow, I heard, was a forger and a thief—but I have never seen him since those old days. In some way he has crossed the purpose of Nixon Carleton—a relentless, heartless foe. But I only feared violence from him. There was no thought of blackmail in my mind until I received that card this morning. Somehow, he hopes to make me pay to keep concealed—well—what Florence has done."

"Florence—what has she done?"

"That I don't know—her actions have been strange—she has—but I must question her. Yesterday Harry Urskine told me that she had been in to see him—had questioned him. Spoken of Darrow and—but no matter. Harry Urskine is my friend—he too has received the three of spades, and has not forgotten those days—or the man."

"And this detective—Terrance Mack? He is—"

"He is a hard man. I understand, a very hard man. Inspector Thurston was right when he hinted that he carried a gun—and was not afraid to use it. If you recollect the desperate attempt to rob the Haverville Trust Company two years ago, you will recall that it was this man who prevented it. But I had another reason—he could have come here as a visitor without the slightest suspicion." Clarence Johnstone leaned far forward, and Old Martin saw the determination in that hard set chin and stem gray eyes. "Martin," he said, "we must meet violence with violence."

5

A Voice On the Wire

TERRY MACK READ his mail while he shaved and dressed. The threatening notes he dismissed with a shrug of broad shoulders. They were neither new, nor were they original. He laid down his razor, flipped back the seal of another letter and shook the contents out upon the table, to the right of the wash basin. Reaching for his razor again he paused, let the soap dry on his face and stared down at the check which lay, face up, below him on the table. It was a check payable to the order of Terrance Mack and drawn on a New York bank, for the sum of twenty-five hundred dollars. He liked letters that started that way. Mechanically, he again picked up the razor, carefully scraped the left side of his face and finally applied the hot towel. Then dabbing his face with cold water, he dried it, lighted a cigarette and read the letter from which the check had fallen. After the customary salutation it read simply enough:

"DEAR MR. MACK:

"I have need of your services. To that end I request your presence in South Newton at once. There is a train leaving the Grand Central Terminal at 11:35 P.M. Tuesday evening. It stops at South Newton to discharge passengers. My chauffeur will meet that train.

"I enclose herewith a check drawn on a New York bank for the sum of twenty-five hundred dollars, which you may return to me if you are for any reason unable to keep this appointment.

"Very truly yours,

"Clarence Belford Johnstone."

The letter was good. The check was better. There was nothing in the wording of the note to tell a story. Neither fear nor worry were hidden between the lines. Yet Terry Mack knew that it all was there some place. Checks for twenty-five hundred dollars were not in the habit of slipping out of the mail as birthday greetings. At least, not out of his mail—and besides, it wasn't his birthday. Long experience in this world had taught him that the only way to make money is to earn it. That thousands of others thought differently only proved it to him. It was through the belief of others in the easy road to wealth that Terry made his living. The sender of that little offering didn't expect him to visit his home along the shore, for the bracing air and a long rest.

He read the remainder of his mail, destroyed one or two notes of a personal nature, pushed half a dozen into the waste basket, and thrusting three others into his pocket, went downstairs to breakfast. The three letters which he placed in his pocket he turned over to his man, Harvey, to be filed away. Harvey was his cook, houseman, private secretary, and chauffeur. Also, in his spare moments, Harvey had been known to tote a gun—and to use it.

Terry Mack read his paper and ate his breakfast in silence. He was not one with the doctors who believe in a simple repast early in the morning. There were grapefruit, a breakfast cereal, and two chops to be disposed of. If Terry Mack gave any thought to the gastronomic results of such a repast, it was that breakfast, after all, is a very important meal. But it is more likely that he simply knew that he was hungry and satisfied that hunger. He was not a big man, but he was broad, muscular, and in his early thirties. When he was hungry he ate.

It was not until he was half through his second cup of coffee that he raised his head and regarded Harvey.

"I shall be out of town for a bit. You may pack my bag." He gave Harvey instructions about purchasing his ticket to South Newton. "The train leaves at 11:35 to-night. I will want a compartment if possible. And you may check my bag at the station; a business bag, Harvey," he added pointedly.

Harvey nodded as Terry Mack rose, passed to the front windows and gazed out upon the street. A butcher's wagon was drawn up to the curb on the opposite side, a woman passed hurriedly by close to the window, and a man entered a brown-stone front down the block. But no figure lurked in the numerous alleys, and no man leaned against a post indifferent to his surroundings. As far as Terry observed, his house was not watched. But there was no reason why it should be watched. Terry was simply a cautious man. Stepping into the narrow hall, he slipped his dark gray hat from the rack and passed out the door.

He had no need to return to his room for anything. The gun which had lain under his pillow during the night now reposed in his left-hand hip pocket. In his right pocket, and not for the purpose of balance, was its fellow—two heavy black colts, which were his constant companions. An affectation, this carrying of two guns! A bit of bravado that would mark his stocky figure as a two-gun man in the underworld. No, Terry did not carry them from the same cause which inspires men to allow the edge of a handkerchief to peep from their breast pockets. One gun was not enough. There was no guesswork about that. He could recollect offhand where two guns were hardly sufficient—but he was not thinking of that now. He was thinking of a check for twenty-five hundred dollars and wondering if it were good. He would not, of course, be let into a trap by the lure of money. There was too much of that lately by ambitious gentlemen who desired him out of the world.

He took the subway downtown, had the check certified, then returning to his own bank, deposited it. He felt better after that. The check had been turned into money and his arrival at South Newton assured. Terry was not a detective for the excitement it afforded him. To him it was a cold, practical business—he was no amateur in crime detection. If ever a man went determinedly and doggedly about his work, that man was Terry Mack. He never gave up a case and he never quit once he was on the trail of his man. He charged high prices for his services but earned the fees. The crooks who hated him and the police who did not tolerate or understand him, knew that he could not be bought off. Once Terry started a thing he saw that thing through.

Returning to his own house in the upper Eighties, he sat down to read while he awaited Harvey's return with the ticket and baggage check. His reading gave him little satisfaction. He turned the two books face down upon his knees and leaned back in his chair. The name of Clarence Belford Johnstone was not in "Who's Who in America" nor was it in his own loosely bound volume of "Who's Who in Crime." He had not expected it would be in the last named volume; he was simply a careful man. The luxury of old age appealed to him.

At two o'clock Harvey called him to the telephone. A low feminine voice came trembling over the wire.

"You received a message," it said, "from South Newton?" There was a long pause, and Terry encouraged.

"Go on." He neither admitted nor denied the question.

A moment of silence and the voice continued.

"I must speak to you. Can you come to me?"

"Speak now. You are in South Newton?"

Another moment of silence, and then:

"No—no—but what I would say cannot be said over the telephone. And what I will say will keep you from South Newton."

Terry laughed. "If you wish to speak to me, you can find me here. I—"

"I dare not do that," the voice cut in. "You must suit yourself as to how important my message is."

"Let me have your address," he said.

"And you will come?"

"More than likely." That did not commit him.

"It is—" The click of a replaced receiver, and silence.

Terry waited a minute, then called Central. A half hour later his complaint that he had been cut off was answered with the advice that he had been called from a pay booth in the Times Square district. The lady on the wire, then, could not have been forcibly dragged from the phone. He shrugged his shoulders and returned to his library. He would have rest and quiet for that afternoon at least. There would no doubt be enough excitement coming his way in the next few days.

At ten o'clock that night the mysterious lady called again on the telephone. But this time she spoke to Harvey, and it was Harvey who delivered her message to the detective.

"She wouldn't wait a minute, Mr. Mack," Harvey explained. "I tried to tell her you were only a few steps away. 'Tell him the address is —— Sixth Avenue,' she said, 'and that it's the lady. Third floor—front room; and he's to wait for me.'"

"Very interesting," Terry murmured. "She leaves the next step entirely in my hands." He consulted his watch. "There's time to make it, of course. And, after all, Harvey—it's the duty of a good detective to learn all he can."

"Quite right, sir," said Harvey, who did not understand at all what Terry Mack was talking about.

"And, Harvey, it would be rather silly and stupid to try to trap a man on the third floor of a tenement house—especially a man who is quite used to such traps."

"It would, sir," said Harvey, stroking his chin.

"Then she wouldn't think of such a thing, would she?"

"No, sir, she would not," said Harvey with emphasis.

"Unless," smiled Terry Mack, "she was a very silly and a very stupid woman—or a very ill-advised one. But, Harvey, surmises and deductions are only for story-book detectives. The only solid road to travel is the road of facts. I think that I shall visit this third floor, front, of the Sixth Avenue tenement."

"Hadn't I better go along—I could watch in the street, to see if you came out all right."

"No, no, Harvey." Terry Mack pushed the button, shutting off the electric light, and stepping to the front window he parted the heavy curtains and peered out. "That would be a sign of weakness and not flattering to my vanity. Besides, I think that I am going to have company on my trip downtown."

6

The Man Behind the Door

AND TERRY MACK was right about his company down-town. If he was aware of the man who slipped from the alley across the street and followed him, he made no sign. But he walked rapidly until he reached Columbus Avenue, swung along beneath the great elevated pillars, and finally climbed the stairs to the station above, and boarded a Sixth Avenue train downtown. He read the advertisements and glanced cautiously up and down the car at his fellow passengers. He thought that the man on the platform who turned his back so suddenly was his man but he could not be sure. He did not watch him closely. Terry Mack had no desire to interfere with the little reception that awaited him in the room of the third floor, front.

The tenement he sought was less than three blocks from the elevated station where he alighted from the train. There was a store on either side of the musty entrance. A jewelry store with a light in the front, and a tailor shop with the light in the back.

Stepping into the shadows of the entrance to the tene-ment, he swung his gun from his hip to his jacket pocket. He expected a trap, yet he had come. There were times, of course, when he avoided a trap, but this was not one of them. It was good to learn at the beginning of a case just what measure of danger was involved. He could be on his guard after that—and besides, it would help him to put a true value on his services. He was a practical man.

If it was the stupid attempt of a sobbing female to make him miss the train, all well and good. If it was something deeper, just as good. One thing was certain. He was going to learn exactly what was waiting for him in that room above.

An electric light burned dimly in the hall on the ground floor as he quickly mounted the stairs. At the top of the first flight he paused. Would the man in the street, the one who had shadowed him from the house, follow him into the hallway. He waited five minutes, and when no sound came from below, continued up the stairs. He had expected to find that the light on the third floor would be out, but this was not the case. It burned just as dimly as had the others, and just as dimly reflected the emptiness of the dusty hallway.

And there was the room; the door partly open, inviting him to enter and wait. He had gone cautiously before, but now he stepped boldly forward, his feet beating heavily over the worn carpet. The thing was old to him. He knew exactly what to suspect. He was to stick his head cautiously in that door and get it cracked for his pains. Just as though he had been granted the power to see through the wood, Terry Mack knew that a figure lurked behind that partly open door. He smiled inwardly—crooks were a great deal like children at play.

He thought that he caught the deep, labored breathing of one who waited—with a gun, or perhaps a blackjack in his upraised hand. Terry Mack shrugged his shoulders. It was all in the game, and he must play that game as he knew it and understood it. He raised his foot suddenly—drew it quickly back—then shot it with all his force against that partly open door. There was a crack and a swish and a dull thud, a moment of silence and the unmistakable sound of a body slipping to the floor. An instant later Terry was in the center of that room, his automatic in his hand as he swung and faced the door.

Again Terry shrugged his shoulders as, taking one hasty glance around that sparsely furnished room, he closed the door and locked it. He had often used the same trick before. There was always enough force behind his foot to stun a man or knock the weapon from his hand, or simply throw him off his guard until Terry could get into action. But this time there was no need for the gun which he now replaced in his pocket as he bent over the man upon the floor.

He whistled softly. This was no attempt to make him miss his train, and delay his arrival at South Newton. The great hulk of a man who lay upon the floor still held tightly in his right hand a knife—rather, a two-edged dagger. His hair was black, thick and matted. Terry turned him over on his back. The bloated evil face was swarthy beneath the several days' growth of beard. A foreigner of some sort, he thought—probably an Italian. At all events he was the common type of paid thug who haunts New York's underworld.

The man must have been kneeling or bending very low, for there was a great red welt on his forehead which could not have been made by the flat surface of the door. The knob had struck him, Terry thought. And a good job it made of him. He would be cold for another hour—perhaps longer. Methodically Terry searched the man. Some bills, a handful of change, a dirty handkerchief, and a thirty-eight caliber revolver. Then, in the inside pocket of the jacket he found a torn fragment of a letter.

Just a few scribbled words.

"Abe Sterns is coming."

And that was all. Terry turned the torn slip over—the opposite side was blank. There was a waste basket in a corner of the room. He searched that for the rest of the letter but did not find it.

Distinctly from the street below came a whistle—just a single note that was not repeated. Terry stepped to the window. A thick bit of calico had been tacked inside the shade to better shut off the light from the street. The man who had followed him must have been waiting below for a signal. Very well, Terry would give him one. He didn't care to have company to the station.

Terry jerked the calico from the window, and stepping to one side raised the curtain. That might be the awaited signal—and it might not. At least, it would let the man below know that something was doing in the room above. Turning quickly he unlocked the door, and closing it behind him stepped into the dusty hall. He made time down that first flight of steps—and paused at the bottom. The door on the ground floor had closed. There was an unmistakable squeak to the rusty hinges.

Stepping back in the shadows of a narrow passage, Terry waited. Feet beat softly upon the stairs, then louder and more determinedly. There was even a slight whistle—a whistle that was meant to be careless and indifferent, but a trembling note crept into it. The solution of this bit of bravado was not hard to find. If there was trouble on that third floor, the man was going to pass by. If he was stopped and questioned by Terry, his unguarded steps and whistle would mark his honesty of purpose in the building.

Terry crouched in the shadows as he passed. He watched the outline of the man halfway up the next flight before he came from his hiding place and made his way cautiously down the stairs. There would be no purpose in questioning the man. He could not even be sure that he was the one who had followed him; that is, absolutely sure. Other tenants lived in that building. At all events it would be some time before the swarthy foreigner above explained to his friend just what had happened. Even then the explanation would be a hazy one. Terry chuckled—a very hazy one indeed, he thought, as he signaled a cruising taxicab and was whirled to the Grand Central Terminal. At the station Terry sought a telephone booth and called up his man, Harvey.

"Look up Abe Sterns," he told Harvey, "and send me the information to Shadow Lawn, South Newton."

He hung up the receiver, turned to the door of the booth—and drew back, leaning against the booth, his ear close to the thin partition.

"Newton—Newton." He heard the name of the town distinctly. And it was a feminine voice—a great deal like the voice he had heard over the phone that afternoon. Of course he could not be sure of that; the telephone wires jingle a voice up slightly.

Head pressed tightly against the partition he listened. But for a slight buzz he heard nothing more. He tried to tell himself that his own name was spoken, but he was only guessing. It might have been a name that sounded the same—or a word either, for that matter. Terry was not one to let his imagination run away with him. But the "Newton" part he was sure of.

He pushed the door of his booth slightly ajar, so that the electric light in the top, which was automatically operated by the opening or closing of the door, went out. In the shadows he watched through the dirty glass for the woman. Would she turn his way and pass the glass door? And he was glad he had not stepped out. There was a man there, standing by the next booth; his back was to him, his shoulders slightly hunched. It was another guess, of course, and he didn't like guesses. But his guess was that this was the man who had ridden on the elevated train with him, and later gone whistling up the stairs.

The thing was possible. Terry's taxi did not make remarkable time to the station, and this man might have had a car waiting for him around the corner. Guesses only—all but that one word "Newton." And that one fact would make those guesses a possibility; not only a possibility but a probability.

And what was the woman telling the party in Newton? Was she notifying some one interested that the plan to keep him away had failed; some one who was anxious to receive that message—so anxious that the shadow did not even take the time to see how seriously his friend was hurt? Something to think of there. And Terry had several thoughts on that subject. The one he leaned most toward was that certain events were planned to take place at Newton—events that his arrival might interfere with. And now—he clenched his hand tightly. Would those interested arrange for those events to-night—before he could reach South Newton?

It was five minutes before the lady made her connection and finished her conversation. The conversation itself was very short. Terry didn't get a look at the man's face, and just the slightest glance at the face of the woman as she left the booth. There was a touch of black hair beneath a tightly fitting hat, the flash of heavy black eyebrows, and the slightest semblance of thin curved lips—and she was gone.

"That party get Newton all right?" Terry approached the lone telephone girl behind the high desk.

"Yeh." The girl looked up, met those gray eyes, the slightly parted lips and even white teeth, and smiled too.

"Thought I knew her." Terry's smiled broadened. "I'm going to Newton, too." He displayed his ticket. "She didn't happen to be Miss Tucker, now?" He scratched his head.

"How should I know? I don't know everybody in Newton. I never even heard of Newton."

"Whom did she call?"

The girl's head jerked sharply. She was not in the least taken off her guard.

"Detective?" she questioned suddenly.

"Yes." Terry laughed. "I'll return the favor some day."

"Theater and dinner, and all that?" The girl scowled up at him. "I know your breed. You'll have to hunt up your divorce evidence somewhere else." And then spoiling her outburst of honest indignation, "None of them ever came through with so much as a box of candy."

The man and the woman had disappeared when he turned from the booth. People were beginning to crowd into the station; the theaters were just "letting out."

And then Terry discovered that his shadow had taken up his job again. He "got his wind" just before he handed in his check at the baggage counter and claimed the bag that Harvey had left there. So he was going to be watched until he boarded the train. And after that, what? He had always thought that a sleeping car was the ideal spot for a murder—the scream of the victim would be drowned by the roar of a train. Murder! He wondered would others think of that to-night. He gulped too as he thought of his berth. Harvey had been unable to get him a compartment, and he didn't fancy lying awake all night with a gun in his hand.

He tried the ticket agent, who seemed to have few customers, as most of the hurrying mass that now began to dot the station were residents of nearby towns and carried their own fifty-trip, or commutation tickets.

The agent was obliging, and having nothing better to do took an interest in Terry's quest for a train that would get him into South Newton earlier in the morning than would the 11:35. The turning and twisting of the time table convinced Terry that the only other train for South Newton did not leave New York until late the next morning.

"I'll tell you what you can do," the agent informed him, when Terry was insistent. "You can go to Newton—you got'a change at Wackhill. Let's see." He consulted another time table. "Yeh, you can make it. 11:10—upper level—last track down, at the other end. You'll get in at 6:10. That's nearly four hours better than the other one. But you won't get much sleep—not so much as you'd get on the through train."

"Yes, I will." Terry laughed. "Just as much—and a good sight easier. Here!" He slipped a bill into the man's hand. "That's for telling any one who inquires, that I asked about the first train to South Newton to-morrow."

With his shadow still on his trail, Terry sauntered to the telegraph office and wrote out a message:

Clarence Belford Johnstone, Esq.,

Shadow Lawn,

South Newton, Mass.

DETAINED, IMPOSSIBLE TO MAKE NIGHT TRAIN, LEAVING ON
FIRST TRAIN IN MORNING.

TERRY MACK.

And here another ten-dollar note went the way of the last one.

"If some one asks about that message, show it to him. Then tear it up."

"You don't want it sent?" The man looked from the crisp bill to Terry, and back to the bill again.

"Not so's you'd notice it, I don't."

With that Terry turned, stepped between a lady and gentleman, and walked straight toward his shadow. The man tried to avoid him, starting suddenly across the station toward the ramp which led to the restaurant, but Terry's hand shot out and clutched him by the arm, swinging him around. He looked into a sharp-featured, mean little face. And the sharp-featured man looked into two flashing gray eyes.

"I'm just taking a good look at that face of yours." Terry shot the words at him, smiling grimly as the man muttered a few unintelligible grunts and exclamations that he did not know him.

"Maybe not." Terry nodded. "But you'll know me the next time. Remember the man behind the door. One more step after me, and I'll lead you up a dark alley and rock you to sleep."

There was a sudden jerk, a backward step, something behind him—and after a futile effort to clutch at the empty air, the man slipped upon the polished floor and went to his knees.

There was a sympathetic sigh from two elderly ladies, a grunt from a hurrying, fat salesman who nearly stumbled over the kneeling man, and the man came to his feet. Terry had disappeared. Could he pick up the trail again? And if he did—would his efforts to follow a man who suspected and knew him be ridiculous, if not exactly dangerous? One minute the man stood in the center of the station—then brushing his clothes with his hand, turned and went directly to the little window and the ticket agent that Terry had left a few minutes before.

7

The Black Sedan

ARDATH JOHNSTONE COULD be described in one word. You might write pages and say less. You could not say more. She was *real*. Pretty? Yes, at first glance; but after you knew her a while she was beautiful. Beauty may be skin-deep with some. Not so with Ardath. There was something beneath that soft delicate skin; something that looked out from the depths of those sparkling brown eyes. Even the little turned-up nose had characteristics entirely different from other little turned-up noses. It was an inquiring little nose. Twenty, black bobbed hair, straight and slender—and we are back where we started. Ardath was REAL.

There was a touch of rawness in that early June morning which the sun had not come far enough out of the water to deaden. But Ardath didn't shiver as she dressed, or if she did, slightly, it was not from the cold. But the freshness of the morning, the soft pounding of the ocean, wiped away her frown and brought a soft humming note from her heart to her lips. She stifled it almost at once as she remembered the reason for her early rising. For the tiny wrist watch upon the bureau marked the time as five-thirty, and the telegram of the previous evening and her own memory of the Newton trains reminded her that she must be at the Newton station by six-ten.

There was ample time to reach the garage, slip out in the roadster and be in to Newton before the servants were up. She wondered why her sister, Florence—for she never thought of her as an adopted sister—had sent the message and why her return to Shadow Lawn was to be secret. But then, her departure had been somewhat sudden. She recalled walking into her room the morning the dead man was found on the beach. Florence had acted strangely; turned on her almost fiercely, and then changing suddenly had dropped her small traveling bag and clasped her in her arms. Florence had said nothing, and indeed for once in her life Ardath was surprised into silence. Just that single embrace, the sudden flood of tears—and Florence was gone.

What had come over Florence lately anyway? She had been so sedate and quiet and attached to the home. Almost a prude, Ardath might have thought if she didn't know her so well. That there had been trouble between Florence and her father, she knew. The cause of it she did not know, though she had subconsciously put it down to household expenses. It was something to do with money anyway. That much she felt sure of. And she laughed lightly; her own troubles always had to do with money, too. But she knew the secret of high finance. When the worst came to the worst, she just crept into her father's arms and waited for the investment to pay dividends.

She tried to recall Florence's message now. It had come over the telephone from the telegraph office in Newton.

MEET SIX-TEN TRAIN FROM NEW YORK IN MORNING. KEEP MY ARRIVAL SECRET.

FLORENCE.

At least, that was her best recollection of the message—at

all events, the substance of it. Well, maybe it wasn't so mysterious after all. Ardath felt certain that if she had walked out of the house as Florence had done, she would be more than apprehensive about the welcome she would receive when she returned. And Florence had been coming and going a great deal the past two months. She had been out late at nights more and more since they had left their city residence for Newton. At least, that was the impression Ardath gathered. And she wondered; after all these years, had Florence suddenly decided to "step out"? But—the main thing was to meet her at the station. She'd stick to Florence. Heaven knows Florence had stuck to her often enough when she played the late hours. Father just couldn't understand—but fathers never do and never will. Ardath sighed.

Ten minutes later she slipped quietly down the back stairs and into the kitchen. Lifting the chain, she passed out the back door and to the garage. She had her own key for the garage. Her roadster was ready. Crimons always saw that it was ready. Climbing into the seat she stepped on the starter, then looked at the clock upon the dash. It marked the time at six-five. She glanced down at the watch upon her wrist. It was still five-thirty. She put it to her ear. It had stopped.

Five minutes to make the three miles to Newton. No, she couldn't do that—but she could come mighty close to it once she got out upon the empty stretch of road. And she was off. Two things in her mind. To reach the station in Newton before Florence would think that she had failed her. And to get back to Shadow Lawn in time to be in the water before seven o'clock. The new roadster was the price of that swim— and besides, there was her pride.

Ardath Johnstone burnt up the road, hardly letting the indicator on the dash slip below forty as she took the curve. She pressed down on the accelerator as she turned out on the long stretch of straightaway, then shot both her feet suddenly forward. There was the grinding of the foot brakes, a sudden reach for the emergency, and the realization that it would be too late. A large black sedan was standing motionless in the center of the road. Whether it was attempting to turn around or had skidded to that position, Ardath did not think of then. She gave all her attention to preventing a smash-up.

She recognized the danger and the inefficiency of the brakes in such a distance. She flung the wheel hard over, felt the car jerk, bend slightly, straighten again and leave the road. There was a jump and a bump, a sharp twist to the wheel which she could not control, and the car pounded against a small tree. But it had lost its speed, and unless she had punctured a tire or two in the jump from the road there could be no more damage than a dented mudguard. She thought of Florence, and turned indignantly toward the big black sedan.

The hasty words on her lips she checked. A new indignation took the place of her former one. Yet it was useless to put it into words. The black sedan was empty—empty, and parked right across the very center of the road. Why, at that point it was almost impossible to get around it without risking a spring in the narrow little ditch her car had jumped.

She forgot about Florence as she stepped from the roadster and approached the big car. She wondered was it a stolen one, or—and a voice behind made her turn. A man had stepped from the thick foliage along the bank at the side of the road. He was dressed in a chauffeur's uniform.

"I'm sorry, Miss—" and as the color shot into her face when she saw the one responsible, "but you were going a bit fast, you know."

"What do you mean by parking your car all over the road?" Ardath demanded hotly, spurred on by the all too truthful statement that she was "going a bit fast."

"I drive for Mr. Cortland." The man touched his cap. "His setter got out of the grounds this morning and I was out looking for him. The dog jumped right across the road in front of the car. Lucky I wasn't going fast. I'm really sorry, Miss."

Ardath Johnstone nodded. She knew Mr. Cortland by sight; a new neighbor far down the beach. After all, she was speeding a bit she admitted to herself, and the man was not entirely to blame. A car coming at a respectable pace would have plenty of time to slow down and perhaps even slip around the big black sedan.

Ardath smiled over at the chauffeur.

"And you didn't get the dog; that's really too bad. Perhaps you aren't so much to blame, and—"

"I'll drive you in to Newton, Miss." The man half glanced over his shoulder at the roadster by the side of the road. "We'll find a garage and a tow car."

"Tow car!" The girl laughed. "Not for that boat of mine. I'll drive in and have the mudguard straightened. She'll slip out of there in no time. Nothing ever happens to that car." She thought now that perhaps the dent in the mudguard might hurry along the new roadster. "You'd better move out of the road though." She turned and started toward the roadster. She heard the man's feet behind her and turned sharply as he clutched her by the arm.

"It ain't safe, Miss." His voice was pleading perhaps, but his eyes weren't. There was something sinister in the curve of his lips, too, and the way the words seemed to slip through the side of his mouth. For the first time the girl noticed that this was not the placid face of the well trained servant. Nothing tangible in her mind; she had never attempted to study faces. Just a natural instinct warned her that this man was not what he pretended to be.

She jerked her arm free of his grasp and faced him angrily.

"How dare you?" Her eyes flamed, but she stepped back a pace as the man leaned forward. There was nothing of the servant in that face now—it was an evil, vicious, sneering face. His attempt to still play the servant would not have deceived a child.

"You get in the car—and I'll drive you to a garage." He repeated the same words but his whole attitude was menacing, threatening; and the hand that shot suddenly forth and gripped her arm could not be shaken off.

Ardath didn't try to free herself again. There was strength in those tightening fingers, and a fear that was cold and physical rather than mental shot through her body.

"I'll not go," she said, and the words seemed to come from a long way off, as if another had spoken them.

"You come along." The man was dragging her toward the car and she was going with him without making an attempt to free herself. She looked frantically up and down the road. Not a car, not a human—just a stretch of emptiness. She was out on the road again when she recovered enough to understand the situation. This man was taking her to the black sedan—forcing her into it. She jerked frantically, helplessly, uselessly; felt herself tightly clasped in the man's arms and fought desperately, kicking at him, even butting her head against his chest and chin. Just one thought now—to be free.

The man cursed softly and tried to pin her arms to her sides, but she wriggled them free and beat at his face with her little hands. She heard the thick brush crack behind them, heard too the beat of feet and felt powerful hands clutch her from behind, forcing her arms to her sides—and she was pushed, dragged and carried toward the sedan.

"Hurry, you fool." It was the newcomer who spoke, and there was fear as well as excitement in his voice. From under a huge arm Ardath saw what the man saw. Coming down the stretch of road from Newton was another car. She could just see the brightness of the morning sun reflected on the nickel trimmings of the approaching touring car.

She struggled and screamed once before a huge hand was placed over her mouth and she was hurled forward into the back of the sedan. She came to her knees quickly—sprang forward and grasped the handle of the door on the other side. A hand clutched her ankle, another pulled at her shoulder. She heard the whir of the self-starter, the grind of the gears, and felt the car backing toward the side of the road to give the approaching touring car a chance to pass. She tried to cry out again, but a hand was pressed tightly over her mouth, something black blocked off the light; she heard the hum of another motor and the light flashed again. The touring car had passed.

8

The Trap

THE SIX-TEN TRAIN jerked into the station at Newton
three minutes ahead of time. A sleepy baggage man bestirred
himself with rightful indignation. The occasion was not a
memorable one; vaudeville jokes about the train service were
lately falling as flat as the mother-in-law gag. The thing had
happened time and time again, but the baggage man was old
in the service of the road. It was hard for him to form new
ideas and customs.

Terry Mack swung to the platform as the train pulled in.
He had slept well, even if the time allotted to slumber was
short; that sudden change at Wackhill in the dull hours of
the morning had been a hop-skip-and-jump affair in order to
make the express from Boston, which had already arrived at
the little station. The sun was already up, the air invigorating,
and forgetting for the moment the experiences of the previous
night and his sudden determination to arrive unexpectedly and
ahead of time at Clarence Johnstone's, in South Newton, he
considered breakfast.

In the morning things seemed different. If any event had
been planned to take place at South Newton, surely it had
taken place in the quiet of the night. Then his early arrival
would be of no avail. But he dismissed that as a thought of the
stomach rather than of the brain. It was just seven minutes past
six o'clock and he had a good four hours start on his scheduled

arrangement. Besides, he didn't fancy the looks of the dingy all-night restaurant across the street. It would be a shame to mistreat an appetite such as his.

A taxi or two were indolently backed to the curb to one side of the platform, but their drivers were not in sight. Then Terry spied the open doors of a garage. That was the ticket. He'd ride to South Newton in an open car. Hard on his already complaining stomach perhaps, but good for his lungs that had breathed deeply of the stuffy air of the speeding train.

Money was no different in Newton than it was in New York. A car was hastily backed from the garage and Terry was on his way.

"Want to take it easy and see the country?" the chauffeur inquired.

"I want to see as little of it as this car is capable of showing me," Terry said.

The chauffeur half jerked his head around, swallowed the question hovering on his lips, and grinned in understanding as he stepped on the gas. Terry's fears had been renewed again. He thought of the man behind the door, the indifference of his friend who had shadowed him, and the telephone call to Newton by the dark lady in black. On top of that there was the arrival of the check for twenty-five hundred dollars. He was needed at South Newton. Needed badly! How badly, he did not know, but he made no objection when the car swirled dangerously around a curve, skidded unpleasantly, and shot along a stretch of barren road.

There was a bracing snap to the air. The breath of the ocean was in his nostrils, and he sniffed in the salt and wondered if Clarence Johnstone's family appreciated the true value of a substantial breakfast. Jerking his slouch hat well down on his forehead, to keep the sun from his eyes and protect the hat itself from the wind, he looked straight down the road. He had to rub the moisture from his eyes to be sure of what he saw, for the car was traveling at a high rate of speed and the wind brought a water that obscured his vision.

A big sedan had come around a curve in the road far down. Or had it? No—on second thought the car seemed to be stationary and directly across the center of the road. Turning perhaps—and Terry's hand crept to his hip pocket, jerked forth a heavy dark object and placed it in the pocket of his light overcoat. He remembered the man behind the door in the third floor, front, of the dirty tenement on Sixth Avenue— and he remembered too the knife in the man's hand. Now he wondered. Had the ticket agent sold him out for a higher figure? Was his arrival on the six-ten train at Newton expected and arranged for? Was this the reception committee?

He set his teeth grimly. Really, these people, whoever they were, knew little about him or they'd hesitate to set a trap of that kind—in broad daylight, too. Most every crook in the great network of New York's underworld knew that he carried a gun—and those who had taken the trouble to find out knew also that he was ready to use it.

Dimly through the biting wind he saw figures struggling in the road beside the car. Two men and a woman, he thought— but he could not be sure. He leaned toward the chauffeur as the siren of his car screeched its warning note to clear the road; then with his hand almost on the man's shoulder and the sentence framed on his lips to tell him to stop, he draw back and smiled. So that was the game. He was to stop the car and play the dubious part of a knight errant, rescuing a young lady.

A very pretty story, too. He wondered if there were more men in the car, and if so, how many. Of course that was the game. He'd be shot down or attacked from behind. Certainly big things were in the air. Even murder was not to be avoided in preventing his arrival at South Newton. He leaned forward again to give an entirely different message to the chauffeur this time. But that message also was not given. For the big black sedan had started to back, leaving plenty of room for his car to pass.

It was turning, too—he could see the front wheels pushed hard over now as he approached. His car had slowed down considerably; Terry slid far back in the protection of the side curtains—and they slipped past. Did he hear a scream above the roar of the racing motor of the black sedan? He turned sharply around and looked through the dirty strip of glass. There was a sudden jerk and he was nearly thrown to the floor of the car.

"A woman screamed in that car," the chauffeur called, and jumped to the road.

Terry peered over the side and looked back. The driver of the big sedan was not bent on attracting his attention now. He was bending every effort to turn the car around and speed off toward Newton. And Terry knew! This was no trap for him. Here was taking place the very thing, perhaps, he had hurried to Newton to prevent.

He flung open the door of the touring car and jumped into the road, calling to the driver of the big sedan. But the sedan was turned now and as Terry dashed forward, a shot came— and he saw a tiny hole in the rear window of the closed car.

And that was Terry's cue. He didn't have to find a bullet buried in his shoulder before he knew that some one was shooting at him. Hostilities had opened—and he went into action. He laid two shots in quick succession through that rear window. He didn't know if he hit the man, and he didn't need to see the falling glass to know that his shots had not gone wild. His shots were not in the habit of going wild. When he fired a gun he could tell you where you'd find the bullets, under ordinary conditions—and the window of that car was generous in its proportions, and the distance not great.

The door of the sedan burst open; a woman screamed and Terry dashed forward. He didn't get the chance to shoot again, and no shot came from the rear of the car. There was only one man there then, he thought; two men altogether, but the driver had all he could attend to. The gears roared into second and the car sprang forward just as Terry was alongside that open door.

He leveled his gun at the driver of the car, shouted for him to stop—when the thing happened. There was a tousled, bobbed black head, two wide frightened brown eyes—and a girl was in his arms. He swayed a bit with the force of the body against his, gave ground to retain his balance, and held that slim lithe body—for after the first force of that one frantic jump she lay a dead weight in his arms.

The sedan was gone, careening madly down the road, ever gathering speed. After all, Terry felt that his plan to arrive in Newton several hours ahead was not a bad move. Deductions, conclusions, or plain reasoning! Call it what you will. But Terry thought differently on that subject. It wasn't the first time he had circumvented the enemy. He simply called it "playing a hunch."

With the girl in his arms he watched the car disappear along the speedway; then he looked down at the white face, the roughened hair and closed eyes. His own eyes grew wide.

"Ardath—" he whispered. "Ardath Johnstone." The girl's head turned slightly on his arm, her lids flickered, opened, and closed again—then suddenly flashed into life. The steady, somber gray eyes of the man looked into the deep, sparkling brown ones of the girl. Her lips quivered, and he smiled—a worn, tired sort of smile.

"Terry Mack," she said slowly and almost painfully.

"Terry—you old son-of-a-gun." Then the eyes closed again. Terry came as near to sighing as he ever had in his life. It was for this that he came to South Newton—for this that a check for twenty-five hundred dollars had slipped out of his mail. He smiled now. He had not connected up the similarity of the names. He hadn't even known that Ardath lived at Newton. There was nothing strange in that. For the past months—ever since last summer when he had met her at a hotel in Bethlem, in the Adirondacks, he had been doing his best to forget that there was such a person as Ardath Johnstone. And now—just a coincidence? Perhaps—such things happen, of course. But Terry Mack didn't believe in coincidence!

9

―

"Let the Ax Fall Where It May"

IT WAS HALF-PAST six of that same morning when Old Martin tapped lightly, waited for the footsteps to cross the floor within, and then entered Clarence Johnstone's bedroom. He made no remark about the door being locked but he looked steadily at the tightly closed shutters before the two windows, which Clarence Johnstone now opened and flooded the room with sunlight.

"Yes, it's come to that." Clarence Johnstone's effort to smile was a dismal affair. "From to-day on things will be different. We'll have some one—to protect the house."

Old Martin rubbed his hands together continuously, which meant that he was more than pleased—or greatly disturbed. It was impossible to distinguish which, for he made use of the same physical exertion for both emotions. There was nothing to read in that expressionless corrugated face, nor the lifeless blank eyes.

"Well," he found a chair and seated himself carefully upon the edge of it, "I didn't disturb you last night—and you didn't disturb me. Did you hear anything—see any one yesterday?"

"Inspector Thurston was in the bank. They have not been able to establish the identity of the body. But they will—they will."

"And your former connection with the man?"

"Hardly that, I think. And if they do, we must be as surprised as they are."

"This detective who is coming. What will you tell him?"

"I don't know until I see the man. We want his protection—not his advice." Clarence Johnstone hesitated a moment. "Still, if we take him into our confidence it will look better—much better. As if he were a lawyer, you know. I think perhaps I should have spoken out."

"You did best—you did best. Have you told Urskine of—the thing on the beach?"

"That's what bothered me last night. I have made inquiries all over town. Harry Urskine has disappeared."

"Fled?"

"I hope so—I hope so. But I am afraid not. There would be no reason for him to keep quiet but his friendship for me."

"You did much for him. Perhaps he don't know the truth."

"Martin, Harry Urskine does know." And the hand that Clarence Johnstone laid upon his friend's arm, trembled. "I am afraid—I am expecting every moment to hear that Harry Urskine has—"

"Like Darrow." Old Martin gasped.

"Like Darrow. He just disappeared when he left the bank. He was in to see me. There was a message from him when I arrived yesterday morning. An unfinished note. My secretary tells me that he was almost hysterical."

Without a word Martin held out his hand.

"I tore it up." And as Martin's eyebrows raised slightly, "There was no use to keep it. I couldn't very well forget it. Here—" Clarence Johnstone closed his eyes before he spoke. "He simply wrote: 'I have heard from N. C. What do you—' And there the note ended. Some one had called him on the phone."

"Who was it? What did he say?"

"Who it was I do not know. What he said can easily be guessed at. For as Harry Urskine hurried through the outer room, he muttered so that both my secretary and clerk heard him, 'There's been murder out at Shadow Lawn—and he's dead.'"

"He thought it was you. That's why they called up from the bank just after you left yesterday. And then what?"

"No one has seen Urskine since. He either fled or started directly out here. If he started to come here—well—" Clarence Johnstone's arms went far apart. "I think I should speak out."

"There's your promise to your dead friend—Florence's father." Martin shook his head.

"There's my duty to the living. I will protect Florence with every cent I own—but a word now to Inspector Thurston might prevent another murder. Besides, there are you and Ardath." And in a sudden burst of anger, "What right had Florence to mix herself up with such company? What right had she to make accusations against—?" He stopped suddenly.

"Yes," said Martin slowly. "You hadn't told me of that."

"No—I had not. And I didn't intend to now. Florence and I have had a stormy session. She actually accuses me—well, has more than hinted that I have deliberately and dishonestly made use of her father's fortune."

"But there was no fortune."

"No—there was not. She has had ten times over what her father put in my keeping. She has been ill-advised and is strangely familiar with the events of thirty years ago. But enough. She must be convinced, must be assured—must be saved from herself—from this Nixon Carleton, for I have never a doubt that somehow she has fallen into his hands. Good heavens! what a dirty scandal it will be—perhaps they may even connect her with this—" He broke off suddenly as a timid knock came upon the door.

"It's Jenkins, sir," a low voice answered his inquiry. "A Mr. Mack is below—a Mr. Terry Mack. I heard you moving about."

"Mack—yes." Clarence Johnstone cut in eagerly. "I shall be down—right down. Is there anything he needs or wants, Jenkins?" He suddenly remembered that the detective had arrived nearly four hours ahead of his expected time.

Jenkins coughed once behind his hand before he replied.

"He spoke of grapefruit, sir—and cereal—and chops, lamb chops," he repeated.

If Clarence Johnstone was doubtful of what he would say to Terry Mack when he met the detective, that doubt was wiped completely from his mind when he heard of the attack upon the road and the attempt to force Ardath into the black sedan. Followed by the faithful Martin, he led Terry into the library, carefully locked the door and told the detective of those days and nights of thirty years ago—of the card on the dead man's chest and his fear that his adopted daughter was somehow connected with Nixon Carleton, and though certainly innocent of any wrong intent, she might be according to law partly responsible for the crime upon the beach. He showed Terry the message he had received—THE THREE OF SPADES IS OUT OF THE PACK AGAIN. He showed him the card that had come in the mail, and even the bloodstained one that he had taken from the body of the dead Darrow. And he told him that Florence believed that he had wrongfully kept her inheritance.

"You see, Mr. Mack," he explained unnecessarily, "the three

of spades was the card that Nixon Carleton palmed that night before he stole the gold and poisoned our meager supplies."

It was a strange story, even for Terry. His steady gray eyes watched the banker as he spoke. Then he asked a few questions.

"The mine was an absolute bust, Mr. Johnstone?"

"Absolutely."

"And you returned to Newton a comparatively poor man but for the trust Frank Marion, your adopted daughter's father, placed in your hands?"

"Yes. I had no right to touch that, of course."

"How much was it?"

"A few thousand dollars—not quite ten."

"But you say you allowed the impression to remain in Newton that you were rich."

"I tried to contradict it but without success. Perhaps I wasn't overemphatic. I was young—the impression perhaps was flattering to youth—and my mother was very proud of me."

"Is there any one else who knows the amount the girl's father put in your hands? Did Mr. Martin, here, see the transaction?"

"No—only myself, this dead Darrow—who was not an honest man, and Harry Urskine. Nixon Carleton has put such thoughts into my daughter's head. No one has ever doubted it before. Frank Marion was a poor man or he would not have prospected in that dismal country."

"And Harry Urskine—where is he?" Terry asked. Clarence Johnstone reddened but his eyes rested full upon Terry's, and his voice was steady when he spoke.

"Harry Urskine has disappeared." And he repeated what he had told Old Martin of Harry Urskine's actions.

Terry shrugged his shoulders—but his eyes had narrowed.

"And you think now that this Nixon Carleton has in some way put a distrust of you in your adopted daughter's mind?"

"I feel it. I know it. Florence has questioned me about it. I simply told her that her father left enough for her needs. I wanted her to feel independent."

"Did she actually accuse you of attempting to defraud her; state reasons; speak of Nixon Carleton—or any one else?"

"She did not mention Nixon Carleton." Clarence Johnstone thought a moment. "I had kept two letters that were written by her father. One was written to a firm in San Francisco. It was about a small sum of money. They had returned it with their check. The other was a letter of a personal nature, that had come back misaddressed. I wanted her to have something of her father's. Two weeks ago she came to me and asked for those letters. I gave them to her."

"Did she say anything—later?"

"Yes, a week later." Clarence Johnstone's voice was very low. "She said, 'I hate one who would rob the dead.'"

"Did you question her then?"

"I did not have the opportunity. She left the room at once. But I fear for her—if she is in the schemes of Nixon Carleton, God help her. He will want money."

Terry nodded. "Has he demanded money from you?"

"Not yet. But his threat on the card, that if I don't keep silent Florence will suffer, tells a story. I want to save her. I will have to pay."

"Now, Mr. Johnstone, how did you happen to engage me?"

"Because of the actions of Florence—of her absence from the house. The message from him. Of her accusations of me. Oh, I saw the handwriting on the wall. It was for her protection—now—it is for all of us. I—"

"But how did you know of me—pick me out in a case where you expected violence—blackmail; pick me in place of a dozen other well-known and nation-wide Agencies?"

"Through my daughter, Ardath. Don't misunderstand me. She did not know. But she talked of you; collected newspaper clippings about you—and I investigated myself. So I sent for you. For if the police fasten on this Nixon Carleton, they must fasten on Florence, too. In the meantime—I fear for Florence—I fear for my daughter, Ardath—and I fear for Old Martin."

"And for yourself."

"In time perhaps—but there will be money wanted. Some place, back of it all, is Nixon Carleton's love of gold. It can't be entirely vengeance."

"You wish me here to protect your family against this man. There is the possibility that I might kill him. You thought of that?" Terry's eyes hardened.

"No—no. Not that."

"It would solve the problem. It would be good." Old Martin spoke for the first time—and as Clarence Johnstone turned on him, "It's your own words—'We must meet violence with violence.'"

And Terry wondered as he stepped to the window and looked out upon the beach. A slim figure was entering the water as the clock in the hall struck the hour of seven. Ardath had told him about her bet with her father. He turned to Clarence Johnstone.

"I will stay here and protect your family." And before the banker could grip his hand in the trembling one he stretched toward Terry, "One thing more," and Terry set his lips firmly. He forgot the girl, forgot all but his business in life. "You may have heard differently, Mr. Johnstone, but I play only one hand—an honest one. I am taking every word you speak as an absolute truth. But in all my cases I have but one end in view—justice must be served. Let the ax fall where it may. Is that agreeable to you?"

"It is agreeable to me," said Clarence Johnstone in a husky voice.

"Aye, it is agreeable to me." Old, Martin echoed the words.

10

Within the Lonely House

NIXON CARLETON LEANED back in his chair and puffed contentedly upon a long black cigar. Perhaps the furnishings of the house were not of the best, perhaps the barren stretch of sand was too lonely for a man who sought the companionship of a great city. But his thoughts were good: those of vengeance that drifted through his mind, overshadowed perhaps by those of wealth. Above all things Nixon Carleton loved money. He was not one to walk the floor, stamp violently, and swear to crush those who had been responsible for his twenty-five years in prison.

Those years in prison sat easily upon his shoulders. The thought of vengeance grew hazy, and his step was faltering and his bearing almost fearful and cringing when the big gates closed behind him and he was once again a free man. He had thought of Clarence Johnstone then, of Harry Urskine and Darrow—and even the name of Old Martin flashed through his mind. But there was no tightening of dry lips, no clenching of wrinkled hands, and no rush of hot blood to the head. He thought of them because there were no others. Most of the companions of his youth were dead or in prison, and those who weren't did not matter. They were not the sort to help a pal, or even remember after all the years. He was an old man now—there was nothing to gain by helping him.

And the thought of Clarence Johnstone, bringing with it

vague rumors that he was rich, did not blur his mind with fury. He simply wondered would a begging, pleading letter bring him in return a few dollars. For Nixon Carleton, the feared gunman and notorious criminal of the west coast, was then a poor, frightened, and somewhat bewildered old man. Even the idea of facing the world was appalling.

After his release he drifted into Chicago and was arrested for robbing a church poor-box. Somehow, he kept his name secret, and his age and apparent feebleness, together with the big heart of the rector of the church, brought him a suspended sentence. But what did he want with a suspended sentence? He regretted his plea for mercy almost as soon as he was free again. It was cold in the streets and the wind cut through his thin clothes, and his shabby overcoat went for a pint of whisky and a "flop" for the night.

Some months later he arrived in New York, and the filth of the great city claimed its own. The underworld accepted him; the crooks tolerated him and occasionally used him for small jobs and as a lookout. And Nixon Carleton talked of the glories of the past and his name that once brought fear along the west coast—and he hinted, too, that he was waiting—waiting for the "great crime" of his life, and the pal that would fill his hands with gold. No one believed him, least of all himself; and when that pal did actually show up in the flesh no one was more surprised than was Nixon Carleton.

It was Darrow who found him. Darrow, whose gift of writing had turned from forging checks to signing liquor permits. It was Darrow who whispered in his ear; renewed again the thoughts of vengeance, and promised to make him rich even beyond his dreams. And that was Nixon Carleton's first step up in the world. He met the man who stood behind Darrow, the man who Darrow called "Chief." But he only saw him in the shadows—a silent figure, whose slouch hat hid his face and whose long coat with its high collar was ever buttoned tightly around his neck. He did not know if he were young or old— just the folded arms, the slightly stooping shoulders, and the uncanny glare of the eyes which he could not see through the dark glasses. But what did it matter? This man called "Chief" was the promise of great wealth. And he, Nixon Carleton, was needed. He was a little proud, and his shoulders straightened and his gait took on a more jaunty air as some of his old-time confidence returned.

There seemed nothing strange to Nixon Carleton that Darrow the man he had robbed and even attempted to murder years before, was his associate now. Darrow was a thief and a scoundrel; both held but a single thought—that of selfish gain.

Nixon Carleton nodded now as he knocked the ashes from his cigar with the tip of his finger. After all, his name stood for something. He was living again in the past and there was a smile on his thick, sensuous lips.

His dreams ended suddenly and he leaned forward in his chair. A man of forty-five, thin of body, sharp of feature, with a touch of gray through the jet blackness of his hair, stood in the doorway. This was Doctor Corellie, a well-known figure to Nixon Carleton.

"Darrow is dead," the doctor said simply. "And—" He stopped. The cigar had fallen to the floor and Nixon Carleton clutched at his heart. His eyes widened and bulged and his breath came in quick, uneven gasps.

Doctor Corellie eyed him a moment, then hurrying from the room returned with a glass half filled with a milky fluid.

"Drink this," he said, thrusting the glass beneath the old man's nose.

Nixon Carleton attempted to rise, fell back in his chair again, and feebly tried to push the glass away. The doctor thrust the glass closer.

"Drink it, you fool. If I poisoned you I'd be cut adrift like a helpless orphan—the helpless orphan." His grin disclosed a double row of even white teeth. There was no attempt on the doctor's part to plead that he would be above such a dastardly crime as administering poison to the old man; and there was no thought in Nixon Carleton's mind that the doctor would hesitate if it was to his advantage. These men understood each other.

"For the moment I thought you did it." Doctor Corellie watched the last of the milky fluid disappear. "You had the opportunity and you hated him enough." He hesitated a moment, then, "But what would be the sense in it?"

"He was murdered then." Nixon Carleton gasped, still holding his hand pressed to his heart.

"Found with a knife in his heart." The sinister face of the doctor shot forward until it was close to the wrinkled old one. "Who's to run things now? Who's to take orders from the Chief? You, of course—I've never set eyes on him." And with a quick, upward glance, "What does he look like?"

"Nothing—nothing at all." Nixon Carleton shook his head. "I've only seen him a few times. He's neither young nor old, tall nor short—and his eyes; they watch you, lifeless like. He's just a man in the shadows."

"Eyes! But you once told me he always wore dark glasses."

"He does, he does—but the eyes are there just the same; you can feel them."

"It's a disguise that wouldn't fool a child." The doctor stroked his chin.

"Yet it fools us."

"You," the doctor said contemptuously. "If he'd come to me— But he doesn't—he doesn't. Why—" he hesitated a moment. "It may be that I do know him—have met him." He stroked his chin. "But if I once see him I'll know him—find out just who he is."

"Darrow knew him—and Darrow is dead," Nixon Carleton said simply.

"You think then—"

"Who else? So long as he pays us well what difference does it make?" Dry lips smacked. "There's to be half a million in it. Three ways, now that Darrow's dead. I've always done as he told me." Nixon Carleton regarded the doctor shrewdly. He couldn't be sure of him. Perhaps he was in the Chief's confidence. Certainly this unknown "Chief" was familiar with all that went on at Shadow Lawn. "I won't pry into his business," he finished, watching the doctor through the corners of his eyes.

Doctor Corellie shook his head. "It's you that should know him; find out who he is. Why should he keep his identity a secret from us? Don't you see the danger to yourself? Suppose," the doctor shot a long slender finger against the other's ribs, "he skipped with everything—suppose this murder was laid to you. Where's your alibi—here at the lonely house. You could easily have slipped out, killed Darrow, and returned."

Nixon Carleton squirmed slightly in his chair. He hadn't thought of that. He listened now to the other, his brow furrowed, a tongue which had moistened dry lips becoming thick and dry itself.

"Find out who he is," the doctor went on in a low voice. "You're in touch with the underworld; you set into motion the necessary wheels in the machine which he simply directs. Don't you see? Suppose, after all, Clarence Johnstone goes straight to the police, and they trace you here. Suppose the plans of this Chief take a sudden setback. Then what? He fades from the picture—a myth, a phantom—something created in your brain. And, my friend, murder is laid at your door."

"Yours too, yours too." Nixon Carleton's head jerked up and down mechanically. "Why do you blame me? Why do you call me a fool? What about you? Have you not also placed yourself in his hands? Why?"

"Why, indeed?" Doctor Corellie glanced toward the ceiling. But he did not tell Nixon Carleton the reason; did not tell him that this unknown man had ferreted out the one dark spot in his life. His certificate as a physician had been taken from him. Doctor Corellie had served his time in prison and now had a good practice in Newton. Then he had received a telephone message from this unknown man, who knew all about him. After that there was Darrow—and Nixon Carleton, until he was involved beyond withdrawal in a plan that went even to murder.

"I was telephoned to come to you," the doctor said suddenly.

Nixon Carleton came to his feet and paced the room. His heart was better now. It pounded, to be sure. But it didn't jump and miss as it had.

"I want," he said slowly, "a drug that will make a man sleep." He smiled knowingly at the doctor. "I am troubled with insomnia."

"So I understood," the doctor said dryly. "The thing is here." He took a small bottle from his case and held it to the light from the window. "Without color and without taste. One teaspoonful, for a short sleep—two, for a longer one—three," he hesitated, "for a sleep that is eternal."

"And leaves no trace in the body," Nixon Carleton thought the words aloud. The doctor smiled.

"Such poisons are of fiction, not of fact. I know of no poison that does not leave as clear a picture of violent death to the scientific eye as a knife, driven through a body." Then suddenly, "You are alone here?"

Nixon Carleton jerked his head erect. He wasn't sure just what that question meant. Then he shrugged his shoulders.

"Apparently I am alone," he answered slowly. "But those I pay watch near by."

"I was not thinking of them," the doctor turned toward the door. "I was not thinking of anything." And turning in the doorway, he said casually, "Harry Urskine has disappeared from Newton." He waited a moment, and when the old man did not answer, he crossed the hall without and slowly descended the stairs. Nixon Carleton heard the front door close behind him. In the gathering dusk he looked from the window and watched the doctor enter the car and drive away. For perhaps five minutes he stared up the deserted stretch of sandy road which led to the lonely house on the beach; then dropping the curtain before the window he began slowly to pace the room.

11

The Man in the Shadows

NIXON CARLETON'S SHARP old ears heard the first knock that came on the rear door which faced the distant ocean. He hesitated as he looked toward the curtains and the approach of night. Then he stepped into the hall, passed to the rear of the building, and opening the door of a room whose walls were lined with books, he entered. There was a table across the center, a big overstuffed velure rocker, and three stiff- backed wooden chairs with worn leather seats. Behind the great overstuffed rocker in the corner was a lamp. He lit this, surveyed the room once, and passing into the hall again descended the back stairs to the kitchen. His feet had hardly trod upon the oilcloth when the knock came again—softer—one—four, then one again. There was no light and he left the kitchen in darkness. But he did not need the signal; he thought that he would know those knocks any time. Others used the same soft signal—but he always knew when the "Chief" was coming. There was an eerie sort of coldness that passed over his body. He shuddered now as he stepped to the door, shot back the bolt and pulled it open.

In the last touch of day he saw the figure that passed quickly in; made out dimly the slouch hat, the bent shoulders, and the upturned collar and blotched blackness of the glasses. The eyes, too—he felt them. This was the Chief—the man he feared and served, but did not trust. It was not Nixon Carleton's nature to trust any man.

Neither spoke as Nixon Carleton turned, and passing back through the kitchen went slowly up the back stairs. He couldn't even be sure of the steps that followed him, yet he knew the man was there. Twice he changed his step; once even took two of the stairs at a time. But always the man behind seemed to anticipate and follow in his footsteps—just the same even tread as if he alone mounted the stairs. That trip up the stairs was always a fearful one for Nixon Carleton—but to-night it was doubly so. There was the thought of Darrow—and the knife in his chest—there were thoughts too of a knife in the back. And he tried to lighten his fears by telling himself over and over that it could not be; that he was necessary to the scheme of the "Chief."

More than once his hand mechanically sought his jacket pocket and the gun that was there. But the hand never touched the gun. It was dark, he had to feel his way above—yet, he feared the man behind him. It was like a nightmare—he hurried now and the tread of the feet behind beat in with his. He stopped dead once but nobody crashed against his own— just silence, but for a warm breath that he could not hear—yet could feel upon his neck. He moved on quickly again; was glad of the thin streak of light before the partly open door.

Nixon Carleton entered the room quickly, crossed the floor, sat down in the big chair below the light, and stared straight before him. He saw the muffled figure enter, slide into a stiff-backed chair near the door, and felt the eyes upon him. And that was all he did see. Simply a man in the shadows.

"Doctor Corellie has been here." The voice from the shadows spoke mechanically; it was a queer, level, even sort of voice.

Not like any Nixon Carleton had ever heard—not exactly like a voice at all—it was mechanical, with a metallic ring in it. He knew of course that it was not a natural voice.

"He has been here." Nixon Carleton coughed; he knew that his voice had taken on the same sort of a mechanical grind and he tried to check it. He pointed to the bottle upon the table—the tumbler of water and the glass beside it. "One for sleep—two for a long sleep—and three—" he waved his hand. The slouch hat had bobbed forward and came up again—boring eyes were regarding him through the black glasses. He felt them.

"Yes, I know." A hand came up and a thumb jerked back over a shoulder. "He's still there?" And when the old man nodded, "We must guard him carefully—until after."

"Not—not the three drops then?"

"No—no." And the second "no" was a thoughtful one. "You bungled things to-day—and last night." And there was a menacing something in that voice; not that it actually changed any, unless the metallic ring had become more pronounced. "I took you from the slums, Nixon. I am going to put wealth in your hands—yet you do not trust me. But I do not ask for your trust—I want your obedience to my orders. The girl got away—but for that things would have been started by now—much money."

"But suppose Clarence Johnstone tells his story to the police—what of me?"

"He will not tell his story to the police—yet. And if he does what does it matter. I am watching; Clarence Johnstone fears. He is a desperate man. He killed Darrow—for Darrow knew and talked with him against my wishes—my orders."

Nixon Carleton gasped. He had not thought of that. Did not believe it now—yet the thing was possible.

"Why not strike now; hold this murder over his head—make him pay for silence." Nixon Carleton's shrewd eyes snapped; but he could not see the face of the man in the shadows.

"No!" The single word jarred out of the darkness.

"Then how are we—?"

"Through his daughter," the Chief interrupted. "But leave that all to me. We are faced now with a new danger. A man that must die. There is no other way. You have bungled things. If Abe Sterns had been behind that door we would not have failed. This time I shall plan and you shall simply execute."

"But if we rush things through and—"

"It would make no difference." A white hand cut through the blackness. "Clarence Johnstone might go to jail—his daughter might die—his bank might close its doors—the latest check that he gave this man might be turned back at the bank as worthless. Yet he would go on until he found you—and perhaps me. You know the sort of a man he is?"

"Terry Mack?"

"Exactly. Listen!" For fifteen minutes the Chief talked, and Nixon Carleton listened. The man was clever. Nixon Carleton could see no flaw in his plan as he outlined it to him. And he could see no danger in it—at least, to himself. And when he had finished Nixon Carleton sat back in his chair. Certainly he admired the man—and the greater his admiration, the greater his fear—for he realized the more he had to fear.

"And now," the Chief came to his feet when he had concluded the arrangement for the death of Terry Mack, "I will see the man inside. You will wait here."

The shadowy outline came to its feet and drifted through the splash of light into the darkness of the hall. Nixon Carleton could hear his steps now; hear the door open, and close too. A moment of indecision, and Nixon Carleton followed; cautiously, noiselessly, and fearfully he reached the door, passed through the light and stood before the closed door of the room the Chief had entered.

There were voices, low, hushed, unintelligible. He stood close to the door and tried to listen—to catch a word, but without success. Then he bent suddenly forward, his excitement for the moment dissipating his fear. Clearly from the room within came the voice of the man who was a prisoner there.

"I know you. I know you. Your voice and your muffled figure and your smoked glasses. But I saw you strike—and even in the darkness now, I know who you are. I—"

Nixon Carleton dropped to his knees, his ear close to the keyhole—but he heard no more. Whether the man had stopped of his own accord or whether a hand had suddenly been laid across his mouth he did not know. How close he had been to hearing the name of the "Chief"—the identity of the man whom he served and feared! And if he had heard it— if—what a protection that would be! He thought of Doctor Corellie's words and—he thought no more; only of his own danger now. The man, perhaps, had muttered the name—and if the Chief should find him there and think he had heard— Nixon Carleton came to his feet and hurried back to the other room, and took his former seat in the large overstuffed chair.

So the Chief found him a few minutes later, when he returned to the room.

"He's noisy and—" The Chief stopped a moment, walked

to the water pitcher and poured himself out a drink. That was encouraging to Nixon Carleton. The Chief's voice had trembled when he spoke. He lifted up the bottle that Doctor Corellie had left and made sure that the contents were still there before he drank the water.

The Chief didn't speak again then, but uncorked the little bottle, measured off a teaspoonful of the colorless liquid and dropped it into the empty tumbler. He corked the bottle again and half filled the glass with water from the pitcher. Then he turned to Nixon Carleton.

"We must quiet him for a bit. If it is necessary to move him I will telephone you." His voice was husky and he coughed. "Get me another glass," he said suddenly. "My throat is parched."

12

Three Drops!

NIXON CARLETON HURRIED from the room, into the hall—and he paused. The fear of the Chief was still strong within him. But it was a different sort of fear now—actual and not uncanny. The Chief's voice had trembled; he had need of water. He was just human and knew fear as others knew it. Nixon Carleton's head swung once and he looked over his shoulder. Clearly beneath the light he saw those rounded shoulders, the tumbler upon the table, and the tiny bottle in the Chief's hand. Once, twice, the neck of that bottle turned, and twice a teaspoonful of the deadly poison dropped into the glass. Again Nixon Carleton shuddered—again he knew the uncanny fear. This, then, was the reason he was sent for an extra glass. The man in the next room was to die—and the body was to be left in his hands—a murder right in his house, or at least the house he occupied under the name of Saunders.

Nixon Carleton went slowly to his own room and to the little washstand adjoining it, and shortly returned with a tumbler. He didn't know exactly what to do, but when he returned to the room his right hand was sunk deep in his pocket and the fingers of that hand wound about a gun.

The figure swung from the table as he entered the room. For a second Nixon Carleton glimpsed a ruddy face—ruddy or lined, he could not be certain—but it was the eyes, the eyes which he could not see, that brought back all his fear and made his right hand jerk from his pocket—empty. And that was all. The man was in the shadows again—young or old—tall or short—there was no way to tell. Those stooping shoulders might be of age, a deformity, or perhaps just an affectation—a part of a disguise which was all the more baffling because—there was no actual disguise.

"We have evil thoughts at times." The mechanical voice came softly to him. "We must conquer them, my friend. If Darrow had listened to me, he would be alive to-day. But he didn't." A warning, or a threat, or just a statement of fact. Nixon Carleton could not be sure. But there he stood, silent, while this unknown man raised the tumbler in his hand, swung on his heels and faced the door.

Nixon Carleton had no childish superstitions that murder was wrong. He could see it and face it, or actually execute it if it was necessary to his own salvation, or even if it was absolutely safe. There was also always the hope in his mind that if things went wrong and he stood before the judge, he could turn State's evidence and perhaps save his own neck. But who would he turn to now? How would he explain this dead body in his house if the police should come? Hard lines deepened into crevices in that wrinkled old face; the right hand again slipped slowly toward his jacket pocket, and his eyes narrowed as through closed lids he watched the hands of the other. He was old, to be sure, but his fingers had lost little of their nimbleness.

Nixon Carleton's hand reached his pocket; the man with the tumbler took a step forward—and stopped. Distinctly from below came a knock upon the door—then others. One—four, and one again.

"I thought we were to be alone." And this time it was the hand of the Chief that shot to a pocket, and stayed there.

"Those were my orders," Nixon Carleton said slowly. "Doctor Corellie may be returning. I'll go and see."

The Chief hesitated—then laid the tumbler upon the table.

"No—" he said very slowly. "I shall go and see. It will perhaps, be good that I, for once, talk directly to Doctor Corellie."

For a moment Nixon Carleton stood on the same spot on the rug. Most of his workers knew of the "Chief"—a few had seen him once or twice, perhaps, as he had—now Doctor Corellie was to see him—and then perhaps he would understand.

And Nixon Carleton suddenly had one of his brilliant thoughts, that had made his name a feared one years ago on the west coast. And with that thought came his former confidence in himself, and also the courage to put the thought into action. He stepped quickly to the table, uncorked the little bottle, measured off a teaspoonful and poured it in the empty tumbler he had brought. He then half filled the glass with water. The tumblers were identical. He took the other one from the table, emptied its contents into the ashes in the fireplace, rinsed out the glass and replaced it. Then he waited.

And as he waited, came fear. Perhaps, after all, he had only caused trouble for himself. He did not know just how long that single spoonful would put a man to sleep. And he wondered too if it acted quickly. But if it didn't he felt sure that the Chief would not leave the house now until the man was asleep—or, perhaps, dead. Cold sweat broke out on his forehead; yet the Chief could not know. At least he could not know for sure. But would such a man as the Chief have to know for sure? Trembling violently, Nixon Carleton sought out the big chair and dropped into it.

A thousand thoughts and a thousand ideas had rushed through his head. In his fear of the man he could almost shoot him dead. But what would that profit him? He did not fully—no, not half understand the plan for bleeding Clarence Johnstone, as the Chief had hatched it out. And suppose he drew his gun and pulled off that slouch hat and the smoked glasses! He would know the man then—and what would it profit him if he did know him? He thought of Darrow. No—he had done the best he could. If only he could discover who the Chief was without the man learning of such a discovery, or at least not until Nixon Carleton could assure his own safety by threatening the Chief with a note that would be left behind if anything should happen to him.

Footsteps were on the stairs. It was too late for Nixon Carleton to draw back and it would be foolhardy for him to slip into one of the seats that were in the darkness. He always sat in that big chair beneath the light. Every one that the Chief talked to sat in that big chair. It was the one weakness of the man, Nixon Carleton thought—a superstition, for he remembered once changing the light, and the Chief's insistence that it should be put back again. Yet the Chief never sat in it himself. It rocked far back when you sat in it, and seemingly without design threw your face from the shadow into the light of the lamp which stood behind it.

And the Chief walked in.

"I sent him away," he said. And Nixon nodded, for he did not trust himself to speak—though he did not know if it were Doctor Corellie or simply one of his own hired gunmen who had tapped at the door. And that was all the Chief said as he lifted the tumbler and walked slowly and steadily to the room where the prisoner lay bound.

There was a single scream from that room—and silence. Five minutes passed, and the Chief returned.

"Have you ever seen this Terry Mack?" he asked suddenly.

"No—I have not." Nixon Carleton managed to get out the words.

"Nor your men that are here?"

"Nor my men that are here, I think. But Clausen knows him." Nixon Carleton winced. "He followed him last night."

The Chief nodded.

"Nor have I seen him," he said slowly. "But I will soon. In the meantime much must happen. The girl must be taken. That is essential, and I, myself, will arrange the details of that. But Terry Mack will not be trapped without a great incentive." He passed toward the door and Nixon Carleton came erect. Was it possible he was going without waiting for the man in the next room to—to die?

"And," the Chief turned for a final word, "that drug which you gave me to administer to our sick friend—if the man should have a weak heart he might die. I will call you on the phone and learn of his condition. But be not alarmed—things that happen when I deal the cards are always for the best. Good night—you are a man whose hands are close to a quarter of a million dollars. Doctor Corellie is worth but little."

And he was gone. Nixon Carleton went to the door and listened; he sighed when the bolt clicked and the door closed, but he was not satisfied. He took an electric torch and searched the lower part of the house. Although he heard the car drive away, he was not sure. He was never sure of this man. The clock was striking eight when he slowly mounted the stairs. There would be a dead man on his hands certainly—but he wouldn't be innocent of a crime that he might be accused of. He would be guilty of a crime that he could accuse another of—and that other would think that he had committed it. And what's more, he would have the name of that man—the "Chief." Old hands rubbed together. For the first time in nearly thirty years Nixon Carleton was feeling himself, and the fear of the man in the shadows was forgotten. His old lips smacked and his decayed teeth bared into a smile; as he approached that room where the prisoner lay, he chuckled. No—he had no intention of letting the man leave the house alive. An enemy was in his hands and he would have vengeance—but he would also hold the life of the dread Chief in his own hands.

His hand crept to his pocket now and the gun slipped into it as his other hand clutched at the knob of the door where the prisoner was. He turned the knob slowly, pushed the door open and peered into the blackness. He could see nothing; his listening, straining ears caught no sound of a man breathing. He drew back once—hesitated—had Corellie, after all, lied to him, and was one teaspoonful enough to bring death? He felt for his flash, dragged it into his hand and sent a beam of light to the comer of the room and onto the white, drawn face of the gray-haired man who lay there. Was he dead?

13

Fingerprints

TERRY MACK DID not spend an unpleasant morning. He started the day right by having chops for breakfast. Ardath, after the earnest insistence of Terry and her father, had gone to bed for a few hours. After lunch she was to drive her father into town. Terry would spend the morning looking over the scene of the crime. Or at least that is what he told Clarence Johnstone. Detectives are supposed to look over the ground where the body was found. But Terry wanted the opportunity to think.

He did, however, visit the beach and the scene of the murder. The tide had come in and gone out again more than once—the beach was smooth as glass. But he stood upon the spot and looked about him. The boat house was the only place where one could hide and spring suddenly out upon his victim. But he dismissed that idea. Crimons, the chauffeur, had told him that the night was bright. Terry leaned toward the conclusion that two men met upon the beach by appointment—and the one had killed the other.

He picked out a dry spot upon the sand and lay there smoking. Clarence Johnstone's story had been a strange one. He wondered if he would have so readily believed it if the man were not Ardath's father. And he wondered, too, if he did believe it. Of course, if Clarence Johnstone spoke the truth, there was perhaps a real reason, if not a good reason, why he did not tell the whole story to the police. An ordinary layman could not understand the emotions which would make him act as he did. But Terry could understand. He knew men—knew, too, what fear would do. There was the fear of the past. To Clarence Johnstone, Darrow had been struck down upon his beach as a warning that the same thing would happen to him—or to his family, if he spoke out.

Of course, he could call in the police and demand their protection—and what's more, was in a position to get it. But, as he explained it, somehow his adopted daughter, Florence, was mixed up in the thing. How deeply she was involved, he could not know. But he feared that, if the hand of the law stretched out and rested on Nixon Carleton's shoulder, it would of necessity rest upon the shoulder of his adopted daughter. He must protect her—and of course, he must protect his own daughter. Thus the reason for bringing Terry Mack into the case.

There was the possibility, too, that all that Clarence Johnstone had told him were lies—that he had actually robbed his adopted daughter, and she had found it out through this Darrow, who had known her father back in the old days. Hundreds of witnesses could be produced to swear that Clarence Johnstone had returned to Newton a rich man. From Clarence Johnstone's own statement only one other man could prove his story that Frank Marion, Florence's father, entrusted into his hands only a few thousand dollars. That other was Harry Urskine—and Harry Urskine had disappeared.

But Terry felt that he must start, believing Clarence Johnstone's story. If other truths, terrible truths, forced themselves upon him, all very well—and he closed his lips tightly. Clarence Johnstone had had his warning. Terry had said, "Let the ax fall where it may." But he shrugged his shoulders; he was paid to perform certain duties; to work along certain lines.

First—the protection of the family. Second—the locating of Nixon Carleton and the hanging of the death of Darrow on him. Third—to find out how deeply the adopted daughter was involved in this thing; if she was an innocent victim of design-ing men, actually believing that her guardian had robbed her; if she was in the thing simply to bleed the man who had brought her up and protected her. Or if she were actually entitled to certain sums of money which Clarence Johnstone willfully withheld from her.

And if Johnstone spoke the truth, this case was not such a difficult one. The police were simply an outside factor. Terry could even wait until this Nixon Carleton struck—until his scheme developed into one of blackmail. And he sat up straight. Could the thing, after all, be simply vengeance? Vengeance on the men who had sent Nixon Carleton to prison? Darrow was one of them, and Darrow was dead. Harry Urskine was one of them, and Harry Urskine had suddenly disappeared. Ardath Johnstone was the daughter of one of them—and—

Terry Mack came to his feet, clenched his hands and walked toward the boat house. He wouldn't wait for the other to strike—again. He would carry the battle to the camp of the enemy. He had noted the window in the boat house, and remembered that Clarence Johnstone had told him that the door was closed when he first passed and was open when he ran from the body.

The door was closed now but unlocked. He pulled it open and stepped within. The place was dark, for the big canoe blocked out the light from the single window. He drew his pocket flash and ran it over the floor. Footsteps were thick in the dust—footsteps that weaved in and out of one another and dotted the floor. That would be Crimons and Harris and Clarence Johnstone. He stepped across to the big canoe and tried to peer out the window—but the canoe blocked the view entirely. He reached up a hand and gripped the canoe. It gave easily and rolled to the left, exposing the window, the light that came through it, the small round clear spot in the glass which had been cleaned by a bit of cloth—and clearly in the glare of light from over the ocean were the prints of fingers. A small hand—not small enough for a child's—a woman's hand, Terry thought.

He was examining it more closely when a shadow crossed the light from the doorway. Terry jerked erect and turned. The man was a stranger to him, but not the man's lips—nor the dominant chin, nor the tilt of the slouch hat. He did not know for certain, but he marked him as a police officer—one above the rank of detective, and he thought at once of Inspector Thurston.

"Terry Mack, eh?" The man in the doorway slipped his lips into a curve which Terry took for a smile—but the eyes remained hard and cold.

"Exactly." Terry let the canoe slip back, and stepped toward the doorway. "I was coming to town to see you this afternoon. At least, I think it was you—Inspector William Thurston?"

"Exactly." The other mimicked Terry. "You found the fingerprints, I see. A woman's—I'll give you a copy of them, if you wish. I thought you didn't believe in such things. I always understood that you went after a man with a gun in your hand—and murder in your heart. And just a warning here,

Mr. Mack—a friendly warning—we don't tolerate any loose shooting at Newton."

"Certainly not." Terry smiled. He was used to the antagonism of the police—rather enjoyed it, in fact—especially in a case of this sort, where he had such a jump on the authorities. "I don't believe in loose shooting either." He shook his head. "You've got to know when to shoot—that's all."

"And when is that—when do you shoot?" The other sneered.

Terry raised his eyebrows, surprised.

"Why, first, of course. You must always shoot before the other fellow."

Inspector William Thurston simply grunted. Then, in a sudden outburst of apparent good fellowship:

"Want to compare notes—want to work in with me?"

"But I don't make notes. And there's nothing to make notes about." Terry shrugged his shoulders. "I've reached the conclusion—that the thing is simply—well, perhaps a bootleggers' quarrel." Terry smiled broadly at the Inspector as he followed him out the door onto the beach.

"That's the conclusion I reached, for the benefit of Mr. Johnstone." Inspector Thurston pulled a cigar from his pocket and jerked it between his teeth. "But I don't mind telling you this, young fellow—get your pay in advance, and watch out that in this investigation you don't run foul to the law."

Terry Mack started slightly despite himself. He looked again, in the daylight, at the face of the man before him. It was a hard face, perhaps a cruel face—but it was a keen, intelligent face and the eyes were stern and piercing. He knew at once that he was not dealing with the ordinary type of police officer of the small cities.

"Mark you," the Inspector went on, his chin protruding further as his head shot forward, "I'm not trying to put suspicions into your head. I don't know what Mr. Johnstone has told you. But I do know this—that the dead man on the beach has struck him with fear. Another thing. He is hiring you for one reason only—to protect him. I know your reputation. Maybe you can protect him—maybe you can't. And there's a hint for you to carry to your boss. He'd do well to trust me."

"Why, what do you suspect?"

"Nothing bad of Mr. Johnstone—you can be sure of that. You know something or you don't know something. But your presence here in Shadow Lawn is enough for me. I've been consulting the New York police and what they know of you. It isn't much. But you're hired in fear—not in reason. I don't have to have a brick building fall on my head. Think it over— Good day." And Inspector William Thurston turned on his heels.

14

The Woman in Black

AND TERRY DID think it over. Did Inspector Thurston know things which he was keeping to himself or did he simply draw his conclusions because of Terry's presence at Shadow Lawn? And to a certain extent Inspector William Thurston was right. Fear was the great factor that drew Terry into cases, for he wasn't the ordinary type of detective. There were clues, of course, and he recognized a good one when he saw it—but most of his cases were similar to this. Sometimes unknown fear; sometimes known fear; and often cases where the police could not be consulted.

He thought of going straight to Clarence Johnstone with the suggestion of William Thurston. All sorts of fancies rushed through his head. Shadow Lawn was a lonely house—a lonely stretch of beach. Nixon Carleton had gathered to himself a bunch of scoundrels—even murderers. Gunmen had been known to attack a house in force; even his life had already been attempted. But he dismissed the idea of a sudden rush upon the house and the death of Clarence Johnstone. That could have been accomplished before—and there would have been no need to attempt to kidnap the girl. Back of it some place would be money.

Clarence Johnstone had not yet been proved guilty of any wrongdoing. He was entitled to keep his secret. Police officers like notoriety, and in towns of the size of Newton they work in close with the newspapers. A word to Thurston might start a dirty bit of scandal. But that wasn't the main thing that bothered Terry. If there was truth in the adopted daughter's accusation, couldn't he—Terry—straighten things out so as to protect the father of Ardath? That was the way he was thinking of Clarence Johnstone now—the father of Ardath. And if there was truth in Florence's accusation, why hadn't she gone to the police about it—or consulted a lawyer? It was all pretty complicated.

He looked up. Ardath was coming across the sand. And his thoughts scattered—overshadowed by the one that took their place. Ardath Johnstone was a wonderful girl.

"Well." She slid up to him, and taking his arm led him down the beach. "First—why are you here? Father tells me it is to unravel the mystery of the dead man on the beach. But I don't believe that. Second—why did these men try to kidnap me?" She held up a hand as he went to speak. "Father told me that they must have mistaken me for another. And I don't believe that. Third—why did you leave Bethlem so suddenly last summer—just when—well, I'd made a bet that in the five weeks I was there I'd turn down three offers of marriage? I squelched two of them in the first ten days—then I wasted nearly four weeks on you—and lost five pounds of candy."

"But I left you ten pounds." He looked down at her.

"It wasn't the money end of it—but my pride." She stepped suddenly away from him and regarded him from the corners of her eyes. "Terry Mack, I believe you were afraid I'd accept—what conceit!" Then, taking his arm again, "Well, why are you here?"

"Because your father sent for me," he answered with a laugh.

"Professional ethics. I recollect now a whole night wasted on that line—so I'll skip to the second. About kidnaping me."

And the smile died on Terry's lips. He couldn't very well lie about that; not that his conscience would bother him. In his business Terry had suppressed the small voice of conscience years before.

"I don't know why—or who they were." He gripped her arm tightly, and there was no smile on his tightly drawn lips. "But I must tell you this, Ardath, and you must, for a time, keep it secret. Some one may try to harm your father through you."

"Held for ransom!" She laughed. "Oh—Terry."

But he did not laugh with her. He held her arm. Clear gray eyes stared into clear brown ones. She could not disregard the gravity in his somber, steady, searching look.

"It all sounds strange and fanciful to you, Ardath—but if you read the papers you must know that the thing happens every day. Your father is a rich man—and all rich men—"

"My father is in trouble." She stopped him suddenly. "So is my sister—then the telegram this morning was sent too—"

"Yes, yes." He cut in suddenly. "Your sister sent the telegram this morning, Ardath? You didn't tell me that; wouldn't tell me that. Yet she didn't arrive on the six-ten train, for I—"

"Don't be silly." She shook her head. "Some one sent the telegram and used my sister's name."

"Of course," Terry said slowly—but he wondered. And he wondered, too, if, after all, he had not seen her sister, there in the station in New York—and if it had not been her sister who telephoned him, and trapped him in the house on Sixth Avenue. If this were true and the woman in black was Florence Johnstone, the adopted daughter, then, indeed, Clarence Johnstone had reason for his fear that she was criminally involved with Nixon Carleton.

"But I don't think you need worry about anything happening to your sister. She's safe, Ardath, and—"

"I know—I know. She just spoke to me on the phone. She arrived in Newton on the through train this morning. I'm going into town to see her—and talk with her. I thought perhaps you would have lunch with us."

And what could Terry tell her—warn her against this sister? But why? She wouldn't believe him, and there would be a long explanation that he was not at liberty to give. No—perhaps the best thing he could do would be to go with her. If he could not warn Ardath against her adopted sister, he could warn that sister to be careful in her actions to Ardath; let the woman know that he saw her in New York—that he knew she had telephoned to Newton. Perhaps he might even threaten her with arrest. That, of course, if Florence Johnstone and the woman in black were one.

Ten minutes later they were speeding toward Newton.

Somehow Ardath must have understood his peculiar position with her father, or perhaps that one long talk on the professional ethics of a detective, last summer, was paying dividends now. For she did not question him again, and seemed to accept without objection his feeble explanation that all rich men are often subject to attacks by cranks, and that any talk on her part would harm his chances of running down the blackmailers.

"There's the police," she did say. "Father don't like the notoriety—or you want all the glory? Which is it?"

"Perhaps a little of both."

"All right, Terry," she finally said. "I'm just a child, without proper understanding, and would go blabbering anything you told me all over Newton." And a little hand came from the wheel and closed about his arm. "But I'll trust you, Terry—my room's full of clippings about you. 'Terrible Terry' some call you; but not with the women, I guess. You saved me this morning—held me in your arms—and— Why, Terry—you're blushing; and I thought we were too well acquainted for that."

He liked this light, bantering mood better than the other, so he played up to it. But he could not help thinking that perhaps he was unraveling the threads of a mystery that would wipe the smile from those red lips and dim the sparkle of those brown eyes. He was disturbed, too, at the way she talked about her sister. Real affection there; she admired and respected her—and loved her. There had been the loving care of a mother, when Ardath was younger; the deep devotion of a sister now that she was older.

"She's had some sort of a row with Father," Ardath concluded. "Money, I guess—we always fight about money with Father—leastwise, I do." She laughed lightly as she nearly ran over a traffic signal.

Five minutes later they drew up before the Arlington Arms Hotel.

"Florence is going to stop here—that is, if I can't coax her to come back home. Father would give her anything if she went about it right."

And Terry was not surprised to see the slender figure that greeted them in the lobby. He had hoped that this adopted daughter would not prove to be his lady of the station. But he recognized her when she first rose and he caught that same glimpse of the profile—the dark eyes, the heavy eyebrows, and the deepening black below the eyes, that he had seen before from the telephone booth in New York.

She acknowledged the introduction with a slight raise of the eyebrows when she heard his name. But she seemed puzzled rather than shocked or surprised, her fingers nervously pounding on the table.

"Terry's my find," Ardath explained, when they had reached the table in one corner of the dining room. "Remember the pictures and the clippings—well, Father dragged him in to explain the dead man on the beach."

"Yes, yes—he's the detective, of course." The dark woman regarded Terry fixedly. "I must, I suppose, wish him success." And her hand slipped along the table and rested on Ardath's as if she were protecting her from some danger. From him, Terry wondered. But the look with which she regarded Ardath was filled with love and devotion—and perhaps a touch of fear.

"He'd do anything for me—except propose." Ardath laughed. "Sis is the winner of the candy," she explained. Then suddenly, "He might even fix it up with Father for you."

"No—I don't think he could do that." The dark-eyed woman shook her head. And Terry saw the softness of those eyes blaze slightly and die suddenly again as she looked at Ardath.

"I might try." Terry decided on bold action. "Ardath said it's about money."

The bent head of the woman flashed suddenly erect—but Terry lost the opportunity of reading what was there, for Ardath broke suddenly in with her story of the telegram from Florence and the attack upon the road.

"It was Terry, of course, who came along—and he was wonderful. Oh, Sis, I'd go through it all again—the way he held me in his arms. Love! Why, you'd think he had hold of a leg of mutton." And Ardath burst into talk of her bet and the coldness of the water, and the wish that the thirty days were up. "But there's Gladys Holmes—" and she was out of her chair in an instant and across the dining room.

Terry and the woman in black faced each other.

"You called me on the phone yesterday—why?" Terry shot the question suddenly at her.

"I—" dark eyes rested full upon him. "How do you know that?"

Terry smiled. He had expected that she'd lie about it. So the suddenness of the attack took her off her guard.

"And when I went to the house on Sixth Avenue there was a pleasant surprise for me."

"The house on Sixth Avenue?" She had recovered now, and Terry thought the slightest raise of her eyebrows and the quizzical turn of her lips were admirable acting. "I do not understand."

"That was in answer to your second call—the first, you know, was rather abrupt," he went on.

"I called but once." She looked straight at him. "I didn't want you to come to Newton. Now—I am glad that you came—very glad, indeed."

"Perhaps," he said, "you were not in a telephone booth in the Grand Central Station last night—and perhaps you did not telephone Newton and tell some one there that I was coming to Newton—that the arrangement to prevent my arrival had failed, and that—"

"Yes, yes—that is true," she cut in. "It is your business to know, I suppose. I would have prevented your coming until—I

had talked with you. It was in my mind to consult you before—"
She stopped so long that Terry encouraged her.

"Before your father hired me, eh?"

Again Terry saw the change in that face—the fire in the eyes and the dab of red in each cheek.

"He is not my father. Yes—I would have seen you. But he even foresaw that. His engaging of you was simply a grand gesture." And she leaned forward. "I would talk with you— meet me at Doctor Corellie's within the hour—9 Garden View Avenue."

He let the woman in black arrange for their meeting. He did not like leaving Ardath alone, but what danger could there be to her in the city? He wondered if this were another trap—but certainly he would be on his guard. Ardath was going shopping; she understood that her sister had an appointment with her doctor and that Terry was to visit Inspector William Thurston. He couldn't very well follow Ardath about town.

15

The Third Letter

TERRY FOUND DOCTOR CORELLIE'S residence without trouble. Florence Johnstone met him at the door and led the way within. She spoke almost at once.

"I do not know what Mr. Johnstone has told you or what you have learned. I have heard much about you," she smiled sadly, "through Ardath. I have brought you here to tell you the truth—and perhaps to seek your advice. You know a great deal, Mr. Mack—do you know that Clarence Johnstone has robbed me—robbed the daughter of his dead friend?"

"I know that you believe that—for he has told me that. Isn't it possible that you have been ill-advised—perhaps even deceived?"

"I am not a child—I have absolute proof. Mr. Johnstone returned to Newton years ago a rich man. The mine was a failure; that I have discovered. Where, then, did he get this fortune? Through my father."

"But people only thought that—"

"I know, I know," she cut in. "Here, see these letters. Mr. Johnstone kept them for me, never knowing to what purpose I would put them." Terry took the two worn old letters and read them over. They were as Clarence Johnstone had said—the one, to a firm in San Francisco; the other, concerning a small sum of money. He looked up at the woman.

"Mr. Johnstone spoke about these—told me you had them."

"Now read this." She thrust another into his hand. It, too, was yellow with age. And Terry's eyes opened wider as he read it.

"DEAR JIM:

"I'd like things to be in your hands, but I don't know if you're dead or alive and I want my little girl protected. There will be relatives who'll contest a will, because after all you and me know that the laws won't recognize my marriage to the baby's mother.

"It's a vast fortune for a man like me to lay his hands to but no one will suspect it—not after my push into the Klondike. It was the stuff that you laughed at less than six years ago—but it brought over six hundred thousand in cash—worth a million if I'd hung on to the ground.

"It all goes to my friend, Clarence Johnstone—as close to me as you've ever been. He's to keep it for my baby, and she ain't never to know until she's of age. It ain't because I don't trust him that I write. He's a white man. But it's human nature to change. It's just so that when the years pass, Jim, you'll sort of look in on things and see that my baby, Florence, gets her rights. It's a pile in cash, but Clarence Johnstone's worthy of the trust. I even shouldn't write; but I do, old pal. I'm kicking over with a belly full of poison. Good-by—forget the letter unless—you understand. Good-by, old pard,

"FRANK MARION."

Terry Mack read the letter over with considerable interest— then he read it again. He compared the third letter with the other two that the woman put into his hand. The handwriting seemed identical at first glance—and even at second. It seemed impossible that some one could duplicate to such a nicety the handwriting of another to that length.

"You have studied handwriting." The woman spoke. "Those letters have been examined by one of the best experts in the city. He has given his opinion that there is no possible doubt but that they were written by the same person. The expert was Franklyn Adams. That is why I went to New York. I wanted to know the truth. And that is what I telephoned to Doctor Corellie from New York."

Terry nodded. He had heard of Franklyn Adams. And he knew that the science of handwriting had advanced so far to-day that any expert could not be mistaken. Five minutes with a microscope and he himself could tell beyond the shadow of a doubt if these three letters were written by the same hand.

"I suppose—you would hardly let me take this letter away with me?"

"Hardly." She smiled. "After all, Mr. Mack, you have been engaged by Clarence Johnstone. It is to your interest to protect him."

"It is never to my interest to protect the wrongdoer. If it was established to my satisfaction and beyond a doubt that Clarence Johnstone had robbed you—or withheld money that your dead father left you, Miss—Miss Johnstone, I would see that he made a settlement—or I would expose him to the authorities. He understands that."

She regarded him steadily for nearly a minute.

"I believe you, Mr. Mack. Yet, in my own interest—and with the advice of those who are aiding me, I must not allow the letters out of my sight. Doctor Corellie has been most kind to me. He, too, has studied in an amateur way the science of handwriting. You may examine those letters here as long as you please."

Terry nodded, and the woman brought him a microscope; she also brought him several books. But Terry did not need the books. He was well equipped to cope with any end of his business. In a few minutes he would know if that third letter was a forgery, for when a man undertakes to forge the handwriting to such length, his task is hopeless from the beginning.

Terry knew that the forger must use one of two methods. Using the first method, he trusts to his skill in imitating the writing of another, and where this may fool the ordinary bank clerk, the peculiarities of the letters and their shadings stand out as vividly beneath the microscope as if each difference was underscored. For every man who writes with a pen has many peculiarities.

The second method is to trace each word from a similar word, after an exhaustive hunt through the correspondence of the victim. This must be first done in pencil, then filled in with ink; and where the peculiarities may be imitated there is a hesitancy to the writing and heavy and light lines stand vividly out. A letter of this type would be the simpler forgery to detect.

In ten minutes Terry was assured that the letter was not a forgery, but was written by the same hand which penned the other two letters. So much for that. The thing now was to discover if the third letter was genuine but for the fact that the amount involved had been changed. But no erasure had been made upon that note, and no acid had been used to discolor the paper. It wasn't guesswork with Terry. He looked up at the woman. He didn't tell her, but he knew that these three letters had been written by the same hand—written from beginning to end. Any expert could swear to that in court.

"May I take one of these letters with me—one of the two that Mr. Johnstone gave you?"

She hesitated a moment—and then nodded.

"Now, Miss Johnstone, you feel that you have absolute proof in your hands that Clarence Johnstone robbed your father—and you. Is that right?"

"All other things considered—I do."

"What are 'all other things'?"

"Mr. Urskine, for one."

"Mr. Urskine has told you—that your father left a great deal of money."

"No—Mr. Urskine has disappeared."

"Have you actually accused Mr. Johnstone to his face?"

"Not actually—no."

"Why not?"

"I—I have been advised not to."

"You are advised in all your actions, then."

"I am so advised."

"By one called Nixon Carleton?"

"No—I do not know the man."

"By whom?"

"Really, Mr. Mack—I cannot consider you as a—well, a friend."

"So—is it Doctor Corellie?"

"Doctor Corellie has been more than kind. He has helped me."

"Has Doctor Corellie advised you not to seek the police?"

"No, he has not—on the contrary, he has advised me to seek the police."

"Then why don't you? Have you done anything—that you

fear the police will find out?"

"I—" she laughed. "No—" she bit her lip before she continued. "Mr. Johnstone has always been kind to me; he brought me up, gave me all I needed and—"

"And you would not wish to harm him."

"I would not raise a finger to save a man who robbed the dead. I—"

"Then why have you not sought the police?"

"Oh—can't you see—because of Ardath. I love her, I love her, I love her. Yet I cannot stay at Shadow Lawn—stay at the house with him. Why, I would not feel that my life is safe. And—believe me, Mr. Mack—if he needed the money I would not take it from him. Why does he not tell me the truth? I would save him from prison—for Ardath's sake. I would never let her know. I do not begrudge her those pretty clothes, the cars, the servants. Heaven knows I would give them to her myself. But he sits there and reads his paper and eats his meals, and even kisses me good night; inquires about my health, criticizes the household expenses as he playfully pinches my cheek, telephones anxiously for the doctor if I am sick, and—oh—a hundred little things that I thought nothing of until I knew the truth. Now—it drives me mad. And the man who was dead—dead; and he smiled pityingly on me when I more than hinted that I knew the truth. Don't you see—can't you understand? I must take it all from the man who robbed my father. Take—when I should give—could give; and my love for his daughter is such, that I cannot speak—I dare not speak."

"You were on the beach the night of the murder. Is that true?" Terry asked suddenly.

"I was—it is true."

"And you saw—any one?"

"I saw Old Martin—but I did not think he saw me.

"What were you there for?"

"I was there—to watch a meeting between two men."

"What two men?"

"Mr. Johnstone and the dead man."

"Then you knew the dead man?"

"Knew him—why, he was the man who gave me the letter that my father wrote. Now do you see—now do you understand why Mr. Johnstone has said nothing to the police?"

Terry was stunned, but for the moment only. Perhaps he would get some valuable information.

"Did you see them meet?"

"I did not."

"Do you know why they were to meet?"

"By appointment—this man, Darrow, was to confront Clarence Johnstone with the truth—I thought perhaps things could be arranged."

"And you think Mr. Johnstone killed him?"

"I did not say that—I do not wish to say that."

"But you understand that you give me that impression."

"Then I am sorry. Old Martin was on the beach that night."

"Ah—you think then—?"

"I am only telling you what I know. Darrow knew the truth, and Darrow is dead. Mr. Harry Urskine knew the truth, and Harry Urskine has disappeared."

"Why do you tell me these things?"

"Because," she answered quickly enough, "I want to save Ardath. I want you to make arrangements with Mr. Johnstone. I want what is mine; I do not want Mr. Johnstone punished.

I want you to talk with him—make him understand that the time has come for him to pay the daughter of the dead man he robbed."

"You would shield him, even after murder?"

"I do not believe he killed this Darrow. I cannot believe it. Perhaps he does not even know the truth. I accuse no one. But Old Martin was on the beach. His love for Mr. Johnstone is almost animal-like. Yet, I will tell you this. I was in the boat house that morning and saw Mr. Johnstone take something from the dead—it seemed like robbing the dead again. But I accuse no one, Mr. Mack. I put things in your hands—for a time."

Terry was not certain if her final words held a threat, but he did think that the woman was sincere. And the mystery of the fingerprints upon the canoe in the boat house was a mystery no longer. Sincere she may have been, but there was the attack on him in New York to be explained, the telegram to Ardath, and later the attempt to abduct Ardath. Florence Johnstone's denial of these things did not dispense with them.

Could all this be laid at the door of Clarence Johnstone? "A grand gesture," as the woman in black put it? Was it simply an attempt on Clarence Johnstone's part to make his story ring true to Terry? But that seemed so improbable. It would mean that Clarence Johnstone had access to the denizens of the underworld. Not impossible exactly. But—and Terry stroked his chin. He didn't believe that.

He left Florence Johnstone with a statement no more definite than that he would see her again. Glancing back over his shoulder he saw her leaning heavily against the partly open door. There was nothing of the defiant, cool, calculating woman in her appearance now. A broken, worried, frightened woman, he thought—uncertain too as he caught the wavering of her lips. It was all very complicated. But where was Nixon Carleton, and what hand did he deal in this game?

Back at Shadow Lawn Terry found a telegram from Harvey. He had almost forgotten the torn bit of note that he had taken from the unconscious man's pocket at the tenement on Sixth Avenue. The body of the telegram was simple enough and refreshed his memory:

ABE STERNS A CANADIAN CROOK STOP HAS SERVED TIME FOR FORGING PASSPORTS.

HARVEY.

16

Back to Nixon Carleton

NIXON CARLETON STARED long at the white face with the streaks of gray hair across the forehead. It was the first time that he had seen this man, who over thirty years ago stood in a courtroom and accused him of murder. As he watched, the head moved slightly and the man groaned. Nixon Carleton breathed deeply. The bulging veins in his cheeks and forehead lost somewhat their bluish hue. The strain had been hard—very hard, he felt, as he stepped across the room.

He glanced hastily at the windows, saw that the shades were tightly drawn, and walking to the man upon the army cot in the corner of the room, leaned over him. He recognized him now; and with that recognition came back the days in prison—and again the threat of vengeance he had made when the gates closed behind him. Here at least was an enemy delivered into his hands. Nixon Carleton sighed; he had saved this enemy's life.

"Urskine," he called softly, kneeling by the side of the bed and sharply jerking up the man's head. "Harry Urskine—" He slapped at the man's cheeks, and the print of his fingers stood out as the head rolled and the man moaned.

The world had dealt kindly with Harry Urskine, Nixon thought. He noted the thickness of his arms, the size of his muscular hands, and the fullness of his cheeks. Not so old as the others perhaps—yet, lying there, Harry Urskine looked like a man in the prime of life; strong, thick fingers twitched and pulled spasmodically at the cords which bound his wrists.

Nixon Carleton threw water in the man's face—even bathed his head. He stamped his feet and mauled the man upon the bed. Why, Urskine might lie like that for hours, and the Chief come back before he had a chance to make him speak. And speak he must! Nixon would promise him freedom if he would speak. Then, when he had obtained the information he sought, there was still the little bottle with the colorless liquid. Even the man over whose head he could hold the murder of Harry Urskine would believe that he was actually guilty of the crime. There would be a different story in their relation then. Nixon Carleton would have the feared unknown—the man in the shadows—in his power. It would be he who would dictate the terms when things were finally settled and the money squeezed from Clarence Johnstone.

Nixon Carleton hunted up a flask of brandy and forced some of it between the tightly closed lips. Urskine coughed and gagged, and twisted slightly. Nixon felt his hands. They were cold, clammy, lifeless—and purplish blue welts showed beneath the tightness of the cords upon his wrists.

Nixon Carleton pleaded with him to speak; called on him as a friend, but to no avail. Then he cursed him for a fool, and in his anger struck him on the side of the head.

The head upon the cot swung again; glassy, moist eyes opened, rolled once, and closed again. But the lips moved now and the man mumbled something. Nixon Carleton bent close and listened.

"Hands! Hands!" the man muttered over and over. "They burn—they burn—they burn."

And so for five minutes more Nixon Carleton pleaded and coaxed, cursed and threatened—but still the man muttered on.

"Hands—my hands—they burn—take the hot irons off—take the hot irons off."

Nixon Carleton hesitated, but time was passing and he had learned nothing. He did not understand the action of the drug. Was his constant talking and bathing his head helping to wear the drug out? Or was it a slow acting drug, and as time went on only getting a tighter hold on its victim, so that even the muttering and the swaying head would be stilled? And the man kept whining like a child, about his hands. Nixon tried rubbing them, but the victim shrieked suddenly with pain.

Nixon Carleton placed his revolver by the side of the electric torch upon the floor and slowly began to untie the ropes that held those wrists. It would give the man relief and at least stop that infernal muttering. There was no danger in it; his feet were still tied, the drug was in his system, and Nixon Carleton had the revolver. And he had that revolver in his right hand too as soon as the last bit of rope was unbound.

Relief seemed to be instant. The man sighed, and opening his eyes stared straight into the eyes of Nixon Carleton. Filmy the eyes were, surely, but not so glassy as before, and though they rolled they always came back and focused themselves questioningly on the steady ones of Nixon Carleton.

"Don't you know me Urskine—Harry Urskine?" I'm Nixon Carleton."

"Yes, I know you—Nixon Carleton."

"That's right—that's right." Nixon Carleton chuckled. "He brought you here against my wishes—but I shan't let him harm you. You know whom I mean—you know, eh?" Mechanically

Nixon thrust the black mouth of the gun against the man's chest.

"Yes—I know."

"You know—I'm going to help you—I'm your friend."

"Friend—"The man seemed puzzled and the eyes began to roll again. "What's the gun for—the gun—Friend."

"Gun—gun. You're excited, Harry." Nixon lowered it at once but still held it close to the man—against his side, so that he could not see it.

"Who was he—this man who brought you here; who just left, you know? We'll punish him, Harry. I'm your friend—who was he?"

"Aye—my friend. What did you do with the gold?"

"Gold? What gold?" Nixon started suddenly.

"From the cabin—wasn't it you? It's gone—we missed it yesterday."

"Yesterday." Nixon Carleton cursed impassionedly. "That's years ago, Harry—I'm here to help you. You were taken here—remember—the man?"

"The man—"

"Fool," Nixon Carleton shook Urskine roughly, "do you want to die here—do you?" He reached down suddenly and clutched up the brandy. The man's eyes seemed clear now, yet his mind wandered; even worse. But he gulped down the fiery liquor and a slight color came into his cheeks. His eyes brightened too—were steady for a moment, then blazed clearly, reasoningly, shrewdly, at the evil old face above him. But Nixon missed that little display of understanding and perhaps hatred that shot into those eyes. He was replacing the bottle upon the floor.

"There, that's better." Nixon placed the bottle by the side of the bed and gave his attention to his victim. "I've been bad, Harry. I'm getting old and I want to die—right—and honest. We'll punish the man who brought you here. You saw him, now—a new face, perhaps." Damn the man, damn that drug anyway—the eyes were rolling again, yet they seemed clear enough, and the mist seemed to have lifted.

"The man—what do you seek with me, Nixon Carleton— and—another drink—another drink."

"You tell me the name of that man!" Nixon Carleton threw all pretense of friendship aside now. It was useless anyway. And the man was shamming. He was better, much better, than he pretended to be.

"You recollect the old days, Urskine. I haven't changed none." His lips curled back into a sneer, his eyes glinted, and his left hand shot to his inner pocket and came out with a knife which he opened. "You saw Fitz and Morrow die, and Frank Marion too. Agony, you called it. But you lie there now and don't answer me, and you'll beg to die like them. So help me—I'll cut you to ribbons. Can you feel that?" He thrust the knife hard down on the man's chest.

"What do you want to know?" The man squirmed. The knife hurt—his eyes opened wide—the hatred was there yet, but fear was intermingled with it.

"I want to know the name of the man who brought you here."

"You don't know that?" Harry Urskine gasped.

"Do you know? That's it—who was he?"

"And what then?"

"I'll let you go free."

Harry Urskine did not believe him. Nixon Carleton did not think that he would and had passed the point where he cared.

He wanted one thing—the man's name. As for murder. His hatred of the old days had returned; an unreasonable hatred, for the hatred for those we have wronged is far greater than a hatred for those who have wronged us.

"I'll tell if you'll let me get—"

A scream of agony was torn from the lips of Harry Urskine. Nixon Carleton's hand had pressed down on the knife, and with a slow movement he scraped it across the other's chest.

"Who was the man?" he asked. And his heart did not beat quickly now. His lips parted and he grinned. The scream of agony did not stir any feeling of compassion within his miserable old carcass. It simply renewed his confidence in himself. He hadn't changed so much after all, he thought with pride. Given the chance, he'd be again the feared gunman of the west coast. He'd have a story to tell in the dives of New York now. They wouldn't laugh at him any more. Perhaps he'd even take things out of the "Chief's" hands and run them himself. At least, he'd dictate the terms.

17

Terror!

OLD LIPS SMACKED. Nixon Carleton was enjoying himself. He was no weakling. He knew how to get what he went after. Again his hand pressed down on the knife—again he began that stroke across; and stopped. No scream had come from those tightly-pressed lips. The face was deadly white and the eyes were closed. The body alone had quivered beneath the sharp blade.

Had he overdone it? Should he have waited to see if Urskine would talk? Was he overanxious, or did the torture of his victim bring him a certain sort of satisfaction—not the man's suffering exactly, but in the confidence it gave him that the years, after all, had not changed him so much?

He bent down, gripped the neck of the flask in the hand that held the knife and straightened again, leaning over the prostrate form. And it happened.

Nixon Carleton was not quite sure that he saw the hands shoot upward, but he must have. But he did know that thick fingers were tightening on his throat—fingers with nails that tore at the skin and bit deeply into the flesh beneath. He dropped the flask and knife and clutched at the fingers which gripped him. Then he saw the hopelessness of that effort; he remembered the thickness of the fingers and the strength that must be in the muscles behind them—was in them. For he could not breathe; the deep, sucking gasps made a whistling in his throat.

He was being dragged forward and downward—when he thought of his gun, jerked it around and fired wildly. The bullet struck Urskine of course; he couldn't have missed—but the fingers never loosened.

Nixon Carleton tried to fire again; perhaps he did. He wasn't sure—but if he did it was a wild shot. Many things flashed through his mind; foremost was his curse against the Chief. Why had he made Carleton clear the house whenever he visited it? A shout now—but he could not shout. Still, the pistol shot would have been heard. Even now he hoped that it might be heard, for he had only half played fair with the Chief; just enough to keep from being discovered. One of his men— one of those creatures from the underworld—Happy Drake, was asleep in the garage behind the house.

Nixon Carleton struggled and cursed against every one but himself. Even the heavy shades and thick wood of the shutters before the windows came in for their share as things grew blacker. There was a sudden twist to his body; glaring, fantastic shadows upon the ceiling—and he went hurtling through space. It was scarcely eighteen inches from the cot to the floor, but to Nixon Carleton it seemed as if he were dropping a great distance. He felt the thud of his body striking the floor, felt the pound of the body on top of him—and then he was swept into blackness; great folds of it that were real and gripping, smothering him, creeping about him—and unconsciousness.

The door was open—the light from the hall seemed to send a dancing stream of weird flashes up and down—and Nixon Carleton's vision cleared. Plainly outlined in the doorway was the figure of a man—a staggering, blindly groping man who half turned once in the light and showed to the bulging eyes of Nixon the face of Harry Urskine. Nixon Carleton tried to rise but fell back again. He groped blindly about for the gun or the flask that had stood upon the floor, but without success. Footsteps came to him—staggering, uneven steps that descended the stairs, stumbling, hesitating, but always going down—down—down.

He counted those steps until he knew that the man had reached the bottom—there was a dull thud then, and Nixon Carleton held his breath. Had he collapsed at the bottom— was Harry Urskine lying there insensible? He'd have to pull himself together; find the flash; or strike a match. That was it—he had matches in his pocket. He felt for the box, found it, and in the act of striking one of the safety matches, stopped and listened. Plainly came the sound of a closing door; the front door. Harry Urskine was out in the night—out upon the beach—and within three miles of Clarence Johnstone's home.

Nixon Carleton struck the match and at once discovered the flash. He tried the switch but it did not light. The bulb, no doubt, had been broken in the fall—it was the flash then that had dug so painfully into his back. Another match, and he had the gun; but what good would that do now? In the dull flicker of the dying match he saw the flask—it was not broken. He drew the cork and gulped down the last of the brandy. He felt better, staggered to his feet, reached the window and flung open the shutters. The night was dark; a thick mist overhung the ocean.

What would he do? What could he do? If Harry Urskine reached the police or Clarence Johnstone that would be the end of their plans—the Chief's plans. He must get Happy Drake; they must search the beach; follow Urskine; get in touch with others of his friends, his associates—those dark, lurking figures that Nixon knew would plunge a knife in a man's back for a few dollars.

Would he fire the gun; shoot through the window? Surely Happy Drake would hear that. But would others hear it? It was a lonely stretch of country there. Should he go below and across the sand to the garage? Physically he knew that he was now able to make the trip—but morally—no, Nixon Carleton was afraid. And his fear was real—not of the darkness of the hall; not of the man who had fled into the night; not even of the police who might any moment come, now. He was afraid of the unknown—the man in the shadows. But it was real fear; a fear that was growing into a terror. What would the Chief do? Hope! Just one hope.

He stretched his arm out the window, tightened his finger on the trigger—then jerked the arm in again. From below came a tapping. Nixon listened; one—four, and one again!

"The Chief, the Chief!" he gasped aloud. Fear kept him away from those steps, but something stronger drove him into the hall and down the stairs. Terror—real, gripping, clutching terror, that seemed to push him from behind.

Mechanically he reached the kitchen, staggered across the floor to the door, threw it open and pitched forward into the arms of the man in the darkness. And the man straightened and spoke as he used a flash.

"I say now—what the devil's all this, old boy? Take a peg to yourself—I thought I heard a shot. You're covered with blood."

Nixon Carleton straightened at once. There was no need to play the baby act now; lie to the Chief.

"Why didn't you come when you heard the shot? Get busy,

Drake—get up the beach. Harry, the man who was bound upstairs, has escaped."

"The Chief'll have your heart out." Happy Drake shook his head. He had been given the name "Happy" because of the sour, uninviting appearance of his features.

"The law'll have your neck." Nixon Carleton clutched the man frantically by the shoulders, gasping excitedly the importance of overtaking the man. "Go—hurry—" he finished, dropping into a chair, and when the man had reached the door, "There'll be five hundred in it for you, Drake, if he's found in the morning with a bullet through his heart."

"That'll be murder, and I—" Drake stopped—Nixon Carleton raised his head. The telephone was ringing. Twenty times a day Nixon Carleton went to that phone; twenty times a day one of his men informed him as to what went on and asked for instructions. It might be Clausen or Randle—or even Doctor Corellie, but somehow he knew that it wasn't. Painfully he climbed the stairs to his own room, and advancing unsteadily to the side of the bed dropped onto it, lifting the receiver from the phone.

"How's the patient—our patient?" came the well-known, mechanical voice of the Chief, with the ring of tin in it.

What would he answer? What could he answer? Should he make up a story of the escape, in which he was sorely hurt trying to prevent it? Or should he simply say that the man was still there—or that he was dead? If he kept silent that Harry Urskine was out in the night, that would mean the end of the Chief. If he spoke out, that would mean the end of him. Or could the Chief—was the Chief in a position to prevent Harry Urskine reaching his friends? His friends—that was it.

If Harry Urskine went directly to the home of Clarence Johnstone, there was hope yet—hope that the Chief could prevent his reaching it. For, with a growing fear in his heart, Nixon remembered that the Chief could do many things—and he thought of Darrow as the voice came again—and this time the metallic ring had changed; it was now as if a sleigh were pulled across dry pavement.

"I asked," the voice said, "what of the patient?"

18

A Cry in the Night

TERRY MACK HAD much to think over but it was all pretty well "hashed up" in his head. There was the dead man on the beach. There were the three letters from Florence's dead father. There was the attempt to kill him—Terry, or at least a brutal assault that would prevent his appearance in Newton. Add to that the sudden disappearance of Harry Urskine.

Florence Johnstone had seemed sincere enough, but so had Clarence Johnstone, for that matter. There was the name of Nixon Carleton to be considered. Take the three of them— which had the most to gain through the death of Darrow, and perhaps the disappearance of Harry Urskine? Nixon Carleton had so far made no demands for money—his only apparent gain then was vengeance. It was hard to see just where he would come in, to collect.

Florence Johnstone gained nothing unless she, too, was mixed up in the vengeance of Nixon Carleton. And why should she be interested? Only one reason—her past was not as it should be. Otherwise she had much to lose. Darrow was her evidence that her father had really left a considerable fortune in the hands of Clarence Johnstone for her. Harry Urskine might also be evidence of that fact. And again, Harry Urskine might be the evidence to the contrary. Whether or not he was a witness for the father or adopted daughter could only be guessed at. Both could claim him now.

The letters might be enough to convince the girl that she had been robbed—but how would they stand in a law court? Clarence Johnstone might deny the authenticity of all three of them. Then what could an expert prove? Nothing but that the letters had been penned by the same hand. There would have to be proof that the hand was that of Frank Marion. Would Clarence Johnstone deny the letters? And that's where Terry hoped to learn something with the single letter he had in his pocket; the one Florence had turned over to him. He would casually get Clarence Johnstone to identify it.

Evidence gathered in town all led to the exemplary life of Clarence Johnstone. Would a man suddenly change his whole nature and turn to murder? Much as he disliked to believe such a thing possible of Ardath's father, Terry had to admit that it could happen just the same—had happened hundreds of times before. Men do strange things when confronted with the "secret past." Respectability is most cherished by those who least deserve it. Guilty, Clarence Johnstone had much to gain by the death of one man and the disappearance of the other. Innocent, he stood to lose— at least, through the disappearance of Harry Urskine who might convince the girl that Clarence Johnstone was innocent of any wrong toward her. So—where did Harry Urskine stand? Whose witness was he?

Terry Mack shrugged his shoulders and went downstairs to dinner. Ardath was the only one who made any attempt at carrying off the situation before the servants. Clarence Johnstone sat and stared at Florence's vacant chair. Curious that! Terry might have taken it instead of having an extra place at the table. But, no—the chair was there, and the table set as if her arrival was expected. Clarence Johnstone was thinking of his promise to her dead father, perhaps, and his daughter would always find a place at the Johnstone table.

Old Martin rubbed his hands and muttered to himself. Twice he stepped to the window and pulled back the curtain.

"It's a bad night," he muttered, "damp and cheerless on the beach, and the mist thick." And when no one spoke, he shuffled to his seat and repeated his words. "A bad night for the good—and a good night for the bad," he added. He liked that, for he chuckled again, and looked at Clarence Johnstone.

Clarence Johnstone jerked up his head, and for a moment the gray eyes flashed into life.

"Will you stop that infernal chuckling?" he said sharply. "There's been enough going on here." He looked apprehensively at Ardath. "If there are bootleggers about—we have Mr. Mack—and the police, handy."

"We might even appease their wrath by buying some liquor." Ardath smiled over at her father—and when his face reddened, "We don't have to drink it, you know. Eh, Terry?"

"Terry." Clarence Johnstone didn't exactly gasp—the word just jerked out in mild surprise.

"Certainly," she nodded. "He's here to protect me, isn't he? It may take years, so why stand on ceremony? Until I get married, or lose my youth, the game will still be played, won't it? Anyway—how much am I worth to you, Father?"

"I wish you wouldn't talk like that. I—"

"I know—I know." She interrupted him. "Old Martin rubs his hands and chuckles and talks about the dreary weather; you stare and gulp and act as though you never saw asparagus before in your life, and expected it to sneak up and hide beneath your vest. And twice I've seen Jenkins wipe gravy off his sleeve—an unheard of thing for Jenkins."

Her father cut in.

"We are disturbed about—Florence. But there is no need for you to be alarmed, Ardath."

"No." She shook her head. "Well then, don't act as if I were already laid out on the table, instead of—"

"Ardath—" Clarence Johnstone snapped to his feet, deadly pale, "you go too far. Humor! Humor!—" He stopped and stamped from the room. In the doorway he turned. "I'd like to see you in the library, Mr. Mack—just as soon as it's agreeable."

The mental attitude of the man was bad. Terry recognized that the moment he entered the library and Clarence Johnstone swung from his pacing and faced him.

"I've been a fool," he said suddenly. "There's my duty to the living as well as the dead. I think that I shall tell the Chief of Police the same story I told you." He waited for Terry to speak, but Terry remained silent and he went on.

"I'll do what I can for Florence after Nixon Carleton is caught. Perhaps, after all, she's an innocent victim." A moment's hesitation, and then, "Mr. Mack, I'm afraid—to-night."

"Of Nixon Carleton?"

"Yes—of Nixon Carleton. I've been living over the past. What would you do—what could you do if he came here to-night? The man is not human in his passion—his hatred."

"You need have no fear of Nixon Carleton while I'm here," Terry told him, and meant it. "Times have changed, Mr. Johnstone. You have engaged me, first, to protect—your family. I shan't hesitate to do that."

"What do you think of the police? Shall I tell them?"

"I could not when you first told me, nor can I now see any reason why the police should not be informed. I think that your fears about Miss Florence are—exaggerated. There are the newspapers, of course. There may be and probably will be a scandal."

Clarence Johnstone strode up and down the room.

"I came to Newton," he said suddenly, "a poor man—a very poor man. Mostly, I believe, I did not talk because of my mother. She was old and sick—and proud of me. It was with her few dollars that I started to build up my—present fortune. Florence's money I never touched. Not that I couldn't have, for Frank Marion told me to use it. But I was afraid. I lacked confidence in myself. I never touched it. I am sorry for that—otherwise she would to-day be rich."

Terry's eyebrows shot up.

"Did you ever tell her just how much it was?"

"Never—the income was not enough even to dress her. I wanted her to feel independent. Her father was my friend. When I died, she would have shared equally with Ardath—and will, even now. But above all I want her confidence and trust again—she mistrusts me, suspects me, and even cohorts with my enemies."

"How do you know that?" Terry asked sharply. He was studying that stern, lined old face now.

"How—but in what other way could the germ of such a base suspicion have grown. I have made no enemies—have had but one."

"But what sense is there in it, Mr. Johnstone? What could Nixon Carleton gain by having this girl suspect you of robbing her?"

"Part of his vengeance—the breaking up of my home—the dragging me into the courts—the newspapers, the scandal—the father that both girls looked up to—and perhaps blackmail to save me from all this—perhaps, Mr. Mack, even the kidnaping of my daughter, Ardath. The one is all closely involved with the other. He will draw Florence so deeply into his net that I won't dare talk; won't dare go to the police. Then, there will be a demand for money.

"Suppose," Clarence Johnstone leaned on the table, "Florence was on the beach to meet Darrow—that he was to pretend that I wronged her and her dead father—suppose that Nixon Carleton killed him—and she knew it and saw it! Couldn't Darrow have first threatened her—demanded money? Then Nixon Carleton could have interfered; stabbed the man—accomplished two things at once. Gotten the girl in his hands, and Darrow out of the way."

"Why 'Darrow out of the way'?"

"Because he had threatened to go over to my side. You see the point. Florence would be a party to the murder—Nixon Carleton would have struck his blow to save her—or at least she would so believe. And—well—if I speak to the police, what of her—what of her?"

Terry whistled to himself. What put such an idea into Clarence Johnstone's head? It was a wild story, an improbable story—an impossible story.

"What gave you that idea?"

Clarence Johnstone hesitated a moment. Then: "Old Martin." And as if he thought aloud, "Weird, fantastic, certainly. Yet, Old Martin was on the beach that night. Perhaps, perhaps—" He stroked his chin and said no more.

Yes, Terry could believe such a story came from Old Martin. And he might even believe the truth of such a story if he had not interviewed Florence. Oh, he didn't pretend to be able to study faces and read what was there. But he felt pretty certain that this girl had not actually participated in the murder. But here was a story that might originate in the brain of a man who was overwrought—nervous—frightened—even guilty.

Easily, indifferently, Terry dug his hand into his pocket and pulled out the letter Florence had given him.

"You spoke of two letters of Frank Marion which you gave to his daughter." Terry opened the letter and spread it out on the table before the staring, surprised gray eyes. "Is this one of them?"

Clarence Johnstone read it.

"Where did you get this?" he demanded. "I—I—" He stopped dead.

"Is it one of the letters?" Terry never took his eyes off the lowered face of the old man.

"Yes, yes, this is one of them," Clarence Johnstone answered, and again, "Where did you get it?"

"It's my business to hunt up things." Terry smiled as he put the letter back in his pocket. "Women leave things around so." He didn't exactly lie to his client, and he wondered then if the client could truthfully say the same thing in return—that he hadn't exactly lied to him.

"And now, Mr. Johnstone, why do you suppose she wanted these letters—just woman's affection?"

"I did think that at first—but not after her actions—our talk. I thought then—that she wanted them for a purpose—perhaps identification."

"With another letter perhaps?"

"Yes—I thought of that—Old Martin thought of that."

"Old Martin thought of a lot of things," Terry said ironically. "Did he help think of me?"

"No—no. He was quite surprised when I told him."

"Quite surprised." And Terry wondered.

"Suppose, Mr. Johnstone," Terry said after a bit, "suppose we went after this thing in the usual way. There's the dead man on the beach—the three of spades upon his chest—the three of spades sent to you. Suppose we hunted up Nixon Carleton, dragged him in, and if he wouldn't talk, made him explain his whereabouts the night Darrow was killed. You see, the card which you lifted from Darrow's chest fastened things rather tightly against Mr. Nixon Carleton. How do you explain his eagerness to be the suspected person?"

"I cannot explain it, unless he had things so arranged—was so sure that he could strike me, touch me vitally, that he did not hesitate to announce his act. Besides, I already felt his presence—feared him—for did I not receive the note which read: 'The Three of Spades is out of the Pack Again.' That was when I wrote you."

Terry went on with his questions. Just to see if the man would have a reason for everything. His answers, his explanations, were ready on his tongue. Terry wondered. There was still the third letter, which had been written by the same hand as the two others. But he didn't tell Clarence Johnstone about that letter.

"Don't you think, Mr. Johnstone, it was rather childish for Nixon Carleton to put the three of spades on the dead Darrow? Wouldn't you then immediately know who committed the murder?"

"But he wanted me to know."

"And place such a trump in your hands? He might blackmail you through your daughter, Florence,"Terry did not mention 'through his suspected theft of the girl's money,'"Yet you hold a greater weapon over his head—one of murder. And again, the police would have found the card and—"

"Perhaps he has an accomplice—an alibi. The card would mean nothing to the police—they could not understand."

"Then why did you take it?"

And for once Terry got over a question which the other could not answer. But Clarence Johnstone did not stammer or turn red or get confused. He said simply:

"I don't know—I don't know." And a minute later, "The past swept over me. You were coming the following day—I was afraid; afraid for Florence."

All true maybe. No one knew better than Terry Mack the strange things innocent, as well as guilty, people do. A moment of silence, then Clarence Johnstone came to his feet, stepped to the phone and gripped it.

"You have questioned me for some time, Mr. Mack. I understand. I have been a fool. Murder will out; scandal—newspapers—I should have spoken out to the police. Now, I will tell Chief Robinson all. I have been wrong."

And Clarence Johnstone waited for Terry to advise him against his determination to call the police. He stood silently, his left hand on the receiver, his right gripping the phone.

Terry was thinking.

Inspector Thurston was already suspicious that something was wrong. Florence would be followed, questioned perhaps, even arrested, since the Inspector probably knew that the fingerprints on the canoe in the boat house were hers. She would talk then—accuse, perhaps—or Doctor Corellie, her friend, would talk for her. No—it was better that Clarence Johnstone spoke out. If the Chief of Police was properly approached, maybe the whole thing could be hushed up—at least, until something definite was disclosed. Terry knew that if he was on the police force he would hesitate a long time before making an actual accusation against Clarence Johnstone.

"Well—" Clarence Johnstone looked at Terry over the phone. Then his left hand fell from the receiver, the fingers landing on the table with two distinct little thuds. The right hand gripped the phone the tighter, and he drew in a sharp breath.

From out in the night had come a cry—a piercing shriek; a scream of fear, that died away in a weird, eerie, shrill note of horror. Terry forgot about Clarence Johnstone, the police, the phone. Just one thing. Where was Ardath? He turned from the window and raced toward the hall. The last he had seen of the girl she was in the house, and the cry had come from out on the fog-swept beach. Besides, it did not sound like a woman, and it didn't sound like a man either, for that matter. Yet—Terry knew, despite the dismal, terrifying wail, that it was not the cry of an animal. Some one—some human being—had been struck with terror.

19

On the Fog-Swept Beach

TERRY REACHED THE hall and the breath which he was holding shot from his mouth. There was Ardath, standing in the center of the big hall. Behind her and dose to the curtains before the dining room was Jenkins—and on the stairs above was the white face of a maid. All had been attracted by that terrible cry, and instinctively they had sought each other near the front door.

"Where is Old Martin?" Terry's words were low and husky; yet he was not afraid—not for himself.

There was no answer from the three silent figures. The maid came a bit further down the stairs—Jenkins, the butler, twisted the thick drapes before the dining room in his fingers. Ardath stood there looking at the front door, the color slowly coming back into her face. She did not laugh now—she looked once at Terry and tried to smile, but she did not speak.

"Where is Old Martin?" The same question was asked again, but this time it did not come from Terry, though it was just as husky and just as deeply down in the speaker's chest. Terry turned and saw Clarence Johnstone in the library doorway.

"Old—Mr. Martin is in his room, sir," Jenkins stammered finally.

"No—no, he's not," the maid called down from the stairs. "I was just in his room. He's downstairs, or—or he's out on the beach."

Out on the beach! Old Martin! Was it he then who had shrieked in terror, or—? Terry wondered.

All four stood listening—there was no other sound. There was no wind—nothing came to straining ears but the steady, monotonous beating of the waves.

"You all stay here—together in the hall," Terry finally broke the silence. "I'll go out and look around." And seeing the whiteness of those faces, "Bolt the door after me, if you wish—I won't be long." And before Clarence Johnstone could lay the trembling hand, that he stretched out, upon his shoulder, Terry stepped toward the door, clutched at the knob, and dug his right hand deep into his pocket.

"Old Martin may be out there—and need me," he explained the necessity of leaving them.

Hand on the knob, he hesitated. Distinctly, clearly to the silent listeners came a sharp report. It might have been the noise from an exploding automobile tire. But none of the four thought of that, and Terry knew that it wasn't that. It was the sharp ping of a bullet. A gun had been fired somewhere off in the night.

"Don't—don't leave us here." It was Ardath who crossed the room as Terry turned the knob. "You can't tell what's out there, Terry—and if—oh, Terry, I'm afraid." She was clinging to him now.

"Why, Ardath." He gripped her tightly by both shoulders and held her so. "This isn't like you. You've laughed over our fears—and waved aside our warnings." For a moment he gazed straight down into wide, frightened brown eyes. They did not meet his gaze for a time, but searched about the floor. Then the little chin came up, the nose tilted just a bit more defiantly, and the steady brown eyes flashed into his.

"You wouldn't have me stand here, Ardath, while some one—perhaps Old Martin—is done to death out there on the beach?" Terry said.

"No, Terry—no." Her voice shook slightly but her eyes were steady and clear. "Go out then—go out and—"

A man shouted, a voice called hoarsely—another bullet spat in the air, and feet beat upon the gravel path. Then steps upon the porch—heavy, unsteady steps—and the moan of a man. Terry pushed Ardath back, gripped the knob tightly, drew his gun and flung open the door.

"Oh— My God— My God! Clarence—Clarence!" An unkempt figure staggered through the door, brushed past Terry's gun. Eyes blazed and stared wildly; gray, matted hair stuck to the wrinkled forehead—and Clarence Johnstone stepped forward and held out his hands as the pitiable, frightened figure lurched forward and pitched into his arms.

"Urskine—Harry Urskine," Clarence Johnstone cried hoarsely, and said no more.

"Harry Urskine—yes." The man cried brokenly as he echoed the name. "I've seen him, Clarence—I've seen him—he's—"

"Nixon Carleton—Nixon—" Clarence Johnstone gasped. "He had— You saw him!"

Terry was standing by the door, drinking in every word—watching every movement of Clarence Johnstone. If Johnstone had anything to do with the disappearance of Harry Urskine or his pitiable condition, certainly Harry Urskine was not aware of it.

"Not Carleton—just an old—old crook—him. But the other—I know him—I saw him. The man in the shadows;

he's—" a pause with the name on his lips as other feet beat upon the front steps. "There—he's coming—he's coming to take me. He's—"

"There, there—calm now—" But Clarence Johnstone's voice was as excited as that of his friend, if not quite so hysterical. "We have help here—you can talk later—shs."

A figure was on the porch, clearly outlined in the dull light that splashed into the mist. Terry raised his gun—spoke sharply, then lowered the gun again. Inspector William Thurston stepped into the room.

He ignored Terry Mack as he closed the door and walked straight toward Harry Urskine. But the man did not see him—he had become a dead weight in the arms of Clarence Johnstone—a weight that Clarence Johnstone could not support, and the limp form slipped to the floor.

"Harry Urskine— By God!" Inspector Thurston gasped. "Some one shot at him on the beach. I saw the figure. I've been watching the house all the evening." Then, as stern eyes rested on Clarence Johnstone, "I thought your story pretty thin, Mr. Johnstone. Now—did he speak—tell you where he was and—?"

"No—no, he didn't." Clarence Johnstone shook his head. "He heard you coming, and thought—thought—"

"Well—what the devil did he think?" Inspector William Thurston eyed Johnstone sharply, and then seeing the maid upon the stairs and Jenkins in the doorway, where he was now backed by the cook and another maid, "Never mind—never mind, sir—we'll cart him off to a bed. He'll talk quickly enough when we get a doctor."

But Terry Mack heard no more. Old Martin was out on the

beach—and it was not Old Martin who had shrieked out in horror; it was Harry Urskine. Clarence Johnstone was safe. Ardath was safe. Inspector Thurston was in the house, and Inspector Thurston seemed a very efficient officer. Also Terry was not surprised that he had been watching the place. Inspector Thurston had more than hinted that he was not satisfied with the explanation of the dead man on the beach. So Terry stepped out into the night.

Terry's pocket flash was useless in that fog. It only blurred up the thick mist, and instead of an asset became a liability—a prowler on the beach with a gun in his hand and murder in his heart could see the light and perhaps take a shot at it. Certainly Harry Urskine had been in fear of something; something real had caused that shriek. He was a man in very bad shape—but not delirious. His clothes were wet and torn; he had escaped from some place. And there was another besides Nixon Carleton involved. Well, when Harry Urskine recovered sufficiently to talk, there would be a pretty story all right. Terry knew that. He hesitated now about going on or returning to the house. He'd like to be the first to hear what Urskine had to say. It was certain that Inspector Thurston would watch the man until he "came around" and spoke. But where was Old Martin? Terry thought a moment, and decided to have a look about the house—at least be the first to talk to Old Martin when he tried to slip back in. Queer, harmless old duck, certainly—but then, queer, harmless old ducks had on more than one occasion sprung surprises on Terry.

Terry did more listening than looking. He could not see five feet before him and heard nothing but the steady beating of the surf. Lights were going up in the house behind him. He could hear voices calling and see figures passing the windows. A huge dark object suddenly loomed up before him. He nearly stumbled over the stones between the lawn and the sand, and knew that the black object was the boat house. He listened but there was no sound—just the thump, thump, thump of the ocean. He tried to locate other noises between the beating of the waves. But there were no other noises—not even the hum of wind—just the ocean and silence.

Terry reached the front of the boat house, and leaning against it faced the ocean—but he could not even see it. Eyes get accustomed to darkness, but not to the mist—at least, not to such a fog as this. Already he was wet through, and drops of water were slipping down his forehead. Then between the thuds of the hammering surf he heard it. Something thudded against the boat house. He turned and looked at the little window, keeping well to the side of it. Was there a face there? It might be a face and it might not. But from the blackness of the boat house something small and white and round seemed to be pressed against the glass. "Seemed to be" was the best Terry could say for it. Stare as he would he could not call that small white object a nose.

There was but one exit to the boat house. The small door which led to the wooden runway, and so to the gravel path across the lawn. The window did not open, and even if it did was too small for a man to slip through. Terry decided to chance his flash—just a quick spurt of light close against the glass. It was much better to scare the man into leaving the boat house than to wait there until he decided to come out himself. To enter the boat house and search for one who hid there was too much like suicide.

He gripped the flash in his left hand and the gun in his right. There was no danger from one within the boat house. The light would flash on and off too quickly for that. The only danger would be from another who prowled on the beach. Terry jerked up his flash, held it close to the little square of dirty glass, and pressed the button.

A circle of light cut the mist and settled on the dirty window. And there was a face—a misty, shadowy thing—distant eyes, the blotch of a nose—and nothing else. The face and the light faded out together. Terry hurried to the door.

Footsteps beat across the wooden floor within, hesitated, stopped, and reached the door. Terry stepped back and waited. Dimly he could make out the door. Was it moving, slowly opening? He put out a hand and rested two fingers lightly upon the surface of the door. Yes—it was opening, very slowly, very cautiously. And it stopped—there was heavy breathing, and the shadowy outline of a head. A sudden lurch forward, and a figure sped into the fog. Terry lurched forward, tripped over the boards, recovered his balance and started in pursuit. But pursuit was useless. Sodden footsteps sounded for a moment and were lost in the dull roar of the ocean. A figure too was quickly swallowed up in the mist.

Terry didn't follow. He ran back up the walk; kept off the gravel path and hurried across the lawn toward the rear entrance of the house. If it was Old Martin that's where he'd go. Terry reached the little rear porch, ducked behind a large pillar, and waited. Not long either; quiet steps slipped over the grass; a foot sought the lower step, and shoulders bent forward. This time Terry did not miss. His left hand shot out and landed on the man's shoulder—then his flash came into play.

"Old Martin." He nodded emphatically when the light settled on that wrinkled, corrugated face.

"Aye—" Old Martin blinked owlishly. "It's Mr. Mack, isn't it? Not a night for a walk—yet I like it. The smell of the salt is deeper, bites sort of, and—well—a bad night for good men and a—"

"Enough of that." Terry shook him. "What were you doing in the boat house?"

"Boat house?" The old hands rubbed together. "Was I in the boat house? You mean the little house where the canoes and the odds and ends of—"

"Yes." Terry crowded the old man back against the wall. In the parlance of the police and underworld, he was "frisking" his man—not searching him exactly, but deft steady fingers were patting Old Martin's pockets and even running down his trouser legs and along his sleeves.

"Stop it—you're tickling me." The old man chuckled. "I'm getting too well along to be playful." And he jumped and giggled when Terry's hands shot suddenly up, jarring beneath his armpits.

"What were you doing on the beach?" Terry demanded. Old Martin was a fool—a doddering idiot; everybody admitted that. Terry knew it too—but he knew something else. When you want to learn things, sometimes a fool such as Old Martin becomes very wise indeed. One thing he was satisfied of—Old Martin carried no gun.

"Come, Martin—" he tried a more kindly tone, "Miss Ardath's in danger—Clarence Johnstone's in danger—and you can help them. What do you know? What brought you out on the beach to-night? What were you doing in the boat house?"

"Aye—three questions, like all in one. You're an energetic young man—very. I wish I knew the answers to them questions. If I did— If I did—"

"Yes, yes—if you did—" Terry tried to be patient but it was very hard.

"Why, if I did I'd know more than you know."

"But I know you were in the boat house."

"Then that's settled—I'm glad, because it was annoying."

In the dim mist Terry could see the old man's hands rubbing, rubbing, rubbing. It was useless to question him further. But he tried again as the old man slipped a key into the rear door.

"You don't want to help—Clarence Johnstone?"

"Him?" Old Martin turned sharply; colorless orbs seemed to shine in the mist, for Terry's flash was back in his pocket. "Yes—yes." And then as shrewd old lips tightened, "But you want me to talk. 'Was I in the boat house?' says you. Ask Clarence Johnstone—he'll tell you. If he says I was there, I was there. I'll wait and see what he says. I always wait and see."

20

Doctor Corellie

TERRY FOLLOWED OLD MARTIN into the house, saw him slip up the back stairs, while Terry passed through the dining room to the front hall. He didn't stop the old man; threaten him with arrest; accuse him of anything. He didn't want Old Martin to think that he suspected him of anything. And Terry laughed—after all, of what could he suspect him? Certainly no living actor that he ever heard of could play such a part. No—Old Martin was real. Terry stroked his chin. Yet, reality did not prevent him from committing murder.

In the great front hall Terry paused. The door was open; a sharp-featured, dark-haired man stood in the doorway. There was a bag by his side, and he had removed his light coat and was in the act of placing it over a chair when Terry entered. Their eyes met across the stretch of hall. Dark piercing eyes shot quickly over Terry's face. Eyes that seemed to pick out each feature and register them back in his head some place. He was a professional man, of course; evidently the doctor, Terry thought.

"Doctor Corellie, sir," the maid said, turning toward the stairs.

"Ah! Doctor—" Terry stepped forward, his gray eyes smilingly meeting those black ones of the doctor. "You're to be congratulated—a quick run in from Newton." He jerked out his watch; it was ten minutes after ten. The clock in Clarence

Johnstone's library was a quarter of ten when the first scream came from the beach.

Doctor Corellie smiled pleasantly. Two rows of white, pointed teeth gleamed in the dim light.

"But I wasn't in Newton," he shook his head. "I was just passing the gate when a policeman stopped me. So, I came in—not one of the family, I hope."

"No," said Terry. And as the voice of Inspector Thurston boomed from above and Doctor Corellie's dark eyes narrowed, "Just a moment, Doctor." Terry stopped him on the stairs. "Mr. Urskine is the patient. It is quite possible that you know him." And Terry's smile disappeared and his lips set tightly. "It would be very embarrassing if Harry Urskine should die in the night—embarrassing for you." For Terry recognized in Doctor Corellie the advisor and confidant of Florence Johnstone.

Doctor Corellie turned on the stairs.

"For me—" He elevated his eyebrows slightly.

"Perhaps I should have said, 'for all of us.'" And then with a shrug of his shoulders, "But I'll go above with you. It will be to your benefit not to object to my attendance by the bedside."

"I do not understand." Again the eyebrows went up.

"No?" Terry smiled. "I'm a detective from the city. You either wish Harry Urskine to live or you wish him to die. I simply wish him to live. I am a seeker after truth."

"I wish all my patients to live." Doctor Corellie smiled—a whimsical sort of a smile. "And I wish Mr. Urskine to live. You are perhaps not the only seeker after truth, Mr. Mack."

"Perhaps not." But Terry Mack was directly on the doctor's heels when he entered the large bedroom at the rear of the house, and placing his bag upon a chair, stepped with that soft, assured, professional air to the side of the bed.

Inspector Thurston was at the foot of the bed—Clarence Johnstone close to the window, and Ardath hovered in the doorway. At the end of the long narrow hall and close to the back stairs which led to the servants' quarters above and the kitchen below, were the white, frightened faces of the servants.

"I think perhaps we had better leave the patient alone with the doctor," Clarence Johnstone said nervously.

"Perhaps *you* had." Terry nodded. "But I studied medicine some years back. I'm interested and may be of some assistance to Doctor Corellie—eh, Doctor?"

"I need no assistance." Doctor Corellie turned sharply, then bent over his patient.

"Nevertheless," said Terry emphatically, "I shall stay." There, unconscious on the bed, was the man who held the secret— the one illuminating fact—in this whole weird, impossible mystery. And he had seen Nixon Carleton—but he had also seen another. No—Terry had no intention of leaving Doctor Corellie alone with the wounded, fear-ridden man.

"I'll sit around too," Inspector Thurston said, as he took a chair by the window. "I don't know a damn thing about medicine. But the doctor can give him something to make him stop that moaning—ease up the pain and let him sleep. I'll be around to listen to what he has to say when he wakes up. We don't want him delirious, you know."

Doctor Corellie turned from his examination of the man upon the bed.

"There's a knife wound on his chest and a bullet in the back of his shoulder. It'll take but a minute to dig it out. But he's been frightened, and if I don't give him a hypodermic, to deaden the brain for a bit and let him sleep, something may snap back in his head. He's a badly frightened man."

"Yes, yes." Clarence Johnstone's voice trembled in the corner of the room. "Do what you can for him. He's been through a lot."

"All right." Inspector William Thurston swung his broad shoulders across the room to the side of the bed. "But we want him in shape in the morning." He looked significantly over at Clarence Johnstone, then back to the doctor. "There's no danger of him kicking over in the night—eh, Doctor?"

Doctor Corellie hesitated a moment, then seeing the hard cold eyes of the police officer fixed upon his face, said slowly:

"None whatever, I should say. And there's the bullet. It would have rubbed loose by the friction from his coat sleeve in another hour."

"So that's the bullet—give it here." Inspector Thurston turned the bit of lead over in a huge hand. "Thirty-eight, I'd say, offhand—what say, Mr. Mack?"

But Terry was watching the doctor bare the man's arm and thrust the needle beneath the skin. He didn't speak to him. He couldn't without the others—or at least the Inspector—hearing him. But the doctor had raised his eyes and met those of Terry. He could not fail to understand the threat and warning those hard gray eyes blazed across the bed to him. One thing was certain. If anything happened to Harry Urskine that night, he'd have Doctor Corellie in jail in the morning. But what right had he to distrust the doctor—and it was such an impossible thought anyway. After hearing what Terry had to say below, even if the doctor was guilty of some conspiracy—or even the murder of Darrow on the beach—he would not dare harm the man upon the bed. The evidence against him then would be conclusive, without the aid of an autopsy. For Terry knew enough to be convinced that Harry Urskine was not in any immediate danger of dying. He was a badly frightened man—little more.

Not once did Terry take his eyes off the doctor, and when he left the room with Clarence Johnstone, Terry carefully examined the windows, the closet, and even bent down and glanced beneath the bed.

Inspector William Thurston stood in the doorway watching him.

"Well, Mr. Mack," he said, stroking his chin when Terry turned from the room, "I won't ask for any explanation from you—but if you hadn't of searched the room, I would have. You see," he hesitated a moment, "like you, I after all wonder if Harry Urskine picked out the safest place possible to recover from his—experience."

But Terry only smiled as he dragged a chair into the hall and locking the door behind him held the key out to the Inspector.

"You might put this in your pocket—or better still," Terry pushed the key into the lock, "I'll leave it in the lock—he might wake up in the night and need me."

"Going to spend the night here in the hall." There was a more of a puzzled statement of fact in Inspector Thurston's voice than a question, for Terry had pushed his chair close up against the door and stretched himself comfortably in it.

"Why, yes," said Terry. "I've grown very fond of Mr. Urskine in our short acquaintance. I want to be as near to him as possible."

"That's very thoughtful." The broad-shouldered officer nodded. "Perhaps I'll join you later. But I think, first, I'll have a little talk with—with your client. Any objections?"

"None whatever." Terry yawned.

"And may I take the key—until my return?" Thurston held out his hand. "After all, Mr. Mack, your position here is not an official one. I'd hate to be unpleasant—but to be perfectly frank with you, I want to hear the first words Urskine speaks—before he's cautioned."

"He's doped up until morning." But Terry handed over the key. There was something dominant about this man. Not that Terry feared what he might do. He could not interfere with his work at Shadow Lawn, but if he stepped in as an official of the law he might make things very unpleasant—very complicated too. And Terry smiled to himself. As if things were not complicated enough as they now stood.

"Doped until morning!" The Inspector echoed his words. "Certainly—but then, you said you studied medicine some years ago." He hesitated a moment, juggling the key in his hand. "I'll join you again in a few minutes. Maybe Mr. Johnstone will talk—before him." A huge fist shot toward the locked door, and Inspector Thurston swung down the hall—a few seconds later his heavy feet beat upon the stairs. Terry stretched back in his seat. He would guard well the life of Harry Urskine.

21

Clarence Johnstone Speaks

THE GREAT CLOCK in the hall below struck the hour of eleven! An electric light burned dimly above the main staircase but Terry had extinguished the one by the door before which he sat, and so was in the darkness. Ardath had gone to bed. The servants could be plainly heard moving about at the end of the house. Clarence Johnstone was below with Inspector Thurston. Terry had heard their voices for a minute—then the closing of the library door. He guessed that Clarence Johnstone was about to tell his story. And a good thing too, he thought. Better he speak before Urskine spoke. And what would Thurston do after hearing the story?

Terry sat suddenly the straighter in the chair. Down the hall toward the servants' entrance a door had closed softly. It was dark there now that the light near the door had been extinguished, and Terry could see nothing. But plainly he heard the door close—and plainly too he heard the shuffling steps. He knew those steps—they were Old Martin's. He was coming softly toward him. What did he want? What was Old Martin doing so cautiously slipping toward Harry Urskine's room?

And Terry cursed inwardly. He had forgotten about the Inspector; time had slipped by. And now he was returning—not so heavily perhaps, but nevertheless that even tread on the front stairs was his. Old Martin heard it too, for his cautious movement stopped; once or twice Terry thought that he heard the old man breathing heavily.

The steps of Inspector Thurston reached the landing and his figure passed beneath the light as he turned and continued up to the floor above. What did he want above? Old Martin? For his room was on that floor and the officer must have known that he had been out on the beach. Had he gone above to interview him—question him? That would be rather a novelty for Inspector Thurston, Terry thought. Then he remembered that Old Martin would not be there. Terry slipped out of the chair and came to his feet. But not silently—the wicker groaned and creaked. A voice came out of the darkness—a voice, and moving steps.

"Mr. Mack—sir." It was Old Martin, and now he was down the hall standing before Terry. "I just want to tell you the truth; I got a word in with Mr. Johnstone on the stairs. I was in the boat house—me and an old rifle—guarding Shadow Lawn, I was—Mr. Johnstone said so. He said I was an old fool, too. It must be so. Good night." The shadow in the darkness turned and shuffled back down the hall; a door closed softly and feet beat distantly on the back stairs. Old Martin was going above to his room. He would meet Inspector Thurston.

But he didn't. For Terry heard the Inspector on the front stairs, and a moment later he had joined Terry in the darkness.

"Went to see Old Martin," he explained as he switched on the light. "He wasn't there but I found this in his room." The Inspector thrust a cold, nickel-plated revolver toward Terry.

Terry took the gun. It was an old revolver—thirty-eight caliber. He broke it open; one of the chambers was empty. He smelt of it. It had been recently fired.

"Where in the room did you find this?" Terry asked.

"In an overcoat pocket—a coat that was wet—the coat that Old Martin must have worn on the beach tonight." He nodded vigorously. "I think, after all, I'll keep vigil with you to-night. I got a few things out of Clarence Johnstone."

"What?"

"Everything—forced him into it. He was half anxious to talk and I told him I'd had a word with his daughter—his adopted daughter, Florence. But, you see, I hadn't—I was guessing. Dirty mess!"

And Inspector William Thurston talked. Undoubtedly Clarence Johnstone had unburdened himself to the law at last. Terry Mack and William Thurston stood on even ground so far as Clarence Johnstone was concerned.

"Did he—speak of Florence; her—her attitude?" Terry must feel his way.

"Absolutely. Personally, I think the girl has the goods on him. I know the town—know the people—I've been on the force here for twenty years. You couldn't get an old party to believe that Clarence Johnstone didn't return to the city over thirty years ago a wealthy man—a very wealthy man. And he admits the gold venture was a bust—that won't be hard to confirm. But that's for them to settle. The murder is my end of it. If she brings a civil suit it'll be hard to collect—if she brings criminal action it will be hard to prove. Lord!" he laughed mirthlessly. "I didn't think it was in the old geezer—and, seriously, I don't believe it is."

"And what do you think of Nixon Carleton—this—you heard about the card?"

"The three of spades, yes." Thurston nodded. "Hard as it

is, we must try to believe Mr. Johnstone's story until we get evidence to the contrary. Vengeance, after all, is a great motive. He should have spoken to me at once. Nixon Carleton is an old man. It won't be hard to lay hands on him if he's in these parts. I won't do anything until something else breaks. If Johnstone is honest, the adopted daughter is mixed up with crooks. But I'll keep his secret a bit yet. If it turns out just blackmail, as he thinks—I'll protect him. If more people would appeal to the police, as human beings, there would be less suicides and even murders. I'm not going to condemn a man who's been an outstanding figure in Newton since I beat the pavements. Come—I'll work with you, Mr. Mack. This may be the work of one, Nixon Carleton, with a far-reaching motive that we can't foresee—it may be the workings of a disordered brain, like—well, Old Martin's. It may be the work of a clever band of crooks who have not yet struck their vital blow. Let's work together." He stretched out a hand, and Terry took it.

After all, Terry thought that they had one common interest—the interest of justice. But he wondered how a thirty-eight caliber revolver with one bullet missing had gotten into the overcoat pocket of Old Martin. Could Terry have overlooked it? But he shook his head. That was impossible—even with a gun of half its size. Who then had planted it there—and why?

Ten minutes later Clarence Johnstone came heavily up the stairs. He walked toward the door before which the two men sat, and behind which Harry Urskine lay. Twice he opened his mouth to speak and each time changed his mind. At length he spoke.

"Good night, Mr. Mack— Good night, Inspector—I shan't

forget—you have been very kind." Without another word he turned and made his way to his room.

"You know," said Inspector Thurston, "I don't know about the money—and his adopted daughter, but somehow I can't connect that man up with—well, even an interest in the death of another."

"No, no," Terry answered mechanically. He was not thinking of Clarence Johnstone then. He was thinking of Ardath. What was the use of talking and guessing and trying to figure things out? A few hours more and Harry Urskine would talk.

Once Terry suggested that they enter the room and have a look at the man upon the bed. Inspector Thurston objected at first, eyed Terry quizzically a moment, and with a shrug slipped the key into the lock and turned the knob. They entered, and Terry snapped on the light.

Harry Urskine lay on his back, breathing regularly. Terry bent over the man and looked closely at him. He half turned upon the bed but slept on. Terry was relieved. Doctor Corellie had been gone over two hours and Harry Urskine slept peacefully.

"We'd better let him drift along until morning." Inspector Thurston yawned. "He's safe enough. It's a tough climb from below if any one did attempt to enter—besides, we'd hear them at the window."

"Right." Terry nodded. But was it right? There was an unexplainable feeling of danger; nothing tangible and nothing that he could lay a finger to. He laughed it away. Inspector Thurston was tired—he might fall asleep. But Terry wouldn't. That much was certain. And his ears were trained over the years to catch the slightest sound. The light in the hall again extinguished, the two men sat down to wait—to wait for dawn.

Inspector Thurston did fall asleep in the chair before the door, and what's more he snored. Loud, wheezing notes they were, and prevented Terry from hearing other sounds in the house—if there were other sounds—and between the snores came the pounding of the surf. The clock below struck two, and Inspector Thurston with a final snort woke himself up.

"What was that?" he gasped.

"The clock below—and your own snore."

"Strange—I thought that I heard a whistle. I've been asleep." And he wiped his eyes. "Why not knock off an hour yourself? I'll keep awake."

But Terry shook his head. He was going to see this night through, wide awake. He hadn't done much; hadn't accomplished much; was far from covering himself with glory. But somehow the lure of the thing didn't get into him as it did with other cases. He wanted a solution—a quick end to the whole affair. He was not thinking of the dead Darrow—or the adopted daughter—or Clarence Johnstone himself—nor even the stranger whom Harry Urskine had named. He was thinking of Ardath, and wishing the whole beastly affair was cleaned up.

This time when Inspector Thurston jerked erect, Terry jerked with him. Distinctly came a whistle from some place out in the night—a long, sharp, single note. Both men listened without speaking. But the whistle was not repeated.

"It came from that side." Thurston pointed to the closed door. "I'll go below and look out—you stay here."

"Right." Terry intended to stay there. This time he hardly heard the Inspector's feet on the stairs—the man could walk lightly when he wished to. But he did hear him below as he brushed against a chair in the hall; just the scraping of it and the soft curse of the man. There was no other sound after the feet crossed the floor below. Inspector Thurston must be at the window, looking out. Five minutes passed—ten, perhaps—yet no sound from below. Was the Inspector still gazing into the night—and what did he see that kept him so long? Terry wondered.

22

Within the Locked Room

THERE WAS THE sound of a single step, a heavy step, some place in the library—and running feet; feet that beat across the thick rug like the soft feet of an animal. Then silence, and Terry strained to pierce it. What could Inspector Thurston be doing all this time? He remembered the fog and the mist, and the uselessness of trying to see into the night. Had something happened to the Inspector there below, and did those running feet seek the back door and freedom? Or was the Inspector pursuing some one in the darkness? Of course it could have been the light patter of a heavy man running silently on his toes. But he shook his head. It was impossible for any one to enter that house without his hearing him.

Terry slipped along the hall to the back stairs, using his flash as he opened the door and stepped softly down them. It was hard to tread noiselessly, for there was no carpet on the steps, but he reached the bottom. The door at the foot of the stairs was open; he flashed his torch about the kitchen. It wouldn't do to be gone long, but nothing could happen to Harry Urskine. It would take force to open that door above quickly, even if any one knew he had left his post. Besides, who would chance it? Who, in that house?

The kitchen was deserted; so was the pantry beyond, for the swinging door was open and Terry could see to the end of the narrow room. He stood there at the foot of the back stairs, listening—but not a sound from above, or the front of the house. And again from out in the fog came a whistle; the same shrill, sharp, single note.

A signal of some sort, Terry thought. Was one out on the fog-swept beach trying to communicate with some one in the house? Would some one leave the house in answer to that sharp note? Or did it mean something else—a signal that a figure was watching and waiting and ready. Ready for what? But Terry couldn't answer that question. There was another one which puzzled him. What had become of Inspector Thurston? It was hard to believe that anything could have happened to that efficient, dominant police officer. No—Inspector Thurston might even now be out on the beach; might even have fastened his huge hands upon the throat of the prowler who sent the sharp, warning notes.

Terry stepped into the kitchen and listened. His flash shot to the back door; the chain was safely in its bolt. If some one had run through the dining room, that some one had not escaped by the rear entrance. Well, he wouldn't waste any more time—he'd go straight to the front stairs and back to his position before Harry Urskine's door. He held his flash in his left hand and his gun in his right as he sought the pantry and the swinging door to the dining room.

For two or three minutes he stood there listening, but there was no sound. Then his flash went out and he swung around facing the kitchen and the back stairs. A board had creaked on the steps. There was no doubt of that. On the door jamb that led from the pantry to the kitchen he waited in the darkness. But the sound was not repeated. Was it nerves? But, no. Terry did not have nerves—or at least, if he had, he was never conscious of them before. Still, this was not like other cases; the cold-blooded man-hunt that he was so used to. Here was an uncertain feeling; a fear that was foreign to him; a coldness and apprehension that was strange to his nature. He shuddered slightly. He was thinking of Ardath and the tragedy that she might be called upon to face any moment. Then he heard it again—footsteps were coming down the back stairs; very quietly, very slowly—but unmistakable just the same.

Terry held his breath and waited. The feet were in the kitchen now, crossing the floor—softly slipping toward the back door. Terry set his teeth grimly—his flash was directed toward where he thought the door to be, and his gun followed the direction of the flash. It would hardly be the Inspector—no need for him to "pussy foot" around like that. Who was it then? Another second and Terry would know. As soon as the chain rattled.

There was a sudden crack, the jingle of falling glass, and a heavy object bounced across the kitchen floor. There was a muffled scream, a quick intake of breath, and the clank of a falling chain. And Terry's thumb pressed down on the button of the flash. A dart of circular white light cut the darkness, wavered a moment, and rested steadily upon the figure of a woman in black. "The woman in black"—for she had turned; wide, frightened black eyes glared dazedly into the light. The woman gasped in surprise and fear. Terry gasped, too—but in surprise only.

"Miss Florence Johnstone," he said calmly as he stepped across the kitchen and stood before her.

"Terry—Mr. Mack." The voice was hardly audible. "Don't—please don't tell any one I was here."

"No?" Terry's eyebrows went up. "Just why are you here?"

"I—I—for Ardath's sake. I—"

"That's pretty thin, Miss Johnstone." Terry shook his head. "What other reason?"

The woman's chin went up a bit defiantly.

"It is my home—I live here," she said.

"And now you're moving again?"

She hesitated a moment, blinking into the light. Terry lowered it.

"Somehow I can't trust you—because of him—Mr. Johnstone. I've been warned against you."

"Doctor Corellie?" Terry cut in.

"I was afraid for Ardath." She ignored his interruption. "That's why I came. I have seen her and she is all right. That's why I am going."

The light from the flash in his hand was drifting about the floor, aimlessly—like his thoughts. Then the flash stopped. The light had fallen upon a small stone. Terry's thoughts and his flash shot to the window together. There was a small hole in the window-pane. He recalled the breaking glass now, and the object that bounced upon the floor. The stone and the hole told the story. Some one had stood outside and tossed the stone through the kitchen window. Had it actually been thrown at the woman? Hardly! These people who threatened Shadow Lawn would stoop to nothing as harmless as that—besides, they couldn't have seen the girl. Terry's heart gave a sudden jump. He knew why that stone was thrown—turning quickly he dashed toward the back stairs.

"Don't—don't leave me," the woman cried suddenly flinging herself upon him. "I came because of Ardath. I braved the night and the fog; the loneliness and the fear of this house.

But now—I'm afraid—I'm afraid—don't leave me here. I have more to tell you."

His flash jerked up and lit upon the woman's face. It was white with fear. And Terry's, too, was white with fear—but a different fear—a fear for the man upstairs. He thrust the woman from him. He thought he saw it all now. Inspector Thurston had been tempted out into the night by the whistle, or perhaps by a noise by the window when he had gone below—oh, by a hundred different things. And then the woman, Florence Johnstone. Had she hidden above? Was she simply there to keep him below? But what was the need of the girl being there—the stone alone would have been sufficient to bring him to the kitchen. But the woman had come down those back stairs.

The woman was clinging to him again now. He leaned down and dragged her hands away. If this was simulated fear it was very good acting indeed.

"You'd trap me here," he whispered sharply, "while perhaps murder takes place above."

"Murder—murder," she cried aloud. "Ardath—little Ardath. Go! Go!" And this time she thrust Terry from her—pushing him up the stairs.

He heard her gasp behind him as he ran; heard, too, the slight thump of her body, and he knew that she was left behind upon the stairs. But he went on. It made no difference now about noise. Time might mean everything. He reached the top step and turned into the hall, his flash cutting the darkness before him, an automatic gripped tightly in his free hand. He tried to tell himself that his thoughts were impossible, fantastic— he hadn't been gone very long. Nothing could have happened.

He had believed in the sincerity of Florence before, why have such wild thoughts now? His flash lit up the two chairs before the door and the darkness beyond it. Inspector Thurston was coming from the direction of the front stairs, hurrying along the hall.

"What's the rush?" Thurston called to him as Terry reached the two chairs and stood beside them.

"Where were you?" Terry questioned.

"Out in the sand—some one was looking in the window. But when I got out there—nothing. Did glass break some place in the house?"

"Yes," said Terry.

"What happened?"

"Clarence Johnstone's adopted daughter, Florence, has come home."

"So—"The other whistled softly. "And why the mad rush?"

"Why—" and Terry hesitated. He didn't put his thoughts into words. The closed door was before him, the two chairs just as he had left them, and a dead quiet from the room. "Nerves, I guess." He tried to laugh—but his voice sounded hollow. "I didn't know what happened to you—I heard noises below— went into the kitchen; and then I thought of the door—and the man behind it—and his secret—and what it meant to us—and to others."

Inspector Thurston stepped to the door and shook the knob gently.

"Still locked." He chuckled. "And here is the key." He dipped his hand into his pocket and produced the key.

"Suppose we take a look anyway," said Terry.

"Not me," said Inspector Thurston. "I have too much confidence in my own ability—and yours." He smiled.

"Nevertheless," said Terry, "I'll have a look behind that door." He took the key from Thurston's outstretched hand and thrust it into the lock. "The man's been through a lot; escaped from something, and might regain consciousness in fear—do himself—" Terry stopped. That wasn't what he was thinking at all. What was he thinking?

Imagination! A case so closely affecting Ardath made him act like a nervous woman; gave him that queer sensation of danger. He turned the key and pushed open the door. Blackness—and his flash cut into it.

Harry Urskine still lay on his back. His face was white and his eyes were open. He was looking straight into the light. Strange, how he stared at it—unblinkingly. He did not speak.

"Thurston—come here." Terry's voice was not above a whisper. Thurston entered the room quickly. Even then Terry wasn't sure. But now that he faced tragedy, he was calm and steady and his hand did not shake as he switched on the light in the room and stepped to the bed.

"Looks funny, doesn't—" Thurston started, but Terry raised his hand.

"Look at the bedclothes over his chest." Terry leaned forward and jerked back the blanket and sheet.

Harry Urskine was dead. A long knife was plunged to the hilt in the man's heart—and beneath the blade of that knife, standing out clearly in the light, was a playing card.

"The three of spades," gasped William Thurston in a hushed, awed voice.

"Exactly—" mused Terry Mack, "the three of spades."

The windows were all tightly fastened; nothing in the room

was disturbed; and the door had been locked and the key in the Inspector's pocket. Nevertheless Harry Urskine had been murdered in his bed. He was dead—and his secret had died with him. But had it? Terry clenched his hands tightly. No— he couldn't bring Harry Urskine back to life, but he could and would drag that secret from its grave.

23

After the Murder

TERRY HAD TO admire the efficiency of Inspector William Thurston. After his first gasp of astonishment he was master of the situation.

"This calls for quick action, Mack. Come!" He beckoned Terry into the hall and locked the door again. "We'll have to check up on every one in the house. I'll start above, with Old Martin. We'll gather them all in the library—family and servants." He stroked his chin there in the semidarkness—he smiled too—but just with his mouth; the eyes were hard and cold. "You check up on the woman—that adopted daughter." He started toward the stairs in front—stopped and swung back to Terry.

"Of course, you must understand that I can't accept the responsibility of keeping secret what Clarence Johnstone told me any longer. I'm not questioning him, you understand—it's a wild story now. Nixon Carleton—a lad over seventy—gallivanting around a strange house, opening locked doors with a key and slipping a knife into the chest of—"Thurston shrugged his huge shoulders. "Mind you—I'm not pointing the finger of suspicion at any one. There's Old Martin—half crazy, and with a fancy, perhaps, that he's acting in the interest of the man he worships. Then there's the adopted daughter, Florence, who might find it embarrassing if Harry Urskine talked—so might Clarence Johnstone. Some one from the outside could have come in and pulled the job—but I think that that some one would have needed help—and what's more, got it."

"You're not thinking of making an arrest?" Terry questioned.

"Hardly that—but I'll talk with the Chief. Even advise him to sleep on the thing for a few days. Then—" hands came apart, "the responsibility's not mine."

"I'll talk with the woman," Terry nodded, "if she's still on the rear stairs." And somehow Terry thought that she would not be "still on the rear stairs."

Inspector Thurston mounted the stairs to Old Martin's room. Terry turned to the rear of the house, hesitated a moment, then swinging about passed up the hall, by the front stairs, and into the narrow hallway across the front of the big house. His thoughts were of Ardath. It was with a sigh of relief that he heard her startled, sleepy voice in answer to his timid knocking on her door.

"Slip into some clothes and come below," Terry told her, and in answer to the question in her voice, "Don't be frightened. Have you been asleep—all the time?"

"Ever since going to bed," she said, and he heard her moving about the room.

"What did your sister tell you—or ask you?" he called softly through the closed door.

"When?"

"Now—a few minutes ago." And in a slightly raised voice when she did not answer at once. "I've seen her—and she told me she was here."

"Here—in the house?" There was no mistaking the genuine surprise in the girl's voice.

"Yes—to-night." Terry grew impatient and slightly alarmed,

too. "Didn't you see her—wasn't she in your room?"

"Why, no—how absurd. I've been asleep; she's stopping in Newton. I—"and in a sudden, quick, sharp voice, "You say she told you—why—what's happened, Terry?"

"Hurry below," was all that Terry said as he turned from the door. Feet were moving in the hall above—doors were opening and closing, and William Thurston's heavy feet could be heard pounding across the upper floor back into the servants' quarters.

Clarence Johnstone's room was back down the hall from his daughter, Ardath's. There was no need to awaken him. His door was open and he was in the hall when Terry returned.

"What's happened—what—" His voice shook, and his face was ghostly in the distant glare of the light.

"It's Urskine—murdered." Terry shot the thing straight at him. There was no use to break it gently; there wasn't time for sentiment. Besides, he wished to watch the man's face; better to see it before William Thurston.

"Dead! Murdered!" Clarence Johnstone gasped. "Oh, my God—my God! Even now—even now."

And Terry wished he hadn't been quite so abrupt. Clarence Johnstone swayed there a moment in the doorway, toppled forward, and clutched at the arm which Terry held out to him.

"You've got to brace up." Terry led him back into the room, eased him onto the side of the bed, and stepping into the adjoining bathroom returned with a tumbler of water. The "even now" may not have had any exact meaning, but it bit into Terry just the same. It was almost like a direct statement that he, Terry, had failed in his duty. And after all, Terry wondered—had he? That Inspector William Thurston shared the responsibility with him brought little comfort. He was not in the habit of having murders committed in a house that he guarded. And he wondered too whose witness Harry Urskine really was. It was quite possible that both Florence and Clarence Johnstone could have a key to that room—either one had plenty of opportunity to get one; and either one could have slipped along the hall, opened the door and stabbed the drugged man. If you looked at it that way, Terry thought, Clarence Johnstone had the better opportunity.

Still, Florence Johnstone had entered the house without his knowing it. It would have been a simple enough matter for her to have brought some one with her and let that some one into the house and then— She had delayed him in the kitchen—but she had also hurried him up the stairs. But she had lied to him about seeing Ardath.

Terry left Clarence Johnstone. The old man's will was stronger than his body. He was ready to go below and face the situation. He asked but one question.

"Was there—anything on—his chest?"

And he simply nodded his head and clutched at his chest when Terry told him of the three of spades. There was no shock in that—he had expected it after learning that the man was dead.

"You see, Mr. Mack, the hopelessness of my position. He brings death into my very house—and the police and you are helpless."

Not very pleasant for Terry to hear that. He set his lips grimly but made no reply. The windows in the room where Harry Urskine was murdered had remained closed and locked. If some one of that household had not actually committed the murder, some one knew who did it.

The back stairs held no weeping, prostrate woman. The kitchen door swung gently back and forth in the slight breeze from the ocean. There was no need to search that house for Florence Johnstone—she had gone into the night and the fog. And the murderer? How had he gone? Inspector Thurston was on the front stairs when Terry was on the back. Had the murderer gone to a room in the house—his own room perhaps? Or had he hidden there in the hall and slipped below while he and Thurston stared at the body, the blood-stained knife, and the three of spades? And Terry found no answers to his thoughts.

Thurston gained nothing in his examination of the servants. He bullied them into a condition of incoherent fright. All of them had slept but little—three of them had heard the whistle—two had gone to the window and looked out into the night. And both had seen shadowy forms—many of them moving about in the mist. Yet, Terry knew that the fog was so thick that one could not see the ground from the second-story window. And he knew, too, that neither of the two servants were lying—that is, consciously so. A few more questions in the manner of Inspector Thurston, and the servants would begin to describe the dress and actions of the figures on the beach. That was human nature. Imagination is strong indeed.

Old Martin constantly rubbed his hands together and nodded his old head as if it worked on a wire. Thurston had found him fully dressed in his room.

"I don't know why I stayed awake." Old Martin gave the information when the servants had been dismissed. "You'll have to ask Mr. Johnstone here—what he says, I say."

"But you kept your clothes on." Inspector Thurston glared at him. "Why? Does Mr. Johnstone know the reason of that?"

Old Martin stared vacantly through those colorless eyes.

"It's an idea of mine. I don't dress like I used to—I mostly wear the same things over and over. It come to me that it was a waste of time to undress and dress—foolish vanities—and if anything happened, why—"

"That was it, wasn't it, Martin?" Clarence Johnstone crossed the room and laid a friendly hand upon his shoulder. "You thought you would be ready if anything happened."

"I'll do the questioning." Inspector Thurston thrust himself between the two old men. "Now, Martin, my man—when was it you suddenly decided that it was useless to dress and undress, and what were you doing with this?"

Inspector Thurston's hand jumped from his pocket and a thirty-eight caliber revolver was thrust close against Old Martin's face.

"See it." The Inspector shot his chin forward. "Thirty-eight—one chamber empty—recently fired—and it was in your pocket—your overcoat pocket—when you came from the beach."

Terry was interested. Old Martin could deny that statement and Terry could back it up. That gun was certainly not in Old Martin's pocket when he came from the beach. That he might have left it on the sand by the porch and returned for it was possible—he had had time enough before Thurston searched his room. But Terry thought that most unlikely. He favored the thought that it was planted there.

"Well—what was it doing in your pocket?" the police officer demanded fiercely.

"Was it in my pocket?" Old Martin shook his head. "I don't know about that either—I'll have to ask Mr. Johnstone. I'll say what he says." The old man grinned and smirked and rubbed his hands together—steadily washing them as if with invisible soap.

One of Thurston's great hands shot forward and rested upon the old man's shoulder. His eyes blazed now—fire lit up those cold, hard, green eyes.

"You'll wait to see what Mr. Johnstone has to say about that, will you?" he sneered. "Do you think a murder can be pulled off right under my nose and a man who carried a gun, with the mates of the bullet that was found in Urskine's shoulder still in it, play the baby act with me? You had the gun; you had the opportunity; you were on the beach; and you were fully dressed. Will you talk here or will I drag you where you will?" He shook the old man roughly.

Two hands were suddenly clutching at the Inspector's shoulder, dragging him back. He turned with an oath and faced the blazing eyes of Ardath Johnstone.

"A great hulking brute like you." Brown eyes blazed into green ones. "I don't know what my father's thinking of to stand there and permit it. But you've no right to come bulldozing people around this house just because you fell down on the job we pay you for. I suppose you slept most of the night. Now you bluster and bully and talk big—and—you leave Old Martin alone. Imagine him killing any one! You must be out of your mind to abuse that poor old man."

She stood in front of the old man now. Thurston's eyes rested full upon her—the fire died out of them and the coldness returned.

"I wouldn't hurt him, Miss Ardath." The growl had gone out of the Inspector's voice but the sternness was still there. "I don't think he'd kill any one either—but he knows something—and he sits there with his silly chatter about your father—sits there while the murderer may be escaping." Then turning again to Old Martin, but this time more kindly, "Are you afraid of some one?" he asked.

"I wasn't afraid of him then and I ain't afraid of him now." He hesitated a moment. "Or maybe I am—I don't know for sure. What does Mr. Johnstone say?"

And the Inspector was on the verge of losing his temper again.

"Tell him the truth, Martin." Clarence Johnstone stepped forward and laid a hand upon his shoulder.

"Well, then—" Old Martin spoke out, "I had no gun—but an old rifle. I left that in the boat house. I was sort of protecting the house—and not taking my clothes off." His face cracked into thick crevices. "We're in a house of death. Locked windows and barred doors are useless. You're young men," he nodded first at Terry, then at Inspector Johnstone, "you live in young days—new days. Nixon Carleton is a page from the past. He didn't care for the police then—he don't now. The years have sapped his youth but it don't take strength to stick a knife in a sleeping man, if the cunning and the hatred and the lust for blood is there. I told him—and I tell him again," he pointed a bony finger at Terry, "you kill Nixon Carleton and you'll kill the spirit that makes for blood and death. There's heart throbs and misunderstanding and hatred breeding between those that should love. It's written on Clarence Johnstone's face. It's written on the face of Florence. It's gripping and clutching at dead, dry bones back in a California grave." His eyes brightened now and he sat the straighter upon the end of his chair. "And I tell you, you've only seen the beginning. There's the cry of vengeance and the cry of blood and the cry of money—and the three are one. For he ain't forgotten, and I ain't forgotten—" a sudden pause. "Leastwise, I don't think I've forgotten—but I'll see what Mr. Johnstone has to say." And he flopped back in his chair again and started rubbing those old hands over and over.

Inspector Thurston shifted from one foot to the other. It was useless to question Old Martin, and it was useless to analyze his actions and fit suspicion into his attitude or words. With the normal person—yes, Terry thought; but with Old Martin— Terry shrugged his shoulders. To try and figure out what was back in that queer old head was impossible. Stupid or shrewd, it made little difference. He was forever falling back on his hands and "I'll see what Mr. Johnstone has to say." No—Terry wasn't going to waste time on Old Martin. Inspector Thurston had certainly not appeared to advantage. Ardath's eyes had blazed into his—and her words— Terry gulped. Ardath's words had a double punch to them; certainly they were not favorable to Terry either. And Terry turned toward the door where Ardath had been standing.

Ardath was gone.

24

Where Was Ardath Johnstone?

THERE WAS NO reason for Terry to be alarmed; yet he was—greatly so. He understood now why surgeons never operate upon their relatives; detectives, too, should keep away from cases where such a personal interest is involved. He couldn't think clearly in this case. The attempt to carry Ardath off in the big black sedan had come early in the game and dimmed his mental vision of events. He wasn't a marrying man. Terry knew that—always thought that; he thought of it now, too. Certainly he wasn't in love. And the thought of being in love wasn't new to him. If he were in love now he had been in love all last summer—through the fall and winter, too. But he had denied any such feeling before and he denied it now. They had been good pals last summer—were still good pals; nothing more.

And here he was! There were clues, many of them—clues that might easily be followed. How quickly his criminally-trained mind would have settled on the one essential thing—and doggedly he would have followed that essential thing to the end. Now what? He hated to admit it even to himself, but he knew the truth. He was afraid to take his guns in his hands, put his nose to the ground and live up to the reputation he had earned. At the end of the road there could be only unhappiness, disillusionment, and even stark tragedy to the girl he—he was just good pals with. And that was the sort of warped mind he had to solve this baffling mystery with.

And back of it all was Nixon Carleton, and a vague idea of some one else—the man in the shadows Harry Urskine had cried out about in the hallway, before he pitched forward into Clarence Johnstone's arms. But there had been no fear of Clarence Johnstone—some one else, who Urskine knew and wished to warn Johnstone against. Or was it just the fancy of a disordered brain—the fear-wracked mind of Harry Urskine? Certainly Clarence Johnstone had not attempted to have his own daughter kidnaped—nor could Florence Johnstone have a hand in such a thing; nor—but some one did. And strange, weird things were happening in this new civilization.

Such were the jumbled thoughts that raced madly through Terry's head as he went in search of Ardath, slipping quietly up the big front stairs and calling her name softly on the landing. But there was no answer. The hushed voices of the servants came to him as he descended the stairs and passed into the dining room. They were even now discussing the murder, and the cook's cracked hysterical voice was raised above the whispers as she called upon her heavenly patrons to strike her dead if Inspector Thurston wasn't a blustering, bullying scoundrel and an eyesore to the fair city of Newton. Never had she been "so sat down upon by a slimy, crawlin'—" and her feeling being superior to her choice of words, she dropped into half-hysterical adjectives again.

There was no reason to be alarmed, Terry told himself—and yet— He hesitated a moment between entering the kitchen and the library. The door to the pantry swung open and Jenkins peered through.

"Oh, Mr. Mack—I don't like to say it—I didn't exactly promise I wouldn't, but I was told not to. Yet, when I think that out there some place is a murderer who—"

"It's about Ardath, Jenkins? Come—she—she didn't go out?" Terry stepped forward and gripped the butler by the shoulder.

"But she did, sir," Jenkins stammered. "She did just that—out in the fog."

"Yes, Jenkins—you should have told me at once. I—but why did she go?" There was no use to bully the man—confuse him by reproaches or threats.

"She went to look for her sister—just a step down by the boat house, and I stood by the door waiting—not watching exactly, sir—one couldn't watch. She has met her sister there before—often, when Miss Ardath stayed out too late and her father was—"

"Yes, yes," Terry cut in hurriedly. "But how long ago did she go out? One minute—five?" It could hardly be more than five, he thought.

"Between that—between one and five—nearer, I can't—" And seeing the white, excited face of Terry, Jenkins stammered, "I didn't know what to do, sir. There'd be the policeman bullying her and me, and maybe Miss Florence—and she told me not to speak. There's strange doings—"

"Yes, Jenkins—and why did you come to me now? But no matter." He pushed by the butler and had reached the pantry door when the voice of Inspector William Thurston spoke behind him.

"Miss Ardath, eh—out on the beach. We'll search the beach together, Mack. Good God—the girl must be crazy!"

"Just a second, now." Inspector Thurston called to Jenkins. "Why did you tell Mr. Mack now, my man—why not sooner—or why at all—did the girl scream?"

"No, sir—oh, no, sir. I'm afraid, sir—a coward, sir—but I'd

of gone to Miss Ardath—I'd of done anything rather than—"

"Never mind that." The dominant chin of the police officer shot forward—his green eyes blazed. "Why did you tell Mr. Mack?"

"No reason, sir—I was afraid—it was so still and weird out there—and the pounding water—and the dead man upstairs—and the one on the beach before. I was just afraid—just afraid," Jenkins stammered.

Terry waited for no more. He passed into the kitchen, through the little huddled mass of servants, and to the back door. It was closing behind him when he heard the Inspector's feet beat across the kitchen; his gruff warning to the servants to stay where they were—and the jerk of the door as Thurston pounded out to his side.

"We'll search the beach together." The Inspector laid a hand upon his shoulder. "It's tough, Mack—oh, don't shake me off; I don't have to have a brick building fall on my head to see how things stand with you. She's a fine girl."

"What—" And that was all Terry said as they reached the gravel walk and hurried along toward the direction of the boat house.

"Your face, man." The Inspector laughed, but there was no mirth behind his chuckle. "White and drawn, and your hand shook. Keep it steady, my boy. If, after all, Johnstone's story is true, you may have to do a trick with one of those guns of yours."

Terry felt a clap on his back and a friendly squeeze to his arm. But he did not speak; he plodded on, unseeingly through the mist. Where was Ardath? How quiet things were as they neared the boat house! Surely she wouldn't venture further along the beach. And what a fool he had been to tell her that Florence was there—and Florence had lied. Ardath had not seen her.

Eerie, weird, uncanny—this staggering through the unseen night. The only guide of the two pair of hurrying feet was the soft crunch of the gravel on the path and the ever steady thud and hiss of the rolling sea. Terry could stand it no longer. What was the use of silence? There was no need to keep Ardath's trip to the beach a secret. The servants knew it—Thurston knew it—by this time Clarence Johnstone and Old Martin knew it. Then why this crunching along the gravel path? Without warning his companion, Terry raised his voice.

"Ardath—" he called shrilly—and again, "Ardath—Ardath!"

"Shs!" Inspector Thurston's startled exclamation came from behind as clutching fingers missed his arm. "If some one wished to strike a blow against Johnstone now, we might rush in and end it all to-night. Didn't they try to kidnap the girl before—won't they try again? Let us go quietly—and maybe through the girl catch them red-handed."

"We'll bait no trap with Ardath Johnstone." Terry turned sharply, startled at the suggestion. There was a ring of anger in his voice. Yet he knew that it was not simply a heartless state-ment—there was a good sound judgment behind it. Terry had often inveigled the enemy into his hands by similar methods. But with Ardath—no; the thing was preposterous. Again his voice cracked and died in the mist.

Inspector Thurston's gruff grunt might have been of dissat-isfaction or of understanding. Terry could not be sure. Just one thing. He had called out—cried Ardath's name over and over, and there was no answer.

In silence the two men walked and ran and stumbled toward the boat house. And then Terry stopped so suddenly that Thurston bumped against him with a curse that died on his lips. Both men stood listening. Was Terry's imagination playing him strange tricks; an imagination that he had thought he did not possess? For it was a nervous, twitching, awesome sort of imagination that swept down and engulfed his mind just as thickly as the mist swept over the sea and engulfed his body.

25

The Card of Death

INSPECTOR THURSTON'S HAND clutched at Terry's shoulder—his heavy breathing hissed in Terry's ear. Neither man spoke; both stood listening; holding their breath as long as possible, then letting it escape in a soft hissing sound. But there were only the mist and the pounding sea and sniffling backwash, followed by the quick breaths and the impatient cautioning of one man to the other.

Both men straightened together. A cry had come; mistily, strangely, muffled through the night. Uncertain at first, as if a hand was held across a mouth, then clear and loud and fearful, like the previous agonized screech of Harry Urskine, came the cry again. This time no hand muffled it—it rang sharply through the fog. It was the cry of a woman.

"Ardath—Ardath!" Terry cried frantically. He was close to the boat house now. Did he see a figure—did he see something that seemed to be floating through the mist? "Ardath—Ardath!" he shouted again.

And this time he got an answer—a little further away, he thought, then nearer as the girl still called in fear and terror. And this time there was a high-pitched note—of hopefulness, Terry thought, as she recognized his voice.

"Terry—Terry!"

And Terry heard no more. Inspector Thurston was talking; shouting in his ear.

"Straight ahead—the other side of the boat house—some one is following her. I'll take the shore side."

Terry gulped something—saw the Inspector's flashlight suddenly sputter into the mist, and clutching at his own light with his left hand and holding a gun in his right, he dashed down to the beach and toward the boat house.

The girl cried out again—Terry answered her as he reached the beach. A man's voice rang out on top of the girl's—very close they were and just the other side of the boat house, Terry thought. The girl screamed once more; no hope in her scream this time. Just a screech of terror.

Terry rounded the boat house, shot his flash forward—and stopped dead. Plainly in the misty light he saw the two figures, struggling; the man's arms were about the girl, one hand over her mouth. And that was all Terry did see—did distinguish in the mist. But that was enough. He didn't dare chance a shot, for as Terry dashed around the corner of the boat house the man's hand was raised, and falling through the air. There was a thud as the heavy object in the man's hand struck the girl— and Terry was upon him.

Terry didn't try to take him prisoner. He didn't thrust his automatic against the man's chest and order him to drop his gun. He might have done this; had time to do this—but he didn't. His light had struck upon an evil face; stubby chin, two slit-like eyes, and thick lips with yellow teeth behind them. The man saw him—saw the flash, for he half turned—bewildered—his mouth hanging open, the gun with which he had struck the girl still clutched in his right hand, and the limp body of Ardath hanging on his arm.

Terry just rushed in, and raising his gun struck, unerringly, viciously, and with all the brute strength and passion that lies buried somewhere in each man. This man had struck Ardath. He wanted to save her, of course—but he forgot that he was a detective; forgot that he was about to make an arrest; forgot that this man might be able to throw valuable light in the blackness of this baffling mystery. In his heart was hatred, vengeance, and the sudden uncontrollable passion that all too often puts the good and honest citizen in the dock for murder.

The man made no sound—just two narrow, staring eyes—a blank and surprised look—and he sunk to the beach without a groan. The girl half fell across his knees.

"All right, Thurston," Terry called hoarsely as he bent forward, his flash upon the white face of the girl. "I got one—and Ardath's all right—thank God." He muttered the last two words to himself.

And there was Ardath, so white and still—with her wet hair streaked across her forehead, her soft, delicate white cheeks smeared with dirt and a tiny streak of blood where sharp dirty fingers had scratched her. Terry had never lost his head before. He was master of himself again though, as he looked down at the sneering, evil features of the man upon the beach. He bent forward, pocketed his flash, but still retaining his gun he placed his arms about Ardath and staggered upright.

There were feet behind him from the same direction that he had come.

"Thurston," he called softly—then louder, and with an anxious note in his voice—"Thurston!" He thought that he could see the figure—at least the outline of it. But it did not move. How still it stood—almost like a queer shadow through the fog—a— And the girl slid from his arms. He knew instinctively, even before the light suddenly spit through the fog and glared into his face. But he knew too late.

"Thurston!" He cried out his warning—shrilly now. Not for himself—for the girl. Thurston had gone the other way, of course. That and a thousand other thoughts crowded through his mind as he jerked up his gun.

He fired once, he thought—but he wasn't sure. At least, he didn't fire at the man. He fired before his gun was up—a hopeless, wild chance that the sudden roar of his gun might startle the other man into a miss. But everything had happened within a split second from the time that flash lit upon his face. There was the roar of a gun—a streak of orange-blue flame through the mist—and a sudden burn about his ear, as if a heated wire had snapped and struck him.

He knew that he was still upon his feet; knew that his fingers had opened, and that his gun had fallen from them. Yet he was helpless to prevent it. The white mist was wet upon his cheeks, the flash was still before him—far distant now and fading into the night. Then the mist rolled from white to black—very black, and his knees began to give, and he sank slowly—knelt so a moment, then rolled upon the beach.

He remembered trying to reach out his hand and touch the girl. He knew that he didn't touch her, but whether or not the muscles of his arms responded to his effort to use it he was not sure. He was slipping toward a vivid blackness—a blackness in which a distant light stood out. A light that grew larger and larger, but which strangely did not seem to hurt his eyes as he stared at it. It was close to his face now and there was something shadowy behind it. He felt something touch his body and sensed the presence of a person. He saw a shadow come before the light and pass across it—saw something gleam, and knew that it was steel—a knife—a two-edged dagger. And his eyes bulged. He tried to lift his hands and grip at the knife, but his hands seemed fastened to his sides, yet he knew that they were not bound—for although he lay like a man in a trance, he knew that seconds only had slipped by since the flash and the shot. His eyes widened, his lips parted—a coated tongue licked at dry lips. The knife had seemed split in two, but now he understood—he saw it plainly. Through the center of that knife was a playing card. The knife turned slightly. He saw the card. It was the three of spades. The knife and the card came lower and lower—then came blackness.

26

Out of the Blackness

THE SEA, DRIVEN by a gale, pounded against the side of the ship; the rail snapped as if it were no stronger than match sticks; the foaming water curled itself into huge, white, hissing peaks and swirled over the ship. And Terry saw the figure; clinging desperately to a log was the white face of a girl. "Ardath! Ardath!" Terry cried aloud, for the white frightened face of the girl seemed to be enveloped in a bright, floating light that hung over the darkened sea just above the girl's face—always above the girl's face, no matter how she and her frail support were tossed about.

Desperately Terry fought to tear himself loose from the cords that bound him to the mast. He struggled frantically but uselessly. Yet in a dazed way he wondered how the girl still lived through the storm—how she was steadily bobbing there before him, always on the crest of a white comber—always in the misty brilliancy that hung above the blackness of the raging sea.

Men called and lights flashed and misty figures seemed to walk upon the waters, and still Terry tore at the bonds that held him. Sometimes he felt that he called out—other times, that his words simply stuck in his throat and rang in his brain rather than his ears. It was maddening—Ardath was being—being—being—

The light hurt his eyes now; something wet ran along the

side of his face and onto his neck. He coughed—struggled once—and sat up. It came back to him now. He was still on the beach beside the boat house and had been unconscious; Ardath was not on the sea, he thought with relief. Then the relief swept quickly to fear again. He had been shot trying to save her—and where was she? Where was the man he had struck, and where was—?

A lantern stood on the beach by his side—a figure was bending over him. He remembered now—the man's hand—the knife—the three of spades. His hand shot up and grasped an arm—and he saw the face that was in the circle of light close to him. It was Old Martin.

"You—you—" Terry clutched at him, gasping for breath.

"Me—yes—Old Martin." The face bobbed up and down, the colorless eyes blinked and danced and stared at him. "I came in time, I did. Thirty years ago I would have held him—but now—he got away—away—"

"Who?" Terry staggered to his feet, thought better of it, and slipped to a sitting position on the beach.

"Him of the knife—I seen it flash toward you—but I didn't know it was you. Not me—" the old man chuckled mirthlessly. "I thought it was Miss Ardath, so I yelled and he jumped. If I knew it was you," Old Martin went on, very deliberately and very slowly, "I'd of let him stick you. Somehow, I ain't the sort of man that wants to die yet. Leastwise, I don't think I do—while Clarence Johnstone lives—and faces it alone."

"Here—give me a hand." Terry clutched at the bony hand Martin extended. "So you'd of let me go—eh, Martin? Why—" Staggering to his feet he leaned heavily upon the old man.

"Mind you, I ain't got nothing against you—not me. But I

ain't called upon to protect you. It ain't right and ain't fair and ain't to be expected. I'm simply telling you so you won't be expecting it another time. You're hired to do things that ain't been done."

"Just what has happened, Martin—and how long have I been lying here?"

"Minutes—many of them—a-clutchin' and a-rollin' and a-moanin' in the sand. And calling too—Ardath, it was, and—" the old man broke off suddenly—clutched at his throat— staggered back a bit. "Ardath—Ardath—" he gasped, "what's become of her—what's become of her?" He turned suddenly and fled—stumbling through the mist.

There were other voices calling, a light or two waving dully in the fog—and once Terry thought that he heard a shot. He staggered to the boat house and leaned against it, breathing heavily. What of Ardath? And what of Inspector Thurston? And what of his own flash? He remembered it then. It was still in his pocket.

A careful search of the ground and he found his pistol in the sand. He turned now; a light was coming—feet were on the gravel path—a voice called—fearful, husky. But he recognized it. It was Jenkins, the butler.

"Jenkins—Jenkins—" Terry called softly.

The light came nearer and Terry stepped toward it. His feet, which had seemed so heavy, now seemed light. He didn't speak again now Jenkins was near him. In a dazed way he allowed the man to lead him to the house.

Jenkins helped Terry wash the wound along the side of his head. Nothing to be alarmed at in that, Terry knew—the flying lead had left a nasty scar along the side of his head just above the ear—nothing more. Like a blow on the head, Terry thought. Although his head throbbed the more, Terry nodded his approval. He had feared he would be out of the running for some time.

But Jenkins could give him little information. He had stood at the back door after Terry and Thurston left the house.

"Then Mr. Johnstone and Old Martin came," Jenkins went on. "I told them, of course, and they stood with me. But finally Old Martin slipped out, and though Mr. Johnstone called him back, I heard his feet beat for a moment on the gravel—then die away, as if he stopped or sought the sand. There was a cry and shots, and grabbing up the lantern I had lighted I ran down toward the boat house. Mr. Johnstone—he came too, for a little way at least. But there was running and calling— and I got confused—and Mr. Johnstone—" Jenkins paused a moment—then, "I haven't seen him since. What's happened?"

"That," said Terry, "we will soon find out." He turned from Jenkins, and passing down the stairs sought the front door. What was he doing in the house anyway? His place was out there with the others—searching for—and again all his fears for Ardath were renewed.

But he stepped to the big front door. Feet were beating across the porch—Clarence Johnstone and Inspector Thurston entered. Thurston simply nodded to Terry as he led Johnstone across the room and pushed him gently into a chair. The old man sat there with his head buried in his hands. He didn't look up and he didn't speak; but there was a moaning, sobbing sort of sigh as he rocked his body back and forth.

"Do what you can for him," Thurston said gruffly. "The girl's gone—I saw the car and fired at it. I'll do some telephoning now."

And Terry heard him give his orders in quick, sharp sentences. Every city within miles would be watched.

"It's a big car, Lieutenant," Thurston finished. "And it carried a New York license, though that may be changed down the road. And tell the boys to keep an eye on strangers and pick up any that don't look good, and hold them for me if they can't talk straight. The doctor and Chief should be out here any minute. I rang them up before, about Urskine—and above everything, look for a short stocky man with a bullet in him. I'm sure I winged one of them."

"And now," said Inspector Thurston, turning to Terry, "what about you? You got nipped, eh?" He looked at the bandage about Terry's head.

"Nothing to speak of." Terry dismissed his wound with a wave of his hand. Then he told Thurston of his experience—and the shot—and the disappearance of the man he had knocked down—and about Ardath. When he spoke of the shadowy form above him and the knife, and the three of spades, the Inspector whistled softly.

"I heard the shots," Thurston nodded, "and I thought you'd explain them later. I always heard you were quick with a gun and I thought—" Was there just a touch of sarcasm in his voice—but he went on quickly. "Your thoughts were of the girl—mine of those who sought her and killed Urskine. Two lights of a car flashed up in the road and I thought to kill two birds with one stone. If you didn't rescue the girl—which seemed certain, then I'd save her anyway by getting those in the car. And I nearly got them too." He stopped and stroked his chin. "But how they got the girl away—and the man you struck! Man—they may be on the beach yet."

Terry was on his way to the door at once, but Thurston stopped him.

"No need." He raised his hand. Both men listened. There was the purr of a motor, the sudden screech of brakes. "That'll be the Chief," said Thurston. "We'll comb the beach for miles."

After that things happened. Half a dozen policemen were in and out of the house almost at once, for Inspector Thurston's orders were quick and thorough.

Chief Robinson, of the Newton police force, proved a mild-mannered man close to sixty years of age. As soon as the police were out of the house and the doctor was in the room with the dead Urskine, Inspector Thurston broke into his story. He omitted no detail—all that Clarence Johnstone had told him went into the surprised ears of the Chief.

"And there it is," Thurston concluded. "On top of Mr. Johnstone's story comes the murder of Urskine and the abduction of his daughter, Ardath. It's a deep game—what are you going to do? You can't keep the murder from the papers."

"What do you advise?" The mild blue eyes of the Chief rested doubtfully and uncertainly upon his Inspector.

"Well—" Thurston hesitated. "You haven't got enough evidence to make an arrest. How much of the truth we are hearing is purely speculative. Old Martin's a fool. Clarence Johnstone's half mad with grief. Florence Johnstone may be ripe for a pinch, but I'd sleep on that. For, after all, we can only base our suspicions through her actions and the vengeance and hatred of a woman wronged, or who thinks she's wronged. My advice is to sit tight. We're not obliged to take the world into our confidence. It's a bad game."

"Certainly—that's the very thing, Thurston. Mr. Johnstone

is a staunch citizen and a friend of the commissioner. We must proceed most carefully. I was tempted to hold him, but now that you advise otherwise—"

"I advise nothing." Thurston's lips curled. "When it's all over there'll be a dirty mess. Let us not make it worse. But the responsibility rests on your shoulders—unless—" cold, green eyes settled upon the Chief.

"Unless—yes, Thurston," the Chief encouraged.

"You might turn the whole case over to me—let me handle it in my way. If you'll give me a free hand, I'll accept all the responsibility."

"That's like you, Thurston." The Chief rose and patted his Inspector on the back. "And I'm sure you'll be most successful. You've cleaned the crooks out of Newton—nothing left but bootleggers—and the people want them." The Chief's smile was an oily one—a political one. "Still, Thurston, your responsibility is after all simply a moral one. The commissioner will look to me; the people will look to me. It's like you—straight and forward, with the push and go of a vigorous officer. But I can't shift my burden."

"You can." Thurston's hand crashed down on the table. "I sat beside the door of a room while a man was murdered, and Ardath Johnstone was whisked away right under my official nose, so to speak. I couldn't prevent it, of course, but people won't see it that way. You can duck the responsibility. If I fail in the case, I'm out—out after twenty years of service—you can make me the goat. And," he leaned far across the table, "there's that other case, which makes necessary identification of Albert Nobel, in Montreal. Why not run up to Canada and leave things here in my hands? I'd welcome the chance."

"Of course I should be there." The Chief spoke half to himself. Politics were politics, and he didn't relish the idea of facing the reporters with the story of Urskine's murder while a police inspector guarded him. "You're competent—better than I am for this sort of work," the Chief went on. "But there is no need of your paying the price of—an error in judgment. I couldn't think—"

"You won't need to think." Thurston set his jaw tightly. "I'll solve this crime. I'll arrest the guilty party. If I fail—you'll have my resignation in twenty-four hours." He raised his hand when the Chief would have spoken. "No—I've got my pride," he said. "I won't be the laughingstock of the town."

Terry Mack didn't wait for them to settle things. He saw the situation clearly enough. The Chief was an old man. Politics kept him in office. He would be quite willing to sacrifice a subordinate for his own protection. It was an old game to Terry. Thurston hoped for success; the wily Chief foresaw the newspaper account of the murder. The commissioner was a great friend of Clarence Johnstone. So Terry figured it out: Thurston would like to have the Chief's job some day; and the Chief was not averse to Thurston landing on the rocks.

But they eyed Terry none too friendly as their heads came together, and Terry left the room. Not that he was particular about listening to private conversation—but he had seen Old Martin pass through the hall. And he might as well leave before there was a request that he absent himself.

27

A Real Clue At Last

CLARENCE JOHNSTONE WAS not in the hall now; Old Martin was already on the stairs, mumbling to himself. Terry overtook Martin halfway up.

But the old man was worse than usual. Terry wasn't going to waste his time questioning him. He was going to warn him— that was all. If the Chief of Police left Newton on other business Old Martin would come in for some rough treatment.

"I'll see Mr. Johnstone and what he has—" Old Martin started when Terry stopped him.

"I'm not going to question you, Martin." Terry shook him by the shoulder. "If you know anything, you better tell me; a friend of Mr. Johnstone; a friend of Ardath; perhaps even a friend of yours. Inspector Thurston will be asking you questions—and he'll find means to make you talk."

"Me—" The old man laughed; a grating, gurgling laugh— like a shovel scraping across dry pavement. "I don't know nothin' only what I've told. He's the devil himself, this Nixon Carleton—but Mr. Johnstone—"

And Terry left him. The door of Clarence Johnstone's room was closed. Hand on knob, Terry hesitated. Sobs came from behind that door—sobs that were not Clarence Johnstone's. It was the soft crying of a woman. Not Ardath, surely. Terry's heart gave a bound—and slumped back with a jar again. The woman was speaking—brokenly; too low for him to understand the words, but the tone of the voice was clear enough. It was Florence Johnstone. Florence, who had left the house a half hour before. Florence, who had been in the house when Harry Urskine was murdered. Florence, who had come because of fear that something might happen to Ardath. Florence, who had lied to him about seeing Ardath. And it was Florence that Ardath had gone out in the fog to find.

Should he knock, or burst into the room? The voice of Clarence Johnstone came to him—unsteady—gulping. What could those two be talking over? Terry pressed his shoulder against the door, spun the knob, and threw his weight against it. But it was not locked. He was hurled almost headlong into the room, but regained his balance and stood looking in unconcealed amazement at the scene before him.

Clarence Johnstone sat in a rocker. Florence knelt at his feet, with her head upon his knees, crying softly. And the adopted father was patting her head and trying to comfort her. Two white, frightened, tear-stained faces jerked up at Terry's sudden entrance.

"Well," said Terry—and "well," again. He could think of nothing else to say.

"I've been wrong—I've been a bad woman." Florence Johnstone struggled to her feet. "He brought me up—cared for me as if I were his own child, and I—I—"

"No, no." Clarence Johnstone stroked the black hair. "I never understood her. I've let her believe that she would be rich. Scheming, selfish, vengeful people have put thoughts into her head. And, poor child—poor, motherless, fatherless child, I—"

Terry understood. A common sorrow had united them. Both thought of Ardath. There was the same love, the same affection, the same devotion—unless— Was it possible that one of these two minds was blinded by a love for Ardath, and played upon by the other? Was the common sorrow clever acting by one? Or were there three in that sorrow—that devotion—was Terry, too, swept away by an overpowering—well—at least, fear of what might happen to Ardath? He didn't know. At the least he felt that the wrong one of these two had done the other was forgotten for the time being.

The woman came to her feet and faced Terry. She did not wipe her eyes; just regarded him steadily through the misty lids.

"I want to speak to you, Mr. Mack—at once, alone," she said calmly. There was no sob in her voice, just a cracked note at the end of her speech—as if something stuck in her throat.

"Yes—"Terry nodded. He wanted to speak to her, too. What would she tell him now? The truth, or more lies?

Clarence Johnstone watched them leave, his eyes staring after them until Terry swung the door shut. Florence Johnstone led Terry down the narrow hall, stopped before a door and swung it open.

"My room, before," she explained. "And my room again—now," she added.

Terry had hardly shut the door before she turned and started to talk.

"What I have told you was the truth as I saw it—then. But now I can't believe that Mr. Johnstone would really, knowingly rob me—or any one else."

"But the letters?" Terry asked. He was thinking of that letter Florence had shown him, which spoke of a vast fortune.

"I shall destroy that. It was forged."

"Yes," said Terry. But he knew that that third letter was not forged.

"My purpose here is to save Ardath—from what, I don't know. Mr. Johnstone thinks that she is in the hands of Nixon Carleton, and that he will shortly demand money. I have come to you because I can no longer believe that Doctor Corellie's interest in me is purely one of friendship. May I tell you just what I heard to-night—what made me come here?"

"Go on." Terry watched her closely. Was she sincere? Was her love for Ardath causing her to abandon the hope of receiving her "rightful inheritance?"

"Last night," she closed her eyes while she talked, "I could not sleep. Dreams of Ardath—thoughts of her father—the night when I was a child with diphtheria and he watched by my bedside! And I thought of the black sedan and the two men who attempted to carry Ardath away in it. I dressed and went to Doctor Corellie. There was a light in his study. I thought that I saw the shadow of two men on the shades. I turned toward the little office door, then stopped and listened. The window was open—clearly came the one word "forgery." It was an excited voice, and the window was closed almost at once."

She hesitated a moment, then went on.

"I tried to listen but heard no more. So I slipped along the little alley to the office door. Doctor Corellie and I have been good friends. I often used his office when he was helping me to prove—well, things against Mr. Johnstone. So I had a key, and opening the door went cautiously along the hallway until I reached the inner door. It was closed, but I heard bits of a conversation. Doctor Corellie was giving orders to another.

" 'Be at the South Newton station to-morrow night,' he said. 'He will wear a red rose and carry a lighted cigar in his left hand. You are to take him directly to the house.'

"The man made some objection and Doctor Corellie went on. 'That makes no difference. I don't know him; no one at the house knows him. It is better so. But Nixon has been in communication with him and trusts him.'"

"Nixon, eh?" Terry's eyebrows went up.

"I am giving the conversation to you word for word. Doctor Corellie has been most kind and thoughtful of me. But that is what I heard. If it is true that there is such a person as Nixon Carleton, and he knows where Ardath is, I thought maybe this man who will be at the South Newton station might lead you to Ardath."

"Why didn't you tell me when you were here before?" Terry demanded.

"Because Ardath was safe. I didn't understand—and don't yet. But Nixon Carleton knew my father—I thought perhaps it was some evidence that would help me. I am only telling you what I heard. Afterward, when I left here and heard the screams and the shots, and Mr. Johnstone told me that Ardath was gone, I decided to speak out."

For a minute or two Terry didn't speak. How much of what the girl told him was true? Or was it all lies? Suddenly he shot his question at her.

"You say you saw Ardath to-night when you were here. What did you say to her?" And he watched her closely while she answered.

"I didn't say anything. She was asleep, and I left. I was satisfied that she was all right. I didn't wake her."

Terry sucked in a deep breath. That statement at least agreed with Ardath's—and after all Florence Johnstone had not told him that she had talked with Ardath; simply that she saw her.

"Can't you do something?" Florence clutched Terry frantically by the shoulders. "For the first time I distrust the doctor. It was he who introduced me to Darrow, who told me the story of my father's wealth, and produced that letter. Oh—can't you do something to save Ardath?"

"Did you hear anything else—the name of the man who was to be at the South Newton station?"

"Yes—didn't I tell you that?" She thought a moment. "It was Abe Sterns."

"Abe Sterns!" Terry gasped. For "Abe Sterns" was the name he had seen on the fragment of the letter in the pocket of the man he had searched in the tenement room, on Sixth Avenue, New York City.

28

At the Deserted Station

TERRY MACK WAS well aware of the danger he faced when he sought the South Newton station just at nightfall. Florence Johnstone had been unable to furnish him with any time of this unknown stranger's arrival. It might be a trap. Very well, he was willing to chance it. At least, he would be doing something. He would welcome any trap which might lead him to Ardath—and trust to his resources to get himself out of it.

He had not mentioned Florence's story to Inspector Thurston, and had cautioned her not to speak of what she told him. The police would not make a good reception committee. He much preferred to watch the arrival of this Abe Sterns alone. He would recognize him as well as the other chap—the red rose and the cigar in the left hand—a double identity.

And who was the man who was to meet this Abe Sterns? Terry was at a disadvantage there? The man might know him, and Terry not know the man. It was certain that this Abe Sterns was being met for one purpose only—that purpose was to be taken some place—some place that this Abe Sterns didn't know the location of. If he knew the location, what was the necessity of having some one meet him?

Terry loitered near the station. A light burned at one end of the platform, facing the tracks. There was another light within, but the station door was locked and the agent had left for the night. On the road that faced the beach, two cars with uniformed chauffeurs waited. The men knew each other and chatted. A train came in and brought the owners of both cars. The cars departed—the station was deserted.

Terry consulted his watch and a time table. It was 10:57. The last train to stop at South Newton had come and gone. There was none other that night. Had Florence lied to him? Or was the deserted station to serve as a rendezvous? Even a stranger would have little difficulty in finding it without questioning any one. There were boxes and a few crates at one end of the platform and Terry made himself fairly comfortable. Occasionally he stretched himself, sought the darkness, and made his way cautiously around the station.

He had to give the station a wide berth, for the fog had blown out to sea on the early morning breeze and the night was fairly bright. There was another bad break, Terry thought. If it had been clear last night and foggy to-night! But it wasn't. He shrugged his shoulders and for the fifth time made the rounds of the station. It was close to eleven-thirty.

Fifteen minutes more and Terry began to suspect that he was the victim of—well, a plot. Hardly a trap, for he had been there since eight o'clock and nothing had happened to him. But why get him away from Shadow Lawn now that Ardath had been carried oil? Inspector Thurston would be there. No—nothing more disastrous could happen at Shadow Lawn. He thought of his duty to his client, Clarence Johnstone, but dismissed such thoughts at once. He was thinking only of Ardath.

It was a fool trip, anyway, he thought. How could this man lead him to Ardath? If Florence Johnstone could be believed, this Abe Sterns was a stranger and—

Terry straightened. Footsteps—feet that crunched along in

cinders. Cinders! Yes, some one was coming down the track from the direction of Newton. Terry slunk in the darkness of the station and waited. Feet beat, sometimes on the ties, sometimes on the cinders—then he made out a figure that turned, sought the platform, and pounded across it toward the light. Cautiously Terry slipped along the side of the station and peered around the corner.

This was the expected stranger, all right. Abe Sterns. He was a tall, well-dressed man with none of the features that mark the criminal—at least, the thugs of the underworld. Just his nervous, shifty bearing as he swung from side to side. But he stood beneath the light. In his left hand was a cigar, on his coat a red rose.

And that was enough for Terry. For the first time he felt that he was getting the breaks. The stranger had arrived first. His luck was turning. He'd take advantage of it. Slipping his gun from his hip to his overcoat pocket with his left hand and clutching it tightly, Terry stepped onto the platform and walked toward the stranger.

"Early," said Terry, as he smilingly extended his right hand to the man.

The man eyed him a moment, keen sharp eyes running from his head to his feet in a split second. His face blanched slightly beneath the light. He started to speak, hesitated, then lowered his hand—and Terry watched it creep toward his pocket.

"Yes, I am early." But the stranger's hand slipped beneath his coat.

And Terry knew that in his greeting he had erred. The stranger was to carry a cigar in his left hand, and sport a red rose in his lapel. But what of the man who was to meet him?

There was to be something of identification there, too, Terry thought. The sudden drawing up of the man's lips and the lowering of a hand that unquestionably sought a gun was enough for Terry.

Terry's extended right hand closed suddenly into a fist and shot forward. There was strength behind that blow and Terry knew it. The stranger knew it, too, as he sagged at the knees and half raised his hand. A moment later he was sitting on the platform and staring into the mouth of Terry's automatic.

"If your digestion isn't good—don't make a sound. You'll be eating lead pellets if you do." There was a certain humor in Terry's voice but a grim sort of humor, which the stranger understood, for he remained motionless. Finally, he whispered:

"Copper, eh? Well, you've got nothing on me. I—"

"Enough." Terry knelt beside the man and went to work. He jerked the man's hands behind his back and slipped handcuffs over his wrists. Then he bound his legs and gagged him. It all took but a few minutes, and though Terry worked quickly he made a thorough job of it. Could he get his work completed before the other man showed up?

With the man lying secure and helpless at his feet, Terry gave his attention to the station window above them. It was locked. Knocking out a bit of glass with the butt of his gun, he reached in, and slipping the catch, pushed up the window.

It was hard work after that—the man was heavy and the window was not overlarge. But with a few prods of his gun, and whispered threats, he got the bound man standing erect before the window. Two minutes later the prisoner dropped to the floor within with a dull thud.

Terry listened. Not a sound about the station—no hum of

a car along the road. He'd have time to complete his job. If he was going to pose as this stranger he didn't want the station agent finding him and setting up a hue and cry that would alarm the whole neighborhood in the morning, and start the newspapers off with a front-page story.

For Terry didn't know how long his job was going to take. He would impersonate this Abe Sterns. The man who came to meet him might spot the whole game, but the chances were he wouldn't. Nixon Carleton might be suspicious, but Terry didn't care about that. Once he was in the same house with Ardath, that would be enough. But perhaps he would be taken some place else for the night—or perhaps the girl wouldn't be at the house where he was taken. He wanted the identity of his prisoner kept secret as long as possible.

With that thought in mind Terry climbed through the station window, and writing a short note, pinned it on the bound man's chest. It read simply:

"To the Station Agent:

"Turn this man over to Inspector William Thurston and keep quiet. If you follow these orders there'll be a hundred dollars in it for you.

"To Inspector Thurston:

"Don't let the capture of this man leak out until you hear from me.

"Terry Mack."

29

In the House of the Enemy

THAT DONE, TERRY climbed out the window and took up his position under the lamp. There was a cigar in his left hand and a red rose in his lapel. The contents of his prisoner's pockets had been transferred to his own.

Five minutes later the hum of a motor came faintly to his ears. He thought that he heard the distant screech of a brake, but could not be sure. There was no further hum of the motor, however, and Terry waited. He felt better than he had felt since first arriving at South Newton. For the first time he was going into action.

And Terry turned suddenly. It was with an effort that he kept from clutching at his gun. The man had appeared so suddenly out of the darkness. Without a sound his rubber-soled shoes were slipping over the boards as the figure approached the light. In his left hand he carried a cigar, in his coat lapel was a white carnation. As he came under the light Terry saw an evil, grinning, sour countenance, as the man twisted his thick lips into a smile.

"Abe Sterns, eh?" A rough hand went into Terry's. "Let's move along—blew a tire coming down the road. I'm Drake—Happy Drake."

"Right," said Terry, as he grasped that knotty hand And that was all he did say. Terry grinned into that evil face—a face that was unfamiliar, yet the face of a common thug. A tire had blown out down the road! The breaks were coming his way at last.

"We'll beat it along." Drake clutched him by the arm and they passed down the platform and so to the road. "I left the car back a bit."

In silence the two men plodded along. Drake wanted to speak, but hesitated. Terry feared he'd make a break. When they reached the car and Terry had climbed in beside the man, Drake spoke again.

"You look like a good skate." He glanced sideways up at him. "Silent and smart lookin'. You'd make a generous handout to a bloat what tipped you off to a piece of change, eh?" Lips turned up at the corner and small eyes grew narrower.

"Right!" said Terry.

"I'll chance spillin' ya some stuff." The man called Drake jerked the car into gear and started slowly down the road. "Things have picked up some since you started. It ain't just slipping the boys out of the country on your forged passports. Don't let Nixon pull the friendly hand stuff on ya and hand you a few hundred berries. Hold out for big jack—and slip a mitful of yellow boys to me for putting you wise."

"Wise to what?" Terry chanced that.

"To the lay." The other stepped on the gas a bit, then slowed down. "Nixon's a bum," he said contemptuously. "It's the guy behind him—they fastened onto a dame and expect to shake down her old man for close to half a million. They ain't foolin' me none—not Happy Drake. I'll holler for my share—if I only knew when the break'll come. But they'll slip the country on your tickets." Then suddenly, "You've got the passports with you, eh?"

"Things are arranged," said Terry, carefully. He sized this man up as a cheap gunman, perhaps one of the pair who had attempted to kidnap Ardath in the black sedan. But his mission was partly explained at least. He was to bring passports. Did he have them? He didn't know just what was in that bulky leather wallet that was now in his inside pocket.

"You don't know the big gun?" Drake asked suddenly. "The man in the shadows?"

"No," said Terry. "Who is he?"

Drake laughed contemptuously.

"Ah!" he said. "Who is he? Maybe it's better I don't know. Darrow knew, and—" He stopped suddenly and spat out into the road. "We'll be there in a minute—Nixon's pacing the house—he ain't got no guts, has Nixon Carleton."

"The girl's at the house, eh?" Terry asked, without looking at the driver.

"Lay off 'a that stuff," Drake sneered. "I don't know. I've tipped you a mouthful—you should slip me all you get above double your price." Then in a half-threatening voice, "I'll know, too."

"I won't forget you," Terry promised. And he meant it. He smiled in the darkness. Would Ardath be at the house—the house of Nixon Carleton?

It was through a lonely stretch of sand and bush that Drake drove the car. Less than five miles from Shadow Lawn, Terry thought, as they approached the big bleak-looking house. Not a light shone through the windows—not a sound as the car bounced into the busted shed that served as a garage.

Happy Drake slouched across the sand to the rear door and knocked upon it; one—four, and one again. The door opened almost at once. A white hand beckoned from the darkness, then rested on Terry's shoulder.

"You're Abe Sterns—come in—you wait outside, Drake."

"Not me—" Drake cleared his throat and his feet shuffled upon the wooden porch. "Things is nearin' the end, Nixon. I ain't to be forgotten. I may have to skip too. I—" He shoved a foot in the door that Nixon was closing on him after Terry's entrance.

"You will be remembered." Nixon Carleton spoke in the darkness. "It's the orders of the Chief. He may be here any moment. It's best to obey his orders. Darrow didn't."

The man on the porch slunk back.

"I'll be in the shack," he said sullenly, and the door closed.

"Upstairs, Mr. Sterns—upstairs." Terry heard the squeaky, high-pitched, excited voice. "The passports—you've got them?" And he directed Terry by the flash which splashed a light upon wooden steps leading from the kitchen.

Terry did not speak until they were in the room above. He took the seat beneath the light, and Nixon sat in the shadows. He chuckled as Terry slipped back into the soft recess of the great overstuffed chair.

"It's odd to watch you like that," Nixon said. "I sit there and he stands here—and I never see him. But he heard of you and put the thought into my head." An old face leaned out of the darkness. "You know your mission—and the price you're to get. But you don't look like him—the description of him—Abe Sterns. I thought he was an older man. I—"

Was his identity to be discovered so early. Terry's hand, too, slipped behind him in the chair, felt of the great cushion and the ample space between it and the back of the chair. But he was not toying in that great crevice; he was feeling for his gun—just as he thought that Nixon Carleton was feeling for his.

He had time to draw and shoot, but what good would that do? He had no proof that Ardath was there. Indeed, it seemed impossible that they would dare to hide her so close to Newton, with Inspector Thurston's men out hunting the whole beach and surrounding country. But he could not see just what Nixon Carleton was doing.

"I am not Abe Sterns." Terry spoke slowly and calmly. "He couldn't come—but I've brought them."

"You've brought the passports, eh? Let me see them." And when Terry hesitated, "It would be bad for you, my friend, if you had not brought them—very bad, indeed. You think you have nothing to fear in me—well, perhaps not. But you will sit in that chair later and see him—the Chief." The voice seemed to be lower now, and Terry could no longer see the man's face.

"Who is this 'Chief'?" he asked.

"The Chief," said Nixon Carleton, his voice coming from one side of the room now, "is the man who will question you—the man in the shadows, and—" He broke off, chuckling softly.

Was this Nixon Carleton crazy, Terry wondered. His voice was taking on a singsong note. Terry's head came erect. Another voice spoke suddenly; a queer, grating voice, with a metallic ring in it. The voice came from behind Terry—deep, guttural, ominous.

"I am the man in the shadows," it said—paused—then, "And you have very nicely fallen into my trap, Mr. Terry Mack—detective and two-gun man."

Terry half jumped to his feet, then sank back in the chair

again. Something hard and cold was pressed against the back of his neck. He didn't need any one to tell him that it was the cold round nose of a large revolver.

"And now, my dear friend, Nixon Carleton," the metallic voice went on, "you may search this man." And as Nixon Carleton came toward Terry, the man in the shadows continued in that monotonous voice. "After all, how simple and childish is the mind of man. It was only necessary, Nixon, to bait the trap with a bit of lace. In this case that bit of lace was Miss Ardath Johnstone."

Nixon Carleton completed his search, laying the contents of Terry's pocket upon the table.

"What, only one gun!" The voice from the darkness came again. "Why, I thought Mr. Mack prided himself on the use of two—but no matter." There was a click and Terry's wrists were snapped into handcuffs, behind him.

Terry had but one thought. What of Ardath? That Florence Johnstone had betrayed him into the hands of the enemy did not matter. But what of Ardath now?

30

A Demand For Money

CLARENCE JOHNSTONE DROPPED the phone and tore his hair.

"It was Ardath's voice," he screamed. "They are going to torture her. And Nixon Carleton; I knew his voice after all these years. Where is Mack? Where is Thurston? Oh, my God—my God! Let him take all I have but give back my—" and dropping into a chair Clarence Johnstone sunk his head in his hands, swaying back and forth.

It was Old Martin who tried to comfort him. And it was Florence Johnstone who ran screaming into the night for one of the two policemen who watched outside the house.

"You call the Inspector's house," a policeman advised her. "He's had little sleep and may be catching a few winks."

Florence dashed inside. Jenkins passed her in the hall with a bottle and a tumbler in his hand. Clarence Johnstone was stretched out on the cot, breathing heavily. For the moment Florence forgot to call the Inspector. When she thought of it again nearly ten minutes had passed. She tried to pull herself together. She knew the Inspector's number—had been told to call him up if anything happened. Now—she dashed toward the phone. It was ringing when she reached it.

"Yes, yes," she said hastily.

"You tried to get me?" It was the voice of Inspector Thurston that came over the wire. "I thought I heard the phone ringing."

"Yes, yes—I want you," she cried. "We need you—Father has heard from Ardath—it's terrible—come at once." She jammed up the receiver. It wasn't until then that she realized that she had spoken of Mr. Johnstone as "father" and that she had not tried to get Inspector Thurston on the wire.

It was close to half an hour before the Inspector reached the house. He ignored Florence and Old Martin and went straight to the prostrate form of Clarence Johnstone.

"Come—brace up and tell me all about it." Inspector Thurston leaned over and looked down into that white face.

Clarence Johnstone gasped, tried twice, and finally sat up.

"It was her voice," he said huskily. "And the voice of Nixon Carleton. She cried out in pain, and I— Oh, my child, my child!"

"He demanded money—was that it?" the Inspector insisted.

"Yes, yes," Clarence Johnstone whispered—then almost shouted, "and he shall have it—I tell you he shall have it. You have failed me—Mack has failed me. I will pay—I will pay. It was Nixon Carleton, without a doubt. He would take pleasure in hurting my girl—" He chuckled like a madman when he spoke. "I shall pay at once."

"How much does he ask?"

"One hundred thousand dollars for the safe return of Ardath."

"And how does he guarantee that safe return? Don't carry on like this, Mr. Johnstone. I'm not trying to alarm you—only help you. We must go cautiously. While he is without money he—he—"

"Won't kill her—won't kill her," Johnstone cut in in a high-pitched voice. "But he'll— No—he shall have the money. I can raise it at the bank."

"And where is this money to be delivered?"

Both Old Martin and Florence Johnstone leaned forward—and even Jenkins, the butler, turned from the table when Clarence Johnstone answered.

"To-morrow morning—ten o'clock—buried a half mile down the beach—there is to be a stick with a handkerchief on it above the spot."

"Good." The Inspector nodded. "I think that I know the spot—there is a place to hide in the bushes not a hundred yards away. We can watch him—broad daylight, too. It will be easy to bury a dummy box."

"No—no—I shall take no chances. My daughter—"

Inspector Thurston held a hand up for silence.

"Very well," he said. "We shall plant the actual money." Now—" he turned upon the three who were close to the couch, "out of the room—all of you. Come, Jenkins; come, Miss Johnstone—and you, too, Martin."

Jenkins hurried from the room. Florence Johnstone hesitated, then followed Jenkins. Old Martin stood in the doorway rubbing his hands.

"Get out!" the Inspector ordered.

"Thirty years I've stood by him, and more. I have a right now—"

"Out—" Inspector Thurston advanced threateningly and Old Martin backed into the hall.

Closing the door and locking it the police officer turned again to Clarence Johnstone.

"It's time you listened to me," he said. "What you plan to do, Mr. Johnstone, is to turn one hundred thousand dollars over to this man. You are a rich man. I do not begrudge your right to pay this sum if you were assured of your daughter's safety. But after that money is taken there will be more wanted. Your daughter will not be returned. Why should they give her up for one hundred thousand if they can have two? And why again should he give her up at all if as you believe he hates you and thinks of vengeance?"

Clarence Johnstone groaned aloud, but he nodded. He felt that Inspector Thurston spoke the truth.

"Now I have a plan. Murder was committed in this house. I believe, Mr. Johnstone, that some one within this house was helpful in that crime. It may be one of the servants, though I doubt it. It may be Old Martin. It might even be your adopted daughter, Florence. It might be none of them. But we must not take a chance this time. Not because of the money but because of your daughter. And we dare not bury a dummy package, for fear perhaps one that I have mentioned will let the enemy know.

"Here's the idea—we'll hide in that clump of bushes—"

"But Nixon Carleton said that if any one watched the money will not be taken, and Ardath will suffer. That's why it's done in daylight, so no one can hide in the darkness. And I can't believe that Old Martin or—"

"Don't believe that, but we must take no chances. No one will know that we shall watch in the bush. Only you and I shall know—others in the house may see us place the money in a box; Old Martin and Miss Florence will be with us when we stick it in the sand. Then only will we tell them that we shall hide in the bush, and we'll take them with us. Jenkins too, for he has heard of the plan. So—we'll take prisoner the one who comes for the money."

"But that will do no good. Nixon—"

"It will do good." Thurston's jaws set tightly. "I will save your daughter, Mr. Johnstone. The man we take will talk. Oh, don't shake your head. I'm in full charge on this case. Nixon Carleton would torture your girl, would he—well, I'll show them that two can play at that game. One-half hour after we have the man that comes for that money, I shall know where Nixon Carleton is, and where Ardath is. I shouldn't tell you this. I hope you won't speak of it afterward. But it's done in police circles every day. I want to relieve your mind."

"But the man who comes for it may be simply a messenger— one who knows nothing."

"That's what he'll tell me at first." Thurston nodded. "They all do. But strangers are not trusted with one hundred thousand dollars. No—one who is greatly interested and high up in this scheme will come for the money."

"I don't know, I don't know." Clarence Johnstone rubbed a hand across his forehead. "But I shall do as you say—and hope."

"That's the spirit." Inspector Thurston patted him on the back. "Now—where's Mack?"

"Mr. Mack—has— Well, he went out last night and has not come back. I am worried about him."

"Probably on some clue or other." Thurston nodded. "I haven't got much use for these private detectives, Mr. Johnstone—but Mack struck me as a chap well able to take care of himself—don't worry about him. I— There's the phone." And as Clarence Johnstone staggered across the room and lifted the receiver, "Catch every word—probably this will be instruction as to how to place the bills."

"Mr. Johnstone—" the words came over the wire.

Clarence Johnstone thrilled—with horror—with terror. It was strange that he should know that voice again—but for a moment he did not doubt that it was the voice of Nixon Carleton.

"The bills should be—five-hundred and one-thousand-dollar notes. Place them in a shoe box. The man who will come knows nothing—do not attempt to trap him—act in good faith. Ten o'clock to-morrow morning."

And that was all. Clarence Johnstone turned to Inspector Thurston, but there was no need to repeat the message. Thurston's ear had been close to the receiver.

"The man who will come knows nothing." Johnstone repeated the words that had come to him.

"That's a weakness," Inspector Thurston cut in. "He would have no need to tell you that if it were true. Shoe box—well, I'll supply that—and I'll accompany you to the bank in the morning."

31

The Money Is Buried

IT WAS HALF-PAST nine in the morning when Inspector Thurston glared across at the little company about the library table. There were Florence Johnstone, Old Martin, Jenkins and Clarence Johnstone, besides himself.

"You, Martin, are an old retainer." Thurston nodded at Martin. "You, Miss Johnstone, owe much to Mr. Johnstone—and you, Jenkins, have been in the family for many years. You know what has happened here. All of you are asked to help—by being silent and doing as I tell you." He extended a bulky shoe box toward Mr. Johnstone. "Put the money in, sir—count it before them and let them understand. This is to save Miss Ardath. All of you are to watch, on the beach. You, Martin, will carry the box."

Old Martin accepted the shoe box after Clarence Johnstone had stuffed the bills into it, and tied it tightly with cord. Jenkins and Florence watched Old Martin carefully as they left the house. It was along the road that they walked until they were about a half mile from the house. Then they cut across the sand and to a thick clump of bush.

"We will hide here," Inspector Thurston saw them safely behind the thick growth, "and watch," he whispered to them as he took the box from Old Martin and handed it to Clarence Johnstone. "I want you to know the man if—if he should get away. I dare not have the police watching the beach or the roads. Now, Mr. Johnstone, you walk back a bit, then straight out on the beach and bury the box, and shove the stick with the handkerchief on it into the sand. Then turn—and go directly home. You must leave the rest to us. Some one with powerful field glasses may be watching far down the beach; the road that we came down cannot be seen."

Clarence Johnstone nodded, took the shoe box filled with money, peeked once beneath the cover at the contents, sighed, and stepped wearily back to the road. Five minutes later the watchers in the bush saw him cross the beach, look dazedly about, and finally begin to dig in the sand. They saw him flatten out the sand too, and shove the stick in. Then he turned, and with an occasional backward glance plodded off toward the house. The beach was deserted—a white handkerchief stood out straight in the breeze.

A half hour passed and the little party grew restless. Florence Johnstone sobbed softly—she knew why she was there—knew that she was suspected. Old Martin rubbed his hands continually together and muttered under his breath. He did not approve of the arrangements. Jenkins stared intently at the beach—the hand that he held in his pocket clutching at an old revolver that had not been fired in many years. Inspector Thurston simply watched the beach, occasionally looking at those beside him.

Nearly an hour had passed when the little party of watchers grew tense. A figure was coming along the beach—a figure that looked out at the sea and lightly swung a stick, as though out for a morning stroll. Four heads bent eagerly forward; the fingers of Jenkins' right hand twitched nervously at the butt of his gun. He wondered now would it go off.

Although the air was mild the approaching man wore an overcoat, the collar of which was turned up about his neck. His cap was pulled well down, and but for an occasional glance shoreward he kept his eyes out over the ocean. In a few minutes he reached the white handkerchief, passed without a glance at it, and continued down the beach.

The eyes of the watchers sought each other. Was this then not the one who sought the money? The figure stopped suddenly and stood looking out toward the sea, then slowly he began to retrace his steps until he reached the stick, and standing between it and the water gazed toward the horizon. Slowly, very slowly, he backed toward that stick and the handkerchief. At length he reached it, knocked it over with his foot, and almost carelessly leaned down and picked it up.

"Not yet." Inspector Thurston clutched Jenkins by the arm. "We are between him and the shore; he can't possibly escape."

The man on the beach gazed down upon the stick which he held in his hand, then tossed it into the water. Taking a few steps to the right he sat down upon the beach, his hands gripped about his knees. For a minute or more he sat so. Then the watchers straightened. The man had suddenly begun to dig into the sand. A few frantic scratches only, and something was shoved beneath his coat and the man came to his feet.

"Go that way, Jenkins." Thurston pointed toward Shadow Lawn—"I'll head him off in this direction."

All four were out of the bushes now and upon the beach. Almost at once the man saw them. He stood still, looking at the four figures, then he turned and hurried down the beach in a direction opposite to Shadow Lawn.

Inspector Thurston drew his gun and ran along the sand,

cutting the man off from making the road inshore. The man on the beach jerked his head around once, hesitated an instant, and dashed madly down the beach.

Inspector Thurston was a big man but not beefy. He lost no ground in that chase, and always he kept the man between the water and him. Old Martin followed—Florence Johnstone stood with hands clasped. Jenkins turned, and a good two hundred feet behind the others, started in pursuit of the madly dashing figure.

Inspector Thurston gained and shouted. The man paused, clutched at his pocket and a black object flashed into his hand. Thurston faced the gun and drew his own. Two shots cracked almost at once. The man turned and stumbled on—he limped. It was quite evident that he had been hit. The Inspector gained more now. The man stopped, turned and fired, wildly emptying his gun at his pursuer. Thurston returned the fire—was almost on him when the man dropped to the beach.

"Good God!" panted Thurston, as he leaned over the man. "I've lost out now—the bullet went straight between his eyes. Tough, Jenkins, I promised Mr. Johnstone that he'd talk."

But Jenkins was looking down at the man who lay on his back.

"It's Doctor Corellie," he muttered.

"Yes," sighed the Inspector. "It came in the way of duty; but I can't help thinking that I might have plugged him in the shoulder."

"It's a wonder he didn't kill you, sir," said Jenkins. "You're not to blame." He laid a hand on the Inspector's arm.

"I know," said Thurston. "But I'm thinking of Mr. Johnstone and that girl of his—we'll have to start it all over again, and next time we may not have the chance." He turned to Old Martin, who had come hobbling up. "Take the money, Martin—he had the box beneath his coat."

Old Martin lifted the shoe box from under the dead doctor's arm and tucked it beneath his own.

Inspector Thurston frowned, then shrugged his shoulders. "We'll have to leave him there for the doctor. He got what was coming to him—but I'm sorry. You won't mind staying here, will you, Jenkins?" But before leaving the body in the care of Jenkins, Thurston went carefully through the pockets.

"Come, Martin." Thurston nodded to the old man, and picking Florence up further down the beach they hurried back to Shadow Lawn.

Old Martin laid the shoe box on the library table before Clarence Johnstone. But it was Thurston who explained just what had happened on the beach.

"There's one scoundrel the less, Mr. Johnstone," he finished. "I'm sorry things didn't work out better; it'll make it doubly hard for us next time. All attempts to trace the phone call have failed. We'll be needing the money again, but you can't keep it in the house." He tapped the box lightly. "If you'll take the money out of there I'll be glad to put it back in the bank for you. You don't look fit for the trip to town."

Mechanically Clarence Johnstone untied the cord, and opening the box pushed his fingers in. Then his hand gripped the contents of the box and his eyes stared into it.

"The money is gone," he cried unsteadily. "See—there is nothing but paper here."

One glance the police officer shot within that box. It was filled with paper. The money was gone. Then he swung on Old

Martin; gripped him by the shoulder and dragged him toward him. Deft, quick fingers searched the bewildered old man. But Old Martin's clothes gave up only a worn five-dollar bill and two ten-cent pieces.

32

Prisoners

TERRY MACK HAD thought that he was getting the breaks at last. He knew that a day had passed, and that he lay bound and gagged in the room at the top of the lonely house. Just a tiny strip of light had come through a small curtained window high up near the roof. Now that had gone and dusk had set in. Another night was approaching and no one had come near him.

Once, early in his imprisonment, he thought that he heard a scream, and that it was a woman's. He thought, too, that it was Ardath but he tried to tell himself that it wasn't. Certainly the scream was not loud enough for him to distinguish the voice behind it. And all that day as he lay there feet had pounded across the room below—slow pacing feet of a man who muttered to himself. That was Nixon Carleton, he thought.

Trapped! What a child he had been! Why had he trusted Florence? Yet, even now it was hard to believe that the woman was not in earnest when she spoke of Ardath. But how could he believe that after what had happened? He turned over and tried to sit up. With an effort he was able to get his back against the wall, but that wasn't much better. His legs were bound with thick rope, but his wrists were tightly fastened behind him, held firmly in steel handcuffs.

It was dark—deadly dark, and Terry was alone with his thoughts. What was going on now that he was helpless? He laughed bitterly. Enough had gone on when he wasn't helpless. Who was the man in the shadows? He had simply heard the voice, and it was like no other voice that he had ever heard—unless it was like the monotonous grind of some stage mesmerist.

Footsteps creaked upon the stairs without and slow-moving feet felt their way along the hallway. A key turned in the door and a man was in the room; Terry could dimly distinguish the figure. The door closed and an electric light button clicked. Terry blinked in the sudden light. For the first time he took a good look at Nixon Carleton. Old and wrinkled, yellow of skin, with sharp teeth that were stained a dirty brown. Foggy blue eyes wavered before his, and the old man laughed.

"Would you like to live, Mr. Mack—and are you fond of the girl?" Nixon chuckled as he crossed the room and knelt beside Terry. He was searching him again, and trembling old fingers released the gag from Terry's mouth.

"They speak of you in the underworld," he muttered. "Two-gun man—always two guns—but you came here with one—just one. But no matter." He looked toward the door. "You didn't happen to recognize the man behind you—the man in the shadows last night?" And there was an anxious, worried look in the old man's eyes; a queer, searching sort of look.

Terry had hope at least of living. Otherwise why should Nixon Carleton bother to worry about whether Terry recognized the man in the shadows? And—Terry jerked up slightly. He had not thought of that possibility. Now—

"Don't you know this man?" he demanded.

"Me—me—" Nixon shot his eyes toward the door again. "It's

you that counts—not me." And bending closer, "You know him?" Then shaking his head, "But you couldn't—not you. You'd not be alive—Darrow knew and Darrow is dead." He straightened suddenly, wiped a hand across his eyes.

"You didn't think much of Nixon Carleton, did you? Years ago they did—and now they will again. Darrow pointed me out in court and Darrow is dead. Harry Urskine pointed me out in court and Harry Urskine is dead. Clarence Johnstone pointed me out in court and—his brat is in my hands. She squealed too—you should have heard her—but Clarence Johnstone did. After I get the money, I— But they won't laugh at Nixon Carleton any more. They won't call him an old fool and slip him a few dirty bills. They'll consult him on matters of importance."

He chuckled softly—straightened suddenly and turned toward the door.

"I forgot," he said suddenly, in a sharp commanding voice. "You are to have a visitor—and you are to listen to her—for to-night you are to talk to Clarence Johnstone on the phone—and you will strongly advise him that he pay the amount we demand. You may think you won't—but you will."

Terry's gray eyes blazed. They might kill him—but they'd never make him squeal for mercy. Not Terry Mack.

Nixon Carleton departed. A door opened along the hall. The rasping voice of the old man shrilled—a girl screamed, and Ardath Johnstone was pushed into the room with Terry. The door closed, the key turned, and the stairs creaked.

Brown frightened eyes peered out of a white face. Frantically the girl beat on the door. Terry scraped his feet upon the floor. The girl turned, and for the first time she saw him.

"Terry—" she cried. Then lower, "Terry." She was across the

room, kneeling at his side. "To think that I—I brought you into this."

Something rose in Terry's throat. There was nothing she could have said—nothing of condemnation or bitterness—that would have hurt him and affected him as much as the words she spoke. He knew then that he loved the girl. And now in her trouble and fear she did not look on him as a paid detective who had failed. She was sorry for him—forgot herself and thought only of him.

"I'll save you, Terry—they shan't kill you," she cried over and over, kneeling beside him while the tears splashed upon his cheeks. "Father didn't know—didn't understand—or he never would have let you come to Shadow Lawn. We thought we were playing a game, Terry—all last summer I thought so, too—and then—and now—I love you, Terry." Suddenly, frantically, desperately she threw her arms about him.

He tried to comfort her; wished that he could take her in his arms—but his arms were held behind him. And what a "woman" he was after all. He tried to put back the tears—but he felt that they were there just the same. And now that he knew the truth and she knew the truth, would he lie there and let them mistreat her? He bit his lip until the blood came. But what could he do?

Ardath was holding him close to her, her arms clasped about his neck, her wet cheek pressed to his. They didn't have to speak—both understood. It was fully five minutes before Terry could get any coherent statement from her.

"I was just grabbed up in the fog," she told him. "Broke away—ran screaming—heard your voice—and then I was struck with something. When I regained consciousness I was here. And that horrible old man—what a beast he is, Terry. Last night—or early this morning—he spoke to Father on the phone—brought me in to speak to him—and then he struck me so suddenly that I screamed. Poor Father—they are going to make him pay—and—you—but I have written to Father to give them what they ask. They shan't kill you." And Ardath broke into tears again and clutched Terry to her.

"Listen, Ardath." Terry drew himself away. He tried to be calm but his voice cracked. He waited a moment, swallowed hard, and got control of himself. There was one chance—a slim one—but he must play toward that. His life wasn't going to be bought off by Ardath's father—and he wasn't going to die now if he could help it. He had always felt that some day he would be killed, and he didn't fear that day. He had hoped that it would be with a bullet in his chest and a smoking gun in his hand. Now—he wanted to live. He thought of the business offers he had refused; the one to head the investigation department of a nationally known railroad. He thought of a home—quiet evenings—children, perhaps—and he looked up at Ardath. There was always the one chance—the breaks had been against him. Now—if—

For some time he talked to Ardath, trying to calm her fears—which strangely were for him, not herself. She untied his feet and helped him to walk up and down the room. He moved his arms back and forth behind him, restoring the circulation to the swollen wrists. There was a wild idea in Terry's mind of attacking Nixon Carleton the very next time he entered the room—a sudden rush and butt on the chin from his head. But he saw little hope in that. Surely there were others in the house, or he and Ardath would not be together like this.

He tried to encourage the girl; speak of the future, and he saw the color come back to her white cheeks. But it faded away again almost at once.

"Is there any chance, Terry?" she finally asked. "Tell me the truth. I will—will die bravely. But this terrible Old Man. He hates my father—and me. Whenever he talks to me I can see that it is with an effort that he controls those bony hands. Oh, Terry—they tremble and twitch to grasp me by the throat. I know it. Don't lie to me—tell me the truth. Is there any chance?"

"There is always hope," Terry started. "Tell me, Ardath—where is this telephone—where did you talk to your father? Is it in a room with books, and a chair beneath—"

"A great overstuffed chair beneath a light," she cut in. "Yes—I was made to sit there while Nixon Carleton paced the room and spoke of my father and his hatred for him. I—"

"Listen—" Terry cautioned. Feet again creaked upon the stairs—more than one pair, Terry thought. He stood in the center of the room. The door was thrown open. Nixon Carleton entered. Behind him stood a man with a gun in his hand. It was Happy Drake—the one who drove Terry to the house. He grinned evilly.

"Strike me dead—Terry Mack." The man slipped the words through the side of an evil mouth, in evident admiration. "You took me in. The Chief played the game well. He's a clever—"

"Shut your face." Nixon Carleton turned upon Drake. "Come here, girl—" stepping into the room Carleton clutched the girl roughly by the wrist and jerked her toward the door. Terry stepped forward—Drake's gun went up. The girl was dragged down the hall—a door closed and a key turned.

"Come!" Nixon Carleton stood in the doorway facing Terry. There was a sinister twist to thick yellow lips, an evil glint to foggy blue eyes.

33

In the Chair Beneath the Light

NIXON CARLETON LED Terry to the room with the books and the big chair with the light over it. But another light burned brightly from the ceiling. Behind him came Drake, with his gun pressed tightly against Terry's back. A false move would mean his life; Terry knew that. Then what of Ardath? And now— Terry started straight for the big chair, but Nixon Carleton laid a hand upon his shoulder.

"We're to unfasten his hands, Drake, and strap them to the chair." Nixon turned to the sour-faced individual.

"What!" Drake gasped. "Take the cuffs off 'a him. Suppose he makes a break for it and—"

"He won't dare." Nixon stared at Drake. "If he does—" He drew his gun from his pocket.

But Drake shook his head.

"He's got the reputation for it—and we don't want no row before he talks on the phone. His hands are fast enough—we can tie his feet to the rungs and—"

"It's the Chief's orders." Nixon shook his head.

"Go on, then," Terry cut in suddenly, "untie my hands." He crouched low. "You'll torture the girl, will you? What do I care for your guns? I'll die fighting. I'll—" he suddenly made a lunge at Nixon Carleton. Nixon waved his gun and jumped back. Drake dashed forward. Terry calmed down at once; he was playing a game. Above everything he did not want his hands bound to the arms of that chair. No—all depended on that—things were bad enough as they were—but there was a chance.

"Untie my hands if you dare," Terry shouted defiantly.

Drake struck him across the face with the long nose of his gun—Terry staggered back, dropped into the armchair—half lay there, breathing heavily.

"Get the ropes about his feet," Drake cried hoarsely. "Do you want me to plug him before we—what's the good of binding his hands to the chair anyway. He can't use them on us."

Terry lay half back in the chair. He let them bind his legs to the rungs without complaint; then sat up.

"So—" Nixon glared down at him. "You'd make trouble, would you? Well—we'll see about that later. Now, Mr. Mack, in ten minutes you are going to have a conversation with Clarence Johnstone—and you are going to say what I tell you to. Oh, don't glare. Ardath Johnstone will be here to help you. For every minute you hesitate she will suffer. See—" he laid a long knife upon the table by the telephone. "We want you to advise Johnstone to pay out the money. One false move—one attempt directly or indirectly to tell Clarence Johnstone where you are will not only mean your death—but a little surprise for the girl. Hold out if you will—wait and see if I really would hurt her. There is no hurry—I am the sort of a man who takes pleasure in his work."

Terry squirmed in the chair, and settled back further. Nixon Carleton grinned. Then Terry spoke.

"They'll trace the phone call—Inspector Thurston will—"

"No, no." Nixon shook his head. "It's a private wire, tapped in on the Shadow Lawn phone. When we want to call, we simply lift the receiver—and one of my workers calls from a drug store in Newton—a drug store, last night—to-night, another place—to-morrow night—" Nixon Carleton straightened slightly in his chair; his gun tapped down on Terry's knee. "I have many workers—when I direct things there can be no failures." He half glanced over his shoulder at the cynical grin on Drake's face.

"You're known, Nixon." Terry looked him straight in the eyes. "There will come a day of reckoning. It may take me days and it may take me years, but sometime I'll lay a hand on your shoulder. If you harm Miss Johnstone, I'll lay a bullet in your heart—if you've got a heart."

"But you won't be around." Nixon chuckled.

"Nixon Carleton," said Terry very slowly. "I have a feeling that I will—that your time is very short."

Nixon fidgeted nervously—he looked over his shoulder again at Drake, who stood in the doorway, gun in hand. Then he laughed.

"Sock him a bat in the lug," Drake advised. "We ain't here to listen to his chatter—nor yours."

"Mine!" Nixon straightened. "Without me, Drake, you would he starving in the city or up—"

"What'd you do?" Drake sneered; and then thinking that perhaps it would be to his advantage to learn all he could, he egged the old crook on. "Maybe I'm wrong, Nixon—but I thought—"

"Who arranged the letters?" Nixon turned to Terry Mack. "That was clever. I found one in your pocket."

"You—you forged that third letter?" Terry asked.

"Me—no—nor any one." Nixon chuckled. "The woman turned the two of them over to Doctor Corellie—he gave them to Darrow to compare with the one Darrow said he had. Then Darrow made copies of those two letters, touched them up to make them look old, and wrote the third. You see, they were all done by the same hand—so an expert could swear to it. Florence Johnstone never knew the difference. Clarence Johnstone wouldn't, for the copies of the originals would fool any one who didn't have the originals to compare them with. It was clever." He chuckled. "Darrow did the work—it was his business. But I thought of the idea."

"And Doctor Corellie?" Terry questioned. He would learn all he could—all that this conceited old scoundrel cared to tell him.

"Doctor Corellie thought the girl would have the money— that the letters were real. He hoped to marry her."

"And you went to all that work simply to fool Doctor Corellie and Florence Johnstone?" Terry sunk further back in the chair.

"No—it was to bring strife into the family. To make Clarence Johnstone believe that Florence was mixed up with—well, with me; and to keep him from going to the police until we could strike him through his daughter, Ardath."

"But why did Florence Johnstone deceive me—lead me into the trap at the railroad station?"

"I thought of that. The conversation she heard beneath the window was found out—one of my men saw her listening there. It was partly a lucky strike—but if she hadn't of been listening you would have obtained the same message from her by another means. It was all very clever." And Nixon nodded his old head and licked his dry lips.

"And this 'Chief'—this man in the shadows?"

"What of him?" Nixon Carleton raised his head slightly. "He acts through me. I lead and he—" Nixon's jaw suddenly dropped, his eyes popped and he swung toward the door. Distinctly from below had come a knock; one—four, then one again.

And in that second that Nixon Carleton turned his head Terry crouched low, thrust his cuffed hands deep into the recess in the back of the chair, behind the cushion. Once, twice, his fingers clutched frantically deeper and deeper. And as Nixon Carleton turned toward him, and Drake, leaving the room, pounded slowly down the stairs, Terry straightened. But his cuffed hands now held a gun. A forty-five caliber automatic. His own gun; the gun which he had let slip down in the deep crevice below the cushion when the unknown man in the shadows had so suddenly thrust a revolver against the back of his neck the previous night. "Two-gun man" was right! Terry's lips set grimly. The missing gun had come back to its owner.

34

Panic

NIXON CARLETON CAME to his feet, stepped to the
wall and snapped out the ceiling light. Just the single light
glowed over Terry's head. Terry thrilled! Coming up the stairs
was the unknown; the man called "Chief." The man in the
shadows. Terry felt that he'd got one break anyway. His hands
were cuffed behind him, to be sure, but in one of those hands
was an automatic. He could twist his body around and fire—
one shot, maybe. He couldn't very well cover all three of the
men. He couldn't even be sure that he would see any of the
men. His chance was a desperate one, of course, still it was a
chance. Five minutes before, his brain was wracked with the
fear that the gun would be gone—that it was not deep enough
down in the back of the great chair to remain unseen. But it
had been—almost too deep for him to reach.

The steps were in the hall without now; slow, even, measured
steps. They reached the landing, swung along the hall, and
approached the door. Drake entered the room and crossed
the light. His gun still hung in his hand. There was a shadow
behind him; nothing to distinguish against the darkness—a
slouch hat, stooping shoulders, and the slightest impression
of two blotches of black against the whiteness of a face. That
puzzled Terry at first, but as his eyes accustomed themselves
ever so slightly to looking from light into darkness he thought
that those black blotches were colored glasses.

Terry sat stiff and straight in the chair. If it wasn't for his legs being bound to the rungs, he'd of chanced jumping to his feet and threatening to kill the first man who moved. There could be a swing to his body then that would make such a move possible—not probable—but possible. But now—he strained his ears. The man in the shadows would speak—and Terry wondered if it would be a voice he had ever heard before.

And the man in the shadows spoke.

"It is close to nine o'clock, Nixon. Bring down the girl; to-night we will play our final card."

The breath that Terry held was released. A disguised voice was not hard for him to recognize—that is, if the speaker used a voice that sounded at all human. But here was a different sort of tone—low, guttural, metallic; of the stomach rather than the throat. It was not a voice that could be used in the drawing-room—in the office—any place, without marking the user as attempting to conceal his natural speech. It was a voice that any man might use and it would sound practically the same.

Terry's gun swung slightly to the side behind him. He could see Drake now; partly distinguish Nixon Carleton as he passed to the door, and could make out but dimly the motionless, stooped figure that stood against the wall, well back in the shadows.

What would he do? Of course the sudden appearance of a gun in his hands would cause an element of surprise that would give him an advantage. All three of the men were armed. He might shoot one; probably Drake, who presented the element of greatest danger, with the dangling gun in his hand. But that would be all. The man in the shadows with a single step could fade completely into the darkness. Nixon Carleton would—

but Nixon Carleton had left the room. No—Terry would have to wait until the girl was there. If he could hold them for a moment only—she would help. But would she? Could he count on quick action from Ardath in a sudden and desperate emergency—and just where would she be in the room? He wished he had told her something of his plans—but he hadn't. Not that it slipped his mind. No—there were two reasons. The one, of raising false hopes—for he did not know if he would ever sit in that chair again, or if he did that the gun would be there. Besides, a sudden hope in the girl's mind might be reflected in her eyes, her actions, and give to the Chief a hint of danger. For it was the Chief that Terry feared. Nixon Carleton alone was none too dangerous—a proud, weak, vengeful old crook and murderer—hardly above the common thug with his distorted, evil, self-glorified mind.

No one spoke—the Chief remained motionless. Drake moved restlessly from foot to foot. It was rather a novelty for him to be standing beside that unknown presence, and he was feeling somewhat the fear that the man in the shadows inspired within Nixon Carleton.

Two—three minutes passed. Terry counted them off by the ticking of a clock which he could not see. Then a threatening voice; hurried feet stumbling upon the stairs, and Ardath was in the room. She looked bewilderedly about her—saw Terry, and holding out her hands started toward him. Nixon Carleton jerked her roughly back, struck her with his open hand, and laughed.

Terry twisted slightly, blinked, and sat straight again. Nixon had been very close to death. It took great self-control for Terry to keep his body straight and his finger from tightening upon the trigger of his automatic. His heart thumped and his spirit fell—Ardath was feeling the strain. When the moment came the girl would not be of much help to him. And that moment must come. Terry would not be taken from that chair without making his fight. There would never be another chance. He set his teeth grimly. Death was almost certain for him—but another would go with him. His eyes tried to pierce the darkness—if he could shoot the Chief the confusion to the others might—

But Nixon Carleton was talking.

"Sit here." He thrust the girl roughly into a chair at the end of the table, close to Terry, and in the reflection of the light behind him. Leaning down Nixon lifted a telephone from a small stand and placed it on the table.

"In another minute, Mr. Mack, the clock will strike the hour of nine. You will speak into this phone to Mr. Johnstone. You will tell him to place the money where the letter told him—all of it. And this time to have no one hiding in the bush, nor Inspector Thurston in the neighborhood. You will tell him that the time is ten o'clock to-night. And at that hour, Clarence Johnstone, Old Martin, Inspector Thurston, and all the household servants must be at Shadow Lawn, as the letter directed. Say that Nixon Carleton will know if they are there."

"And if I do not deliver this message?" Terry leaned forward. Nixon Carleton was close beside him. Drake was partly in the light. The man in the shadows could be seen dimly in the light that came through the crack in the drawn curtains before the door.

"If you do not—see!" Nixon Carleton bent suddenly, clutched at the arm of Ardath, twisted it behind her back and raised it with a sharp jerk. The girl screamed with the pain. And Terry acted.

He swung suddenly sideways. His hands and his gun were now in the light. The man in the shadows cursed softly—Nixon Carleton clutched at his head and muttered unintelligibly. Terry spoke.

"The one who moves is dead." He tried to make his voice ring with a conviction that he did not feel. "Drake—drop your gun. Ardath, take—"

That ended Terry's conversation. Drake's hand went up and Terry fired. He saw the man pitch forward against the table, clutch at it, and sink to the floor.

Nixon Carleton cried aloud in fear and dashed toward the door. The man in the shadows shouted a warning. A gun in his hand seemed suddenly to pierce the darkness and flashed into the light.

Terry fired wildly, a split second before that other gun went off. He saw the man in the shadows stagger slightly; a white hand jump to his left shoulder as his gun roared. Would he miss? Hardly! The man had not lost his head. He aimed from darkness into light and the distance was not much more than ten feet. He was going to make sure of his first shot. Nothing Terry could do would save him.

And Terry did not see that spurt of yellow-blue flame. He only heard the roar of the gun as it echoed in the room. A figure shot before him—a wailing, crying, running thing that sought the door. It was Nixon Carleton who dashed before that gun and saved Terry's life.

Nixon stagged once, and stood swaying in the center of the room. The man in the shadows cried out hoarsely, and this time there was no metallic ring in his voice, but a high-pitched shrill to it—like the cry of a wounded bird.

"Him—him—" the voice shrilled. "And I killed—him."

That was all. Nixon turned toward Terry, who was trying frantically to find an opening to the man in the shadows. Terry twisted and turned in the chair, but Nixon's staggering, wavering body was between them. Then Nixon Carleton turned again; glassy eyes stared vacantly at Terry, and slowly slipping to his knees as if in prayer Nixon pitched forward on his face—but not before Terry had seen the purple hole in the side of the man's head.

Terry fired then, toward the door, toward the dimness of the light from the hall. But he, too, was feeling the hysteria that had dominated the actors in the drama which was taking place in the lonely house along the sand.

Feet beat up to him as a man ran down the stairs. A door slammed below—a moment of silence—a soft purr and the roar of a motor. Then came the grind of badly meshed gears. Terry knew that the "Chief" had escaped—the man in the shadows. The daring, scheming mind behind this whole dastardly plot had fled—and what's more he had fled in panic. Also he had cried out before he left that room—cried out when he shot Nixon Carleton; and the voice was not feigned then—but was a natural, if an hysterical one.

Did Terry recognize that voice? At first he thought that he did—then that he didn't—then that he did again. It was so impossible. He looked over toward Drake; the man did not move. He looked toward Nixon Carleton—his face was close to the light there below the table. He was dead.

And Ardath! She had slipped to the floor when the firing first began.

"Ardath," Terry called softly. "Ardath—it's all—all over now."

But she did not answer. Terry pushed forward as far as his bound legs would permit his body to hang across the table. She was there, slumped against one of the legs. And as Terry looked down at her white, upturned face her eyes opened.

"It's all right, Ardath—come, help unfasten me." Ardath looked up at him—her lips quivered—she tried to smile—tried to force to the surface the courage, the moral courage, that her frail young body could not now sustain.

"Terry—Terry—I—Terry, you old son-of-a-gun." And she fainted. She had laughed at fear, joked at the prospect of being taken by these people—thought of only Terry when danger was greatest. And now that the danger was over, she fainted— like—like the woman she was. Terry smiled. That was as it should be, as he would have her. It wasn't a woman's game, and he didn't think he would fancy having breakfast every morning of his life with a wife who could step nonchalantly over a corpse as she passed to the kitchen to make his coffee.

But was the danger over? Why had the man in the shadows gone into such a panic over the death of Nixon Carleton—for surely it was that. He had been steady enough before—calm, cool, and collected as he raised that gun to shoot Terry. And now when the panic would be over, mightn't he return to finish the job? Hardly that, Terry thought. He couldn't know that Ardath wouldn't unbind his legs—but he mustn't take any chances. This was a desperate scoundrel. Terry had gotten the breaks once—when he most needed them. Now he must act quickly.

It was twenty minutes later when Terry kicked his feet free, and as the last rope fell to the floor Ardath climbed to her feet.

They laughed. He wouldn't have to call the police after all—not yet anyway. He'd see Inspector Thurston in person—yes, that was the best thing to do. He must act cautiously now.

Ten minutes later two figures crept from the lonely house. The man stumbled after the girl, for his hands were fastened tightly behind him with steel. The key to those cuffs might have been in one of the pockets of the dead Nixon Carleton, but Terry didn't have the heart to ask the girl to search for it. He knew it was bad business not to—but he loved the girl.

35

At Shadow Lawn

INSPECTOR WILLIAM THURSTON was at Shadow Lawn when Terry and Ardath arrived. It was some time before Terry could get in a word with the Inspector. There were tears and hugs and hysterical laughter. Terry had to tell his story; Ardath had to tell hers; and both had to listen to the account of the death of Doctor Corellie and the mysterious and unexplained disappearance of the hundred thousand dollars from the shoe box which had been buried in the sand.

Ardath refused to leave Terry's side when the Inspector wished a word with him in private.

"There's no necessity for it." She shook her head when they three were alone. "What could you keep from me now—I've gone through all that's possible. Besides, Terry's not fit for it, Inspector Thurston; he collapsed twice on the beach. And he nearly fainted again when the handcuffs were finally filed off his wrists. No—I'll stick by him. Get your talk over, for he's going to bed. Oh, don't look at me like that—" and she turned her head slightly. "I've got certain rights in Terry Mack, now."

Inspector Thurston shrugged his shoulders.

"I didn't arrest Martin," he explained. "And since hearing your story I doubt very much that he was the brains behind this. It doesn't seem possible that he could stand in the shadows and deceive Nixon Carlerton and you—and Ardath here. Besides, there was that bit of shooting you spoke of." Inspector

Thurston regarded Terry shrewdly.

"I have no reason to suspect Old Martin." Terry leaned wearily back on the couch. "Yet, it would not be entirely impossible for him to do it. There was no attempt of the man in the shadows to make his voice sound unnatural; there was just the one object of that metallic ring—that of disguising the natural tone of his voice. His face was never more than a semblance of white through the darkness; his eyes, black glasses; his form dull and stooped."

"Did you get any hint at all—just the slightest suspicion that you might know him again? Even an idea, Mack—if you thought of half a dozen suspects we could trace their movements. Was he old or young?"

"Very old," said Ardath. "I'm sure of that."

Terry hesitated, then shook his head.

"No—" he said. "I have pretty sharp eyes, Inspector, and I can't be certain. I'd be almost willing to swear to the fact that I had never seen the man before. He cried out when Nixon Carleton fell—but his voice was harder to disguise then, for there was a high-pitched, hysterical note in it. I doubt that Martin knows anything—but has he been in the house all the evening?"

"I just got here fifteen minutes ago." Thurston stood up and paced the room. "Martin had left the house. I had a man to watch him. That man sent word that he lost Old Martin on the beach. But," he spread his hands far apart, "those are the breaks of the game. I've rung in at headquarters on your story and the lonely house you described so well will be searched and the bodies removed later. Technically, Mack—" he smiled, "you should be under arrest. You have no official standing. It is, after all, a confession of a killing you've made."

"Quite the contrary," Terry said, somewhat stiffly. "As a citizen I tell you that I was lured to a lonely house, threatened, and attacked. In defending myself, men were shot. There were three present—two are dead. I make no confession in this matter. I make a complaint—and call upon you as Inspector of Police of Newton to arrest this third man. That is all."

"There, there." Inspector William Thurston stepped across the room and laid a hand on Terry's shoulder. "You're knocked out, old man, and perhaps I'm a bit jealous of your success. Better slip into bed and we'll have a doctor for you. By the way, you say you shot this man—this third man—this man in the shadows?"

"I hit him in the shoulder—how bad, I don't know; but I saw his hand go up and clutch at his right shoulder."

"That may help matters—right shoulder, you say." Thurston made a note of it. "I'll have the hospitals watched and notify all physicians. Come! I'll give you a lift up the stairs." The Inspector thrust back his shoulders and stood over Terry, who had suddenly slumped down in the chair.

Terry leaned heavily on the Inspector's shoulder as he slowly climbed the stairs. Ardath paused at the bottom, calling for Jenkins.

"Listen, Inspector," Terry whispered. "I haven't told a soul yet—but I'm trying to figure out how that money disappeared." His eyes rolled slightly as he looked up at the ruddy, hard face of Thurston. "But to-morrow we'll search. Maybe it's still on the beach. Don't breathe a word to any one."

Terry's words trembled on his lips; the hand on the Inspector's shoulder shook violently. Thurston wondered was Terry slightly delirious—he almost had to lift him the last few steps.

"There, there," he said kindly. "Don't worry about things—we'll fetch you a doctor and—"

"Jenkins will see him to bed." Ardath was coming up the stairs behind them, with Jenkins at her heels. "I know you have a lot to do, Inspector."

"Very thoughtful," said Inspector Thurston. "But we of the force always have the time for a comrade—even if we don't seem to look with a kindly eye upon the private detectives. But you're right—I'll have to be taking charge of things down at that lonely house."

Inspector Thurston turned and pounded down the stairs. Ardath, with Jenkins at her heels, followed Terry into the room. Terry slumped into a chair with a groan—the door closed and a key clicked in the lock.

36

Unmasked

FAR DOWN THE main thoroughfare from Shadow Lawn a car turned, and moved cautiously over a narrow sandy road. Twice the figure in the car was obliged to pull up sharply and climb from behind the steering wheel, and descending to the sand mark carefully in his mind the slight twist to the roadway. He cursed softly in the darkness, for the lights on the car were not lit—and though stars were twinkling in the sky no moon was out and the blackness was intense.

Once only did the single occupant of the car strike a light, and then it was where the sandy stretch widened and made possible the turning of a small car by a careful driver. It was a match that the driver lit; it sputtered between his cupped hands and burst into a tiny flame. For a moment the stooped shoulders, the tightly buttoned coat, and the white face beneath it was visible. But the features were not recognizable, for black glasses covered the eyes, and the nose and mouth were peculiarly in the shadows. Luck or careful manipulation of the match might be responsible, still this man had the knack of always remaining in the shadows.

And the match was held in such a way that the light could not be seen beyond those cupped hands but for the small splash that blinked upon the sand. He was a good fifteen minutes in turning that car and facing it again toward the main road, and he was careful too that the motor purred softly—at no time did he race the engine. Satisfied that the car was well placed for a quick start toward the main road, the figure stepped out boldly through the darkness toward the beach. The gun in his right hand was barely visible against the whiteness of his fingers. That is, visible to him as he looked down at it and clutched it more tightly. But five feet away the blackness of the gun and the whiteness of the fingers were intermingled and lost in the night.

With a measured, steady step the figure of the man in the shadows traveled through the blackness down to the beach, swung suddenly close to the water and plodded toward Shadow Lawn.

Perhaps half a mile from Shadow Lawn the man turned and walked over the wet beach until the rush of the pounding surf played about his ankles. Up and down along the beach he made his way, feeling for something in the dark. Twice he felt in his pocket, fingering a flashlight and clutching at his box of safety matches. But each time he brought his hand out empty and continued his search. He cursed softly at times, yet he did not strike a light. He must find what he wished—and he must find it in the darkness.

For perhaps ten minutes he waded through the water—then he went in a little deeper, so that the water splashed about his knees and sucked at his feet. Finally his foot struck against wood; he half stumbled, and regaining his balance bent down and felt of the old breakwater. Carefully he followed it toward the shore until he stood by an upright. Planting his back close against this old log he pulled a tiny compass from his pocket, glanced down at the radium illuminated dial and leaned firmly against the worn, bent, and rounded wood that for years had held its place in the sand.

"Sixty-two—toe to heel," he muttered as he slowly placed a heel before a toe, glancing ever down at the compass. "I can't miss it. I've done it over and over."

Slowly the man proceeded, counting off the steps half aloud. Sixty-two such steps completed he knelt upon the beach and felt cautiously about with his fingers, digging into the loose sand. Five minutes, ten perhaps, he moved cautiously about on his knees. There was a pause to his moving fingers, a quick grasp at a sharp object, an uncontrollable exclamation of satisfaction, and a sudden frantic digging of fingers in the sand.

Only a minute then and he felt the shoe box, placed his gun by his side and dug both hands into the little pit he had made. The box came up easily enough; he thrust it beneath his arm, chuckled half aloud as he started to his feet, then remembering his gun bent quickly to recover it.

There was a flash of light, a sharp whistle, running feet, and men calling to each other. The man half crouched there on the sand; then he swung to his feet and gazed frantically and unseeingly around him. Ever that light blazed into his face, through the blackness of the glasses reflecting the greenness of his eyes.

Lights were everywhere now. He tried to hide his face—saw the uselessness of it and straightened suddenly. Lips smiled into the light, but the eyes remained cold and hard.

"I guess," said a voice out of the darkness, "the game is up. You don't need to remove the glasses or the slouch hat so far as I am concerned, but others will be—just a bit surprised. There, I wouldn't reach for that gun. You saw what happened to Drake." And as the man in the light bent ever nearer the gun upon the sand the figure behind the flashlight spoke again. "There's always a chance to beat the chair, you know."

The figure straightened again, lifted a hand and tore off the glasses and the slouch hat.

"At your service, Mr. Terry Mack." He bowed mockingly, but his hard stern lips trembled and his green eyes wavered as other men crossed the beach and gripped at his arms.

"Thank you," said Terry, calmly. "I think that you have done the wisest thing. For I would not have hesitated a single moment about placing a bullet straight between your eyes, Mr. Inspector William Thurston—alias, The Man in the Shadows."

Another voice spoke from the blackness.

"Yes, it's him—it's him. It seemed impossible even when you spoke to me to-night—and I never expected there would be such a disclosure when you sent me the telegram to return from Canada. Why, the telegram was waiting when I got there."

Inspector Thurston turned sharply. In the dazzling, jumping lights he recognized in the speaker Chief Robinson.

"Well," Thurston said sullenly, "you got me—tricked me. Mack's faking that he was weak and sick did it. When he spoke about the money being still on the beach I decided to get it to-night—before others searched for it in the morning."

"That is just what I thought you'd do," said Terry. "I never felt better in my life."

"But how you knew the money was there beats me," said Thurston.

"I didn't." Terry smiled. "I don't know how you worked it yet, but if you didn't take it away with you—and Johnstone looked in the box before he buried it, and no one had it—why, the obvious conclusion was that it was still there."

"But when did you first suspect me?" Thurston asked.

Terry reddened slightly.

"I don't know," he said at length. "I might put a string of clues together that would call for mighty clever deductions—but I'll be honest in this matter. You could have killed Harry Urskine, of course, but I didn't for the moment think that you did it. I have a childlike, innocent belief in the inherent honesty of paid man-hunters. Oh, their souls are no better than other men's but the reason that few of them go crooked is perhaps more psychological. They know only too well that crime does not pay—none better." Terry stroked his chin. "But when Urskine was murdered—no—I didn't suspect you then."

"But you wired me to return," Chief Robinson cut in.

"Just playing a hunch," said Terry—but that was hardly the truth. Yet, Terry saw no use in telling the Chief that he wished his presence in Newton to protect Clarence Johnstone and Old Martin from William Thurston. He had a strong suspicion that once Chief Robinson was out of the way Inspector Thurston would make an arrest—and Terry didn't want the scandal that would follow. Besides, he felt all along that Old Martin was innocent, and feared the third degree that Thurston might give him—for he never suspected Thurston then.

"But when did you first really suspect me?" Thurston was insistent.

"The time you cried out when you shot Nixon Carleton. I thought that I recognized your voice then. Of course I only half believed. Then I went over things. Certainly you had the opportunity to be the guiding hand in this game. Ardath was taken and money demanded. Certainly then you even had a motive. And when I heard that the money had disappeared— why—well, I set my trap for you. Tell me—why did you lose your head and cry out when you shot Nixon Carleton?"

"Because," said Inspector William Thurston very slowly, "Nixon Carleton was my father. It is not a complicated story, gentlemen—rather a simple one," he added as Chief Robinson gasped.

"We will hear that story," said Chief Robinson, "up at Shadow Lawn."

37

A Confession and Chops

"I HAD NOT seen my father, Nixon Carleton, since I was less than seven years old—nearly four years before he went to the Klondike." Inspector William Thurston smoked as he talked in the big Johnstone library. "But I knew of him. My aunt, with whom I lived, changed my name when my father stood in the dock for murder. It was not a coincidence that I came to Newton twenty years ago. My aunt believed that Clarence Johnstone might help me. She said that he was a good man and had adopted the daughter of Frank Marion. I took her letter to Clarence Johnstone and came to Newton.

"I had hardly arrived before I received word that my aunt had died. At the hotel here I was, of course, registered as William Thurston. I did not hold the same views as my aunt, who was a good and charitable woman. I put myself in the place of Clarence Johnstone and knew that I would have nothing but hatred for the son of such a man as Nixon Carleton. So I destroyed the letter and kept my identity secret.

"Besides, luck favored me. Newton was in a real estate boom. There was opportunity; and just twenty years ago last month I went on the police force. Few questions were asked; they needed men badly. I think that I was an efficient if not an honest officer. Those were the days of big graft. I got my share." He smiled. "That I lost most of it in speculation does not matter. But the blood of my father was in my body. Prohibition came, and with it came Darrow. He had seen my aunt just before she died and discovered that I had come to Newton. He was a forger and a thief. Then—not so long ago—Darrow saw my father, Nixon Carleton, in New York City and I planned this thing that you, Mr. Mack, finally frustrated. I knew enough of the former activities of Doctor Corellie to, through Darrow, make him an unwilling helper and—"

"You killed Corellie—why?" Terry interrupted.

"Let me come to that in my own way." Thurston raised his hand. "When I am through, if I have left anything unsaid, question me. Once into the thing I thought to make it the one perfect crime; to so cover my tracks and confuse the authorities that I would never be suspected. No one knew me, but Darrow. And then Darrow became a problem. Things did not move quickly enough for him. He was always needing money. At length he threatened me. He spoke of my past; of my father—even hinted that he would make a deal with Clarence Johnstone. I did not believe him. Did not fear him then. But I looked into the future, saw the money which we had made squandered by Darrow and Darrow ever on my heels. Well, Darrow had threatened me, Darrow was the only one that knew me. Darrow might talk to Nixon Carleton or Doctor Corellie—and Darrow must die. When I felt that I could trust him no longer and needed him no longer I sent for him to meet me on the beach near Shadow Lawn. He came and he died, and I left the three of spades upon his chest.

"The card was not there simply to confuse. I knew that Johnstone would be on the beach very early. I had watched him for several mornings. I wanted to make him afraid to go to the police. I had planned things so that he would think his adopted daughter, Florence, was somehow tied up with Nixon Carleton. That at the end Nixon Carleton would pay for the crime did not concern me. I had no sympathy for him—cared not what happened to him. Of course, when I killed him—well, it was a shock. For the moment I lost my head, and so went the perfect crime."

William Thurston paused and wiped his forehead.

"Let me see—yes, there was Harry Urskine. I arranged for his disappearance because I did not wish him to tell Miss Florence the truth—that her father left very little money. That once, I worked in a hurry—did the job myself, and Urskine recognized me." And Thurston told of the poison and Urskine's escape. "Of course I had to kill him—there was no other way. It was rather simple after all. Terry Mack sat by Urskine's door while I went below. Doctor Corellie had orders to be on the beach. The situation was desperate. I had to talk to the doctor—tell him to throw a stone through the window to attract Mack from his position before the door.

"Doctor Corellie was a shrewd man—he knew me. He did not say so—but I knew it—and that's why I killed him later. He told me that Florence Johnstone had listened by his door—a man planted across the street from his house by Nixon Carleton saw her. He told me, too, that he had followed Florence out here and that she was in the house.

"Softly I mounted the stairs to wait until that stone would coax Mack from the door—and Mack was gone; I guess my footsteps below, which I purposely made loud, attracted his attention. Then it was the work of a minute only. I had the key; I had a knife; and the card was for my future protection, for who would believe an old man's story that a guiding shadow stood in the shadows and directed him? When Mack came up the back stairs the door was locked and I appeared to be ascending the front stairs.

"The taking of Miss Ardath Johnstone was a piece of luck, though I never counted on luck—nor did I need it. Each night men waited for the chance. Somehow I would have tempted her out—but she went herself." Thurston turned to Terry. "Old Martin saved you that night, Mack—if he had come a second later I'd of plunged the knife in your chest as I bent over you on the sand.

"About the box of money. Its very simplicity assured its success. Doctor Corellie had my instructions through Nixon Carleton not to dig beneath the stick with the handkerchief upon it but to dig ten feet to the left of the stick. And ten feet to the left I had planted a shoe box full of paper. He did not suspect. Nor was I in danger of being shot, for Nixon Carleton had removed the bullets from Corellie's gun. Nixon was willing—with Corellie dead his share went the higher."

"And it was planned by you that I should be attacked in New York and that a woman should ring me up, eh?" Terry asked.

"Some of it." Thurston nodded. "Nixon spoiled things. I wanted you out of the way of course." Thurston smiled reminiscently. "I played in bad luck—I even planned to make my resignation a natural thing when once I had the money. Chief Robinson knew that I would leave if I failed—I planned to fail—but not in this way. But I made one other mistake—that no one noticed."

"Not the calling of Florence Johnstone on the phone the night Clarence Johnstone heard from Nixon Carleton, and heard Ardath scream?" smiled Terry.

"Yes—yes," said Thurston, his eyebrows going up. "You discovered that, eh?"

"It made me nearly sure of you." Terry nodded.

"I was not home—I was afraid that would look bad. I expected they would call me at once. So I waited close to twenty minutes after Nixon Carleton had sent his message to Clarence Johnstone—then I called, as if from my own house—pretending that I had heard the phone ringing and been half asleep."

"You planted the gun in Old Martin's pocket, too?" Terry asked.

"Yes, it was just to mix things up worse." William Thurston straightened slightly. "Each move I planned carefully—the only known fact would be the killing of Doctor Corellie. I had killed him in doing my duty. I was an officer of the law. I could not be suspected; I had not touched the money. But I make no excuse, gentlemen. I had no love for my father, Nixon Carleton. I would have let him rot in jail without raising a hand to save him. But to kill him—well—it was a shock. I am here before you without an excuse to the law, but I hope that I will have one before God—for after all the blood of Nixon Carleton, thief and murderer, flowed in my veins. Time may change my thoughts. I shall not cry for mercy now. The man with the blood of Nixon Carleton is only sorry that he failed."

Terry raised his head and sniffed the air. Ardath had left the room. Unnoticed, Terry slipped into the dining room, and sitting down at the big table took out his pen and began to fill in a check from a pocket checkbook.

Again he raised his head and sniffed the air. Something was cooking in the kitchen and some one was humming. For the first time in several days Terry thought of his stomach. Passing through the swinging doors he entered the kitchen. Ardath was at the stove.

"What in heaven's name are you doing?" Terry went quickly across to the gas range and lowered the flame beneath the pan. "You'll burn those chops." He smacked his lips. "Besides, they should be broiled, not fried. Anyway—"

"Oh, Terry," Ardath crept into his arms, "I'm just practicing."

Terry looked again at the chops.

"I think," he said slowly, "I shall be able to afford a cook."

"What's that in your hand?" She was looking at the check.

"That," he said, "is a check for twenty-five hundred dollars, payable to your father. For after all I saved you for myself, not for him."

"How noble!" Ardath slipped a hand from about his shoulder and plucked the check from his fingers. "And how silly—let me give it to Father. Perhaps, just perhaps, he may endorse it over to me as a wedding present."

One of Terry's hands closed down on her little one. He slowly opened the fingers, and taking the check put it in his pocket.

"Young lady," he said in mock severity, "I am not married to you—yet."

"Oh, Terry," said Ardath. "Terry—you old son-of-a-gun."

And Terry could not understand why she put her head down on his shoulder and began to cry. Nor could he understand why her eyes and lips smiled as the tears rolled down her face. Like the sun through an April shower, he thought.

About the Author

OPERATOR—WHITE
PLAINS—YES-YES—MR.
CARROLL John Daly. No!
NOT John Daly of Los Angeles.
Sssh! You'll make him mad if he
hears that again. Pretty tough on
a gentleman of Mr. Daly's standing—yeh—land of liberty and freedom—talk about the Soviet! Too bad
Race Williams hadn't been around just then;
he'd fixed that guy. Yeh—

Oh—hullo, Mr. Daly! Coming fine, thank you. Yes—they
want the story of your life—yes—all set.

(Mr. Daly on the wire.)

Year of birth—1889. Color—white. Sex—male. Height—
five feet, nine inches. Color eyes—blue. Color hair—light
brown.

Hullo! Hullo ! Mr. Daly—this is not the auto license bureau.
Black Mask! Yes—story of your life—yes—

Very well—let me see. Ah, yes—Race Williams stands five
feet, eleven and one-half inches; weighs one hundred and
eighty-three pounds and is thirty years old. His hair is dark
brown and his eyes are black. He shaves his whole face, and
does not usurp the prerogative of gentlemen in their preference
for blondes. For that matter, he prefers neither; he admires a
clever woman and respects a good one—when he finds her. As

a matter of personal taste, Race opposes the 18th Amendment, but he finds it good for his business. Society pictures rest his mind; allow him to think of other things, so to speak; but a good thriller wakes him right up. Race likes action, you know. There is nothing soft-boiled about Race, but when it comes to casting his vote, he says yea to no man; he votes for the best man in his opinion, regardless of party.

Now, now, Mr. Daly. We know Race Williams almost as well as you do. What hey want is—yes—that's it—*your* life.

I can think of a great many wonderful things about myself but I can't without immodesty say them.

Let me see—I was born in Yonkers, N.Y., September 14, 1889, attended half the prep schools in the state, with a fling at The American Academy of Dramatic Arts; a short period in the study of law and a longer one in stenography. I owned and operated with another chap the first moving picture theatre on the Boardwalk in Atlantic City; then theatres at Asbury Park, Arverne, and a stock company in Yonkers. Thousands were taken in at Atlantic City and thousands were spent out at Yonkers.

I have been broke on the very edge of the Sahara Desert in Africa, and equally as free from money on Forty-second street, New York City. I have seen Paris on a thousand dollars and a week later seen London on eight dollars, and that eight borrowed from a friend.

About my work. I like it. It's easy. As easy as digging for coal in a mine ten hours a day. But I like it. About the picture you have—that was taken some time ago. I have since tucked my shirt in.

There—I think that quite a bit for a lad who never has accomplished much of anything.

Thanks, Mr. Daly—but if I could write the stories you do, I think I'd leave out that last line… Give my regards to Race— Coming in to see us soon, is he? Fine— What? A whole Race Williams book? What's the name? When will it be— Hullo! Hullo ! Operator—somebody has cut me off— What? Mr. Daly has gone back to work? Oh—very well.

www.ingramcontent.com/pod-product-compliance
Lightning Source LLC
Chambersburg PA
CBHW020252030726
47499CB00001B/171